stereovision

a NOVEL by STEVE EGGLESTON

Prologue

Six miles above sea level. The view is a privilege. Newton, Da Vinci, they never saw this. My horizon is more distant than any of theirs. Why? Because I know how to book a flight.

I try to stay awake, I try to stay amazed by it, but it's lost its wonder. I imagine the look on Leonardo Da Vinci's face when I tell him that we can fly above the clouds, yet I normally sleep right through it. I'm used to it. Six miles above sea level. I'm used to it.

This is what it means to be alive right now, in a society such as ours. We live with a chemical dependence on the ingenuity of others. If we were to take away everything that we don't know how to build or fix, many of us would be naked in caves, or worse. We've become numb, even callous towards these technological accomplishments, but we skipped the part where we become proficient. We're dependent on what we don't understand.

This is what I do now. I fly around the county. I stand behind podiums and I read excerpts and I answer questions. I enjoy doing this. People ask me about science and the universe, about the role of science in our culture, about the future. I cherish the question I've never asked myself, and more times than not, it's a child asking me that question. Children are curious about the world. They're aware of how little they know, and they want to know more. Adults, on the other hand, they generally ask a question hoping the answer will confirm what they think they know.

Recently a child asked me what questions an alien would have for us if it arrived on our planet. I've been chewing through this one since. The concept of life on other worlds is fascinating, and taking into account how many hundreds of billions of galaxies there are, and how abundant in the universe the ingredients for life are, it's mathematically probable that we are not alone.

When I think about life elsewhere in the universe, I normally keep my imagination fastened to a science-based reality. I ask myself, would the life be carbon-based? Maybe if the world was rich in sulphuric acid, would life be silicon-based? What if *we* were the far superior intelligent being, would we exploit these life forms for our own purposes? Given the way we treat animals on our planet, I think I know the answer to that question. These are the thoughts of an adult with a scientific background.

But you don't sell movie tickets by being scientifically accurate. Not today. Your customer base isn't interested in a movie about microbes. They want flying saucers. They want danger. They want, *take me to your leader*. Hollywood moves faster and reaches a wider audience than the peer reviewed papers written on the topic. Many people, children especially, have a fantasy in their minds when they wonder about life on other worlds. Octopus aliens zipping around in flying saucers. At least they're considering the possibility of it. They're not so egocentric to assume that life only exists here. If Hollywood helps perpetuate that curiosity, great.

And what would these aliens ask us? This isn't really about aliens. It's about us. These questions would teach us more about ourselves than them. My mind goes there when I'm half awake on a plane, trying to stay captivated by the miracle of flight. So, thanks to some squirrely kid in Des Moines, I've been having daydream conversations with comic book aliens.

I imagine they might ask what a prison is. Or what a school is. And why we need both. They'd be curious about religions, sports, and entertainment. They might ask why we have separate languages, separate countries. They'd wonder why we introduce greenhouse gases into our own atmosphere, while fully aware of the consequences. But I think that, more than anything else, they'd wonder why it is that only a fraction of our society is scientifically literate, making decisions and driving technology that affects everyone. And we should be asking the same question.

Inevitably, I did doze off. I sleep every time I fly. And when I awoke I was eye level with the sunlit peak of Mt. Rainier, shoving its way up and out of a typical Pacific Northwest rainstorm. I had a brief moment to admire one of the most dangerous volcanoes in the world before sinking down below the wet clouds where people forget what blue skies and sunlit mountain peaks look like. *This plane is a submarine,* I heard a kid say from a few rows back.

The familiar routine of taxiing and baggage claiming escaped the foreground of my daydream. I snapped out of it in the back of a sharp turning taxicab where I had blindly placed my faith and a bookstore address in the hands of a stranger. My only concern was a tip toeing curiosity of whether I had gotten the time wrong. I was either fifty minutes early or ten minutes late. That's what I was preparing myself for.

The books I write are simple. I make a case for science. Why? We live in a society that sends humans into space, then crosses its fingers and hopes for the best. Some people discover stars, others wish upon them. The gap is wide between the scientifically literate and illiterate. My message is basic; Learn. Ask questions. Seek evidence. Demand evidence. Oddly, it's often the simplest notions that invoke the most complicated responses, and because of that I have a steady writing career.

Every audience at every book reading gives me an opportunity to interact with a fuzzy sampling of my readers. I knew what to expect. I knew who would be seated in each row. I sketched the audience in my mind at a stoplight.

I drew college kids who were breaking rank and rebelliously embracing the science that debunked much of what they had been taught throughout their lives. They'd show up late, sit in the back, and raise their hands like they were hailing for a cab. They kept clumsy opinions that you hoped would age into more tested and confident theories. Their statements tailed up at the ends like questions. These college kids and I, we had a special bond. They knew what I expected of them. It was up to them to lead us into a new scientific age. Even a good microscope costs less than a video game console, and they were reminded of that every time we spoke.

But it was always a mixed group. Dependably, front and center, you'd have the relentless pack of eloquent critics. They had personal reasons for showing up and challenging me. And dammit, I just absolutely love these people. Oh, it wasn't always this way, but I've grown to appreciate the role they play. My best sound bites come from responses to their aggressive questions. And until they understand that the burden of proof is theirs, I'll always have at least a few of these wonderful people at every reading.

In the end, I feel for these people. My entire pitch is a needle in their balloon. What they believe, it's so deeply woven into their identities, and I come along and point out that they lack evidence. They were never taught that it was required. How can you live 40, 50, 60 years believing in something and then some skinny scientist starts publishing books suggesting that your take on reality is flawed? These people are as faith-based as they are carbon-based. In a way, we all are. We put faith in all kinds of things, some more than others.

Filling the gaps of rows in the middle, I'd have the passive scholars who tuck in their shirts and rarely ask questions. Like educated Styrofoam, they formed a buffer between the soft and the sharp. I know very little about these people. Nothing I say stirs them. I imagine they work and live in airtight scientific communities. But until the whole of our society is a scientific community, I'd rather live on the borders, and interact with those that have very little understanding of science. That's why I fly all over the country in airborne submarines. We need science.

Sitting near a tree under the rain clouds with close to fifty minutes until my scheduled book reading, I noticed a little girl tossing coins in a fountain, wishing out loud for world peace. She locked eyes with me, recognized me, ran over to her mom and yanked a book out from under her arm. Before I could blink, she was an inch from my face.

"Are you him?" she said, pointing to the picture on the back of the book. It was a much younger picture of me when my hair was round and wild. "Are you that guy, Philip Duke? We're going to listen to you read."

I quickly took out my notes. Fortunately I was so early. There was now only one person in the audience that mattered. I'm here to tell kids the truth.

stereovision

A red-tailed hawk floats above a 10-kilowatt wind turbine, hidden in the drab and colorless sky. Something small with a tail fidgets in a clump of grass, but the hawk isn't hunting. A rooster crows, a squeaky door opens, a pair of size 21 boots roll gravel with each step as rays of sunlight begin to poke through.

Long winds, scattered with crystallized chimes from tree ornaments, rush past the man's face, catching his knotted beard. Ladle sized knuckles rub the sleep out of his waking eyes. The flickering grey silhouette of the morning hawk is blurred into two separate images. Before the man can focus, the hawk flies off to a dead standing tree miles away. This is every morning on The Farm.

Like a statue, fixed and focused on the horizon, the massive, wool-clad man they call Logjam swallows deep breaths of air, his hands soaring high above his head. The first arrows of refracted light catch the red hair on his patchy knuckles. Within minutes, sunlight will have flooded the Field of the Morning Hawk where children giggle and tumble the width of Logjam's shadow.

Normally, a thin, blurry figure would take shape and climb a short hill up to the field and stand alongside Logjam in a comedy of comparisons. But on this morning, Logjam stood and welcomed the sunlight alone, and he understood why. For close to a year, the author Philip Duke had been crawling, hands and knees, through the task of completing his novel. It came to an end late into the night, in the hours that don't matter. And now Philip was miles under his covers in his warm bed as Logjam welcomed the sun without him.

"Did he really build that typewriter?" they had asked Logjam, only weeks earlier, unaware that Philip was listening from the corners of the hearth room. He was striking keys, zipping the makeshift carriage back to the starting position. Everyone was used to Philip's disengaged presence, and were surprised when he snapped up and corrected them by saying, "I just restored it, I didn't build it." Logjam countered with, "But it wasn't a typewriter to begin with." Everyone laughed, and the conversation ended without any clarification on the matter. The two men's eyes met, and Logjam wondered, *You're not going to stay here much longer, are you, friend?* Philip's bed sheet face stretched into a grin, and Logjam understood.

Logjam knew this day was coming. He imagined it often. When the book was finished, Philip would walk along the trail to the spot where his enormous friend stood, the spot where the grass below has suffered from the daily ritual of a 300-pound man stealing sunlight. He would stand beside Logjam, welcome the daylight, and inform him that the time had come. It was inevitable, nobody stays at The Farm forever, but Philip would be missed. Logjam would miss his friend.

On this day, Philip would notice Logjam's braided hair, like he did on most mornings, curious as to how he could have braided it already, or if he slept with it braided, and if so, how the braids kept so tight. His hair was like rope. Children on The Farm dreamed of swinging from it. Every detail of Logjam's appearance delightfully mystified Philip. He admired the thick warfare of red beard on Logjam's face. He thought his arms looked like sandbags, and that his gallon hands were nimble like two ballerinas.

Philip was indebted. He knew that Logjam and everyone here at The Farm had helped him. They had saved him from himself. And on this summer morning, he would have meaningfully thanked Logjam. He would have brought to words all the grateful thoughts and feelings from the past year. He would have, but instead, he was stuck in bed, catching up on the hours of sleep he lost dancing over a makeshift typewriter. So, Logjam admired the sun alone. Philip's absence may have spoken loud enough.

Logjam thought often of the first morning Philip spent with him on the Field of the Morning Hawk. "It's deceiving," Philip had said, his voice kidnapping the silent morning. "The sun *does* appear to move. It tricks us into believing that we are placed in the center of it all. Most people who have ever lived on this planet have died believing that the sun circled the earth, for the sole purpose of us." Logjam listened, letting his soft fingers polish the whale tooth that hung from his neck. Philip's words were a comb in the tangles of his imagination.

The sperm whale tooth necklace was a gift from a traveling band of Hawaiian slide guitarists who were staying at The Farm many years earlier. A celebration was held on the night before they moved on, and the musicians told the story of the goddess Hina and her son Maui. Hina had complained to Maui of how quickly the sun flew through the sky, too quickly for her tapa cloth to dry. Maui, eager to please his mother, took a rope and tied it around the sun. The sun begged to be let go, negotiating its release by agreeing to travel slower through the sky. The children on the farm were enchanted by their story, and the adults were entertained.

The musicians hoped to pay homage to Logjam. They had noticed his routine of greeting the sun, the routine that predates the wind turbine, the solar panels, the herb gardens, the soaking pools, and the length of stay of every person currently living at

The Farm.

As a token of their gratitude, the musicians then presented Logjam with a gift that had passed through many generations of men in their family. Logjam found the tooth had a smooth touch, and he rubbed it often, thinking about Philip's words, and revisiting the story of the Hawaiian myth. He imagined a time when the sun was alive, when gods and goddesses were writing the laws of nature, and debated whether he enjoyed the well-combed truth over the tangles of fantasy.

By the time Philip finally found his way out of bed on this morning, the sun was high, and Logjam was packing his truck full of belongings. Philip yawned and curved and twisted all the way up the grassy hill, up near Logjam's straw bale home, and climbed up into the bed of Logjam's truck, interrupting him.

There was an instinctive nature between the two men. It had been this way since the time they first met, back when Philip arrived in pieces. They knew how to speak to one another, and they learned how to skip most of the unnecessary words. They would start a conversation several exchanges in. People would notice them catching eyes, nodding, and walking away, knowing precisely what the other person meant. Philip wouldn't have climbed up into the back of the truck if he had wanted Logjam to continue packing it. So, Logjam stopped what he was doing, and waited for Philip to speak, but no words came.

Philip was in no rush to let Logjam get back to work, and they both knew they'd be frozen in time until Logjam explained why he was packing the truck. Not a detail of this silent interaction was lost on either of them, and Logjam knew it was his silence to break.

"If you've noticed, I've spent some time restoring the old chapel from when my father and his brothers lived here. It was an old building, it needed work." Nothing energized Logjam more than a meaningful chore.

Philip turned his head in the direction of the chapel, which had looked dumped and discarded the last time he saw it. He hadn't noticed. The past few weeks had been full of activity that Philip missed.

"I know that you are leaving soon, Philip. You finished your work." Logjam paused, letting his kick drum breath land and become a smile. "I'm asking you to stay until I return. I'll be back in a week."

He wouldn't have asked this without good reason. Philip knew that. They said no more to each other, and Philip watched the chaos of dust clouds kick up from Logjam's truck as it drove down the old, narrow road toward the highway.

Individual hair lengths dragged across the bartender's round head, and his chipped tooth only added to his gallant smile. The bar was crowded. He was never happier.

He hadn't noticed when the picture went out, but his patrons alerted him. "Yossi, YOSSI!! The game!!" He knew just where to hit the mounted television with a broomstick so the picture would reappear. And it was just in time.

No one in that particular Manhattan bar saw the pitch, but they saw Reggie Jackson's knee graze the dirt as he swung his bat up through the ball. The home crowd was sick and silent throughout Dodger Stadium, but Yankee fans erupted into euphoric violence, spilling beers, hugging, kissing, spitting. Everyone in that bar, and in every bar in New York, knew the Yankees were going to win Game 4 of the 1977 World Series.

Philip Duke

I used to have a recurring daydream. I'd see myself reaching for something, standing on my toes. When that didn't work, I'd get on a stool. Whatever it was I was reaching for, I could almost feel it, but it would disappear. I'd put the stool on a box, the box on a desk, the desk on a table. I'd keep reaching. I'd feel it again, just barely. I'd have a brief, delicate understanding of what it was, and then it'd be gone.

My mom and I moved across the San Fernando Valley to an apartment in Canoga Park in 1972. I turned five that October. I don't remember living anywhere else. We still lived in that same spot, number 304 on the third floor, the day I graduated from high school.

I can close my eyes and see the floor plan. I remember how many steps it took to get from one room to another. I can hear the slapping sound of a picky eater shutting the refrigerator, wishing there was something more exciting to eat. I remember our apartment manager, Mr. Leahy, who lived below us, coming up to replace the refrigerator door gasket, asking me if I knew what a hex screw was. He had a tool belt. He had a kind voice. I can still hear it.

I was a busy, messy, introverted kid. I asked *why* a lot, and then I'd go find out. There has always been, deep within me, a need to gather evidence. I was born a scientist. I have always been curious.

Science Experiments. My bedroom was constantly covered in science experiments. It wasn't just my bedroom either, my research spread throughout the limited space we had. I'd keep colonies of mold, and rusty nails wrapped up like mummies with copper wires. I painted light bulbs. I took apart plants and the electronics around the house. Things would spill, things would break, and things would make noise. I wanted to understand it all. My mom allowed me to become a scientist. She stayed out of my way.

We didn't always have the things I needed, but Mr. Leahy did. At some point in the hectic subconscious of a curious kid, he became an ally to me. I'd comfortably knock on his door at all hours and ask him for duct tape, and more duct tape, and then one day I found a cardboard box filled with rolls of duct tape by our door. But that didn't keep me away; I needed wires, fertilizer, food coloring, magnets, paper clips, washers, ink, and shoelaces. I probably didn't thank him either. I never questioned good fortune enough to be grateful.

In the months prior to my tenth birthday, I had been using duct tape to measure the sunlight as it crawled across my floor. Every month I marked, with tape, where the sunlight would reach and at what time. One strip of tape on the floor meant 6:00 AM, and the next one meant 6:30 AM, and so on, multiples of thirty minutes. I had big plans. I was exploring sensory activation, I was learning about solar power. This was going to be an alarm clock. I'm sure Mr. Leahy would have had all the necessary supplies. But I abandoned my project on my tenth birthday due to an unfortunate incident. I took the tape off the ground, and started using a standard alarm clock; one that Mr. Leahy gave me.

Nothing extraordinary happened the day before my tenth birthday. It was a Friday in October. There was a crescent moon in the sky. I wandered the playground at recess, alone, thinking about science, the universe. I was probably trying to imagine a sky with two moons, a Martian sky. My mom had told me she would take me to the museums on my birthday, so I'm sure I bugged her quite a bit about that.

Museums. There was nothing better. I knew of no better way to spend a day. Museums presented me with the rare occasion of impressing people, and feeling good about myself. I'd know as much about the exhibit, if not more, than the employees. This was really all I had. For a few brief moments some strangers would notice the smart kid, me, bringing attention to myself. And if they weren't annoyed, they were impressed.

So much of my life was a reminder that I was different, inadequate. I didn't play sports. I wasn't a confident, jock type of kid. I was overlooked. My teachers were annoyed by me, and didn't tap into my intelligence. I was just a lot of work for them. I'd finish the assignments, and I'd be bored. I don't remember my elementary teachers. I don't remember their names. I think if I had forged any bonds I would have remembered them more.

The plan, on the morning of my birthday, was that my mom would let me sleep in a bit, and we'd have breakfast, and pack some sandwiches, and drive downtown around 10:00. There were four museums all within a block from each other, and you could buy a pass that would get you into all of them for the whole day. That was the plan. That was the glorious plan. I was on fire the night before my birthday. I couldn't sleep. I pictured all of it, lying in bed, eyes wide open.

I woke up that next morning to the confusing sound of my mom frantically trying to get me out of bed. I looked over at the ground where my parallel lines of duct tape told me it was early, early like a school day, or a work day.

"Get up Philip, hurry, I gotta go to work."

I'm sure I got mad. I'm sure in her busy, distracted way, she ignored me, and got me out of the house in time for her to get to work. She didn't work every Saturday, and she didn't always work a double, but on this day she did. This meant I wouldn't be going to the museums, but instead I'd have to go to North Hollywood and spend the day with my grandmother and her boyfriend, Hal.

Hal was terrible. He drank and smoked inside, he talked about God and duty and creation, and had a chip on his shoulder towards me. Every time he opened his mouth around me, it was a way to remind me about all the good men who took a face full of bullets protecting the freedom we have in this country. He must have been convinced that I needed to be reminded.

This was an age in my life where I was beginning to read about the universe, our solar system, our planet, how it was all created. I was becoming more and more literate in physics, astronomy, and biology. I started to develop an innate sense for science. And then I'd be around Hal, and he had this way about him, it seemed to oppose science. I didn't have it organized into words yet, but I sensed that science contradicted him. Hal was unscientific.

Hal would talk about a god with a white beard living in a fluffy toilet paper heaven, and a cartoon devil poking around in a volcanic hell. His god put animals on the planet for our enjoyment, like little moving presents. In his naïve perception of reality, we were at the center of it. He conveniently arranged the order of all things, which sat him, his gender, his nationality, high above all else. He wanted to believe all of this, and humans are gifted in believing what we want to believe.

I looked at Hal as the ultimate coward. Afraid of the truth. Fearful of science. He didn't understand it, didn't want to. I watched him ignore the science that he depended on, waiting for the water to boil and mix with his crystallized, processed coffee. He'd unknowingly listen for science, for the sound of the kettle, the sound of water boiling, bubbling sound waves, temperature of vapor pressure equal to atmospheric pressure. To him, coffee was ready. Coffee was what my grandmother would pour for him. Nothing more. Every kitchen is a lab if you're curious enough, and if your mom doesn't mind you making a mess and breaking a few things.

It wasn't long after showing up at my grandmother's house that I'd take my book and wander across the street to the pool. I didn't like the pool, but I liked my grandmother's house less. My mom packed me a bag with a towel and trunks. I'd told her not to, that I wasn't going to go swimming, but she must have known I'd change my mind.

It always interested me that we, as a species, swim despite having all the land we need. It's like we're anticipating something. So, as a ten year old, I didn't go in the pool to swim, I went in the pool to better understand why we swim. That's the kind of kid I was.

The community pool in North Hollywood was likely designed to be a fun place for kids, but just like every pool, or playground, or sports field, it's a stage for evolution, accidentally reaching for impossible order. These kids were rough. They yelled and splashed, and held each other underwater. I stayed at the far end of the pool, dipping my feet in, survival by non-participation. I hid like a deer mouse.

My understanding of evolution at the time was that chaos will eventually find order. Give an organism billions of years, with billions of options, and order will pursue. I now know that we will never fully reach order, like a distance cut in half an infinite number of times, the gap never fully closes. Order is a relative term.

My library book about Mars was damp when I came back to my chair. It's not like any of these kids were thinking, *let's not splash water in this direction, that skinny kid seems to be enjoying his book.* I should have known my surroundings better. But I sat and felt sorry for myself. I was still upset about not going to the museums, and about Hal mouthing off to me the moment I walked in, pointing out the way I was dressed and the lack of respect I had for adults. He wanted me to look adults straight in the eyes and say *yes ma'am*, and *yes sir.*

I was getting sunburned and I wasn't very interested in my rubber hot dog that I bought from a vendor at the pool, so I walked back over to my grandmother's house, and I did my best to avoid any heat from Hal. I walked right up to my grandmother, looked her in the eye, waited for Hal to be paying attention, and I asked, "May I please make something to eat?" That seemed to satisfy Hal for the meantime, and I took my sandwich over to the corner of the kitchen where the light was good and I read.

I can remember what I was reading at that moment, about how the public got swept up in the possibility of life on Mars due to a mistranslated Italian description from

1877. Astronomer Giovanni Schiaparelli used the Italian word *canale*, which he likely chose to mean channel, not canal, when describing the Martian surface. Regardless, the report was sensationalized, and for generations people kept alive an interest in intelligent Martian life. Never mind the polar ice caps, the volcanoes, the tectonic sites, and all the characteristics that make it my favorite planet. Mars, with about half the diameter of our planet, has a mountain, which stands three times as tall as Mt. Everest. I dream about standing at the foot of this mountain.

I was contemplating striking up a conversation with Hal, assuming even he would find these facts interesting, and possibly correcting parts of our relationship. Before I could arrange the right words, I heard him ask my Grandma, "What kind of kid reads indoors on a sunny day like this?" On cue I took my sandwich and my book outdoors to read, out on the porch, and I stayed there until I saw my mom's station wagon hours later.

I was filled with self-pity. I had high expectations of this day. I remember feeling small in an unfair world. There's a Mark Twain quote that a friend of mine once shared with me, which I have since considered as a thesis statement for my tenth birthday. *Nothing that grieves us can be called little: by the eternal laws of proportion a child's loss of a doll and a king's loss of a crown are events of the same size.* I lost more than a doll that day, but the quote still fits.

Normally, birthdays didn't mean much to me, as with most calendar days. I never got excited about Christmas or Halloween, I always felt that these were arbitrary dates on our non-scientific calendar, but this birthday marked ten trips around the sun. A year for every finger. I thought of it as a milestone.

Soon after we got home, the phone rang. My dad and I weren't close. He moved around a lot, and I rarely saw him. My mom did what she always did when my dad calls, she walked as far as she could away from me, pulling length from our coiled up phone cord. I must have learned from an early age not to listen when they talked, that nothing good was happening. I had already heard things I didn't want to hear.

I heard my mom say, "I'll call you right back," and she came in and asked me if I wanted to go to a baseball game at Dodger Stadium with my dad. I didn't know what to say, and I let a long *ummmm* level off into eternity. I wasn't at all interested in sports, but, as my mom explained to me, this was the World Series. Just the math alone intrigued me. Seven games, first team to win four takes the series. I agreed to go to the game. I didn't think my day could have gotten worse. I was wrong.

There were technical details of this day that I still recall. My dad was 45 minutes late. Even I know that when you're late you normally apologize, but instead he flew in and was impatiently trying to rush me out the door. I remember it all so well. I remember where he was standing. I can picture it perfectly. It's ugly. His face was ugly to me. He stuck his chin up in the air and leaned against the wall with his hands at his hips, and snapped at me to hurry up. I had to go to the bathroom when he arrived, and at my age I was well trained to go right before I left the house.

I still replay the event in my head. I try to go back, and get inside the brain of that little ten year old, and stand up to my dad. He got mad at me, and he was the one that was late. He was 45 minutes late. I went to the bathroom a few minutes before he was supposed to show up, and then I stood by the door, and by the time he actually did show up, I had to go again. And I'm still bothered by it. He was wrong.

I was sensitive. My mom never lost her cool with me. We would scratch at each other, but she always kept her voice from rising. And if she ever did get mad at me, I could handle it. I knew she loved me.

When we got in the car, my dad drove like a maniac. I didn't feel safe. When you're with your dad, you should feel safe. Then we got to the ballpark, and he was upset about the parking, and how far we'd have to walk. I remember thinking, *all these other cars were driven by people who got here earlier, so that's why we have to walk so far.*

We got to the park at the end of the second inning, which I didn't think was a big deal, but he did. He was still rushing, dragging me to our seats. I couldn't walk as fast as he wanted me to; there were a lot of stairs.

I'd never seen Dodger Stadium before. I'd never seen anything like it. My dad knew exactly where he was going, where our seats were. He knew the stadium layout perfectly. He must have been here before, many times. I wondered to myself, *how come I've never been here? Isn't this something you take your kid to?*

The moment we sat, I could tell this was an important game. The atmosphere was very tense. People were screaming. People don't act like this at museums. I remember asking my dad why everyone was yelling. He shot me a glance, like, *what do you think, kid?* It was clear, his interest was not in whether I had fun, or learned anything from the experience. He wanted to watch the game, and to be left alone. I wondered why he even invited me.

I couldn't care less who won, and I was amazed at how much it mattered to everyone. I wanted to remind people how little difference it made. I wanted to climb up the aisles, and sit down with each person and remind them none of this mattered. I wanted to say, "Hey, I'm Philip, I'm ten and I know that none of this matters. Why do you care so much about this?"

Everyone looked gullible to me. A bunch of gullible people getting tricked by a fancy company, something that happens when you don't analyze further, when you don't think scientifically.

But the game itself held my attention. I was fascinated by the physics of it. My exposure to baseball had been kids swinging plastic bats at school, so to see a 90 mph fastball in person was exhilarating. I think I could have been a baseball fan. Maybe not the score keeping, or getting worked up about the results of the game, just the game of baseball. It was science accelerated, it was chaos finding order, and while the outcome came with probabilities, it was unpredictable. I might have enjoyed this game, but bad stuff got in the way.

My dad was tense. He acted like it was life or death. This wasn't fun. I went back to feeling sorry for myself. It was my birthday, and my dad wouldn't leave his seat to walk me to the bathroom, or to help me get some food. He handed me a few bucks when I said I was hungry. I was cold and he told me to knock it off and watch the game, that I should have brought a warmer jacket. I didn't own one.

Then something happened. It was the 6th inning, and a man, who I learned later was Reggie Jackson, was up to bat. I remember he hit the ball so hard, and so fast, and it launched out of the park. It made a beautiful sound. The second he hit it, I knew it was going to be a home run. What a remarkable human accomplishment that was. I got excited. I couldn't help it. I celebrated that magnificent display of physics. Everyone around me was dead silent, and my dad was furious, and he looked at me and saw me jumping around, and he smacked me on the back of the head, hard. It made my eyes blur, and he yelled, "Would you shut the fuck up?"

This wasn't really a dad, he didn't spend a lot of time with me. He loved me, I'm sure, but I imagine the art of being a dad takes practice. You can't just show up every once in awhile and be a dad, just like he couldn't show up at his job every few months and be good at it. My mom was a good mom. I didn't give her enough credit. She didn't always understand me, but she was patient. My dad though, he just wasn't good at it. I don't have any good memories with him.

I hardly remember the last few innings of the game. I was cold, hungry, and uncomfortable. It wasn't fun anymore. The Dodgers lost, and the melodramatic fans were sure life was coming to an end.

It was a clear night, and had everyone turned off the stadium lights, we could have seen the Orion Nebula, and we would have all been reminded that life was not over, in fact, the very opposite was true. And I'm pretty sure I had that exact thought on my tenth birthday. I imagined a reality where tens of thousands of people got together and looked at the sky. In my imagination, this wasn't ridiculous. To me, it's ridiculous people don't do this.

I didn't yet know the dangers of mixing alcohol and a steering wheel, it was never in any of my science books, but my dad should have. He'd buy a beer at an embarrassingly marked up price every time the beer vendor climbed up to our section. With all the money he spent on beer he could have bought me a warm jacket with the Dodgers logo on it, at least he'd be financially supporting the team, and I would have been warmer.

I woke up right before the moment of impact. I can still remember it. A tiny capsule of a memory. On. Off. A flash of light and a screech and a consequence. I can remember so clearly feeling like I was in free fall. Of course the car never left the ground, but that's how it felt. It felt like we were falling, like we were lost and powerless.

The rest is a dim memory. I woke up again later in a hospital. I had suffered a concussion and had a few scars, one of them permanent, a few inches down my neck, where some glass cut me. It wasn't my birthday anymore, and I would never be young again.

The scar. You can't miss it. It's this strange wormy discoloration that twists when I turn my neck. I'm not embarrassed by the scar. I'm not concerned with that. But I grew tired of people asking, "Cool scar, where'd you get it?" and I'd say, "my tenth birthday, I was in a car accident," and my tone would drop so that only an asshole would ask any follow up questions. But at times I would run into those assholes, they'd ignore my tone and body language, satisfying their own curiosity, they'd keep asking until I'd finally say, "My dad got drunk, totaled his car, with me in it, and I haven't seen him since."

Whatever I feel about my dad, I feel this way because I wanted to like him. He could have been a great dad, he had a funny personality, he was smart, but he was smart about all the wrong things, and that made him ugly to me.

My dad was clever enough to win my mom over, who at first wasn't very interested. He was a driver when he met her, and he had taught himself several mechanic tricks for keeping his truck running well, which he liked to brag about while she poured his beer. My mom was waiting tables at some smoky trucker bar, putting up with more than she wanted to, most likely settling on a life of serving others. The image I conjure up is sad and desperate. I try not to think of this place. I hope it doesn't exist anymore. But hope has no place in reality. That bar is likely out there, hosting its own brand of reckless evolution, whether I hope it is or not.

Life went on. I became very serious about science over the next eight years, and many opportunities arose from this. I secured internships at museums and science camps. I met people who I had only read about in books. I won a few awards, one of which was a junior NASA achievement award. I created a spectroscope for a middle school science fair project, and a telescope that my high school most likely still uses. I was on my way to a life of science.

During my senior year, it happened to be that a local artist was painting a mural in the cafeteria, and she used real students as the subjects. The students voted, and I was chosen to be illustrated looking through a microscope. This surprised me. I didn't know people even knew who I was. And I rarely looked under a microscope. It never interested me as much as a telescope did.

Students suddenly knew me as 'that science kid.' I didn't mind that, but their imaginations ran loose, and I had a reputation. I don't remember all the exaggerations, but I heard wild claims that I could do calculus in my head, or that NASA was hiring me out of our high school, things of that nature. It was flattering for about a day, and then it bothered me.

This strange reputation made me anxious and drove me to be even more introverted. I'd sit with my face in a book at lunch, avoiding everyone. Their exaggerations were a sign that they didn't understand me, so they sensationalized me as someone they could laugh at or be entertained by. Like Mars. Like the canals of Mars. They skipped over what was accurate and interesting about me, and turned me into some mad scientist character from a budget movie.

I've always thought it was strange that other people weren't constantly thinking about science. They didn't ask where the earth came from, what stars were. Or maybe they didn't need to, they were already given that information, but incorrectly. And there's something very instinctual that happens when you are outnumbered, but you feel very strongly about your views. You become very insulated. Very few people at that age valued science as much as I did. I needed science. I needed to think scientifically. It was therapeutic. I needed a system of truth, of accuracy. I needed it more than I needed others. I lived within a bubble of science, mostly alone. A bubble the size of the universe.

Then high school was over. I squeezed through without making any friends. Never went to any parties, or dances. Never had a girlfriend. I was aware that these things existed. I was aware of what kids my age were doing, but you just couldn't peel me away from what I was up to. I'd sit up in my room with Dirac, Herschel, Keppler, Penzias, and Wilson. I'd close the windows and close the blinds, and I wasn't in my Canoga Park third story apartment anymore, I was just another curious student of the universe. I liked to think that these icons, these brilliant scientists would smile at the thought of a clumsy teenager trading in his youth to be among them every night of the week.

Columbia University. New York City. 2500 miles away. I had choices when it came to college. I wanted out of Los Angeles, out of the smog. My lungs weren't suited for this city. I wanted to study physics and astronomy. I admit I don't remember exactly how I landed on Columbia. I knew of several notable physicists and astronomers that had studied there, and maybe I wanted to be like them. Or maybe it had something to do with its location, Manhattan. There were museums in New York that I wanted to visit. New York, and Manhattan in particular, is the setting of many important events in scientific history, and not all were positive.

Or maybe I wanted to go where Yankees came from, Yankees who show up and hit home runs and ruin little ten-year-old's birthdays. I imagined walking past people who must have been elated when Reggie Jackson hit that homerun. Before I was slapped on the back of the head, I was elated too.

But really, I don't remember why I chose Columbia. I don't remember any of the other colleges I was considering. I imagine there was something very subconscious about the decision. Regardless of why, this is what I did, and if I hadn't, my life would have been different.

I took a bus across the country. Between sleeping and reading, I thought to myself, *this is our magnificent planet.* I was so familiar with the surfaces of other planets, that I forgot about the surface of my own planet. I rode that bus over mountains and through deserts, across one of the more vast and diverse lateral distances on Earth, and I was reminded of the powers of the universe, its ability to create worlds like ours, and everything in it. It was reaffirming to me why I chose to study astrophysics, because I wanted to study everything.

I had never left California before the moment the bus crossed into southern Nevada on highway 15, and I probably knew more about the surface of the moon than I did about what was on the other side of that state line. The bus ride was one part enlightening, and two parts terrifying. With every mile I was taken farther away from everything I knew. I had no idea how I was going to fare in this setting. It wasn't going to be easy, not for a kid like me.

For the first time, I was away from my mom and our apartment, and Mr. Leahy, who I hadn't seen much of since I was younger, but I still missed him. I was away from everything I was familiar with. We had lived in the same apartment my whole life. Most days were identical to the next, and those were good days. I'd sit on the couch, or in my room, and read or build something. And my mom would clean or cook or find a minute to rest, and we coexisted very predictably.

College shook it all up. My whole life, I had always been the smartest kid around, so I didn't mind my lack of social skills. There was balance. In college, I was just as socially unskilled, and I wasn't the smartest kid either. And I had to get used to that real quickly, because I was never going to be the smartest kid.

It stung a little when I saw kids throwing the Frisbee around, laughing and feeling comfortable around each other, feeling socially comfortable within themselves, and then I'd overhear those same kids discussing quantum electrodynamics or renormalization techniques, concepts that at the time were way over my head.

But maybe this was what college did for me, more than anything; it adjusted my position in the universe. I had to adapt to new surroundings. It was a challenge. And when it comes down to it, I'm always a little tougher than I realize. I don't sink. I'm buoyant, I suppose.

I'd travel home each summer by bus, and work at the museums. Sometimes I'd volunteer there. I'd do anything to be at those museums, still making up for my tenth birthday tragedy.

My mom had left Canoga Park and was living with her boyfriend in Venice Beach. She was never more than twenty years older than me, and young enough to start over. Throughout my childhood, I don't remember her having a man around. I was happy that she wasn't alone. It put me at ease knowing that while I was 2,500 miles away, she was doing well.

By my junior year I stopped going home. My mom was a new person, living a new life. We had grown apart. She was less predictable. She had opinions. She was more vibrant and confident, and younger looking. She had love in her life. I never once realized how little she took for herself, until I saw her take a little for herself.

When I look back at undergrad, my experience was likely very common, but that's what made it a unique period of time. Nothing in my life up until that point was at all common. Normality was rare in my life, so it felt anything but normal. I had an exciting, slow merge into the place where I would fit in.

Any anxieties I had as a freshman had eased. College life grew on me. I became more accustomed to my surroundings. I could have stayed forever. I would have taken every class offered. I would have taken geology, or zoology, maybe even neurology. I didn't need to graduate, and I didn't have it mapped out yet what I was going to do with this degree. That was never really something I considered when I was in school. I was there to learn. I never considered a career. I didn't want one. I just wanted to stay in the cosmic bubble where everyone valued science and evidence and everything was peer reviewed. I didn't want to graduate to the real world with their horoscopes and their superstitions, and their religions, and their New York Yankees.

But I did eventually graduate, which felt like a free-fall, so I reached for something familiar. I harassed the local planetarium on 81st until they hired me, and I took the only job they offered. I collected tickets at the door. I enjoyed a low stress job that allowed me to be at a museum every day. I felt like I had won. I had some loans to pay back, but other than that, I was doing great. I had a shoebox studio apartment in a crowded part of town, and I bought some thick curtains.

In my spare time I read every book, every paper, every quote from every lecture I could find on string theory; the relationship between quantum mechanics, the study of physics at a microscopic scale, and general relativity theory, the branch of physics dealing with the larger objects. I never wanted to contribute anything to this discussion. I just wanted to read everything I could find on it. It fascinated me that the greatest minds at the time could not reconcile the two.

Big things are made of little things, and big things behave differently than little things. And I think once we understand how the big and the little coexist, we will understand much better how the big things came about, and that will be a very big achievement for science, possibly humanity.

Metaphorically, the big things in life, companies, governments, societies, nations, religions, they are made of the small things, such as people. And they behave differently from people. They have a different set of laws. I often examined this parallel, and asked if it had something to teach us about science, or if the very opposite is true, that science has a lot to teach us about societal structures. I imagined a world free of the larger social structures, but even I know that's ridiculous. It's in our nature, we create bigger things, and we surrender ourselves to them.

I questioned if this was good enough. I had an Ivy League education, but I worked a wage job that I enjoyed. I could eat and pay rent. I could do this forever. There was nothing else I needed. I didn't need to advance any further. I could continue to read every book published, I'd have plenty of time. I could build telescopes and go to museums at no cost. I had an employee pass.

I wondered if I could remain free, and not get sucked into the larger structure. In my most rational thinking, I would remain. I would collect tickets at the planetarium. I would be a scholar of the universe, but free of the astronomically large structures of society. This was a rational path to take in my life, but I have never been very rational.

A year later I was a grad student, studying astronomy at the Columbia Graduate School of Arts and Sciences. I eventually got my PhD in astrophysics, focusing on the electromagnetic spectrum. It happened just like that. I got sucked right into the larger structure. I became a part of something bigger.

Time raced by. This isn't to say it was easy. It wasn't. I struggled. I may have been the worst student in the program. No, I was definitely the worst student in the program. But even with the intense challenge of completing a very demanding doctoral program, I still loved every minute of it. I catch myself saying this a lot, but I could have done it forever. Once I settle in, I can stick with something forever.

I began working full time back at the planetarium as the director of the youth outreach department. This was a busy, demanding, stressful job. I observed the kid at the door collecting tickets with a cynical grin. I'm sure she didn't know how good of a spot she was in.

Essentially, my job was to coordinate and oversee every aspect of the youth programs and the museum exhibits aimed towards our younger patrons. There was research involved, direct teaching, training the instructors, meeting with the design teams with the plans for the exhibits, exhibits that I oversaw.

I appreciate kids. I know quite well the excitement of being a kid in a museum. I walked the floor a lot, talking to kids. One day a young girl asked me how far away the Orion Nebula was, and since I'm a fact memorizer, I told her 1,344 light years away. She asked how far a light year was, I told her roughly six trillion miles. That figure paralyzed her. It wasn't something she could grasp, but she had some fight to her, and she didn't give up on it. She looked like she was off fly-fishing in the creek and, to her surprise, caught a blue whale. Sharing that information with her, and watching her deal with it, was gratifying. I may have benefitted as much as she did.

I heard the girl's mom continue the conversation with her while walking away, naming various events in history that have occurred over the past 1,344 years, while these photons from the nebula were traveling at the speed of light towards us. This was a scientifically stimulated kid.

I remember this kid well, and I often wonder where her life took her. Maybe astronomy wasn't her ticket, maybe she's a chemist, or she's into anthropology and she's off somewhere immersing herself in another culture. Maybe her job is not in any field of science, but instead, she enjoys hobbies of scientific nature. Maybe she still visits the planetarium.

Probabilities are about all we have in predicting outcomes. I theorize that children who are exposed to science, children who are allowed to explore, encouraged to explore, and investigate, and ask questions, have a greater probability of success, health, and happiness. I am evidence of this.

My mom didn't know a thing about science, but she let me explore, she let me break things. And I had the kindness of my neighbor, Mr. Leahy, bankrolling my field research. As introverted as I am, I will always feel an obligation to treat every curious minded kid I see just as Mr. Leahy treated me.

It was the spring of 1995. The unmanned Galileo spacecraft was a few months away from exploring Jupiter and it's moons. Back when I was ten, I read an article about the blueprints for this spacecraft. I thought about where I'd be when the spacecraft eventually arrived at Jupiter. I'd love to go back and tell that ten-year-old where I'd be, working at a museum. I think I would have been pleased to know that.

I rarely spoke to my mom, but when I did, it was evident to me that she was well. She was happy with her life. She was treated kindly. She was working at a flower shop part time, and volunteering at a school for kids with special needs. She didn't have to work as much. She lived a very simple life with her boyfriend.

Up until then, there had been no positive romantic relationship modeled for me. So it had appeared to be an unnecessary aspect of life, something to avoid, something I'd been perfectly happy without. I never felt like I was missing anything by being alone. But every once in awhile, I'd be looking through my solar telescope on a clear day, observing solar flares ripping off of the sun, something I've done hundreds of times, and I'd be reminded of how fine our star was, 93 million miles away. Hours looking through a telescope can be an insulating experience, and the older I got, I felt the need, an irrational need perhaps, to form a bond with another person, and share with them how spectacular our universe is. Maybe that's entropy, that force kicked into gear long before us, our planet, our solar system, that affects everything we do. Maybe it's evolution, instructed within me. Maybe I just met a beautiful girl and I wanted to do something about it. Kennedy Kravitz. Bartender's daughter. Short and feisty Kennedy.

I had noticed Kennedy several times in the past year. She brought her class to the planetarium on a field trip. I had also seen her in the park near my apartment, jogging with her dog. She would run in the rain, and I was impressed with how prepared she was. I thought it took some planning. Her gear was rainproof, and she had a leash that she attached to her waist. She had some kind of gadget, kept dry within a waterproof case, which I assumed was monitoring her heart rate.

I was drawn in by the lack of common ground. I didn't run, or have a dog, or have any mechanism in place to keep myself dry. The best I had was an umbrella and an old raincoat.

Kennedy was a person who functioned at a high level. She appeared to know what she was doing. Some people, myself included, are chaotic in comparison. I sputter around, guessing often at what I am supposed to do. Kennedy was more programmed. You could take someone like her seriously. Even her appearance had an intentional consistency to it. Her hair looked like it had been drawn by a cartoon artist. Her eyes were olive pits. Her face achieved a hypnotizing symmetry. She was luminous.

Before meeting Kennedy, I had criteria. I knew that I could never consider a girl as a partner if she didn't have an appreciation for science. If she mentioned astrology, we were done. If she used any of the popular lexicons of pseudoscience, like karma, we were done. If she drank more than one drink of alcohol at a time, we were done. If she had a favorite sports team, we were done. If she was overly caught up in celebrating holidays, we were done. And most of all, if she bugged me about my scar on my neck, we were done.

And then I met her, and within our very first conversation, she said something like this, "I'm sorry, I'm a little hung over, I was at the Yankee game last night and then my friends and I went out for Cinco de Mayo. I don't even know what Cinco de Mayo is but I love holidays. What can I say? I'm an Aries. This hangover is Karma for all the times I cut in line last night. By the way, that's a huge scar you got on your neck." But attraction is an interesting thing. My criteria didn't hold up to the laws of attraction.

The day I met her, I was getting a bite to eat at a cafe near my home. Coincidentally, there was an enormous group of tourists that was taking up most of the shop. Had that group gone anywhere else to eat that day, at any other time, perhaps I would have never met Kennedy.

I got a cup of coffee and a bagel and sat down at the only table left. A few minutes later Kennedy came in, ordered some food, searched around the shop, and, with nowhere else to sit, asked if she could share the table.

We introduced ourselves. It felt like we had to. I could tell she wasn't in the mood to make small talk, but I was nervous that she would slip away forever. I remember once, out of the blue, Mr. Leahy told me, *ask the kind of questions that you would want to answer*. He appeared to me at that moment, beamed in just to help me keep Kennedy from vanishing.

So, I said something like, "You must be a teacher, right? You took your kids to the planetarium, where I work, I remember you. What's your favorite thing about teaching?" That was all it took. She gave a quick apology about being hung-over and being an Aries, and Cinco de Mayo, and then we settled into a long, exciting conversation. It was at least two hours of us going back and forth. Easily the longest conversation I ever had with another person.

And then she looked at her watch, realized she was late, and sprinted out of the bakery. I was dumbfounded.

Attraction is a science of its own. If I had read the transcript of our conversation, I would have no explanation for why I wanted to see her again. I didn't even like the name Kennedy, I thought it was a pretentious name. But sitting at that little, round, wobbly table and actually being around her, I was under a spell. I must have read a dozen published papers on pheromones after our first meeting.

For the next two months, I visited that cafe almost daily, hoping that she would return. I got to know the owners so well that they invited me to their son's Bar Mitzvah. I normally would have declined, seeing no reason to partake in a religious experience that meant nothing to me, with people I hardly knew. But I had my reasons.

I had this slight trace of a memory that when Kennedy came into the cafe that day, months ago, the owners struck up a conversation with her. I might have been mistaken, but I thought they asked her how her dad was doing. Maybe I was being hopeful. It's amazing what we can convince ourselves of.

So I showed up to the Bar Mitzvah with a gift, an adjustable sky chart for stargazing. I dressed as nice as I knew how. I didn't see Kennedy anywhere, and was starting to think this was a mistake. I started looking for ways out. And although this religion had no authority over me, I felt governed by it while I was in that room. There is something powerful about a room full of people who all believe in something. I was outnumbered. The math was against me. I had had very few run-ins with religion before this, but it was strange for me. I didn't feel like I could just leave.

And then I didn't want to leave. Kennedy showed up late, during the reception. She walked over to Mrs. Cohen, the owner of the cafe, who immediately pointed at me. There had been an empty seat at my table all along, the table I hadn't yet gotten up from. Kennedy came and sat down, looked at me and said, "We're being set up, did you know that?" I responded, "It's you again."

We began dating immediately. We moved fast, I suppose. It was the most exciting thing that had ever happened to me. And so it came to be, that I would fall in love with a girl named Kennedy.

The director of the planetarium was a man in his 60s named Art. He was a cowboy, had a drawl, and wore a big shiny belt buckle and bolo ties. He had worked off and on at NASA for decades, and was stationed in the mission control room in Houston during the heated Apollo 7 mission. He told me once, "I like to think no one loves the universe more than I do, so I may ignore you from time to time to keep that fantasy intact."

A few months after Kennedy and I began dating, around midnight, I got a call from him. He must have said something convincing because an hour later we were bumping around on an old logging road out near Pine Barrens in his Chevy Suburban. I didn't know what this was about, why we were driving up here. I looked in the back, where there was probably a seat once, and there were telescope parts and lenses and blankets, all scattered.

We got to the top of the hill, he parked the car and said, "The board is going to vote you out of a job... because I am suggesting that they do exactly that." I didn't have time to respond before he added, "Philip, we have to cut your division. We gotta let you go." Admissions at the museum were low. I'd known that for a while. We couldn't get people in the door. The board had to rethink the budget. I didn't take it personally.

He set a telescope up in seconds, and we admired the Andromeda Galaxy, at a distance of 2.5 million light years from us. The light we see from this galaxy predates the emergence of our Homo genus. Moments like these remind me that everything is fine. Art knew I'd see it that way. We can lose jobs, but we can't lose the universe.

I found it humorous that he called me up to this hill to fire me. On top of that, before we left, he informed me of a NASA research position up in Alaska, studying ice, and that he already confirmed with NASA that I'd accept the job. Art was the type of guy who could do that. When I read the transcripts from the Apollo 7 mission, I hear his voice no matter who's talking.

I got home and Kennedy was at my apartment because we were supposed to go jogging that morning. I was several hours late, and I hadn't slept. I explained to her that the reason I was gone all morning was that I no longer work for the planetarium, but that I now work for NASA... in Alaska. It was all worth it if it got me out of jogging with Kennedy. You have to hate yourself to enjoy jogging with Kennedy.

It was tough for me to say goodbye. Leaving for six months to go study ice in Alaska left an uncertainty between Kennedy and me. I knew I was going to miss her. I was going to be nocturnal, up above the Arctic Circle, where the nearest town isn't one. I'd be up all night measuring soil temperature, measuring ice temperature, measuring air temperature. Then I'd crawl into my warm bed above the busy harbor and pull the curtains and sleep until about two in the afternoon. I knew I was going to enjoy this job.

I had a portable trailer lab, warmed by propane tanks. Everything about this job was low budget. This was the kind of work I always wanted to do. I hadn't done much with this PhD I had dangling at the end of my name. This felt like real work.

It was noisy in the harbor. I'd wake up, walk down to a spot where I'd have lunch with all the transient oil field workers. This feeling of being out of orbit with the rest of the population, it worked for me. I could have done this forever. From the moment I flew into Deadhorse, I embraced everything about this experience, but I missed Kennedy more.

Three months into this position, I took a two-day bus ride to Fairbanks. I got to a phone and called Kennedy. I had to make the conversation brief. I sensed that I missed her more than she missed me. I could understand that. I was in a world of solitude, above the Arctic, working in the ice. She was still in New York.

I soon had to make a decision, I could work for NASA, and travel, and do absolutely everything I ever wanted to do with my life, or I could go back to New York and try to make it work with Kennedy, and find work there.

It was an easy decision. NASA was a guarantee. It was exciting. Everyone wants to work for NASA. And I was the least likely candidate for this job. I couldn't get a recommendation from anyone back at Columbia, so without Art, I wouldn't have had a shot at this kind of work. There would be no logical reason for burning my bridges with my employer after one assignment. Kennedy was wonderful, but they weren't going to stop making girls. There'd be others. Besides, I still didn't know her that well. I didn't want to live in New York, either. In New York, I was unemployed.

I chose Kennedy. I didn't even hesitate. We melted back into each other. I stepped off the plane and Kennedy became the center of my life.

Life was slow back in New York for me. I had enough money in savings to hold on to my place and live frugally for a while, but not forever. While I was gone, Kennedy had some conflict at work and decided to quit being a teacher. But she always had her father's bar to fall back on, so while she worked evenings, we had our days to spend together. We drank tea, read books, listened to music. She was into jazz, and I had never listened to any of it before. There was a science to jazz, a chaos that had no interest in finding order. Most organisms find a routine to their survival, an order. Jazz was indifferent to its own survival. I got a feeling that I had never experienced before when we listened to jazz. I'd ask her to put on a record, and I'd lose myself in it. That was a gift she gave to me.

We were different. I'd share what I knew about the universe, facts that would normally drop jaws, and she'd try to be excited, but it wasn't her thing. And that was fine. I had always figured I'd meet a woman who loved the stars like I did, but this was good, in a way, that she had other interests. I think it gave our relationship some heterogeneity.

Along with records, she liked to collect old books. She didn't read them, she just liked the way her walls looked with books lining the shelves. During a rainy day when I had no interest in going outside, a title of a book caught my eye. The name of the book was *Iridescence*, by Gilbert Wiseman. I had never heard of it, or him, but the title stopped me. I had studied colors, wavelengths, ones we can see, ones we can't. So I pulled the book off the shelf and I flopped on the floor with several of Kennedy's bright colored pillows under me, and I began to read.

The very first line of the book, in the prologue, was anonymous quote, "It is scientifically impossible to bury a tire." Anonymous or not, someone doesn't understand science or impossibilities. But I read on. And on. This book was covered in glue.

I didn't move for hours. This was the first time I enjoyed reading about history, culture, and religions. I had been obsessed with science since before I could read. I never enjoyed my history classes. Every time I had to do a biographical research project it was about a famous astronomer or physicist. I'm familiar with important dates in scientific discovery, or the evolutionary timeline of our species, but I never enjoyed history. I didn't care about the Civil War, or about some tribe in the jungles of South America, unless of course they made significant advancements in astronomy, which many of them did.

Wiseman's book was really just a dusty collection of fables, with almost no real scientific evidence. Yet, I couldn't put the thing down. I knew very little about the Virgin of Guadalupe, or the Taj Mahal, or the Ming Dynasty. He wrote about the superstitions of nomadic people in Eastern Europe who roam the countryside to this day. He wrote about indigenous Sami reindeer herders up above the Arctic Circle in Finland and Norway, singing their spiritual chants under their magnetic skies. He even wrote an entire chapter about Chilean refugees after the 1973 coup d'état, and while it seemed out of place and irrelevant, it was fascinating. Gilbert Wiseman was a talented storyteller.

This book woke me up to something, human behavior. It fascinated me. I always thought I understood other humans because I had a clean grasp of the evolutionary process, and because I excelled in biology and anatomy. But I knew almost nothing about societies and culture. For thousands of years, people had been guessing and interpreting, building cultures around these collective curiosities.

Without the scientists before me, I would have been just as curious about the world, but I would have had a difficult time finding any of the answers. I might have concluded that the planet was flat. I would have bought the geocentric model. It's convincing. I would have looked up at the stars, and let my imagination fill in the blanks. I was fortunate to have grown up at a time when modern science was accessible. Wiseman's book brought me closer to that period of time, when we did guess. His book helped me identify with those curious times in our past.

I asked Kennedy as she was getting up to leave if she had ever read this book. It was slightly sticking out from the other books, so I assumed she had. She responded that she didn't know she owned it, but if I liked it so much I ought to contact the author. *Contact the author? Who does that?*

On the back side of the cover was a picture of Gilbert Wiseman, a jolly looking man a bit older than I was, and the picture was at least a few years old. The caption read that he was an anthropology professor at The Evergreen State College in Olympia, Washington. Without thinking, I dialed information, and easily found the number for the college, who then easily patched me over to Mr. Wiseman's office, who answered after the first ring. I told him, "Hello, I just read most of your book, and I need to use the bathroom, but I'll call you right back." I don't always plan things out well.

We then spoke on the phone until Kennedy came back home from work. I had a lot of questions for him. To go through the book I was reading with the author was incredibly informative and entertaining. I didn't want to let him off the phone.

I finally got around to sharing a bit about myself. When he learned that I had gone to Columbia, he wanted to talk about the Manhattan Project. I almost laughed.

Manhattan was just a code name. The real work was going on in Tennessee, and in the desert of New Mexico. Or at least that's what I thought. Gilb corrected me.

There were warehouses all over Manhattan that housed uranium, places I had walked by and knew very well. 270 Broadway, a building overlooking downtown Manhattan, was the original headquarters of the project before it was moved to Tennessee. Pupin Physics Lab, on the campus of Columbia, where the first nuclear fission experiments took place in the basement. I knew about Enrico Fermi splitting the uranium atom, but you could search the whole campus and learn almost nothing about its role in the Manhattan Project. Most of these activities took place very quietly, like when the football team helped move tons of uranium across campus, unknowingly.

These were the sort of things Gilb knew. Not Gilbert, Gilb.

Before we got off the phone, he had convinced me to come out to Olympia for a couple of days. There was an open faculty position in the science department at the college. He thought maybe I would enjoy Olympia. I just needed a job, and I didn't have a head start on anything in New York, I hadn't been looking. Gilb easily convinced me. The first of many times he would. So I booked a flight, and I interviewed for the faculty position at the college.

I knew, when I was sitting out on Gilb's porch, under a blanket of fog that prevented us from seeing anything in the sky, after spending the day walking around town with Gilb in the rain with no umbrella, and visiting all the antique shops that he frequented, that I wanted to spend my life with Kennedy, in Olympia. And it had nothing to do with the Gilb's porch, or the rain, or the antique shops, or even Olympia. It had nothing to do with the most interesting interview I'd ever been on, either. We took a hike down to the beach at the edge of campus, and some tie-dyed, ponytailed man eventually introduced himself as the dean of students, but not before he offered me a taste of some leaf he picked along the trail.

I was sitting on Gilb's porch, and I knew that I couldn't make it without Kennedy, and Olympia was a new place where we could start over, and I told her all that very soon after I got back from Olympia. I wanted to spend my life with her. I was convinced that the earth was formed in the chaos of a dust cloud just so I could meet her.

Our wedding was quiet. We held it in the park where Kennedy used to jog, and where I used to notice her. My mom and her boyfriend, and the Cohens, and Art from the planetarium were the only people I invited. Kennedy only had her dad there. Gilb sent us a peacock feather. I never asked him why. That was the first time I realized we were friends.

The day after our wedding, we drove across the country and moved into our little blue house on the Westside of Olympia near the college. Gilb knew a guy that was renting a home, so it was easy for us to move right in. Kennedy found work at a cozy pub that brewed its own beer, and I began teaching physics and astronomy to a bunch of art majors at a damp college in the middle of the forest, a place where kids go to get an education, not a career. This was a place in touch with quantum mechanics.

The next five years were some of the happiest years of my life. Olympia, Washington. Geoducks, animal parades, tandem bike commuters, The Evergreen State College, Gilb Wiseman.

And then, tragically, time stood still.

The news flashed the same photograph of the boy, over and over, until it was washed into the public's consciousness. Cigarette in his mouth, teardrop tattoo below his eye, gang signs locked in the air. Never mind the photographs from little league, or his school pictures, or the one of him hugging his sister at her First Communion. When the public thought of the longhaired Latin boy who got hopped up on some wild drug, who attacked the storeowner and tried to take the cop's weapons before they beat his head in, they thought of that photograph. Everyone in Chicago knew that photograph.

The boy died as a result of blunt force trauma to the head. People who knew him said he was a troubled kid. They said he had been crying for help. His teachers said he was a product of his environment. Those who comfortably lived outside this environment called for tougher action in the fight against crime. The police sergeant claimed that he and the other officers were doing their job, that the boy posed a serious risk, that their stun guns weren't slowing him down.

Sam and her friends decided to vandalize the building of the newspaper that mischaracterized the boy they knew from their street, from their church, and from their school. Sam was faster and got away, but her friends didn't.

Sam Rios

I changed my mind a lot. Chemistry, then biology, then psychology, then neuroscience. That's how it happened for me. College students ask me if I always wanted to study neuroscience. It would have been a lot simpler if I did. I tell them, *each time I reached the horizon, I looked out and saw there was something else out there.*

In high school it was all about chemistry for me, testing water quality, pH levels. I memorized the periodic table. I had access to a lab, and I was about the only one who used it. In college, I shifted my focus to biology. It was more fun. I wanted to study the trees, conduct ecological research, and eat mushrooms. Evolution enlightened me. It taught me who I was, where I came from.

But I again shifted focus. Humans. Human behavior, human psychology. Why humans do all the things we do. We're complicated and we have complicated needs, and from what I've experienced, it's tough to be a human. We make problems for ourselves, and create more problems trying to fix our problems. We burden each other; we burden the planet. If humans disappeared overnight, nearly every other life form would flourish.

Why do humans pollute the waters or butcher the forests, creating the environmental issues that I had studied in chemistry and biology? Why do we overfish and overharvest? Why do we rely on excess?

We follow. We do what we're told. We're gullible, greedy, and fearful. Skills that kept us alive in past ages are now racking up a bill that this planet can't afford to pay.

I kept with psychology for a few years, but I didn't stay there. There had to be something deeper about us. The human brain. The human brain has cured diseases. It has allowed humans to explore the oceans, the sky, and our solar system. The human brain has discovered its place in the universe. It evolved and expanded and adapted. It is a beautiful organ.

I had a college professor, Philip Duke, who, to my knowledge, knew very little about neuroscience, but his off-topic, sloppy lectures are the reason I now study the brain. He taught me about this species, and our path as living organisms, tracing us directly from the formation of the planet, and our solar system. I already knew about evolution, but I never considered that we were currently just another arbitrary stage. That was a powerful message to me at the time.

He sparked a curiosity in me that led to my career, which led me to meet my husband, and all the wonderful things in my life that I now enjoy. And yet, for years, I held a grudge against him. I held a heavy, useless, irrational grudge. It was my brain doing its thing.

So, that's where I landed. I now work in academic neurology. My job combines clinical research and teaching. I've published papers about epilepsy caused by brain abscess, and women with spinal cord injuries who could reach orgasm. The best part about my job is that I get to see my husband, my favorite adult, every day. We work in the same clinic. It's how we met.

I live in North Kenwood now with my family. We have a comfortable home, in a comfortable neighborhood that smells like flowers. We move slowly over clean sidewalks, beneath tall elegant buildings, past dogs that don't bite. It's not far from the Lower West Side neighborhood I grew up in, which smelled like lighter fluid, where longhaired boys got themselves killed.

You look at me, and you don't know what my ethnicity is. I look like a Mexican, or maybe I'm Asian, or Hawaiian. I could fit in everywhere, and nowhere. I like that about me. I know that look on your face when you don't know my ethnicity. It makes you uneasy, and I know why. I know how your brain works.

Our home was a Catholic home. Everybody was Catholic. Every wall was Catholic, some of the plates, and the candles. We even had a Frisbee with the pope's face on it. My mom didn't know it was a Frisbee and started filling it up with cat food.

We were superstitious. Every time a plate broke my mom would whisper a prayer in Spanish. We all feared God, my brothers and I, and we all thought we could avoid his omnipresence. I'd steal bottles from the liquor store, stash them under a dark coat, and drink them alone in a dark alley, hoping God wouldn't see me. I never questioned any of it. This was what I believed.

I'm a pack animal. I always have been. I got mixed up with gangs and drugs, all before my first day of high school. My friends and I vandalized a building. We had our reasons. They got caught. I moved faster, and they didn't snitch. Nobody does.

But my mom knew. She said the Virgin Mary came to her and warned her that I was going to get myself killed. I don't remember if I believed her or not, it didn't matter. It wasn't like I could've convinced her she was wrong. People in my home spoke in permanent ink.

My mom sent me to live with my Filipino father and his wife and their newborn baby in Visalia, California. I didn't know where California was. I had never looked on a map. I probably had some media influenced perception of California as one long beach with volleyball nets every so often.

No one knew me when I arrived, and those who remembered me from when I was a toddler, they didn't recognize me. So, it was a fresh start in many ways. The voices that told me who I was, that I'd never amount to anything, they were all gone. The only person in my ear was my dad, telling me to get ready for church, telling me to do my homework.

In Chicago, the word 'school' meant nothing. It was a location. It was a place we'd go sometimes, out of habit. It was like a base. There was no reward for doing well in school. We lived in a world of instant, immediate consequences. There was never any positive consequence for school. No one thought about the future. It wasn't until my dad held me accountable and modeled to me what responsibility looked like, that I actually started taking school seriously.

The first week of my freshman year in high school, we had a test in history. I had been present for every day of school, and my dad was making sure I was doing my homework, so I did well on the test. I got all but one question correct. It felt good. I brought the test home, and I showed my dad. He was proud, but not too proud. He asked me why I got that one question wrong. I've often wondered how much impact that moment had on me, that tiny fraction of a moment where he was proud, but withheld.

On the next test I did get a perfect score, 100%. It wasn't difficult. I hardly studied. I just paid attention. I had a good memory. I could remember everything that the teacher had said, almost word for word. By the end of the quarter, when I got my report card, I had a 4.0, and I was elevated into more advanced classes.

My father provided structure. He was employed, conservative, and he worked hard. He was a good father. Back in Chicago, no one cared where I was. No one kept tabs on me. I was wild. Living with my dad, I had a curfew, and chores. He never drank or smoked, didn't allow any of it in the house. He was a stoic man, distant from people, and he was tough to please.

My dad was religious, Protestant, and was never shy about reminding me how misinformed my Catholic upbringing had left me. He assumed I learned about God at church. No, we'd sneak out and smoke in the bathrooms during mass. I learned about God through scary stories that my mom and my aunts would tell me. I feared God. God was like the mean principal of the world, and the world was no bigger than our neighborhood in South Chicago, from 18th to Roosevelt.

Going to church with my dad was a lot different than anything I was used to. I had to pay attention. He paid attention to whether or not I paid attention. I listened to the stories, tolerated the music and the nice people, but now that I was forced to stop and think about it, I had my doubts. I wasn't sure I really believed.

I felt a sense of community at church, nothing stronger, nothing deeper. But that sense of community could be confusing. From time to time I would catch myself being pulled in. Pack animal mentality. I know this about myself. If I was stressed, or feeling low, or maybe a cute boy wasn't paying any attention to me, I could feel the church yanking at me, and it felt emotionally manipulating. I'd watched the hundreds of other members of the congregation looking hypnotized. They looked gullible to me, and they looked like they were okay with it. Like they were just fine with surrendering logic. It seemed so easy to me. Such an easy puzzle to solve. You could scrutinize the claims of that Bible even a little, and it doesn't add up. I didn't know it yet, but I was starting to think like a scientist.

Throughout high school I gravitated towards science. I became increasingly aware of my surroundings, scientifically. We lived in cattle ranching country. And the rivers were polluted. I started to question things. My brain was more activated, and I was curious. I started to connect the dots. I wasn't just a fact memorizer, but I had inquiry skills. I started writing essays on the topic of water pollution, and fearlessly, pointed fingers towards the billion-dollar cattle industry.

It was the same feeling that had burned inside of me when the cops killed the longhaired boy, the boy I rode the bus with in Kindergarten. I wanted to hold the newspapers accountable for running such a careless article, so I talked my two friends into vandalizing the building with me, breaking windows and spray painting the walls, and I made them think it was all their idea from the beginning. Now, I was more guided in my activism. I decided to write my own articles.

I got invited, along with other students from high schools in the area, to go to

Washington DC and speak in front of Congress about water quality. They yawned. I can remember reading my speech, looking out at all the grey haired politicians, and they were yawning. So, I called them on it. I went off script, and said something like, "There will be still be water pollution past the election cycle, your children and grandchildren will inherit this problem. If yawning is really how we fix this, they're going to wonder why we didn't just yawn more."

My dad never seemed too interested in my newfound environmental causes, but he was proud that I was asserting myself, and although he was never rich, he found the money to send me to Washington to speak in front of all those dormant politicians. When I told him what I had said, he smirked.

High school continued along this same pattern. I was smart. I did well. I was in the most advanced classes. I was praised highly by every teacher, and I suppose I got used to it. But every once in awhile, I would sit and think about my mom's vision of the Virgin, or whatever actually happened in her head, and I was grateful for it. My life had direction, and I was motivated to go make a difference in the world. My dad had, in a short period of time, instilled in me a desire to work hard and prove myself. I found that, at the core, I had a lot of his qualities.

I graduated valedictorian in my high school class, and received a full academic scholarship to UC Berkeley. I declared myself a chemistry major. I got comfortable working in labs in high school, and figured I could make a career out of this. But after a year, I switched to biology. I had participated in a research trip in the forests out on the coast. Half the team was chemistry and the other half was biology majors. I fell in love with biology during that time. I fell in love with nature. And the biology majors were having more fun.

I was starting to take on some radical views about the environment and politics. The girls I was living with would go and meet up with an anarchist group in Oakland, and they brought home literature. My pack mentality kicked in again, and before I knew it I was hiding from the cops after we monkey wrenched some expensive logging equipment.

I got away again, spent a summer in a tree in the middle of Oregon, keeping it from getting cut down. Just another woman and I living up in a tree. These were blurry times. My pack mentality had violently kicked in. I believed in our causes, and the actions appeared normal and justified.

I found myself 150 feet high in an ancient western red cedar with all the amenities I'd ever need. There were traverse lines to trees in the area, where other sitters were staying. They had built water-catching devices, had even installed solar power. There were cargo lines and sprout farms. It was a village. I started to feel more comfortable up in the tree than down below. Up in the tree, we were harnessed in, and we could move freely.

The woman I was with showed symptoms of appendicitis while we were in that tree together, and I finally convinced her that we needed to go get help, that her appendix was going to burst. There was no other choice. A tree sitter in a nearby tree helped us get to the hospital, where they removed her inflamed appendix.

I've never pieced it together, but somehow, when we were waiting in the hospital in Eugene, the cops came in and arrested me. They just yanked me out of the chair in the waiting room and cuffed me. I was charged as an accomplice to the crime against the lumber company back in California. I avoided jail on a plea bargain, but I had a fine, and I lost my scholarship, and neither my mom nor dad would talk to me.

The woman whose appendix nearly burst let me come live with her in Portland, Oregon, and I worked at her bookstore and cafe, trying to pay off the fine. These were low times for me. It all happened so fast. One moment I was given a scholarship to study at a major university, and the next I was pouring coffee. I thought my life was over. I thought I blew it. Saving trees meant nothing at that point. Cut them down.

Then something happened that changed my life. I say this, and it's easy to miss the importance of this statement. What I mean is, something happened, it was random, and it changed my whole existence. I wouldn't have my met my husband, we wouldn't have adopted our two children, and I wouldn't have my career.

A strange looking guy came in the coffee shop and put a poster up on the bulletin board. That poster would change my life. We couldn't tell if he was an adult or a kid. He was just a round, wimpy looking guy. My friend who had the appendectomy and I were trying not to laugh as he fidgeted with his stapler, trying to staple a poster to our community board, and change my life. There were several thumbtacks he could have used, but he used a stapler. And that means nothing, whether he used a stapler or a few thumbtacks, but had he used neither, had he never shown up, had he just not existed, or chose not to staple a poster to the community board, I wouldn't know my two children. The bond I have with my two children is covalent. There is nothing that I value more. I have cried, years after we adopted them, because of those first 63 days of their lives that we did not share with them. I want those days, too. It hurts me, right now, knowing that my two children spent their first 63 days, from their birthday on July 20 until we arrived in Manila on September 21, 2009, without their mom.

We went over to the board and read his poster. It was promoting an event where a discussion panel would give thoughts on the topic of life after death. The invited guests ranged from a cultural anthropologist, a scientist, a minister, a priest, and a rabbi.

It intrigued me. Life after death. What would a scientist actually think about that? I was starting to ask myself the same question. I never feared death, I always believed that whatever happens is supposed to happen. When I was living 150 feet above the ground in a tree, we could have died at any moment, yet I slept soundly. But now that I had lost my scholarship and was living on my friend's couch, I wasn't as confident about my path anymore. I wasn't sure if there was anyone looking out for us, and I didn't know what I believed. I wanted badly to hear what a scientist had to say. I knew that I could trust a scientist.

I wrote down the date and location on a receipt and put it in my coat. I didn't think about it again for weeks. But it just so happened that on the day of the event, it was a chilly, early summer day and I was wearing the same coat, and I accidentally found the receipt folded up in one of the pockets. A cold front over the Willamette Valley, causing me to wear the coat, find the receipt, changing my life. My job, my husband, my kids. A chilly, early summer day. I grabbed the coat at the last minute when I walked out the door that morning.

The event itself wasn't too interesting, but there were two speakers, both professors at a little liberal arts college up north who I felt were speaking more at my level. One of them was round, one of them was skinny. The skinny man was the scientist, the man who I came to see, the man who was going to tell me what life was all about. I actually thought that, I thought he was going to explain everything to me. That didn't quite happen.

He spoke completely from a scientific standpoint. In a way I appreciated it. He gave very few opinions. He simply explained what happened to the body of any animal after it dies, and how death is a very important part of evolution, that it makes room for the next generation. The way he phrased it, it reminded me that we are very much a part of the animal kingdom. In the face of all that religious doctrine I've been exposed to, of man over beast, of God creating us in his image, I favored the position of us being a part of the animal kingdom, as opposed to being above it.

The rounder, happier looking professor did speak about God, but from a much more spiritual standpoint, not claiming any religion to be his own. He also talked about our connection with the animal kingdom, and with nature, in a spiritual way. That had appeal to me too. I was one of those kids that really held out hope that our cats would go to heaven. As an adult, I liked the idea of our spirits having a connection with the animals around us, like we all looked out for each other. I wanted that to be true. It just didn't really make any sense, though.

At the time, I felt like I would have landed pretty evenly between these two views. I wanted to believe in a god, or goddess, or some kind of higher power. I didn't want to admit that this was all there was. I knowingly held out hope. I was hoping the scientist had something scientific to say about a higher power. I didn't ever understand the Big Bang. I'd like to think there was someone, or something, that sparked it.

I spoke with the professors afterward. They were approachable. I positioned myself so that they couldn't really get past me. I basically told them my whole story, all the way back to the longhaired kid who I used to ride the bus with, and vandalizing the newspaper building, and my dad in Visalia, and losing my scholarship, and getting yanked out of the hospital waiting room by the cops. I spoke to them for a long time, not letting either of them really get a word in. They looked genuinely amazed with my life story. They may have even doubted it. Wouldn't you?

Eventually, the skinnier one, he said to me, "Would you ever consider attending Evergreen?" A month later I was in Olympia, applying for financial aid, looking for a place to live, figuring out what I was going to do with my life.

I sent a letter to my dad giving him all my contact info, letting him know I was starting over at a liberal arts college, and that I wanted to study psychology. I had become fascinated with human behavior, with my own behavior. I felt good about my new direction in life. I didn't expect to hear from my dad, but I wanted him to know where I was, and what I was up to.

Soon after I sent my dad the letter, Lena, my dad's wife, called to let me know that my grandfather had died. I hardly remembered him. He was a very distant, stoic man, even more so than my dad was. It was just the way these men are, I suppose, these men of my family that I don't know.

So, without invitation, I took a bus back to San Francisco, where the funeral was to be held. My dad didn't speak to me. But, I shouldn't have felt too bad, he didn't speak to anyone, and I wasn't really there for him. I actually felt obligated to say goodbye to my grandfather. Whatever that meant. Maybe I was just curious.

The ceremony was religious, with people reading Bible passages. I was surprised to learn that my dad's entire family was Catholic, and that my dad converted because of his wife, Lena, who was a Protestant. Perhaps I'll never understand my dad. I've accepted that.

He and his brothers walked out on a pier and scattered his ashes. I watched the ashes fly away, and I experienced some heavy, confusing emotions. I couldn't explain it; I'll never be able to explain it. It could have been my mind playing tricks on me, but I felt something far too powerful to understand. Those were the ashes of a human, spread and carried away into untraceable pieces. It was all that remained of him, of this man that I hardly knew, who was tougher than dirt, and had grown up working the fields of California.

Half of me belongs to this culture. But I was removed from it. My brothers back in Chicago had a different dad than I did, so I was the only one in that family who was ethnically Filipino. It was a part of my past that I knew nothing about.

I met a cousin that I had never known. I didn't know she existed. She was the only speaker who didn't read from the Bible. Instead she took a quote from Carlos Bulosan.

We do not take democracy for granted. We feel it grow in our working together, many millions of us working toward a common purpose. If it took us several decades of sacrifice to arrive at this faith, it is because it took us that long to know what part of America is ours.

I didn't know who Carlos Bulosan was, I was not a part of this culture, and yet, when my cousin read this quote, and I saw the years of hard work on the faces of my family, I recognized something in myself. It wasn't a clear thought, it was a bit blurry, but I sensed that I had much in common with these people.

I'm like them, I'm driven, I work hard. I don't quit.

I said goodbye to my family, knowing that not a person there would miss me. They didn't know me. And I read *America is in the Heart*, by Carlos Bulosan, on the bus ride back up to Olympia. And I'm glad I did. It helped explain me to myself. I trusted myself forever after that.

For two years, I studied psychology. I put all of my energy into the program. I didn't date; I had very few friends. I was home at night, studying. Nothing else mattered. My apartment was a bed and a desk and a stack of books. I was grateful for a second chance to do something with my life. Nothing was going to get in my way.

In the spring of 2001, my last semester, with all of my psychology classes out of the way, I enrolled in a class, poetically titled *The All-Encompassing Cosmic Experience*, taught by Philip Duke, the skinny professor from the discussion panel back in Portland two years earlier. It was thematic for me to take a class from him, since it was he who suggested I consider going back to college in the first place.

Philip came out wearing clothes that were far too big on him. He looked skinnier and paler than I remember. He had a blank stare on his face as he walked up to the podium. On the giant white board behind him he wrote:

The All-Encompassing Cosmic Experience – April 2, 2001
Welcome
Thank Jupiter?
Reimann Hypothesis
The Five Ages of the Universe

What I didn't know at the time was that these three or four topics would have almost no shot of making it into his lecture. The students all knew this. They'd laugh as he began to list the bullet points on the wall. Philip had every intention of lecturing on these topics. He was oblivious to his own tendencies.

On that first day, he handed out a syllabus of about a dozen required readings, and the expectations of the course. All you had to do was read some of the books and show up at the evaluation and discuss what you learned. I read it twice to make sure I wasn't missing something. It didn't seem right. I had been task driven, taught that nothing came that easy, since I rolled off the bus back in California as a teenager.

I almost left to go speak with my enrollment counselor, to see about finding a new class for me. If I had, tragically, I would have never met my children, my angels. I still revisit that memory, just to make sure I stay.

I remember the exact moment when Philip began to speak. I hadn't heard his voice since the forum in Portland two years earlier, but it brought me right back. His voice may have been the reason I came to Olympia in the first place. You couldn't ignore it, and you wouldn't want to. He was phenomenal. Here was this scrawny looking man, his face was sunk and he looked horrible, and yet, when he lectured, his voice thundered. Five minutes in, I knew this was going to be the most informative class I would take at this little liberal arts college.

Each day I'd get there early to get a good spot in the front, because the lecture hall would fill up, past occupancy. People who weren't even enrolled would crash the class just to hear him lecture.

And that's all he did, lecture. Occasionally, he would provide a slide or have an artifact, like a stone meteorite, which he'd pass around, indifferent to the rarity or value of it. He'd explain that it was fusion crust, and that complete fusion crusted stones are very rare, that collectors would be willing to spend a lot of money to own something like this, and then he'd pass it around the room like it was a paper clip.

I had a hand recorder, which I used to record every class in college. Even back when I was at Berkeley, I used the same hand recorder, and I would rush to my computer and type out the transcript and save it on my hard drive. I still have all my lectures from all of my classes in college, but the only ones I ever looked at again are from Philip's class. They read like a police chase. He couldn't stay on topic. I'm fortunate to have his voice in my head as I read through them.

After 23 minutes into the first lecture, my hand went up. The lecture had already derailed, and we were talking about religion. I'd been fighting with where my spirituality lays, what I believed in, if I believed in anything at all. I wasn't the gullible kid living in Chicago, and I wasn't the teenager in California that wanted to prove everyone wrong. I wanted to believe there was a way to blend spirituality and science. I needed to believe that. By odd chance, out of dozens of raised hands, he called on me, and this was his lengthy response to a question I had waited two years to ask him.

Min 23:   There *is* much we can learn from religion. The infrastructure, the convenience of religion, how available it is ... if you were to find yourself in any urban or suburban, maybe even rural setting, you'd find you could probably walk to the nearest Christian church, assuming you are not too particular about the denomination. In most cases, you will be welcomed in, and for free, you would be exposed to an hour-long sermon. A typical experience may include a moment where ... those in attendance are asked to give a reasonable donation. I imagine if you were a visitor, or a poor college student, you could be forgiven if you passed on this. Forgiveness seems to be their thing. (laughter)

These organizations aren't taxed, but they do keep a payroll of employees and have some overhead, so they rely on consistent donations from congregation members. They operate very similarly to a business. Larger congregations, or those located in more affluent areas are going to benefit from their financial base. They will acquire new technology, perhaps more expensive ... I don't know ... things ... whatever churches have. Better pews, a more life like Jesus execution sculpture. (laughter)

My point is this. Churches are relevant. Whether you go to church or not, whether you are affiliated with any form of organized religion, you're familiar with church. You're familiar with what church is all about. You know where they stand on issues. Currently, churches are doing a great job of making themselves available to the population, and spreading their messages to the population. I say currently because the way they used to do it wasn't so great, they used to kill people. That's cheating, in my opinion. I don't think they cheat as much as they used to, at least I hope not. But ... a dozen centuries of evolutional bottle necking and so many of us are the descendants of followers, the ones who dared speak out weren't always given an opportunity to reproduce. So it's almost a radical act to proclaim yourself free of theological ideology. (question from the audience)

Free of theological ideology? What I mean is ... Well, let me explain it this way ... pleading ignorance to the existence of theological ideology might be a better way for me to put that. Let's say you were having a conversation with a devout Christian follower, someone who took the Bible literally, word for word. Let's say you were agnostic or atheist, which, seems to be a safe call here at Evergreen. Let's say this person asked you if you believed in God. You'd have a hard time responding with something like, *I don't understand what you mean by the word god.* You'd have a hard time making the case that you aren't familiar with the concept of a singular male god that the Christians and Jews have given us, the Abrahamic religions. You couldn't say you've never heard of god. Of course you've heard of god. Most of the people in this room grew up going to a church or a synagogue ... and are now in recovery. (laughter)

What I mean is ... the fact that you can't claim ignorance on the subject reflects the position, or the leverage, these religions have in our culture. Every one of us can be expected to give a straight answer whether or not we believe in god ... or ... if we believe in *their* god.

Now, let's imagine you were to respond with, *no, I don't know what you mean by god, I've never heard of this concept. But I believe in unicorns, do you believe in unicorns?* Watch how scientific this conversation would get.

The Christian would probably respond with, *there is no evidence of unicorns, why would you believe in unicorns?* (laughter, pause)

I know I'm about to get way off topic here, but ... I like to tell people that there have been tens of thousands of gods worshipped throughout human history. I believe in one less than Christians do. They can't fathom that thought, because to them, their god isn't just one of those pagan hocus pocus gods that people sit around the fire and chant to. Except, that's exactly what it is. Their god is traced back to ancient mythology, and survived through thousands of years of religious tournament. Like a tournament. Like a basketball tournament, someone has to win. So, Christianity won, and there are a lot of theories as to why. Some of them are monstrous.

People ask me if I am an atheist or agnostic, and honestly, I don't really think about it much. I don't think about god that much. Really. I have a lot of opinions about the religions that claim a god, but I don't spend a lot of time wondering about the concept of a deity. I have other things to think about.

I think about science. I think about physics. I think about the universe. And ... and if that's what god is, then sure, I think about god, but I've yet to see any rational need to worship this force. It's doing just fine without my worship. In fact, it would be egotistical of me to feel like my worship is needed.

The power of this universe, it has existed for close to 14 billion years, so, I can't imagine it sits around wishing that this particular life form, *us*, would stop what we were doing and worship it. Our egos are so swollen that we really struggle with the concept that we're arbitrary, that we are … we are but a relatively intelligent stage of life on a fortunately tilted planet swinging around a star which is halfway through its hydrogen burning phase, a star which is one of over a hundred billion stars in this galaxy, one of over a hundred billion galaxies in the universe.

That makes people feel small. Maybe we were never supposed to feel any bigger than that. Our egos, our religions, symbiotic to one another, have misled us to believe otherwise.

But, when asked, when really pressed on whether or not I am agnostic or atheist, I generally do say that I am an atheist. It's not that I'm convinced without a doubt that there is no god. If tomorrow someone showed me evidence of a god, I would be very enthusiastic. I would want to see that evidence. But I've never in my life seen any evidence as to the existence of a god.

On the other hand, I am agnostic to unicorns, because we discover new species all the time. If you showed me evidence of unicorns, you wouldn't be the first person to discover a new species. Stranger things have happened. But if you showed me evidence of a god, if you were able to scientifically prove the existence of a god, you would be the very first person to do so. You might win a Nobel Prize. You'd at least be in the running.

But, I've wandered off, far from your question, which I don't even remember any longer ... oh, wait, yes, what can science learn from religion? I was just thinking about this the other day, or a few years ago, I don't know. (laughter)

I was starting to explain, before I got off track, that I believe religion has done a good job of spreading their message, once they stopped killing people. What I'm trying to say is that having churches set up throughout the land, accessible to people, that's a good model. Science could learn from this. Science could rival this, because science could meet several of the identifiable needs people have when they enter a church, and science could fulfill it in a more honest way.

People are looking for answers, community, support, help, and perspective. Science can do this. Science can be kind and caring.

So, how did science get so far behind in this race? Why is religion kicking our butts? Why is there a church on every street in America, but you've got to pay to get into a museum, and there's a whole lot less of them.

Religions represent what we can't figure out. Well, that shrinks by the hour. But there was a time when we didn't have anything figured out. Humans had a sizable gap of time, at least from our vantage point, between the moment when we were capable of a grand curiosity, of contemplating the stars, our own existence, the possibility of afterlife ... hold that thought, just hold that thought for a second, I recently read a great quote, something like … *that belief in the afterlife is the product of an ego so delicate that we cannot fathom the future of the universe without ourselves* … ok, but … what I was saying, we had a gap of time, a sizable gap of time, between our dawn of curiosity and the advancements necessary to provide any answers. We didn't have telescopes in the earliest centuries of the last millennium, we didn't have the Hubble Telescope or quantum mechanics before the twentieth century, so I understand the abundance of misinformation, to a degree. We're creative. We make things up. It's easier to just make it up.

This period of time between the developed cognitive awareness necessary to be curious and the technological advancements necessary to provide answers, this period of time gave us a storm of religions. And there are people who are irreversibly invested in these religions, still; various religious figures, authority figures, et cetera, et cetera. They have done their best, at times, to slow progress, to extend this period of ignorance as long as possible. Example? Galileo Galilei. We know about him. We know what they did to him. To be fair, though, the church didn't really have a hard time with the heliocentric theory, the Jesuits may have even supported him on that. Galileo got himself into trouble for mocking the Pope. Remind me sometime to talk about Galileo, what a guy.

Ok, what was I saying? There are people who have done whatever they can to keep the public from thinking for themselves, they are irreversibly invested in their religions, they have done their best to extend this period of ignorance ... and people *do* want to know what's out there, they want to know badly, dangerously. But we need to get better at skeptically analyzing what we're being fed. Even a fish won't bite if he suspects there's a hook attached. I've had a long day, class. (laughter) I've gotten off topic, again.

Let me wrap this up. I was explaining how science has a lot to learn from religion, and that religion has had a head start, but ... I'm not too concerned with the recent events of the last few thousand years. This period of time, this age of viral religious growth, the age of religious empires, it is comparatively small. And I predict that faith based religions are not a permanent feature of our species, either. This is just a phase, a small phase.

Consider, again, as always, that the universe is about 14 billion years old, and that our planet is about 4.6 billion years old. Humans who look and move like us are roughly 200,000 years old, and we first used writing as a means to communicate about five or six thousand years ago, when our economic needs became more complex, causing us to store information outside of our brains.

Let's really compare how brief our human existence is so far. Humans are recent when we compare ourselves to ... say ... flowers. We are young in comparison to flowers. Flowers have been here for over 100 million years. Insects, land plants, all about 500 million years on this planet. Don't quote me on that, I could be off by a tad. Hopefully that gives you a bit of a perspective that we are still developing. 200,000 years as modern humans. 200,000 years is nothing. Our planet is 4.6 billion years old. 200,000 years is a blink. Even the genus Homo, two and half million years since the emergence of the genus Homo; even that's nothing.

Let's put this into perspective. Let's condense the history of our planet into a month, a 30-day month. 4.6 billion years, condensed into a 30-day Gregorian month. We'll call it April, since, I believe, we are currently in the Gregorian month of April (laughter), because, honestly, I often forget. I try to live based on lunar months. That's a whole other ... we'll get into that another time, don't even get me started on that sloppy Gregorian calendar (laughter).

Ok, so, we condense the history of our planet, the timeline of our planet into the month of April ... let me see here, I wrote this down, I was hoping I could wedge this into a lecture, even if ... Ok, if the age of our planet was condensed into the month of April, every day would be about 153,000,000 years. Every hour would be about 6,400,000 years. Every minute would be 1,070,000 years. Now, keep in mind, 200,000 years as modern humans. That lands us somewhere in the last dozen seconds of the last day of April. We're recent.

Let me tie this up. I emphasize that we are recent because that forgives us. We are playing around with this thing we call 'curiosity', and our reaction time is slow, and many of us haven't realized that many of the ... things that we have been historically curious of, well, we now have the answers. But the answers don't line up well with what we had believed, what we had hoped would be the answers. So many generations before us, believing the same thing. That's a lot of force. That's an 18-wheeler slamming on the breaks. We carry the momentum of those that lived before us. We like the idea of a heaven, a destination after this earthly place, of a heavenly father looking over us, the romance of a virgin mother, or whatever else people believe, we tend to believe because we want to. But that doesn't make it true.

I think we'll eventually figure it out though. It's just a strange time to be alive. Never have we enjoyed the availability of so much information, yet so many of us are drowning in ignorance. I think we'll eventually sort this out. Or ... maybe I'm being hopeful. (laughter)

So ... okay, here's what I believe is the best way to answer your question, based on how I see it. I submit this ... not that religions start acting more like science, although if they did, there wouldn't be too many religions left ... I submit that the scientific community begin to act more like religions. I know, this is a long, long answer to your question, but what if ... every community had a building, similar to a church, that operated like a church. A resident scholar, living modestly on the donations of the congregation, would hold lectures, would present scientific data, and he or she would be trained in the art of holding audience, of explaining concepts in ways that a diverse audience could grasp, similar to the skills of a preacher or a minister. This resident would be available to meet privately with people, perhaps if someone needed some counsel, for which I believe science can be a useful tool.

Basically, hijack the church model, every damn thing about it, even call it church, but teach science instead. Teach people to be scientifically literate, for the sake of a better quality of living, for the sake of responsible community citizenship.

I would gladly donate weekly to my local science church. Science church ... I like the sound of that ... I would even offer services as a resident scientist. It would be an honor. I would live like a monk, in modest quarters, spending my days studying. We really could take every aspect of how a church operates, and model a new kind of church with a different message. We wouldn't do this to piss them off, but to pay homage to an earlier stage of curiosity.

Sunday is a convenient day, most people don't work on Sundays, we can have mass on Sunday mornings, why not? Perhaps these church sermons would not be too different from ... these lectures here, on campus, but without the student loans. (laughter, some applause)

Cycle this through a couple of generations and perhaps ... we will have flushed the religions out of our politics, rewarding ourselves with a scientifically literate electorate, making decisions for the good of everyone, relying on the latest and most accurate science. We would still have liberals and conservatives, but they would be agreeable to each other. There would be mutual respect. We would have a conservative and a liberal agenda towards addressing the needs of our society, while considering science. The differences in our approaches, we could live with.

As a species, we need to refocus. We need to shift our energies. Science can save us. It's about the only thing that can. And with every generation that we don't do this, that we don't make this shift, we are in more jeopardy of killing ourselves off. We have so much more potential. We haven't even begun to see our potential. But I have confidence in us.

I've heard people compare intelligent life to mountains. That if a mountain was to get too large, it would crumble under its own weight. And that if a species becomes too intelligent, that it will also kill itself off. I don't know if I agree. We are flawed by our own shortsightedness, not by our intelligence. Our intelligence should save us, it always has.

Think about humans. Think about why we are here, and why we have emerged from the Serengeti with the skills we have, and why we have held our place in the animal kingdom. We were an unlikely candidate. Like an underdog.

It's possible we've lost our path ... we've endured kingdoms that have engulfed us, religions that have misinformed us, colonization that have oppressed several of us, industrial revolutions that have poisoned the earth, but these are all recent events.

So ... yes, religion does have something to offer us, many things. Perhaps not what religion has intended to offer us, but it has much substance, nonetheless. Throughout history we have always built upon the past, whether we agree with it or not. This new age of scientific inquiry, abundant throughout the population, would, I believe, usher in a new epoch. An age of science, an age of thinking scientifically, could save us. And I expect that it will.

I hope I answered your question. Now, I should get back to the lecture I had planned. (laughter)

If I had taken a photograph of Philip, you would have asked who that dangerously unhealthy man was. But if you were in the same room, listening to him lecture, you would have felt what I felt. I was in awe. Philip was larger than life at his podium. For him to take the time and effort to discuss my question, it was validating and empowering. People didn't always take me seriously, not at first.

My original question was directed more towards how to blend science and spirituality, but this was as close as I was going to get with him. What I was left with, what I think he was trying to say, was that all of our questions stem from curiosity, but only science is dedicated to answering these questions with the truth. He was hopeful that we would eventually begin to value science more as a global society.

When I look around at everyone I've ever known, myself included, I perceive that we are inexperienced with the truth. We believe what we want to be true, or what we don't want to be true, or what we're told is true -- or maybe we're rebellious and we believe what we're told isn't true. But we are mainly indifferent towards what is truthfully accurate. Reality is a variable, and we like our variables to be dependent on our motives.

I've struggled with reality for most of my life. I wasn't good at recognizing it. I believed what people wanted me to believe. They told me I wasn't smart, that I wasn't capable of anything. I've believed a lot of bullshit about myself. When I was in Chicago, I believed life was about pushing other people down to get ahead. I believed that was the only way someone like me *could* get ahead.

When you grow up in a place where crime is contagious, and your teenage friends are getting locked up, and people are afraid to come to your community, you feel that you're not worth much. When the media is pushing a perception about you and your neighborhood, and they write articles from the standpoint that your community is plagued with poverty, that people should avoid walking alone in those neighborhoods, and investing in those neighborhoods, that gets into your psyche. I believed every word I ever heard about myself. It's not what I wanted to be true, but I believed it because I was afraid that it was true.

Within a month of living under my dad's roof, he challenged me to reach my potential simply by expecting it of me. He wanted to believe his daughter was bright. He had high expectations of me, and I met them. I had to. Was I just as gullible to believe that I was an intelligent, capable person?

The truth is irrelevant. Had I stayed in Chicago, with that crowd, we know how my life would have ended up. My friends weren't doing much with their lives, probably didn't finish high school. I would have been just like them. There were forces at work that wanted me to do very little with my life. Many people from where I grew up are dead or in prison, that doesn't happen by coincidence. There are forces at work, forces that are tampering with reality, and how we view ourselves.

But if Philip was correct in his prediction that we will eventually begin to think more scientifically about our surroundings, and ourselves, I believe poverty will be a quick casualty of that new age. If we are to seek the truth, and favor reality, we will learn that we are intelligent, and capable of providing for ourselves.

This is what that Carlos Bulosan quote meant to me, that my cousin read. I had to recognize my place in this world; I had to overcome the forces at work. My view of myself was blurry, like when I rub my eyes in the morning, and they're slow to focus, and there's two of everything.

I went from believing I was nobody, to believing that nothing short of an A was acceptable. I went from fearing God, to privately mocking the nice people at my dad's church with their arms in the air, praising, worshipping.

Once we learn the truth about ourselves, once we have focus, we can then find our place in this world, and what we are supposed to do. Rarely does anyone other than ourselves ever say anything accurate about ourselves. To do so, would be an act of love.

Maybe Philip had no intention of communicating this, maybe it was just me, hearing what I wanted to hear, but what I got out of his lectures, many of his lectures, was that there might be nothing we know of more spiritually rewarding than the truth; That if there is any meaningful spirituality to be experienced in this existence, it is met with the knowledge of ourselves. Maybe Philip meant that, maybe he didn't.

I think about my grandfather's funeral often. I still picture the faces of my relatives. They knew hard work. I was affected, very positively, by the common ground I found between them and myself. The more I think about them, the more I know myself.

I was driven, ferociously, to find my place in this world. These were important years for me.

All throughout my time in Olympia, I lived in the middle of town, above a cupcake shop, near a historic park. It was an old building, the elevator would shake, and the lights would flicker. The park reminded me of some of the parks back in Chicago. I liked the park, but it had its downsides. From my window I could see drug deals going down all night. There were homeless teenagers and their dogs with spiked collars, and thugs with neck tattoos.

Some people were bent out of shape over the environment of the park. But it really never bothered me much. I didn't mind taking my schoolwork down there on a nice day. If there was a homeless guy asleep on the bench near me, I didn't mind. It took more than that to scare me off.

In my apartment building, down the hall, there was a girl that was probably my age. I'd see her at school; she was a student there. At night she would walk over to the park and bring a rope with her, light the end on fire, and spin it. I could see her dancing around from my apartment window. She was odd and quirky and wore strange, unnecessary hats. I never knew how to approach her. I wanted to ask her what the hell she was doing, but in a nice way. I wanted to know how she lit the rope, if she used an oil, or dipped it in lighter fluid. She was moving too fast and I couldn't make any sense of it.

I saw a photograph of her twirling her fire rope, blown up at an art show in the library later in the semester. A caption below the photograph explained that she was an art student from Iceland, and was focusing on studying human movement through art. And for a fraction of a second, I was envious of her playful nature.

She attached an essay, explaining her project, and I didn't read most of it. But she included a quote, and I don't know if it was something she came up with, or something she borrowed, but it read: I *believe there are two ways to heal people, through medicine, and through art.*

It's always amazing to me where I will find some insight. I appreciate art, but it's always been a luxury that I couldn't waste my time with. I was on a tight path. I already felt like I blew a few chances, so I kept my life pointed aggressively in one direction. My room looked like a prison cell. This education was a lot like a prison sentence, one I was trying to get over with as quickly as possible.

There are days when I am still like this. My husband will have to put me to bed, or I'd work late into the night. Sometimes he'll take me out for walks, through the market, just to do something silly like buy a bar of soap. My children are great reminders as well. When I'm too serious, they sense it, even in their young ages, they can tell when I'm overextending myself, and they'll make me art projects, little finger paintings that I'll keep forever and ever even after I die.

I could have used the positive energy from my husband and kids during my time in Olympia. I don't know how I made it through life all those years without them. I remember looking out my window one night. I was trying to study, but I was distracted, over thinking things, wondering what Philip's take on some psychology paper would have been.

Out my window, I saw the Icelandic girl twirling, and laughing, spinning her fire rope. Maybe twenty feet from her, there was an exchange between two ragged men. They weren't even trying to be discreet. Money and capsules swapped hands. Not far from them, a homeless man was talking to himself, incoherently.

I understood why people didn't like the park. They looked at all of it; the freaky fire girl dressed like a mix between a panda and a ballerina, the drugs, the homeless people. It made them uncomfortable. I'd see flyers from some downtown association, trying to rally the cops to start busting the junkies, or to enforce the park curfews. It was a historic park and it meant something to them.

These concerned citizens reminded me of the way I felt about all the cattle ranches along the highways in Central California. I didn't grow up there, so I wasn't used to the smells. I would avoid going by there if I could. I hated everything about them. I could be tolerant of a park with homeless teenagers, but a cattle ranch that was having a serious impact on the environment; I couldn't get on board with that. We all react from a place of comfort, a threatened place of comfort. When what we care about is threatened, we get up off the couch. I was encouraged that my comfort had some ecological importance.

That was the difference. The cattle ranches were causing actual harm. It wasn't just visually displeasing. The cattle ranches were a major source of nitrate pollution in the waterways, which flowed into the larger rivers. But this meant nothing to people. It was a profitable industry. And they didn't like it when a dark skinned teenage girl from

Chicago started speaking up about it.

I wondered what Philip thought about it all. I wanted to know his take on pollution, and how humans will ignore their environmental impact, the destruction they cause in the name of profit, or just basic habits. I wanted to know his take on everything.

Sometime in May, in the 31st minute, I raised my hand, and I asked him.

Minute 31: I'm aware of the region that you're speaking of. I'm also from California. I've driven that stretch. My mom still lives in Los Angeles, although I don't visit as much as I ought to, but I have driven through that part of the country. And, economically, it's very successful, for some people, I suppose.

I like to think of the environment as a cosmic issue. What pulls at us who are environmentally concerned, I believe, is the value of this planet, the understanding of the value of this planet. I'd like to add some muscle to that viewpoint; to that argument. Unfortunately it becomes an argument.

A good planet is hard to find. And planets, good or bad, are impossibly difficult to get to. In 2018, the orbits of Mars and Earth will align in such a way that NASA believes we may be capable of orchestrating a round trip mission with a duration of under two years. And Mars is not livable. Yes, there are hypotheses, I emphasize, hypotheses, which involve the terraforming of Mars, introducing greenhouse gases to the atmosphere of Mars. Mars has polar ice caps, could we melt them somehow? That's what people are asking.

Let's not hold out hope for this. It would be easier to just change our habits here, on the planet we already live on. It would be thousands of years before humans would be capable of colonizing Mars, and just getting there ...

Now, as far as your question, it's something I think about often. Why are people ignorant of their environmental impact? I believe one of the causes is a lack of scientific literacy.

You don't have to be overwhelmingly knowledgeable in any specific field of science to be scientifically literate. There's a published biologist, and there's a curious kid who likes to look in the microscope at all the bugs in the backyard. If you consider how much there is to know, the published biologist knows only a tad bit more than the backyard biologist. They are almost equally useful in society.

But when someone isn't even curious, when they don't value evidence, when they are scientifically illiterate, that's when dangerous things happen. That's when the disillusions appear.

If you've got a lot of money tied up in an industry, and the scientist comes and tells you that you need to shut down operations because your profits are arriving at the cost of the environment, well, that's a great start towards not giving a shit about the environment, or science. And hell, if you have the power, you might try to make sure other people don't value the environment, or science, either.

Science has a habit of giving people information that they don't want to hear. But that's *our* fault. You're out of sequence if you've got your profits, and then science shows up and tells you something you don't want to hear. You should have considered science beforehand.

In this country, and in many countries around the world, we reward the daring businessperson. We reward their vision. We've mistaken their careless ignorance for ambition. These oil tycoons, these lumber company CEOs, these billionaires of industries dependent on valuable resources, they are shortsighted, scientifically and economically. Anytime your business model is not sustainable, you're selling off your capital and calling it income.

There are equations that take skilled mathematicians months to solve, sometimes years. There are hypotheses that scientists are working on that will often eat up the bulk of their careers. If they make an error, at any point in their work, then the result is going to be flawed. They wouldn't say, *well, I've gone too far, I've invested too much, I can't turn back now.* At all costs, they would correct their error.

To me, that's daring. Not the billionaire who ignores the inconvenient information and continues on into the bliss of ignorance. That guy's a fucking coward. (applause)

Now, what to do about it. You think you can present a logical argument to someone who appears to be illogical? Well, let's take a closer look at what logic is.

Logic. Inductive, abductive, and deductive reasoning. There are numerous studies under the umbrella of logic, but most of us just deal with common, everyday logic. It's cold outside. Be logical, wear a coat. Or hey, let's leave early because there is traffic during this time of day on the road. We follow these corollaries because they have proven to be true. We've learned from experience, and we've strengthened our reasoning skills. A child may not have the cause-and-effect skills to remember their coat on a cold day, and they would be clueless at guessing how much time they need to drive from one place to the next during busy hours.

But we can be very childlike when it comes to logic. Phobias are often born from this. If you have an irrational fear of heights, every time you stay away from heights and you survive, you may be strengthening your phobia. Your reasoning skills are being influenced. The path of logic might go like this: I'm alive, I'm afraid of heights, I stayed away from heights, I remained alive, therefore HEIGHTS WILL KILL YOU! (laughter) It's difficult to debunk your own phobias.

I've strayed from your question, you were asking about pollution, right? And what we've arrived at is that people act illogically, or, maybe our logic fails us. Allow me to stray even further (laughter). My wife has a fear of flying. We had to drive across the country because she wouldn't get on a plane. When she was a kid she used to have nightmares of plane crashes. Maybe she was exposed to images, or imagery, of a plane crash at a young age. Maybe she was too impressionable to be exposed to those images.

Maybe. But she knows that she is being unreasonable. She has an irrational phobia. She knows the odds are one and several million that anything wrong will happen on an airplane. Yet, she can't fly. It's a phobia. It's irrational.

Logic often loses in the face of fears, and many of our miscalculations in life are derived from fear. I've met people who are such radical fanatics of their ideology, whether it is a business, a religion, even a sports team, that they exhibit panic-like behavior when faced with opposition to their beliefs. I think the term is cognitive dissonance, the reaction when information differs from beliefs. The difference though between my wife's fear of flying, and the man whose income depends on a non sustainable industry, my wife knows she's being irrational, but logic isn't going to do either of them any good. I don't know if I'm explaining it well. Let me try again... (laughter)

We're pack animals. We've always been pack animals. Let's go back to the Serengeti, the research lab we call the Serengeti, where a lot of our survival skills were sharpened. We had to survive in packs, and often that meant disengaging logic and trusting the majority. Maybe you didn't think a flood was coming, but the leader of the pack, the more experienced leader of the pack did. He or she had the insight to make a prediction that went against your less refined decision making skills. So, you disengaged your own logic, and you trusted the majority, and that may have saved your life.

We may be conditioned. We may be wired up to change our mind when we find ourselves in opposition to the majority or a stronger or more powerful voice. We may do it without realizing it. Using simple logic may not be a luxury. It may not be relevant whatsoever.

Now, my wife has me in the corner on a few things too. I'm aware of my faults. My wife is talking to me about plastic. I never thought about it. So, now I'm reading articles about all the hundreds of millions of tons of plastic in the ocean. Plastic right here in the Puget Sound, and one of many ways of decreasing how much plastic ends up in our oceans is to just bring our own grocery bags to the store. How hard is that? A kindergartner can do that. But I forget.

Or yoga. I know yoga is good for me, but I just can't seem to get into it. She tells me I need to stop eating so much wheat. So I look it up, turns out there is an abundance of evidence supporting what she tells me, but I had a sandwich for lunch today. I love bread. I'm aware of what I'm doing, and I don't try to refute the evidence, I don't try to argue from the standpoint that I'm right. I know I'm wrong. I'm a scientist, I can admit when I'm wrong. (laughter)

Let me answer your question this way, we're strange. We're a strange species. We act very strangely, and we do things that are not in our best interest, and unfortunately we do things that harm other people, animals, and nature. This is alarming.

I don't really have a better answer for you, but, it's just one of those fuzzy, blurry discussions we can have about our species' silly relationship with the truth. People are going to ignore the truth, we all know that, and we all probably do it. Our logic often fails us. Sometimes our logic gets hijacked by greed, by fear, or even the comfort of a sandwich.

I want to tell you all a funny story. It involves a very ... um, interesting ... insult. It may offend you, please, try not to be offended. (laughter) What I mean to say is, try to listen to the story, and keep in mind that I am not wishing to offend any of you. I know that I'm in Olympia, Washington, and we tend to get a little uptight about certain things. (laughter)

I was in Alaska, long ago, working for NASA. Let me first premise this story by telling you that, while I may boast and brag about my Ivy League education, about my PhD in astrophysics, I very well might be the worst astrophysicist currently living. (laughter) I take some pride in this. I barely passed each and every course, and when I graduated, I couldn't get any of my professors to write letters for me. I actually had a professor tell me that I was the least qualified doctoral candidate he has ever worked with. I'm okay with this. I'm quite content teaching all of you art majors the wonder of the cosmos so you can one day become bartenders, where ... you can serve cosmos. (laughter) If I were to keep in touch with any of my old classmates, their stories of cutting edge research would not leave me with any envy. They have no idea what a burrito from The Evergreen State College cafeteria tastes like. And let me add this, I teach the universe to hundreds of students every year who have no interest in becoming astronomers. I feel fortunate to do that.

Now, most astrophysicists don't work in the freezing icy tundra and sleep above a busy harbor like I did. But, like I said, I celebrate my path. Most astrophysicists don't get handed a sport rifle and are told to watch out for bears.

I used to go sit in this diner in the harbor. It's odd what you remember, but I remember this man, this big cowboy, he was either working on a fishing boat, or he was working in the oil fields, and his buddy was telling about him about how spectacular some glacier was, and he turns to him and says, *I'm just here for the money*.

That phrase stuck with me for some reason. Where was he coming from? Was he desperate for money? This was a fascinating character. I remembered his face. I could still pick him out of a crowd.

Some time later, the diner is more crowded this time, and the same cowboy, he's sitting up at the bar, right next to me. I'm having a conversation with the owner of the diner, and we're talking about Vietnam. Why? I don't remember. And I made a comment, something like, *well, we all know how that turned out*. The owner of the diner laughed because … it was likely relevant to our conversation. We didn't win the Vietnam War, whether you were for it or against it.

So, before I knew it, this cowboy turns around and says something like, "What did you say about Vietnam, you hippie faggot pussy?" (lots of reaction, some laughter) Yeah, strange choice of words, highly offensive, but this was a diner full of crab fisherman and oil field workers, so I shouldn't have been too surprised.

I somehow got myself out of that jam without getting my face smashed in. I've got a set of survival skills that allows me to avoid confrontation, because there would be no other way to survive a confrontation. Look me. (laughter) ... and I was left analyzing what he meant by this insult, and what he thought he meant.

Let's start with the first part. Hippie. I get it. People hate hippies. The hard working class, the boilermakers of the world, they hate hippies. They picture hippies smoking a bunch of dope and throwing the Frisbee around. Where ... did ... they ... ever ... get that idea? (laughter) But really, when they're waking up early, putting their stiff work boots on, drinking shitty coffee, hippies are sleeping in 'til noon and sipping some organic fair trade. At least that's what the boilermaker, or the oil field worker, or the crab fisherman thinks. I bet what he meant to say was that I was some kind of ungrateful coward. He must have believed that the brave people who fought in Vietnam were fighting for our freedom here in 'Merica. Maybe he even fought in Vietnam, himself. Regardless, he interpreted my words to be disrespectful, ungrateful, and he responded in a knee jerk way by calling me a hippie. That was the first and only time I've been called a hippie.

Okay, next, the F word. Faggot. Yikes, that's an offensive word. I'm glad I belong to a culture where that word is unacceptable. But, it's a word people still use. I don't know much about this topic. I understand that homosexuality is a completely normal occurrence in thousands of animals. Hell, gut worms have been observed ... um ... being gay. But only in humans have we observed a backlash to homosexuality. I don't completely understand it. I don't even care to. This strange behavior we call homophobia, I'm sure there's a very scientific reason for it, I'm sure psychologists can make sense of it, but I don't care to. I've always felt, if you understood how beautiful the universe was, you'd never spend another moment worrying about who's having sex with who ... whom? Who?

I mean, I could show you photographs of Saturn's moons, the gravity of the moons plucking at the fibers of the rings like a harp, and it's so gorgeous you'd forget about anything going on here. You definitely wouldn't worry about gay people, happily living their lives.

Lastly, of course, the P word, also horribly offensive, but probably the silliest. Being called this term, it prompted me to do a little research on it, and I learned it was a false cognate, that the word has a Latin root describing cowardly behaviors, and it has a Germanic root meaning tamed cat. Regardless, the word has been used as an insult for a cowardly man, by associating him with vaginas. I'm assuming that the man in the Alaskan diner wasn't a properly trained linguist, and was clearly labeling me as a vagina, and by doing so, had made the association that vaginas are cowardly.

Well, I disagree. (applause) We got far off topic, and I don't remember why I told that story in the first place.

I have always enjoyed the story about the man in the diner in Alaska. While it's not very funny, and those are hurtful, divisive words, the way Philip broke it down and analyzed that phrase, it reminds me of our easily threatened nature. I imagine the man in the diner to have been many times the size of Philip, yet threatened by some part of a statement that he misinterpreted. And that is human nature. We are an easily threatened species. We react in silly ways.

Back in Central California, my articles that I wrote as a high schooler were met with hostility, even from people who had no ties to the industry. When the word spread that I had traveled across the country to speak in front of Congress, there were many people who challenged me on it. I was thinking, *I'm trying to keep our water from being even more polluted.* Yet, people couldn't understand what I was doing, they were threatened. It was silly.

I started having long discussions with Philip after class every night. He said his wife worked late at a bar, and he hardly slept at all anyway. I wanted to give him a chance to explain some of the bullets he posted on the wall. The class was designed to explore the cosmos, and he kept answering unrelated questions about the environment and human behavior. He would remind us that the cosmos is everything; that the universe created everything, and no question is unrelated.

I was finding more and more ways to get closer to Philip. It was a strange pull he had over me. He fascinated me and I wanted to listen to him. But in conversation, he was very different from when he lectured. He couldn't make eye contact and his voice was wobbly. He wasn't as funny or witty. Everyday he looked worse and worse. He didn't take care of himself. But he still commanded the attention of the lecture hall. He could have read a cookbook from his podium, and we would have enjoyed it.

It had been two years since the night of the forum in Portland when I first met Philip. Gilbert Wiseman, the other professor from that night, briefly popped into our class one evening and spoke to us about the upcoming forum, which was an annual event. He said there would be room for three or four students in the van if anyone was interested in attending. It was one of those large, wheelchair accessible vans that every Evergreen student takes at least one field trip in, and I hadn't yet. We would be staying the night at a hostel as well. The whole trip sounded perfect to me. I hadn't gotten out of Olympia much. I didn't have the money to travel. I had been overworked, and stressed.

Gilbert was also fascinating to me, in more of a cultural, artsy way. He struck me as an odd sidekick to Philip. The few times I was around him, he was in a good mood, cracking jokes that he would laugh the loudest at. He was very poetic when he spoke, full of imagery.

I was envious of these college professors with their intellects on display. I wanted people to look up to me, to respect me. I wanted to be an expert in a field, and be recognized for it. I've allowed others to define me for so long, it would have been nice for it to be in a more positive way.

When I graduated from high school, I gave a speech. It took me an eternity just to get to the stage, and I actually heard boos. It was no secret how people felt about me,

I was still an outsider, preaching about how environmentally harmful all these large-scale cattle ranches were. The "boos" didn't bother me, I didn't mind being the activist. But, if I'm honest, it was another example of me letting others define me.

I remember, strapped into that van, being honest with myself, knowing that I'll probably always be this way. I do care what people think about me. It's hard not to. I'm affected, positively and negatively, by how people view me. This is ok. I'm a pack animal. I wanted to be respected, but with that respect comes responsibility. I wanted to have a positive impact on people. People could look up to me, and maybe they'd think, *if she can do it, so can I.* I'd be humbled if a group of college kids hopped in a crowded bus just to hear me ramble on stage. I would show gratitude. I would never take my position for granted.

During the drive down to Portland, it appeared that Philip was sleeping, but he would look around every once in awhile, rubbing his eyes. He was very different than the man who ripped through audiences with his lectures. He slouched like a teenager, and didn't say a word.

We arrived at the gymnasium and the students found their seats. I found a spot up front where I could see the stage. The same strange looking man from two years earlier, the one who had put up the sign in the coffee shop and had altered my life forever, he was there again. He was carrying an older man's briefcase, and organizing notes for him.

The setting in the gymnasium looked familiar, like nothing had changed since the last time I was here. All the guest speakers were the same, standing in their familiar spots. I heard Gilbert say several times that this wasn't a debate, that this was a respectful discussion forum. I wouldn't have been surprised if each and every one of them had the same canned speeches from the last time I was here. But that's not what happened.

Philip looked like he should have been admitted to a hospital. I couldn't have been the only one that noticed it. He looked downright sick. It took some time, almost twenty minutes before Philip spoke, and when he did, I think he may have gone off script. And I recorded it, of course.

Min 19:   What happens after ... What happens to the body? You're asking me what happens to the body after ... after death? You know that answer. You know what happens. You don't need a scientist to ...

You know, I often preface statements on this topic by reminding people ... that I am a scientist, and I think like a scientist. I've grown tired of having to do this. Tired of it.

I gather evidence, I scrutinize evidence, and I arrive at a conclusion based on evidence. I shouldn't have to preface with this, I shouldn't have to warn you that I am about to tell you the truth. People who do not value science should be doing the prefacing, like, *hey, I'm about to drop some bull shit on you.* (some laughter)

(long pause) When I think of life and death, I have to examine the evidence. I rarely consider any longer what remains of our consciousness after we die. Most of the mythological interpretations of life after death include the sustained consciousness of an individual. You would be you, and

I would continue to be me, somehow, somewhere. I see no evidence for this. This is run off from mythological tales, the source several thousand years upstream from Christianity and Judaism.

I am carbon based. I have hydrogen in me. Does hydrogen die? These atoms can be traced back all the way to the beginning. As long as there has been a universe, there has always been a trace of us, so I predict there always will be a trace of us. The atoms that make up you and me, they have a long journey ahead of them after we stop functioning as beings. I'm okay with that. It means this is all temporary. It means you have to do something *right now*. You have to make life happen *before* death. Don't count on life *after* death. You don't have the evidence to back that up.

I'll admit, I wish I could continue to be me for eternity. I like it. It's all I know. I *wish* it was the case. But I've learned to accept this, and yes, I'm okay with it. It's a bold journey to explore the truth about ourselves. It's a bold and brave journey to look up in the sky, and to ask questions, and to accept the answer. If there was proof that my wife and I would go to heaven and be together, that would be marvelous, but I haven't come across any evidence to support that. When I ask questions, I have to be prepared to accept the answer.

(long pause) I think ... I think it's criminal that people are being taught to believe these unproven theories, and they are being misled about themselves, and it is happening to people at a very young age, before they have the reasoning skills to combat it. They have to relearn the truth later in life, or at least unlearn the falsehoods they have been told. They have to learn that they are not central to anything. The earth is not central to the solar system; the solar system isn't central to the galaxy. And people feel small when they realize how enormous the universe is, and they feel insignificant when they realize that we are central to nothing, and these religions, they build people up for a disappointment. It is criminal that people wish and hope for something, they spend their whole lives wishing and hoping for an afterlife, and they waste the life they do have. (some applause)

But ... but ... I've always been open ... to everything. We should always remain open minded. I just don't lend faith to theories without a shred of evidence.

These faith based religions, I'm struggling lately, I'll be honest, I'm struggling with your messages, I'm struggling with the impact of these religions.

Stellar nucleosynthesis ... the universe created us. Hydrogen, oxygen, carbon, et cetera. And look what happened. Here on this planet. Simple cells became complex cells, and then complex cells became multicellular, and then we got some fish, and some amphibians, and this took billions of years. And then, we've got apes doing very ape like things. Eventually you and I climbed out of the trees. But evolution isn't just the ability to evolve; it's about having the necessary combination of pieces to survive. It's a matter of *one in a billion*, billions of times. Every one of us is holding the winning lottery ticket to billions of lotteries. You can't make up something more magnificent than that. And we can look at it like it's just by plain dumb luck that we are here, or we can embrace the magnificence of our existence, and make our lives matter. It's important to remember that we are descendants of living creatures who wanted to survive. It mattered to them to survive, so it matters to me too.

But, I want to say, very directly ... listen, your religions, they're not innocent. Look at what they've done. Look at how they are misleading people. I hear people say that their god answers their prayers. Why would god do that? Why would your god answer *your* prayers, but ignore the thousands of children each day that die of malaria, starvation, AIDS? The jumbo jets full of children that die each day, painfully, slowly. This happens. You know it. I know it. If your god is able to save the innocent children that die each day, but does nothing about it, is that god worth your worship? I'd say, your god either isn't very powerful, doesn't care, or doesn't exist. And when I ask people why their god allows people to suffer, what do they say? Every time? Every single time? They say *god works in mysterious ways.* What a cop out.

These religions mislead people, and they suppress conflicting information. And this has been going on for too long. Look at ... um ...

Galileo Galilei. I admire him. Not because he was brilliant, but because he was brave. He stood up for the truth. I imagine there were several people living throughout Christian Europe that were just as brilliant as Galileo, but we don't know who they are, because look at what happened, look what happened when people spoke out. I suspect a lot of brilliant people kept their trap shut. Religion slowed us down, and it made us think things about ourselves that were never true. And I can't stand it anymore. (mixed reaction from crowd)

Look ... I ... I live my life as if ... well, I strive to live my life as if every day is important. I care about people. I am equipped with functioning emotions. I bond, chemically, with others. I ... I can only say it this way ... Science never set out to be the arch enemy of religion. Science is the pursuit of truth, and if science is your opponent, that should explain everything you need to know. We're made of stars. You should all know that. Science is truth. Science is love.

The panel lost it's warm and fuzzy feel after Philip's rant. The more religious speakers began to debate with him, and it got awkward for everyone. Philip hardly added more content, he simply repeated, several times, the same phrases; *but where's your evidence?* or *the burden of proof is on you.* And Gilbert didn't say another word for the rest of the forum. Then it was over.

Afterward, the other students went off to a bar, and Gilbert and Philip were nowhere to be found, so I went wandered off on my own, through the neighborhood I used to live in. I thought about where my life was going, who I was, something I thought about often.

I connected with what Philip had said that night. These were similar thoughts to mine. I knew the importance of each day, of making life count, of experiencing life *before* death. I thought about the quote from Carlos Bulosan, and my hard working family in California that I hardly knew. I thought about my hysterical mother, with her beliefs that were more superstitious than religious. Her fear, her failed logic. I thought about the longhaired boy from my childhood, the boy who got himself killed by the cops, whom I used to ride the bus to school with.

I thought about the day of the accident, the day the bus flipped on its side. We were in kindergarten. The boy who got killed by the cops, he was on the bus too. He was sitting next to me, like always. They said the boy went a little crazy after that. They said his mom couldn't control him, and that he was twitchy all the time. No one ever took him to a doctor.

I stepped onto the bus, took a few steps to my seat. That was the last time I'd ever use my legs.

The bus swerved to avoid hitting a pedestrian in the road. The road was slippery. I remember the screeching sounds the bus made, then everyone fell on each other, and the boy who got killed by the cops, he hit his head hard. He didn't say anything, he didn't move. His eyes were closed. He was bleeding.

We weren't screaming, we weren't crying. We were in shock. I was breathing short, quick breaths. The bus was on its side, across the width of a city street. The bus driver was climbing out of his seat. I remember him screaming at us to stay calm. We may have thought the crash was over at that point.

And then the truck hit us. We were T-boned by a delivery truck, the driver was checking his map. He hit us at the exact spot where I was trapped. The body of the bus broke apart, and my legs and back were crushed under the front wheel axle. My spinal cord was severed in the sacral region, leaving me paralyzed from the waist down.

We got a settlement, it paid for things, things that I needed because of the injury. My mom and her husband used a lot of it, too. We lived in a bigger house for a while, but that just meant more aunts and uncles and cousins taking up space. We burned right through the rest of the money before I ever left for California.

That accident hasn't slowed me down. It didn't slow me down after we vandalized the building, and I got away. The security guard walked right by me and asked if I had heard any noise. It didn't keep me out the trees in Oregon. I preferred the life of the tree sitter, roped and harnessed. I was Peter Pan. I was more mobile in that tree than I was out of it.

When people doubt me, when they doubt what I can do, I don't waste any time proving them wrong. Now that I have my family, my husband and kids, they take care of me, they've softened me up. I've gotten comfortable. I don't have to hide from cops, or climb trees. We go for long walks together. You just can't get happier than I am.

On the last day of the quarter, I had my scheduled evaluation with Philip. I was thoroughly excited. I thought we had formed a bond. He was so influential to me. I felt like he was very instrumental in the new direction my life was going. I wanted to share every thought I had with him. I thought he'd be happy to know that he reached me.

I entered the room. He was stiff. I was expecting him to be more personal with me. Then he looked right through me, and he asked me what my name was. *What my fucking name was?*

I wanted to scream, *my name is Sam! Sam Fucking Rios!* How did he not know my name? We used to visit after every lecture. I traveled to Portland with him. He didn't even recognize me. I looked like a stranger to him. And he started to look like one to me too.

Philip was a brilliant man, but his philosophies were lost on himself. He spoke of a connected community of humans, and how we are all related. He used the term *genetic silverware, with very long handles.* He spoke about how we are all one, how every person you meet shares an ancestor with you, an actual person that breathed and lived, and how pleased that person would be to know that two of his or her descendants would meet again someday. He reminded us that we have a responsibility to treat every person as family.

I could hardly conduct my evaluation. It was painful. It was scarring. Philip's words had changed my life, the way I look at the world, but I left our meeting with the devastating conclusion that Philip was a fraud. I felt sick.

Of all places, I moved back to Chicago, and began taking all the prerequisites necessary to begin a graduate program in neuroscience. That was over a decade ago.

I now do exactly what I wanted to do. I teach. I conduct research. I meet with patients. I've published several papers. A few years back I co-authored a paper with a neuroscientist on the topic of females living with severed spinal cords who were able to achieve orgasm, affirming that the vagus nerve bypasses the spinal cord. I couldn't help but wonder what Philip would have thought about our research. Maybe he read it.

Working at the clinic involved a lot of long hours, and late night meetings, sometimes working around the cleaning crew, the people we didn't notice who cleaned up after us. We'd be meeting in the boardroom; a vacuum would wander in on its own. We'd ignore the person pushing it and lift our feet so the vacuum could do its job. Lifting our feet off the ground was the closest we'd get to showing any appreciation.

Inconveniently, the elevator on the third floor didn't line up well. There was a lip, and my wheelchair had to fight to get over it. The custodian of the building must have noticed and installed a small ramp, about an inch in height, just so I could smoothly get on and off the elevator.

And that's how Scott and I met. I tracked him down to say thank you, and to introduce myself. If I ever minded being paralyzed, if I ever felt sorry for myself, I don't now. If I could walk, I'd never have met my husband, surely.

I found art. I found a need for it. My kids and I paint. The refrigerator is our gallery. We're good, real good. If nature had made it possible for a woman with a severed spinal cord to orgasm, I could find a way to appreciate, and create, artwork. We're not only designed to survive, but enjoy survival.

I see my family from time to time. But I'm weird to them. They think I've changed too much.

I still talk to my dad. We have surface level conversations. He and Lena came out a month after the twins came home with us, but I haven't seen him since. He hardly said a word to my husband. It freaked him out. I thought it was funny.

Surprisingly, I do go to church every once in awhile. It's not a spiritual experience. It's just a time to remember where I came from. I don't have any animosity towards church like I used to. Scott grew up Catholic and he likes to bring the kids, and I just go on holidays. I figure, when the kids are older, they can make up their own minds. They know their dad believes, and their mom doesn't, and they can find their own path.

Not long ago, I was at a bookstore. Something pulled at my eyes. I saw his name, Philip Duke. It sent shockwaves through me. I had no idea he had written books. There were several books under his name, so I examined the publication dates. I wanted to start with his earliest work. I wanted to go in order, chronologically. I went to the front desk and asked if the book in my hand was his first. They informed that they actually didn't have his first one, but they could order it.

Today, a book titled *Between Yellow and Red* arrived in the mail.

After Dennis got busted by the cops, Ray lost his banjo player. But he gained a banjo. He took his share of the pay from the show and went to buy a loaf of bread at a bakery. He put Dennis' share in an envelope and figured he'd keep it safe for him.

That's where he saw her. She was putting up a friendly flyer, advertising herself as a music instructor, that she could teach any instrument.

He had a banjo, but he didn't have a bastard's chance of playing it.

Gilb Wiseman

It was late. I was tired. It was hailing. My eyes were sliding all over my face. My forehead rolled like dough. I was driving to somewhere from somewhere.

I pulled off for gas and saw a beautifully colored bus parked off to the side. I couldn't take my eyes off it. Painted in bright blues and yellows, it looked like it belonged in the kids' section of a bookstore. There were red and black flags I didn't recognize. A man in his 30s worked on the engine. He looked inconvenienced.

Forces greater than me dragged me across the parking lot, through the heavy hail. I didn't have a choice. I had to check it out. There were other adults drinking tea, speaking in Spanish, pacing. I don't remember what I said, or who I said it to, but minutes later I was drinking tea with them and listening to their story.

Arturo, the man working on the engine, was a teenager back in 1973, when Salvador Allende, then president of Chile, was ousted. He lived in a shantytown outside Santiago, and watched the soldiers drag his father and uncles away, along with others suspected of communist ties. He never saw them again. Every September 11th Arturo and his family drive to Seattle and deliver a street performance in protest of the CIA's involvement in removing a democratically elected president.

Arturo shot a sideways look at his wife, and I must have interpreted it correctly because I invited them all to my home and they accepted. Arturo was able to drive the bus slowly to my house. He worked on the engine long into the night as I chatted with his family in my living room. The group never made it to Seattle, but instead, downtown Olympia was treated to its very first Chilean protest performance, exactly twenty years after the coup d'état.

Arturo and his family stayed with me for close to a week before he could fix the bus up enough to hit the road. I never wanted them to leave. I was sober the whole time they visited, and for a few months afterwards.

Over the course of our visit, Arturo became my friend. He would wake up earlier than the rest. We'd drink thick coffee and he'd tell me stories of racing motorcycles in Russia, diving in the Galapagos, or reindeer herding with the Sami people of Scandinavia. I was skeptic of his tales initially; this was a lot of life for a man who looked to be in his mid 30s. But as the week went on, I came to realize that an exile can move around a lot if he gets an early start in life.

Arturo noticed a picture of a woman on my wall. Maybe he noticed it all along, but he waited until the day he left to ask me about her. It was a beautiful picture of Aishwarya. It still melted me. I couldn't take it down. But Arturo was intuitive. He read my eyes and didn't wait for me to speak. He just slightly rubbed his finger over the picture. "Your heart works," he said with a smile, in perfect English.

I learned two things from Arturo and his traveling band of activists. Inside details of the 1973 Chilean coup d'état was the first thing, which I knew nearly nothing about. The second thing I learned was that it was okay to continue to love what you lose. I probably knew it already, but the way Arturo worded that phrase, that my *heart works*, I understood what he meant. I loved her in a way that wasn't going to stop just because she left.

I grew up in a hailstorm of fortuitous obscurity. Or just random, odd chance. Regardless, it was a hailstorm. It was a common weather occurrence. We lived in Colorado, Wyoming, a little bit of Montana.

While most kids rode a bus to school, ironically, I never did. But I lived in a school bus. I know the sound of hail crashing on the roof of that bus. I can still sense the warnings the sky gives when it's going to hail. I can taste the updraft in the air.

My mom was beautiful. I'm not shy about saying that. She gardened, and hemmed, and sculpted, and fermented, and scavenged. Everything she did was beautiful and bright and magic. She had an energy that would pierce people. When I was close to her I could hear her soul humming. She taught me about nature and weather and love and the spirit within all of us, the spirit that binds us to all things.

She was a music instructor. She could teach any instrument. A man named Ray picked up the phone and responded to her ad, and she came over to his home to teach him banjo. He was living on an acre of tall, green grass up on a hill in a school bus. On the top of the bus was a garden, and the electricity he used was generated by a bicycle. She was 6 months pregnant when she arrived. She never left.

She once told me that the grass was so green, and the school bus was so colorful, that she felt a cool burn in her eyes, and every breath rattled in her diaphragm as she walked up the trail to the top of the hill where Ray was fumbling with his banjo, guessing at how to tune it. She said she knew there was a beautiful person inside, that she could feel his heart beating before he opened the door.

I was born in that bus with Ray behind her, holding her. I have a picture of my head crowning, and Ray behind her, and a stick of incense burning, poking out of a closed book on a shelf in the background. I don't know who took the picture, but it's holy to me. I keep it in an envelope with several other pictures that have faded, but this one looks like it was printed yesterday. I can't explain that.

Together, Ray and my mom made the bus into a home. And they traveled around the Rocky Mountains for the next ten years. They taught yoga, practiced a westernized Buddhist lifestyle, and grew vegetables. They played shows. Ray was an excellent singer, but he never learned banjo. He was missing most of the fingers on his right hand due to a Komodo dragon mishap.

They loved each other. They were equals. You could feel it when you were around them. They trusted each other. They gave themselves to each other. This was a family. We were bonded in spirit.

My favorite toy growing up was a microscope. I'd pick up pine needles and magnify them to explore colors I didn't know existed. I was mystified. I'd put my eye in that lens piece, and I could experience God's hidden artwork.

My God appears in the genius of nature. I'd sit near a tree, encased in euphoria. My eyes would brim with electricity. This was no abstract feeling; I could feel it and I could see it. All I have to do is remember those moments, whatever mood I'm in, and I'm there again. The problem is, I often forget to remember.

Everything I experienced, I felt the need to share. I've always been a storyteller. Often it was Ray who would stop what he was doing, and patiently listen to every word that made its way out of my mouth. It was a lot of work getting those words out; I was a heavy stutterer as a kid. And Ray never made me feel rushed.

I'm still a storyteller, and to this day, I picture Ray patiently listening. He's the audience I consider most.

I have a memory from when I was 6 years old that I often replay in my head. It was a warm day, and my mom was playing the flute and Ray was standing on his head, doing some yoga pose, breathing like a walrus. I laughed, and then he laughed, but he never lost his balance. He was wearing a bright purple and blue pair of pajama bottoms that my mom made. Ray was a hairy man. Hairy chest and face and long braided hair.

I wandered off that morning, away from the flute playing and the walrus breathing, and I got into a hornet's nest. I walked right up to it as if I had placed it in that hollowed out tree myself. I don't know how I knew it was there, but I did. I could picture the queen hornet chewing up the scrub oak bark, carefully placing the cells. I saw the genius of nature, and I was drawn towards it, carelessly and clumsily.

And then nature reacted. I must have screamed. I can remember Ray calmly walking over to me at that moment, picking me up, walking me back to the bus, and rubbing some oily, balmy liquid over my welts.

He was calm. I sensed what he was trying to tell me. At no point was he trying to comfort me mentally, he knew I was in pain and he had very little means to alleviate it. I remember how strong that message was. *Gilb, this hurts you, this is what the hornets are trying to tell you, and this will continue to hurt. Please remember this message.*

This experience spoke volumes to me. It reminded me that the pain I was experiencing was temporary, and that I should remember the elements of this moment so that I don't mess around with hornets again. To be cautious around nature is to be cognizant of how wonderfully powerful it is. He was teaching me cause and effect.

The way Ray handled it, he turned what could have been a traumatic experience into a good memory. Strangely enough, it's actually a warm memory for me, and I've had a special relationship with hornets since. It wouldn't be my last encounter with them.

In the eyes of a young kid mesmerized with plants and animals and the infinite wilderness, Ray had it all figured out. *Spirit provides,* he would say, reminding me that if I listened, if I was tuned in enough, that the spirit of nature would lead me. It would provide me with the answers I was looking for.

Ray spoke often of his unyielding belief that the spirit of the elk was watching over him. Ray would study me, concentrating, trying to figure out which animal I was connected to. He said the native people of the land would have a ceremony when a child turns ten, and the leader of the tribe would rename the child after the spirit animal. I didn't understand all of what Ray would tell me, but I lived as if every word he said was true. I saw him speak to trees, or the clouds, and when it hailed, I used to think he made it happen.

Ray was a dad to me. And I lost him right before I turned ten, before he would reveal to me my animal spirit guide, before he could explain the rest of life's mysteries to me. I would have asked him better questions if he was still around. I had more to learn from him. I didn't know it at the time, but he was sick, and he was trying to cure himself with crystals or some shit, and I lost Ray because he didn't go to a fucking doctor. And that's all I have to say about that.

His funeral was an informal service with cider and a string band. Several people spoke, people I had never met before. Before dusk, my mother spoke, and told us a story about Ray. I don't remember it word for word, but I remember what I got from it.

She said there was a time when he didn't know what he wanted to do with his life, so he bought a cheap motorcycle and went to Mexico to surf his life away. He fished, drank beer, rolled cheap cigarettes and slept on the beach at night. Everyone left him alone for the most part.

One day, an elderly woman who he'd never seen before came and sat down next to him, startling him. He didn't see her coming. She asked him who he was. She was curious. To this, he replied, *I'm no one.*

It took a few minutes for the woman to get back on her feet, but she eventually did, and turned to walk away. After taking a few steps, she pivoted, then returned to him, and sat back down again. She asked him a different question, *who* he used to be.

He thought about it for a while, and realized he didn't really have an answer, and didn't want to talk to the woman any longer, so he replied, *I don't remember.*

That seemed to satisfy her, so she began the long and treacherous act of standing, knees wobbling. He felt sorry for her, so he tried to help her, but she refused his help. She finally got up to her feet, and began to walk back toward town, away from Ray. The sun was setting and he enjoyed this part of the day, and didn't want to be bothered any longer. The warmth of the sun was on his face, cooking him.

But then he heard her feet stop, and once more, she turned to walk back to him, sitting down again, which took minutes. This time, she didn't ask a question, but explained to him that she was old and tired, and it had taken her all day to walk to the beach to confront him, for her life was very bleak and the curiosity of a stranger's identity was impossible to ignore. She told him that she wished not to live any longer, that her family members were all either dead or had moved away and forgotten her. Since Ray was a *no one*, then surely he wouldn't mind helping her end her life. She asked him to carry her out past the surf, and to hold her under water until she died.

This shocked Ray. He immediately refused, and fought for reasons why she still had meaningful years of life ahead of her. She wasn't listening. She appeared distracted as she searched through her handbag. She pulled out a small mirror, and held it up to Ray's leathery face.

Ray laughed, catching on to her ploy. He looked into her hand mirror, and hardly noticed his neglected face. She then told him, "If I have so much to live for, imagine how much you do. You are free to waste away here, but there are many people who would love to have the years you have ahead of you."

He agreed to help her walk back up to town, where he met her family, who had neither died nor moved away. At some point over room temperature beers he asked the lady what she would have done if he had agreed to help her die. She laughed, and pretended the incident never happened.

My mom was originally from Seattle and we moved back up there after Ray died, so we could live with her mom and dad. This was a much more stable life for me. We had everything we needed. And I hated it. This was the land of bedtimes and bike helmets and looking both ways. Practical things that are universally good ideas, and I couldn't stand it. This was the land where dirt stays outside, and toys stay inside. This was safe. This wasn't learning from our cousin, the hornet, and her divine message.

My grandparents would describe our lifestyle in that bus as dangerous and nomadic, but it wasn't. It was just miles beyond their understanding. They were traditional, Jewish, and conservative. And their daughter, my mom, had gone a different route. My mom had earned money by reading palms, making jewelry, playing and teaching music, and before she met Ray, she often danced for men. I'm not ashamed.

Love, and family, and spirituality, and respect, were all modeled for me in those first ten years of my life. The next eight years gave me the structure I needed to be successful, and that sometimes makes me feel like a traitor for admitting it. I wouldn't have grown up to be a professor without my grandparents, but I wouldn't have had much to teach without my mom and Ray.

I went to college for a long time, studying anthropology. I then set off traveling through Latin America, hiking up volcanoes and temples, and sleeping on beaches. I searched for the beach Ray had chosen to surf his life away. I imagine I found it several times.

I experienced the miracle of the Virgin of Guadalupe in Mexico City. I saw her tilma with my own eyes, and wrote about it in a book years later.

Science has struggled to make sense of the material of the tilma, and the image it contains. A reflection of the eyes of the Virgin, when magnified, shows the figure of the saint, Juan Diego, who, according to legend, was given the tilma by the Virgin in 1531. But even more miraculous than what the image contains, is that the image appears to change color from the angle viewed, an illusion we call iridescence. Human hands have yet to master this technique.

I was heavily influenced by this realization. It reminds me that we are not here to understand everything, but to be open to everything. There will always be much we don't understand.

My mom passed away when I was 30. I took a sabbatical from teaching and traveled again, this time through Colorado with a feather in my hat, just looking at mountains and whispering to myself. I carried her ashes, and searched for a sign, something to tell me where to spread them.

I used to sit on my mom's lap as a boy while Ray drove and I'd stare at these mountains. Those memories aren't in my past. Other memories are, but not these ones. These memories are forever. They extend in both directions eternally. They will have happened forever, they will continue to have happened. This is where I remember my mom, passenger seat with her son on her lap, singing to the mountains.

I parked on a nameless road, low on the dry side of a mountain, blurry with the impending desert, and I walked a trail. The sun was melting and spreading into the heat of the distant horizon, and the sky was orange. The wind tasted like sugar.

Ray used to talk about the significance of the color orange, and the entire wavelength between yellow and red. He spoke of monks wearing saffron robes, and I followed his story through ancient trading routes where saffron spice was traded, derived from some sacred flower in the Iridaceae family.

The trail had thinned to the width of a whisper. Grass had combed over most of it. But I walked further; I don't remember why. I had no reaction when I came across the hornet's nest, fractured and empty on the ground. I still have that hornet's nest, but I left my mother's ashes in its place. Ray helped me spread them. I had been searching for a sign; I wasn't surprised when I found it.

I wouldn't know how to get back to that spot. The unmarked roads and trails may have well disappeared behind me.

That night I dreamed of an orange sky, and children wearing bright orange, and the hand-collected stigmas of a rare flower, whose name I've never learned. I took this as a sign, and sold my VW van for a plane ticket to India, to go learn how to pray.

India gutted me. I thought I'd be more prepared for it. I had survived scorpions in Mexico and the thin air above volcanoes. But India was something else entirely. I hadn't realized it, but I'd been fighting against the tide since I got off the plane. I flinched when crowds engulfed me. I'd reel in slow careful breaths, trying to avoid the unpleasant stenches. I'd inspect my food and nibble on it, and leave most of it on the plate.

I finally gave up. I surrendered. I had to. I found myself in the belly of a long bus ride, surrounded by humans and livestock. I had grabbed some bottled water and drank as much as I could before boarding the bus. People were coming and going, but I was trapped, hour after hour. At some point, I just said *fuck it*, and pissed all over myself. And to my surprise, I deeply offended several people. And all I could do was laugh, and that turned into a cry, which turned into a hailstorm of emotions.

But then I laughed again, and for the rest of the trip I rode the waves of uncertain and unpredictable chaos that I had been skillfully avoiding. I stepped into a restaurant and ordered something by pointing to a picture of a jackfruit. I was sitting in my own piss. I pulled a human hair at least a foot in length from my food and I never stopped chewing. A fly came too close to me and I swatted it. That's when I first heard her speak.

"I wonder why you felt the need to kill that fly." Her voice was a cat's tongue in my ear. Soft like a cloud, abrasive like sandpaper. I turned and replied, "I didn't kill it. I just slapped it away." And we would bicker over the facts of that moment during late night baby talk for years.

Aishwarya. She became my wife, my lonely, homesick wife. Her decision to follow me caught up to her, and she left me, and I can only imagine she is happy now.

Four years of watching her smile fade and I never stopped believing. I believed that I was supposed to go to India, that I was guided there by a higher power, and that I was supposed to find Aishwarya. The moment I saw her, I knew she was going to be my wife.

Regardless of how low she sunk and how alone she felt living in a city she didn't know existed, in a state she didn't know existed, in a country she had only read about in movie subtitles, regardless of how far from love she was, I never gave up on us. I always believed she'd eventually learn to love this life we were building, and I could see my children sitting on her lap while I drove through the mountains, pulling over to stand on my head and breath like a walrus.

She just didn't love me, and I didn't want to know that.

And then she was gone. It took me several days to read the letter she left. It wasn't very well written. What's funny to me is that I don't even remember why I loved her.

My mother's last name was Wiseman, as is mine. Ray's last name was Plum, but I never took his name. My mom had always told me to stay away from alcohol. It had ruined the life of someone I had never met, whose last name I don't know, and that in my blood was a fight I couldn't win. And then one day, when I didn't feel much like winning, I went searching for a fight through a bottle of whiskey.

From the inside, the glass bottle had a warm feel to it. You can spot traces of oak, from its time aging in the cask. I lost a lot of time inside that bottle, looking out at my life, losing hope in everything I believed in, forgetting about the importance of hailstorms and hornet's nests, and drinking until I didn't care. I was a drunk, and it's not a very interesting time in my life. I was pathetic, I made enemies, and I try not to think about it.

My sponsor corrected me once when I said I was only an alcoholic for a few years. No, I was born an alcoholic, and there's a man out there who never met his son because he was born one too.

I had two months of sobriety under my belt and was in my office one night trying not to open a bottle of whiskey. Every choice that landed me in that spot felt involuntary. My shoe laces tied themselves, and the wind picked up and blew me over to the liquor store, and the exact change leapt from my pocket, and this cute little fifth of a gallon followed me all the way home. So, I went to work, sat down in my office and there it was again, within arms length, on my desk. It must have followed me there too.

I was sick with the thought of what I knew was going to happen. I knew I was going to drink that whole bottle. I knew I was going to be a drunk for the rest of my life. I had no choice. I was cornered. I was begging for mercy. *Just get it over with*, I thought.

My armpits were sweating. My palms were melting on my forehead. I wanted to be someone else. I wanted to leave me. I wanted to leave a poorly written note to myself, and never see myself again.

And then the phone rang. I snatched it out of the air. *Hello! Oh God Hello!!* I thought it was a prank, some guy said he was reading my book, but needed to take a piss. I couldn't make any sense of it. But then the phone rang again, and I answered it with a bit of paranoia.

We spoke all night. Philip. Lovely Philip. He wanted to have a chat about my book, *Iridescence*, which he said he'd found in his girlfriend's loft out in New York. I had written it not long after the Chilean actors left, during a brief spell of sobriety, and it was a successful book, but the buzz had recently died down.

I was born to tell stories. I live through my stories. And Philip, his voice materialized out of nowhere, through the miracle of a telephone wire stretched across the country, he called me up and wanted me to tell him stories *about* my stories. He must have asked me a hundred questions before I finally stopped and asked him who he was. But by then he had saved me.

I grew in size and in stature, and I towered over the cute little fifth of whiskey, who conceded defeat by pouring itself out the window. That phone call saved my life.

Philip was brilliant. Not just a little brilliant, but scary brilliant. Over an hour into the conversation, I learned he was an astrophysicist, who had just returned from Alaska, where he was conducting field research for NASA, studying conditions similar to Mars. It was out of my grasp.

The conversation shifted to the universe, and he said combinations of words I had never heard before, never known. We spoke about evolution as a cosmic experience. He used terms like epochs and nebulae and brought me up to the formation of our solar system, through collapsing molecular clouds. I knew nothing about it, didn't care about it, until now. He made it matter.

He talked about looking through his solar telescope at the sun, our star, 93 million miles away. I couldn't believe I'd never done that. I thought about the sun all the time. I never considered what it must look like, or what it's made of. I never thought about it as a star. Stars are far away. They're bright lights in the sky, things I know nothing about.

I will always love Philip. I am in his debt. I will always be loyal to him. No favor is too big. Even now, if he needed me, I'd be there. I wouldn't hesitate.

I was on the hiring committee at the college. We were screening applicants for a teaching position, and I suggested to Philip that he consider the opening. He was unemployed at the time. Before I knew it, I was giving him a tour of the campus.

I've been known to sensationalize a story, to reshape it for the sake of the audience, but I couldn't help thinking that Philip and I needed to know each other, that there was a reason he was here, and that we both needed something from the other person. This all felt so guided, powerfully guided, like so many other moments in my life.

Philip was charmed by the informal nature of his interview. The other members of the hiring committee met up with us at the trailhead and we walked down to the beach, at the edge of campus. We took turns asking Philip questions, all kinds of questions, personal and professional. His view of the universe flattened us.

I was wondering what some astrophysicist from New York would think of this Charlie Brown neighborhood, but Philip was so simple, he had such basic needs. Olympia was not below him. He appreciated it. I liked that about Philip.

I called him to let him know it was a unanimous decision to offer him the position. I may have led him to believe that it was already his, because in that short time since he flew back to New York, he had convinced Kennedy to move to Olympia with him, and had asked her to marry him.

We all instantly became close. Philip and Kennedy filled a void in my life. Friendship. I had pushed most people away during my drinking years. I was surrounded by people I knew - coworkers and neighbors, people I recognized in town - but I had few friends. I now had two wonderful people in my life that I spent a lot of quality time with.

Most Sundays we would get together, Kennedy, Philip and myself. We would light a candle and talk about things, or listen to jazz. More times than not, Philip would eventually disengage and slowly pull away. It was normal for him to be in the corner reading a book before the night was over. We all knew that was just Philip being Philip. He was an introvert. He disengaged. He never meant any harm by it, and he had no problems with Kennedy and I continuing to visit long after he had checked out.

I would watch Philip and Kennedy interact, and I tried not to speculate, but I didn't see a lot of love between them. I saw two people who were so different in every possible way. They wanted very different things out of life. They had different dreams.

Philip would look at the weather report each day to see if the skies were going to be clear, and if so, he'd be looking through his telescope. He liked to go downtown, where curious strangers would ask what he was doing. He loved answering that question. Everything about him changed when he talked about the universe. He stuck his chest out, and his voice was authentic, like a brass instrument. He'd turn a city block into an observatory.

Occasionally a young kid would come around, and he took special interest in explaining everything that was remarkable about the sun. He had his facts down, facts that I learned to memorize, because I liked watching him in his element. *The sun is 93 million miles away. Photons travel at the speed of light, 671 million mph, taking 500 seconds to reach us.* He'd explain sunspots and solar flares. A kid's eyes would light up when he explained how big the sun was, how hot it was, how it was formed. And then he'd really blow them away. He'd explain to them that this smaller than average star they were looking at, our sun, was one of over a hundred billion stars in our galaxy, and that our galaxy was one of over a hundred billion galaxies.

I'd feel such a rush of energy when he spoke about the universe, but then the crowds would disperse, and he'd put away his equipment, and stare off into a blankness, and his shaky, tin voice would return.

Five years flew by. I saw more and more dissatisfaction in Kennedy. She used to be a schoolteacher before she moved out to Olympia. Now she was a bartender. She made sacrifices to come out here.

Her passion for teaching was apparent. When she spoke about teaching to me. She described a classroom where kids learned instinctively, comfortably, and without pressure. She talked about a classroom where kids understood why they were learning and were free to explore. She had empathy for kids with troubled lives. She wanted to give kids problem solving skills that were practical in the real world. What she described reminded me of the homeschooling I got from Ray and my mom.

She had a dream about opening a school out in the woods somewhere, with farm animals, and tools, and art, and trails, and fishing poles. She believed our society was paying the price for all the intelligence that was left undiscovered. She lit up when she talked about it. I encouraged her to push forward, to try to make that dream happen. She said I was the only one who believed in her.

Philip was a beautiful man, central to himself, and his gentle view of life and science was inspiring. But Kennedy wasn't happy, and Philip didn't know. Kennedy reminded me of my mom. They looked alike. She had dark hair, dark eyes. She was warm and beautiful. She had soul to her. Philip was insular. He was deep within himself.

He was always working on something. He was meant to do great things, we all knew

that, but being Kennedy's life partner wasn't one of them.

We all have our struggles. In Philip's perfect world, every kid would know the

periodic table, maybe in the place of some baseball statistic. We'd all interpret our

surroundings scientifically. He's lost a lot of sleep and energy worrying about this,

wishing things were different. Evidence, proof, he values these things, he depends on

them. I like to wing it more, I've never taken a map with me when I explore, and I never

trust everything I see either.

I have my struggles too. I have my battles. I've traveled this planet. I've spent

enough time crossing borders that birds fly over. I don't get it. I don't understand all this

nation building. I don't understand patriotism. I see a lot of blind, ignorant nation loving.

That's never made any sense to me.

People in this country have a false sense of superiority, like being born an

American makes us better at everything. I hear people say that we live in the best

country in the world. They talk about the freedom we have in this country. Stop it. This is

obnoxious.

I've seen the same sun shine over darker faces, herding their animals, sleeping

under the same moon, carrying their children, the same wind in their hair, the same

stars in their eyes.

What are nations? Lift that line off the ground. It doesn't exist. It's fiction. It's a

social fiction. If no one believed in it, it wouldn't exist. I don't believe in any of it.

I was ten years old, my first day in a new school. Any school would have been a new school. A bell rang, and then, simultaneously, like they had been trained to do so, every kid in that room turned perfectly towards the flag and put their hand over their chest, thinking it was their heart, and recited their pledge to this nation. I jumped. I didn't know what was happening. The other kids laughed at me, made me feel like I was the one who was strange. *Me? I'm the one that's strange? You all just turned simultaneously and talked to a piece of fabric, you robots.*

But all they could think was *how could you not know the Pledge of Allegiance?* It was a wall too big and too wide for them to get past, and I was seen as not American. I can still hear my teacher say, *Well you're going to have to learn to respect your country.* But I knew all about the Duwamish tribes that inhabited the Seattle area before we came and built schools and raised flags and embarrassed little kids who felt out of place in a classroom but loved to learn. Ray used to like to learn about the native people who first inhabited the land any time we'd relocate somewhere new. That was the way he'd show respect.

I'd love to go back and tell them, *it doesn't make you a better person because you love this country more than I do.* Their actions directly motivated me to spend hours of my life researching all the reasons why countries, especially ours, didn't deserve a pledge of allegiance.

I have to restrain myself. I know there's no fight worth fighting, but I see that same dude all over Olympia, sporting his red, white and blue, his soaring eagle of freedom, all that bullshit. He's out there every day, walking around with his sandwich board pushing all his pro-America, *love it or leave it* nonsense. I'd like to ask him, *you ever heard of Project MK Ultra? How about Paul Robeson? There's a reason you've never heard of him. He was a communist. You ever heard of United States Public Law 103-150? How about things you have heard of? Trail of Tears? The Dred Scott Decision? Internment camps? McCarthyism? Attaboy, go wave your flag, you fucking puppet.* But I say none of it. I smile. I remain polite and peaceful. And that's my struggle.

I start thinking about this and my blood boils. I know enough about Ray's parents to know that they were a little different and had an FBI file kept open on them. Or maybe they made that up. Ray's dad once told him, *you're nobody 'til the FBI thinks you're up to something.* I think some of that pinko wisdom rubbed off on me.

It was early fall, 1999. God, I love telling this story. I have a cousin on Ray's side of the family, Jimmy Eagle, who gets himself mixed up in the anarchist groups down in Oregon. He came up around this time with some propaganda about globalization.

That bank you put your paycheck in, they invest in drilling for oil on indigenous lands in Columbia, and that company you buy your hundred dollar shoes from, they got kids working in sweatshops, and all the rainforests are getting mowed down so fat cattle can roam and fat people can eat them. That's globalization, man. And these bastards are having themselves a summit up in Seattle, last day of November.

I'm not one to believe everything I hear, but I did my research, and most of what Jimmy Eagle told me was based on some kind of truth, to a point. Yeah, there were companies who had invested in oil drilling on lands belonging to the U'wa people, and one of these companies was a bank here in the United States. And, it was partially true that a lot of the meat we eat comes from ranches in South America, ranches that took the place of hundreds of thousands of square miles of rainforest.

But I had my own reasons for wanting to join the protests against the World

Trade Organization Conference of 1999. I figured, the more people who go down there and make noise, the better chance it'll make the news, even for just a short segment. I pictured someone sitting comfortably in their sofa, eating their dinner, watching the news, thinking about how great this country is, and then some footage of a few hundred people chanting appears, and maybe it gets them thinking. Maybe it annoys them.

We like to think that the world is a better place than it used to be. And that's probably true. Developed countries aren't openly dabbling in the slave market anymore. We're not openly pushing indigenous peoples off their lands so we can make a profit anymore. But we're doing a lot of it quietly, behind the scenes, hoping people won't pay attention. My motivation for protesting? Let's annoy some people. You don't get anyone's attention unless you annoy them.

I had brought the protest up to Kennedy, and I didn't get more than halfway through my pitch when Philip came over from some corner of the room where I didn't think he was listening, and he enthusiastically agreed. I had heard him lecture on deforestation and the devastating effect on global warming, so this was in his ballpark. He was a lot like me, sick of people being gullible, sick of people believing everything they hear.

Kennedy agreed as well. I never doubted her. In our own discussions, she wasn't shy about her frustration with our consumer society. She had worked in a school where a kid was shot over his ridiculously expensive shoes, shoes that were assembled at embarrassingly low wages, somewhere in a country far away where we don't have to think about it.

In the weeks running up to the WTO Conference, it became clear that there were going to be a lot more than a few hundred people and a guitar. Union leaders, teachers, religious leaders, environmentalist, and three concerned global citizens listening to jazz in a little blue house on the Westside of Olympia, we were organizing, planning our strategies. We were going to be annoying, really annoying. And we were going to make more than the evening news.

Protesting in Seattle with Philip and Kennedy and fifty thousand other people was the most unifying moment we all had. It brought us all together. It gave us a cause, at least for that one day. We bailed the moment rubber bullets started flying, but I do like to think that our presence added to the annoyance. Delegates weren't able to get from their hotel rooms to the conference. That's annoying.

I had hoped this would energize us, that this would bring Philip and Kennedy closer, but we quickly resumed our normal routine not long after the protests. Philip and Kennedy got back to their normal distant selves. Kennedy went back to dreaming about a school in the woods. Life went on.

Dates didn't mean anything to Philip, but I picked him up in my truck exactly five years after our first phone call, to the date, and I told him I wanted to go on a hike. We traveled north up the highway into the Skokomish Valley. I had, and still have, a strong feeling that Philip and Kennedy came into my life for a reason. I wanted to celebrate it that day. Kennedy was working a day shift, so it was just Philip and me on that trip.

I saw the occasion as an appropriate moment to confide in Philip. I had been carrying around a secret, a secret about the last moments of my mom's life. I wanted to share that story with my close friend. I wanted to bond with Philip, to get inside his soul a little, and to share what was deep inside of me. We headed out on the trail and I immediately began talking about my mom, and the last moments I shared with her.

She was dying, painfully, slowly. She talked more and more about Ray everyday. She was frail. Her quality of life was poor. She deserved to be at peace. So, I helped her.

I'm right back in that room every time I think about it. I held her hand the whole time. In the other hand I held the picture of me, her, and Ray, the day I was born, incense stick poking out of a book on the shelf.

This event, this moment with my mom, her last moments inside her body, everything that was happening, it was hitting me in waves, waves like the beach where the old woman told Ray to get up off his ass. It was hitting me in rhythms, pulsating like the pain of a hornet bite. I saw the wind in the room blow through an organ pipe, and it came out a different color, an orange that painted the walls. I felt her dance away with Ray that day.

And when she left, I could feel them both present, together. I felt something I hadn't felt since the morning I walked into the bus and saw my mom holding Ray's lifeless hand, the one that had been rearranged by a Komodo dragon when he was learning how to breathe in Indonesia. When I walked in and saw Ray lying there, I felt something I wasn't prepared to understand.

But when my mom died, I understood it better.

I wanted Philip to feel that moment with me, to really be there with me. I wanted him to understand what I felt, the peace I felt about where she is now, with Ray. I knew their souls were destined to be with each other.

When they were together, their energies would blend in a way that that made everything and everyone around them happy. Plants, flowers, vegetables, all grew better around them. I remember relatively wild animals coming closer and fearing us less.

I knew where my mom was, where her spirit was. I was at peace with it. I shared this with Philip up on the trail in the Skokomish, and he discarded it. He responded with, "You don't know where your mom is, nobody knows."

I punched him. I didn't know what else to do. I'd never punched anyone before. I said to him, "Hey man, I'm going to punch you hard in the face, but you can handle it, you're an adult." And then I punched him. He didn't even try to stop me. We looked ridiculous. I helped him up, and I asked him if he wanted to punch me back, and he said, "I'm sorry Gilb, I haven't slept in a while. I'm not at my best lately."

That was the first sign that something was wrong, very wrong. I'd noticed he wasn't looking good. I knew he stayed up late at night stargazing. I didn't know just how poorly he was doing.

We were silent for most of the hike. He didn't seem to take it personally that I punched him. He just motored through the hike, focusing off into the distance.

On the way home, in my truck, I told him about the day he called me, how I had wandered over to the liquor store, how I dragged my feet the whole way. I didn't want to buy that bottle of whisky. I knew that if I even took one sip, that I would spiral away. I had lost Ray and my mom to cancer. I never knew my biological father. I had lost my wife, who just never really loved me. I thought my life, my career, and how everything was falling apart. And then Philip called. It just couldn't have been a coincidence. I know that.

And to that, he responded, as if he knew his line, "Gilb, I called you because you wrote a good book," and then he said something else, something I may have known all along. He said, "and because Kennedy told me to." We didn't say much else to each other that day.

I spent every moment I could after that, trying to help Philip. I picked him up and we volunteered at shelters, and I had him bring his telescopes over to my friends' homes. I had him explain the universe to children. I did everything I could for him, but I couldn't help him.

A date on my calendar was dangling in front of me. It was an important date to me. Every year Philip and I took part in a discussion panel on the topic of life and death, and how members of the scientific community and religious communities interpreted death. I had helped organize this event before Philip moved out to Olympia.

The idea arrived from an unfortunate circumstance. I was at a funeral of a boy who had committed suicide. I knew the kid through a youth outreach program. Sitting in my row at the service were a minister, a local storeowner, a high school teacher, and myself. We all carpooled to the funeral in silence.

My friend Sal was a minister at a very progressive, very left leaning non-denominational church in Olympia. He had helped feed and clothe the boy whose funeral we were attending. Sal had grown up in a strict Roman Catholic home. His family was from Italy and he was the only one of his siblings born in the United States. He grew up in San Francisco, so I've often theorized that he got balanced out somehow. He left the Catholic Church while in college, and began studying theology, in hopes of becoming a minister.

He says he didn't lose his faith, that he gained one, and that he was probably a closeted atheist growing up. He found God when his car broke down outside a church in Oakland, California. An African American gospel choir was rehearsing on a weeknight, and he walked in hoping to use their phone, but forgot all about his car and sat and cried, and felt his God at work. And I think it's a gorgeous story, even if it doesn't blend with my beliefs.

But I'll admit I was stumped, watching Sal during the funeral. I noticed he was praying, his hands were clenched and he was trembling. He was whispering to himself. I wondered what he was praying about. Aware of how insensitive this sounded in my head, I had to ask myself, *the boy is already dead, what could Sal be praying about?* And I'd still like to know.

Jefferson is a man I've known since my very first days in Olympia. He owns a restaurant downtown where he keeps a pianist on staff who plays raucous Old Western music. The entire restaurant is engulfed in a western theme, and all he serves is spaghetti. That's it.

When he's not running his restaurant, he teaches laughter yoga. He is the ultimate opportunist. He says he follows his instinct, but he can't explain it. He's not sure any of it is real, or coincidence. Everything he has ever done in life has been a success. He says he just visualizes it, and it happens. He considers himself agnostic, open to all, not sure of anything.

Neil, the furthest away from me in our row, is a high school teacher. He was a student of mine back in college. I knew from several of his essays that he was an atheist. He made an effort to point this out. He was sure, absolutely sure, that there is no God, no afterlife.

Neil was a very caring person with strong morals. He gave everything he had. In his spare time, he would volunteer at soup kitchens, which is where he met the boy who had died. This instinct to care for his fellow human didn't come from a religion, but from his own conscience.

In all honesty, atheists often make me uneasy. I can only wonder where he believes the boy is now. I don't understand where the atheist believes this all comes from, all of this. All the matter of the universe, it had to come from somewhere. To truly believe that it all just spontaneously popped out of nothing, I don't get it. But, I respected Neil. I knew no one more generous.

I don't consider myself an atheist because I do believe in God. I don't consider myself traditionally religious because I don't have any scripture to follow. I don't consider myself agnostic because I don't have doubts, I know what I believe. I believe in nature. I believe in the spirits of nature and of humans, and a powerful force that helps guide us, if we're tuned in enough to notice.

So, the four of us drove home from the funeral in silence because we didn't know how to discuss what we were feeling. All four of us had different beliefs about death. I had to wonder, *why can't we talk about this?*

I knew an Irish priest who taught at a high school in Portland. He wrote a book about the Virgin of Guadalupe that I used in my classes. We used to get together and drink whiskey. I would drive all the way to Portland just to get drunk with a priest because it made me feel less alone. We got sober together too, several times.

I'd had the idea of organizing this event since the funeral of the young boy, and I ran it by my friend, the priest. He had the use of a fancy private high school gymnasium, which I was hoping he'd offer. I described it all, every aspect of the discussion forum, and he was on board.

It ran smoothly for years. I looked forward to it this time of year, every year. I believed in what we were doing. We brought people in from all over, from several different systems of faith, and the discussion was always positive. This was always intended to be a discussion, not a debate. We purposely went out of our way not to disrespect each other's views.

I got Philip involved in this event because he was brilliant, he was well spoken, and he came from a scientific background. I figured that would add a new perspective. But I could see him visibly struggle with the format each year. He wanted to go on the offensive. Philip isn't a mean person, but he has very little patience for systems of thought that do not abide by the scientific method. He couldn't understand why I didn't just prove them all wrong and be done with it. He told me that scientists are expected to find flaws in each other's work. It's what keeps the community accurate.

Regrettably, I had written much on the Bible, debunking it as irrelevant mythology. In an essay that was published, I wrote about the resurrection of Jesus and how the chronology of events in the Bible didn't match from Mark, Matthew, John and Luke. In another paper, I cited Joshua 10:13, and openly questioned the idea of a sun staying fixed in the sky so a nation could avenge its enemy. Many times I explored the meanings behind different verses in the Bible that appear to endorse an oppressive role for women in their marriages. There's enough in Deuteronomy, Chapter 22, to send chills down my spine.

I challenged Christians, I accused them of being selective, treating the Bible like a menu that they could order what they wanted off of. They seem to have no problem accusing homosexuals of living a sinful life, while ignoring equally confusing laws about getting tattoos, eating shellfish, wearing denim. I accused them of using the Bible to settle arguments. *If God said it, that settles it.* But when the Bible contradicts itself, they offer a different explanation; *the word was instead inspired by God, and was muffled by humans.*

I went after Judaism as well, how at every Rosh Hashanah ceremony it is specifically stated that the Earth is less than 6,000 years old. I challenged the notion that the Torah was written by a single author, Moses. I argued that the only remaining copy of the Torah after the Babylonians sacked the Kingdom of Judah was a translated Greek version that landed in Alexandria. As it turns out, I was an eager grad student who wanted to be noticed, who wanted to tell stories. I didn't quite have my facts straight.

I regret doing this. This was a habit of mine back when I was a graduate student. I felt threatened by religions that defined their god in absolute terms. But setting out to prove what others believe as wrong is a practice that has no place in anthropology. And furthermore, Ray never defined what he believed in by proving others wrong. So, I should have known better.

I wrote Iridescence as a rebuttal to myself, as a way to celebrate the many different ways to look at this wonderful existence. The energy spent trying to prove each other wrong is divisive, and it's not very productive. There are betters ways to use our energy.

As an anthropologist, there are subjects you can't avoid. Death is one of them. How cultures have perceived death is a fascinating study. Every culture has to deal with it, and we're all left guessing. Speaking about these *guesses*, in a respectful format, is why we created the forum in the first place. And maybe I still felt guilty about the essays I published back in college.

This year, 2001, the last year of the event, the last year that Philip and Kennedy and I all lived in Olympia together, I had reservations about Philip participating in the forum. He was falling apart. His insomnia had gotten worse. He was even more distant and withdrawn. I don't know how he finished off the semester. He was a zombie walking around campus. His eyes were sunk and he had lost weight. But he insisted on participating. So, just like every year, I reminded him of the protocol, and begged him not to go on the attack.

We packed a van full of students and headed down to Portland. I drove, and Philip sat in the front seat deep in his own universe, eyes beaming off into nothing. Those who didn't know him, I can only imagine what they thought of him. But he still functioned; he still had a briefcase full of notes. I had stepped in once to announce to his students that this event was coming, and I stuck around to watch him lecture, and you wouldn't have known he was suffering from insomnia. He was brilliant, as always. So I trusted he would remain professional at the forum.

A woman named Sam traveled down with us. I remember her well. She was paralyzed from the waist down. She had been living in Portland a few years earlier and happened to come to the forum. Afterward she had approached Philip and me. She told us her life story, how she was searching for purpose, and had gotten in trouble with the law. Philip suggested she attend Evergreen. And there she was, a few years later, a few weeks away from graduation. Those are the instances when I am reminded of the forces at work that are guiding us. I couldn't help but admire her. She looked up to us. She was an academic pilgrim. I had very few interactions with her, but I felt her spirit. She was a powerful, strong willed person. And I think that was lost on Philip. He may not have realized how important his position was as an educator.

As soon as the forum began, I had a bad feeling in my gut. I looked over at Philip and he was mouthing words to himself, shifting his weight back and forth. The moderator eventually asked him a science question about the stages of a dead body. I was hoping he would amuse the crowd with some stats on how quickly body temperature drops. I don't even think he heard the question. He instead unleashed a lengthy attack where he discussed the psychological disconnect humans have with death *because* of religion, how religion doesn't prepare us for death, and misguides us as to what happens to us after death. He received loud cheers from about half the crowd. I never wanted the crowd to be so divided. Half the crowd cheering meant half the crowd wasn't.

But he wasn't done. He spoke of the evolutionary effects that religion has had on us, that it has shaped us into believing in fairy tales. That there was a price to pay for speaking out, and that we are descendants, many of us, of those who obeyed. He spoke of Galileo as brilliant, but even more brave, and wondered how many more thinkers there were like Galileo that kept quiet, and how much that must have slowed us down scientifically.

He derailed the forum. He went on the offensive, and the different religious leaders tried to counter, but he ignored them. I'll admit, he didn't debate, but he broke the format. The moderator lost all control. He stopped asking questions, and everyone took turns trying to counter what Philip was saying, and then the event was over. I didn't speak a word during the rest of the forum.

He walked off the stage when it was all finished, without shaking hands with anyone. At first I couldn't find him. We were in the gymnasium of a Catholic high school, and he had found the weight lifting room, and was sleeping, or at least appeared to be, on a workout bench.

When I found him, I was angry. I wanted to get loud. I had told him several times that this is not the place for him to get even with the world. This was not that stage. If he wanted to do that, go do it somewhere else. I had some bottled up anger towards him. He wasn't a good husband, he hadn't been that good of a friend either. I had reached out to him endlessly, trying to help him. I knew I was going to say some things I would regret.

But as I walked up to him, he was drooling out of the side of his mouth, his head hanging off the edge of the bench. I stopped and collected myself. My thoughts shifted.

He was brilliant up there that night. He was well spoken. His voice filled every corner of the room. Philip was a phenomenal public speaker. He really punctured the crowd. And maybe that was the first time I saw him for who he really was. Not who I wanted him to be, but who he was. Science was everything to Philip. It wasn't just a hobby.

To Philip, this was serious. He really felt like our human race was in danger. I can't say I agree with everything he said, but I understood where his urgency came from.

I let him sleep. He ruined my forum, but I was proud of him. This was his calling, his purpose. I know he considers the well being of the entire human race, future and present, when he acts. Philip is a wonderful man, but he had tough times ahead of him.

That summer, the summer of 2001, Philip hit rock bottom. Without the hours of teaching to keep him regulated, he drifted further and further. Kennedy was worried, but I think her biggest concern was how she was going to get out of this marriage. Or, at least it should have been.

I would come visit and he'd be on the couch, eyes blank. I'd read to him. It felt silly at first, a grown man reading to another grown man. I brought my manuscript over, one that I had been working on for the past year. It was fictional, my first attempt at that genre. I chose to center the book around the color orange, incorporating the place orange holds in different cultures around the world.

Every time I came over I would bring Philip an orange, just to be comical, and he'd sit up and eat it. I felt like his older brother, bringing him food, reading to him. I wish I would have had a brother, someone else who could have remembered how beautiful my parents were. I was going to dedicate the book to them. Ray and my mother had a special place in their hearts for the color orange.

After I had read through the entire draft, I was discouraged with the quality of the story. I knew it needed some work. The characters were imbalanced, their personalities blended too much. There was too much about the story that you couldn't take seriously. I was disappointed. Every story I've ever told has been exaggerated and enhanced, so I assumed I'd be a good fictional writer.

I put it away, and told myself I'd continue working on it in the fall. I then picked up

Philip's book. I thought it was a good idea that I showed him what he was capable of.

Years earlier he attempted to write a book. He had put together a manuscript and it was very entertaining. I honestly enjoyed it. I wanted him to keep at it, but he lost interest. I kept a bound copy in a safe place, and every so often I would remind him of what he had started, trying to motivate him into finishing it. He used a typewriter. He didn't like computers, and he wrote it in one draft. No one would believe me. Over 100,000 words I imagine, and it took him a few weeks. That's unheard of.

The book featured a man who was chosen to visit Mars in 2018. He wasn't an astronaut. He was just a pilot who had volunteered for the mission, having passed hundreds of psychological and physical tests. After the shuttle launched, there was a problem with the chamber and he was told that if he didn't abort the mission that he would surely die of radiation. He chose not to abort, and the world watched him die before the computers on the shuttle carried out the mission without him.

The main character, I believe his name was Joshua, he knew how important it was, and it may have been another decade before the cooperating space committees were able to put another mission together. 2018 was chosen because of the proximity of the planets' orbits, and so completing this mission was more important than the life of one man.

Philip described the psychological tests in great detail. It was almost painful to read. Hallucinations were induced. Unlivable conditions were simulated. Several times he was convinced he was going to die and was expected to perform a task. Philip eluded that one of the reasons he was chosen was that they felt he would sacrifice himself if the situation arose. And it did.

He'd said the book was unfixable, that almost every aspect of the mission he had described would have been inaccurate. The way I saw it, it really only needed a few minor alterations, and it could have been successful. But, I don't know anything about Mars. I'm just an optimistic, loyal friend, to a fault.

Joshua, the character in his story, died with about half of the book left, and then Philip spent the second half of the book digging into his childhood. I suspected this was more autobiographical than he let on. He spoke about a building manager that looked out for him, lending him a bike lock and tools to work on experiments. He spoke about an alcoholic father, a car crash, and a scar. I told him, we both have it; we both have that fight we can't win in our blood. He smiled and reminded me the book was fictional. I was proud of him because I could have never put something together like it. I was proud the way a brother would be.

It was midsummer, and I went down to a wedding in Oregon where I have a pocket of family, and stayed a few weeks. I needed some time away from Olympia. Every year I tried to take a few weeks and get out of town. It couldn't have come at a better time. Philip was getting worse and worse, my attempts to get him in to see a doctor had failed. I think I needed to get away from all of it for a short time. I needed to recharge my engine if I was going to continue to be there for him.

These were Ray's brothers and sisters I was visiting, and their kids. I safely referred to them as first cousins. Ray's supposedly communist parents had raised all their kids to be trouble making, beach combing citizens of the world. None of them even had social security numbers. Every time I saw these people, I felt like I was spending time with Ray. They couldn't help but be just like him.

My cousin, Jimmy Eagle Plum, the anarchist manifesto reading cousin of mine that always had a new conspiracy theory, he and I spent some good bonding time together down at his sister's wedding, and he decided to come back to Olympia with me for a few weeks. Jimmy Eagle knew of a family that was working on a straw bale home, and he felt like he could help them out.

Jimmy is a clever guy. He could do anything. He's worked on wind turbines, climbed trees as an arborist, grown and trimmed weed all over Humboldt, worked construction, and worked on fishing boats. He's done all the jobs I wouldn't have a clue how to do, and I don't think he ever graduated from anything. I liked spending time with him. He was intelligent in all the ways I wasn't.

When I eventually did come back to Olympia, I quickly stopped by to see Philip. I missed him. I was worried about him. I got to the door and knocked, but no one answered. I could hear noises inside, like someone was home, so I knocked on the door, but again, no one answered.

Kennedy finally opened the door as she was leaving for work, surprised to see me. I asked her if she could hear me knocking, and she broke down in tears. I had never seen her with so much emotion.

She walked off, still talking under her breath, leaving her front door open. Not caring. After getting in her car, she cried some more, resting on her steering wheel, with her foot on the brake and the car in reverse.

I couldn't just let her cry like that, alone, so I sat down next to her, and we spoke. And that's when she told me about the incident, in detail. It was difficult to process. It was incredibly disturbing. But even after everything Kennedy told me, I still couldn't feel negatively toward Philip. I knew he was out of his mind. I knew he would never really want to hurt himself. There were times when I was up against a wall, where I was desperate. We don't judge people for what they do during these times.

Kennedy and I sat in her car, speaking plainly. We were transparent with each other. I was grateful to connect with her. I felt the forces of nature at work. We had a powerful, healing conversation. And in that conversation, several times we spoke of a school, out in the woods. I don't think she ever made it to work that day.

I left. I grabbed Jimmy Eagle, and we went out searching for my very important friend Philip.

A fast talking, finger snapping, well dressed Powerman walks into the conference room where two older gentlemen are dressed in identical business suits. His leather bound briefcase is an assembly of one image projector and a freestanding projector screen. He pops the briefcase open at one end of the table, and at the other end, he quickly assembles the screen. The Powerman walks around the room slowly, alternating his hands like pinball flippers as he speaks.

"My client... if you allow him to test the market, will receive offers that you cannot match. If you do not extend his contract, he'll be gone. And my client..." The older gentlemen, forced to listen to the Powerman's pitch, attempt a synchronized eye roll, "he's currently ranked among the top goalkeepers in Europe at the moment."

The Powerman's redundant statement is not going to convince the owners of the small Spanish club, just barely avoiding regulation into the second tier of professional football, to part with the amount of money the Powerman is negotiating for on behalf of his client.

A remote magically appears in the Powerman's hands, and the attention of the room is directed towards looped images on a screen of a goalkeeper diving across the goal line.

"My client... he's loyal. He wants to continue his career here. Personally, I think it smells like pirates."

The businessmen, stiff and bored, yawn as they pour water from a carafe with floating sliced lemons. One of them says to the other, "¿Pero quién coño es este gilipollas?"

Kennedy Kravitz

Everyone I've managed to piss off, they live in a room where all they do is discuss my faults. They talk about how I'm passive aggressive, opinionated, and dishonest, I'm not always fun to be around when I don't get my way. They sit around and they all agree about how horrible I am. Some of these people have legitimate reasons to dislike me, some don't. Doesn't matter. They get together, and they have a great time. They get real comfy in that room. There are big fluffy pillows. Sometimes I think I designed that room to be as cozy as possible. I don't know why I do that.

I live with anxiety. I have a scab on my arm; I've picked it for years, never letting it heal. I have to leave the room sometimes to pick it. That can't be normal.

I used to have nightmares about my mom's family. She had so many brothers. They were ugly and loud. My mom was already starting to lose her mind when my dad had to kick them out of the bar. I was relieved when she said, in a little girl's voice, "This time, they'll all go away for ever and ever and ever." She was right. We never saw any of them again.

I was named after those lunatics. My mom's maiden name is Kennedy. But my dad says he secretly named me after Robert Kennedy. He just didn't tell my mom that. I have a much older half brother, too. My mom had a kid long before she met my dad. He's done well for himself by staying away from us all.

My dad owned a basement bar in Manhattan. He originally came here from Israel to be a chemist, had gone to college, but learned how to brew beer instead. And then he ended up with a bar.

The way he tells it, it was by pure accident. He used to brew ales for his friends, one of which was a bar owner. I'm not sure if it was legal, but he'd sell his beer at his friend's bar.

The man that owned the bar got behind on some bills, and needed to borrow money. My dad, being a nice guy, tried to help him out by letting him sell the beer and keep the profits, as kind of a loan. Then he couldn't pay that loan back, so my dad, being a nice guy, took the bar off his hands.

My dad had a couple of old TVs that he repaired and propped them up so he could watch movies when business was slow. And business was often slow. The bar was in a great location, but it had no appeal to it. My dad knew nothing about this kind of business, and I think he was starting to regret his decision. But then someone came in and asked him to turn the Yankee game on. He came back the next day with a few more people, and asked the same thing. In his own convenient storytelling ways, before he knew it, my dad had a sports bar.

I couldn't have been older than eight when he had me running around the bar cleaning up after people. Why hire someone when you have a kid that'll do it? I spent a lot of time in that bar in Manhattan, and I didn't mind. No one ever thought of cigarette smoke or whatever else I was exposed to. The language of drunks. I was safe. I was near my dad.

It was all a game to me. Some girls my age were taking their dolls' orders at make believe tea parties, and that's all my dad's bar was to me, a big tea party. I don't think it was ever legal to have a kid working in a bar, but my dad never paid attention to rules. And I can remember off duty police officers letting me play with their handcuffs, so clearly they weren't too concerned either.

We were hurting financially for a while when my mom lost her job. This was 1976, '77, and '78. The Yankees went to the World Series all three years, which meant more crowded nights at the bar. We had double occupancy during those games. I don't think the bar would have made it without those World Series runs.

I grew up believing in magic. The bar was a superstitious place. My dad could have bought better televisions, but the old models from the 60s that he had dangerously propped up; he said they brought in customers. He'd say that any time the picture went out, something good happened for the Yankees. I remember him poking at the television set with a broomstick, and the picture would come back, and a Yankee base runner was rounding third.

His customers believed him. They wanted to believe. Grown men willingly played along with all these silly rules. No one at the bar could talk during a no-hitter. Educated and skilled adults, believing wholeheartedly that their voices in a bar miles away from the stadium could jinx a professional athlete's performance. I believed it too. I'd shush city council members.

Police officers and firefighters made the bar theirs. I felt invincible. We'd get pulled over, they'd recognize my dad, and then I'd be playing around in the back of the cop car like it was a jungle gym. "I can't give Yossi Kravitz a ticket, it's bad luck," I heard a cop say.

But my dad may have had them all fooled. These superstitions, I don't think he actually believed any of them. He needed to get people into the bar, and he had to make his bar different. He seemed to know that people would fall for it. They wanted to believe in magic.

We lived in Glen Rock, New Jersey, thirty minutes from Manhattan, if my dad was driving. He didn't like our nice, little town. He was more at home in the city. That bar meant a lot to him. He was proud of it, and he didn't have much to do with my mom. He never understood what was happening to her. He avoided her. In one hand was a fun day at the bar, where your customers love you and give you money, and in the other hand is a woman who is losing her mind and hiding bowls of cereal on the shelves. I get it. I understand why he chose the bar.

I lived in two different worlds. I went to school with all the kids my age, and tried to fit in as normal, but then I'd go sidekick it with my dad in the city. When I got older, my dad didn't ask me to come in the bar as much. He must have known that a teenage girl didn't want to go work with her dad, but I still came and helped out during busy times. Business was good enough and he hired some people and started selling merchandise.

I was always much closer to my dad. We had the same sense of humor and cynical brand of storytelling. My mom embarrassed me. She made me anxious. The way my dad would ignore her - that made me anxious too. Relating to other people became tough.

In college, my boyfriends were all much older than I was. One of them was a sports agent, and his clients were European professional athletes. He'd be in Spain or Germany, and he would come home with souvenirs that I didn't care about. At first, my dad liked him, because his job sounded exciting, but he soon saw him as a powerman, a slick businessman. That's what he called my boyfriend. Powerman. He didn't like people like that in his bar, said they brought bad luck. He may have meant it this time. Before I could see it that way, I got pregnant.

Powerman was wealthy and motivated. We would have had a comfortable life together. We would have seen the world. I'm sure he's out there doing exactly that, right now.

When I learned I was pregnant, I went to my mom. She's crazy. That's how I describe it. Crazy. I say she's crazy, and then I laugh the way people laugh when nothing's funny. But with all the bat shit in her head, I still would confide in her from time to time. I knew she would give me straight advice, and she wouldn't ever tell anyone what I told her.

When I told her Powerman got me pregnant, she said, in a kid's voice, "Well, that's an easy fix, just have an abortion. A big, fat abortion. And then don't see him anymore, not him, Kennedy, ewww."

So, this is what I did. And maybe this will tell you a few things about the kind of person I am. I walked up to a boy in my college class, and I said, "I need to talk to you … Oh, and my name's Kennedy." He seemed like a nice, honest kid. I thought of boys my age as kids. I remember I told him I needed his help. I needed to go have an abortion, and I couldn't do it by myself. And so out of the goodness of his heart, he needed to just come with me, and pretend like he knew me, and then leave me alone forever. He agreed. Boys.

But that doesn't mean the abortion was easy. I cried. And I had issues with men for years afterwards. I think it was the right decision, I hope so. I still don't know how I feel about abortion, I just think of it as something that happened, something I did, and it's over now.

I wish I had told Powerman the truth, that I was pregnant, but that I wasn't anymore. I wish I had told him to just go away, because I didn't like him, because no one did, because he was a dirt bag.

Instead, I avoided him. I stopped answering his phone calls. I hid behind the bar twice when he showed up looking for me. I wish I had chosen to be more direct with him, and with people in general. It's a flaw of mine.

My mom got worse, and she couldn't take care of herself anymore. My dad didn't know how to deal with it, and starting living in an apartment upstairs from the bar. The bar had done so well that he bought the building. He no longer had to hit the television with a broomstick. His business model was simple. He kept the bar clean, he smiled, and he never fixed his chipped tooth, even when he could afford to. And he may have led people to believe his bar was magic.

Yossi Kravitz, my dad, was the most popular bartender in New York. He turned himself into an icon. He used to make predictions, and he was right enough for people to come pay attention. He was wrong a lot too, but he'd get away with that somehow.

In 1987 and 1991, the Giants won the Super Bowl. Both times, he had convinced people he was making it happen. He played on people's hopes. He told people the Giants won every time someone bought a round for the bar at halftime. Of course, they lost sometimes too. But people would line up to do it. He had shirts and hats made that read *I bought a round at Yossi's.* News crews would come by, and people from out of town would travel long distances just to watch games at his bar.

One year a group of college students traveled up to Manhattan, all the way from Durham, North Carolina, just to watch the UNC vs. Duke game, thinking it would bring good luck. My dad was always looking to have fun, so the moment they walked in, he said, "Welcome, have a drink on me, your team is going to lose."

I happened to be in the bar that day. I saw him leave at half time. Magically, just a few minutes later, he came back with a North Carolina hat on, and sat with the college students, heckling them. He thought they would enjoy some friendly rivalry, but they were far too serious about the game, especially when Duke lost, and they left in a sour mood. Not everyone got my dad's humor.

I needed a career of my own. I didn't want to be a professional bartender's daughter. I didn't really want much to do with the bar. I was proud of my dad, of course, but bar life wasn't for me. Bars are desperate places.

Some of my friends were in a teaching program. It seemed like a decent career choice. I thought that many of the skills I learned from working at a bar would help serve me in the classroom. But I wasn't one of those people who had a 'calling' to teach. It wasn't like that for me. I wasn't even sure I'd enjoy it. College was like a button that I pushed. It really happened like that. I didn't give much thought into it. It was something I was told I was smart enough to do, so I did it. I filled my college application out in the bar and I got a little bit of spilled beer on it. If you grow up in a bar, college life isn't really too spectacular.

I got hired to teach fifth grade at the elementary school in Glen Rock where I grew up. And then I did something else that surprised me, I moved in with my mom and started taking care of her. Someone had to.

I worked at that elementary school for two years. It was a nice school with nice kids, and nice supportive families. The kids all knew they belonged. It was just like when I was a kid. We had a great PTO; they bought us all computers. Kids at this school had a good shot at doing well in life, and I was proud to be a part of that. It was validating. Life was good.

My mom was a lot of work, but I felt like I owed her. I was never there for her when I was younger, and, I probably would have been married to Powerman and would have had all his little Powerbabies had she not scribbled her advice to me about having an abortion. The older I got, the more I knew I wasn't supposed to be with anyone like Powerman. I needed someone kinder; someone like the boy who helped me out at the clinic.

A time came that my mom had to be institutionalized. I couldn't help her. She needed doctors. She didn't have anyone. My brother was long gone; he was a lawyer in California. He would send money, just envelopes with checks in them. My dad, my brother, they didn't really know how to help. They were absent. They didn't know just how bad it got. She was delusional. She was hearing voices, having conversations with the walls, filling the empty shelves with cereal bowls.

So, that's what we did, we put her away. We put our own mom away. I guess we had to. Sometimes, there isn't a right thing to do. Every choice felt wrong. But now I needed a new job. The whole experience made me want to leave Glen Rock forever.

I'm such a sucker sometimes. I was home, in my sweats, eating ice cream, watching some horrible movie about a teacher in a poverty-stricken area. Goosebumps climbed up my arms. Within a week I found a job at a middle school in the city. I found an apartment I could barely afford in an East Harlem neighborhood. They said it was gentrifying.

I was scared living there, but I didn't let my dad think so because he was scared of me living there too. So, I got a big scary dog, twice the size of me. I babied that dog so much that he would rip your face off if you touched me.

The bell rang on the first day of school, and some of the most impoverished kids in the country walked through my door, and I didn't have a clue what to do. I threw my lessons out the window. I spent the rest of the week just talking to them, trying to get to know them, letting them get to know me.

School was a place they were told to go, so they went. A habit. But most of them had no interest in learning. And I couldn't see why they would want to. It'd be like if I was being chased by a monster and someone ran alongside me and asked if I wanted to learn how to finger crochet. No, NO! I'd want to learn how to run faster, how to hide. Or maybe, how to fight monsters.

I was scared of their world. I didn't understand their world. They thought where I lived was the nicer part of town, where you'd see white people buying up old warehouses and turning them into trendy art deco studios.

It would have been easy, as an outsider, to generalize them, to box them up, and miss what made each and every one of them unique. Such a big part of their lives was unidentifiable to me. I'd get caught up on that. I wouldn't have gotten very far teaching a classroom full of the same kid, living in extreme poverty, not if I thought of it that way. Every student had to be unique to me, and I had to develop a very different relationship with each of them. Each one of these kids needed a teacher who saw them as a unique person.

That went against my nature as a human. Stereotyping is easy. It feels almost natural. It would have been a convenient shortcut. I had to fight the urge to group them all together. That would have been less intimidating. I think that's why we stereotype in the first place. It's got to be. It's easier to simplify what's different from us. It's safe. It makes sense.

But that self-serving human nature wasn't going to make a difference here. I didn't put on my ugly sweats for nothing, and sit on the couch for nothing, with a pint of ice cream, watching a horrible movie about a precious girl from the suburbs braving it in the ghetto where she had the brilliant epiphany that those people matter too. I might as well have stayed home if I wanted it be safe, if I wanted it to make sense.

The only way to help them fight their monsters was to learn about these kids, and to learn about their monsters. I had to get closer. Their lives were foreign to me.

My life was normal to me. I did normal things. I didn't know what it was like to knock on your neighbor's door, not because your mom's boyfriend overdosed in the bathroom, but because you had to go pee, and there was a man who happened to be your mom's boyfriend unconscious in the bathroom. I didn't know what it was like to cry in the park because the landlord pinned the eviction notice on a dead cat. I didn't know you could learn the names of the presidents by pairing them with 14 story housing projects in your neighborhood. I've never been shot at over the shoes I was wearing. These are real things that happened to real people.

If I was going to be anything other than useless, I had to get closer. I had to spend time in their neighborhood, in their lives. These kids had to be more identifiable to me. It mattered. This was the first time I was doing something that mattered. And you're not a hero for being brave enough to experience what others are forced to deal with.

It was never easy. I'd tell people where I was going, where I was working, and they'd be nervous because I was a young, white, attractive female. And I was scared, too. I grew up in a bar, and I used to clean Fruit Loops out of a bookshelf. But nothing prepared me for this.

These kids came from rented and borrowed and stolen places, and sometimes, they came from nowhere. I decided the classroom needed to be theirs. It was the only place they had that could be theirs. I was turning into that woman from the movie. I'd ask myself daily, *what would she do?* And just like the movie, I had a principal who was going to fight me every step of the way.

This wasn't exactly teaching; this was something else. And that's what got under my principal's skin. That school was one big power orgy for her. And she couldn't stand knowing that I was over in my room cultivating positive relationships with my students without single filing them, without bullying them. I wasn't under her power. I didn't fear her. I was an herb garden in her industrial complex. Maybe she saw that horrible movie too, and when the young, spunky teacher finally got pushed out, she probably cheered like she was watching the Olympics. I wasted a lot of energy fighting an uphill battle with that principal, whose name I don't remember, but I bet she remembers mine. I bet she hangs out in the comfy room with all the other people I've pissed off.

I had the kids in a circle doing some mental gymnastics, with hip hop playing in the background, and some of the other kids were potting plants, and then I had two girls doing something that looked like a card game, but was really a poetry lesson.

And my principal came in. I knew the sound the door would make when someone other than a kid opened it. She gave me a look, pointed her finger at me, thinned her eyes like she was mad, and then pointed to the hallway, as if I was supposed to follow her out there.

I ignored her. If she wasn't going to treat me like a professional, then the hell with it, I wasn't going to treat her like a boss. When she realized I wasn't paying any attention to her, she spoke up, and her tone did a very condescending tumble roll, "Mizzzzzz KRAAAAAvitz, I really need to speak with you, in the haaaaallway." I ignored her again. My students were laughing. It was perfectly clear to everyone in the room exactly what was happening.

She repeated herself, "Mizzzzz Kravitz, these kids need more structure than this, and you need to start teaching the curriculum." I was quicker though, and I said, "Hey, you tell me one kid's name in this classroom, and I'll do whatever you want." I loved those kids, and she wasn't going to win that round.

My life was in a good spot, I gave everything to my job, and I didn't have much left in me to give to another person. Dating seemed like an annoying chore. I didn't need it. My job came first. I probably got that from my dad. And I felt like I was cursed, that I'd get pregnant again. I still believed in superstitions. That was in my head every time I was with someone. I'd occasionally go out on the town, and guys would hit on me, and I'd be so inconvenienced by it, like they were trying to sell me a vacuum. No fucking thanks. I had a vacuum. But it wasn't called a vacuum. It was called a vibrator.

The night before I met Philip, I was out with some old friends from college, friends I didn't see too often because I didn't keep in touch with them, mostly because they didn't keep in touch with me, because I can be difficult to be around. Like when I spend twenty minutes in the bathroom trying to pull a chin hair out, and then lie that I was making out with a guy, or when I walk along the bar making sure everyone is using a coaster. My friends tolerated me, they didn't always like me, and they probably spend time in the *room* too, with my principal, and Powerman who has hopefully realized by now that we are no longer dating.

It was Cinco de Mayo, which I don't know anything about, but I was looking to party, so I talked my friends into wearing sombreros and we ordered a lot of margaritas, and we looked like idiots. We had Yankees tickets, and the game went extra innings. I made my friends stay the whole game. Then they dragged me over to the Upper West Side and we bounced around the trendy bars in the district.

Towards the end of the night, some slimy lawyer gave me his business card. Who gives someone a business card? I attract those types of people, the power driven, high-octane lawyers and agents, the kind of people who give women business cards, out of convenience. If I had wanted to meet someone, and trust me, I wasn't looking, I would have wanted to meet someone quirky, someone who would feel out of place taking their suit to the dry cleaners. Like a scientist, or a college professor. Someone who enjoyed what he did for a living and wasn't trying to make a killing. If someone buys whole bean coffee by the pound, that's as sophisticated as I need someone to be.

After tossing the lawyer's card in the trash, I crashed on my friend's couch. I'd had far too much to drink, and I didn't feel like making my way back home at that hour. I must have slept in until noon the next day.

My dad had a lot of Jewish friends around Manhattan that he rarely saw, mostly because he never really identified as religiously Jewish, just culturally. Bar hours and Jewish holidays land in the same slot, so he never went to any of the traditional Jewish celebrations where he would have seen those people. After waking up in time for lunch, I walked into a cafe over on 81st, and the owners recognized me as my dad's daughter. *Yossi's daughter this, Yossi's daughter that.* If they knew my name, they didn't use it.

Mr. and Mrs. Cohen. I hadn't seen them since I was a kid. I barely recognized them. I almost left the moment I walked in; it was overcrowded with tourists, but when the owners recognized me, I didn't have a choice.

It was busy, and the only available seat was at a small table where a tall, thin man was seated. I could have taken my food to go, but, the man looked harmless and I felt like sitting for a moment. It had been a rough 24 hours. A long baseball game, then drinks until the bars closed, then Mrs. Cohen pinching my arm fat like I was five.

The tall, thin man, who I would forever and ever know by the name Philip, sparked up a conversation with me right away. I wasn't in the mood. Reggie was home alone, needing to be let out, and I just wanted to sit quietly before I rushed home. But we locked eyes, accidentally, and I saw a spark, and some depth. He had my interest. Before long, we were back and forth, talking about everything.

He wasn't trying to pick up on me; he just wanted to have a conversation. He did something for a living that he was passionate about. It wasn't about money. He wasn't flashy and he didn't have expensive clothes on. These were the qualities I respected in a man. He wanted to hear all about my classroom. It felt good to speak, with pride, about what I did for a living, a sharp contrast from having to defend what I was doing to an administrator, which was often the case.

I eventually realized what time it was, and how long my dog had been alone, and how I was still wearing the clothes from the night before, and I jumped out of my seat and raced home. Maybe a part of me got caught up in the connection we had made, and I got nervous and split. I never gave him my number.

A month or two passed, and I was still getting hit on by the powermen of the city. I kept the idea of Philip alive, that we'd run into each other somehow, but even in my daydreams I was cautious. I thought maybe we could be friends, get to know each other better. He could bring his telescopes into my classroom to show my kids, or we could be jogging buddies. Now I know why people have business cards. It was stupid of me to leave the cafe like that. New York's a big city, I felt like I dropped a grain of sand on the beach, a grain of sand I would have hoped to get to know better. I was at the mercy of coincidence.

I'd been a good person most of my life. I assumed I had some Karma coming my way. So I waited. And then a horribly tacky invitation came in the mail. The Cohens must have gotten my address from my dad. Their son was having his Bar Mitzvah at the Old Broadway Synagogue in Harlem, which was really, really close to where I lived. I wasn't going to go, I wasn't going to waste my afternoon listening to some kid's voice crack.

By some dumb luck, I ran into Mrs. Cohen again at a bagel shop in Midtown, and she's the kind of person who asks questions with only one answer, so now I had to go. And I think she pinched my arm fat again.

I don't like these formal, religious events. It's better to be a red headed, freckled Lutheran at a Bar Mitzvah than a non-practicing half Jewish woman. Better to be out of place than misplaced.

My mom grew up Catholic, but probably forgot, and I wasn't going to remind her. And my dad was Jewish, though he seemed to have left that part of him behind. I didn't have religion in my life. The only time I ever saw anyone pray was in the bar, bottom of the 9th, two out.

But here I was, all dressed up in my bad attitude, arriving late at the Cohen's kid's Bar Mitzvah. Mrs. Cohen pointed me over to an empty seat, right next to the skinny astronomer from the cafe, Philip.

So she set us up on a blind date at her son's Bar Mitzvah. She pinched my arm again. I was okay with it. Just a little.

I sat down and smiled. We didn't say much at the Bar Mitzvah, they're not as intimate as you might think, but we walked off together and caught a cab somewhere and went and did something and I was cute and he was clumsy and I made sure he had my number.

We started dating immediately. And we skipped all the fun stuff and went right to the part where we were old and farting around each other. We were comfortable; almost too comfortable. I wasn't used to anything like this.

I had a boyfriend, a geeky boyfriend that treated me well and told me things about the stars that I didn't care about, but I pretended to listen. And we'd go jogging, and he'd pretend not to have asthma. And we were happy, for the most part. At least he was nice to me.

Reggie and I showed up at his apartment one morning in the summer, and he wasn't there, which was odd because he was normally very prompt. We sat and waited all morning, and I was getting impatient. He finally showed up, looking like he hadn't slept, and explained to me that his boss took him up to the hills to look at some far off galaxy and then fired him, but that he was going to Alaska for the next six months, probably longer, to study ice. I blinked and he was gone, and I had no way to get a hold of him, again.

Philip had so many qualities that I wanted in someone, but he didn't know how to have a girlfriend. When he was gone in Alaska, I figured I would have heard from him more, or that he would send me a letter, anything. Three months in, he finally called me. He told me he had no way of calling me before that. I thought, *you work for NASA, you guys can call each other from the moon, and you can't call New York?*

During that time he was gone, I can't say I was keeping my hopes up we'd stay together. Six months is a long time to be in New York without the person you think may or may not be your boyfriend. But I still had that image of the skinny man in the cafe, talking about everything that has ever mattered.

While Philip was gone, I lost my teaching job. They finally pushed me too far. And my union wasn't backing me up. The principal was forcing me to sign a provisional contract stating that I would teach exactly what I was told to teach. I finally just said *fuck it*. I couldn't teach like that. I quit. I walked right into my principal's office with my building keys dangling from my middle finger.

I knew I'd miss the relationships I had with my kids, but I was done. That authority junkie principal finally won, and I sat on the couch in my sweats with a pint of ice cream, and watched that movie about the girl who grew up wiping spilled beer off the bar, and finding cereal on the bookshelves, where there were never books. You know, the movie about the girl who lost her job while her boyfriend forgot how to use a phone up in Alaska. That movie also sucked.

Without a job, I went back over to my dad's bar. I was fortunate to always have a backup plan. We'd talk about Philip, and I could never get a read on how he felt about him. I don't think he knew. He'd only met him a few times. Philip was the exact opposite as Powerman, so at first everyone liked him. He wasn't pushy. He was polite. He was quiet and soft and careful. But he was also very disconnected, very distant, like he was somewhere else all the time.

When he got back from Alaska, I expected him to say that he was going to go off on another research trip. He had been very excited about this job. I thought this was a new career for him. I figured Philip would just be some guy I knew that had the world's best first impression, then fall flat and out of my life.

But instead, he got off the plane, and I could tell he genuinely missed me. He actually did. And he had gifts for me, and he said some of the most beautiful things to me on the cab ride home. He spoke about the billions of years this planet has been around, and that he felt fortunate to be alive at the same time as me. He made science romantic.

He said he was going to find work in New York, even if it wasn't in his field. He said the only thing that mattered was being close to me. It threw me off. I couldn't have expected that.

But I shouldn't have been so hopeful. He settled right back to his introverted, disconnected self. When I explained to him what happened at work, he responded in a way that still bothers me. He said, "Well, at least you have your dad's bar." He didn't understand the passion I had for teaching, and that I was politically driven out of my job. It was tragic for me. Sure, I was grateful that I had my dad's bar to go back to, but dammit, Philip, I just lost my job. That's something that you talk about, and you empathize. My boss didn't take me up to the mountaintop. She didn't recommend me for a position with NASA. This was war, and I lost. You're supposed to call her a bitch and buy me something.

We settled back into our comfort zone, our boring comfort zone. Maybe that's what Philip meant on the cab ride home. He couldn't wait to be two old retired people together. He would come over daily and read books. I'd want to make conversation, so I'd ask him a question, and he wouldn't hear me. I'd ask him again, and he would look up, not really knowing what I had said, and not listening. My dad was a great listener, not because he had great hearing, but because he was ready to listen. He was tuned in to the people around him. Philip was the opposite; he was tuned out.

I was still in love with the conversation we had at the cafe. His voice was different that day. I couldn't even remember it anymore. He'd gotten too comfortable. This was a comfortable coexistence, not an exciting relationship.

I started to do some real heavy thinking. I knew I needed to be straightforward with Philip if we were going to continue, and tell him about everything that was bugging me. So, we had a long talk, and he heard me, and he told me he would do whatever he needed to do to keep us together. In some ways, this confused me more. I could never understand what he saw in us, or what he got from being in that relationship. He could sit and read in anyone's apartment. But he chose mine. Over and over.

And then a pivotal moment in my life occurred, which I've both regretted and felt grateful for during different times in my life. Philip was over at my place, on the floor pillows, reading late into evening. To be fair, we did have a fun day together, we went to the market and bought some fruit and cheese, and we sat and listened to a King Curtis record that we picked out. I could introduce him to all these old, lesser known jazz and blues records, and he genuinely enjoyed them. I don't think he ever listened to music before we met, ever.

But then the night went on, and he found a book to read. Hours went by. I said, "Hey I'm going to work soon," and he didn't notice. I repeated, "Hey, I'm going to work in a few minutes." And he didn't even look up.

Finally, I got up, and grabbed my coat, and I started to leave, and Philip looked up and said, "Hey, this book is amazing, have you read this?" No, I hadn't read it, or maybe I had, but I didn't know what book he was reading. And then I said something crabby as I walked out, like, "If you like it so much, why don't you call the author and tell *him?*"

I couldn't believe it. When I came home from my shift, he was on the phone with the author of the book. He actually thought I was serious. I was amazed. I heard his voice, when he was speaking about astronomy on the phone, and he sounded just like that guy I met at the cafe, just like him.

And I thought, *maybe it was me. Maybe I didn't bring the magic out of him. Maybe I didn't wake that part of him up.* The next day, I asked him what he wanted to do, if there was something he really wanted to do. It was a nice day, and he wanted to go into the city and look at the sun with his telescope. I thought, *that's going to burn your eyes,* but he explained that he had a strong filter on, and that we'd be okay. I was skeptical, but I agreed.

For a skinny guy, he carried the telescope around like it was a newspaper. He was a different person, strong and confident.

He set the telescope down on a busy Midtown street corner, lined it up so he could see the sun, looked through the lens, and let out a shout of excitement. I asked him how many times he'd done this, and the answer was in the several hundreds. That really shook me. He loved the sky that much.

People, strangers, they came from everywhere and wanted to look. I saw adults act like children, men hopping around with excitement like at my dad's bar, like the Yankees were winning, all just to see something they'd never seen before. The sun, through a telescope. Philip's voice was explosive. It was beautiful.

And then he realized that I hadn't looked through the lens yet. He stopped everyone, lowered the height, because I'm short, and set it up so I could see through.

Something really did happen. I had never thought about the sun as something worth looking at. Philip could have spent everyday of his life doing this. That's not me, but I did enjoy it a lot more than I thought I would. We had fun, and it was something to build on. Every time I thought this relationship was over, we figured out a way to make it work again. I put my head on his shoulder in the subway car on the way home.

When we got home, he told me he was going to fly out to Seattle, that the author of the book had suggested he look at the college. There was an opening.

My initial reaction was *no, no way*. That stupid comment of mine, to contact the author, was going to bite me in the ass. I live here, in New York. I can't move to Seattle. And worse, it wasn't even Seattle, it was some little town south of it, Olympia.

He was only gone a few days, but when he came back he had a hunch that he was going to be offered the job. *Damn*. I was hoping that Introverted Philip would show up and put them to sleep. I was hoping he'd go find a corner of the room and read a book during his interview, and then think to himself that went well.

But, it sounds like Dynamic Philip showed up. It was almost supernatural, the differences between these two people. Dynamic Philip is about 3 inches taller, with a more robust frame, and a voice that will cause a unicorn to go into heat. Introverted Philip gets picked on by mice.

And when Philip asked me to marry him and move to Olympia, Dynamic Philip did the deed. There was no saying no. I'd walk on fire for Dynamic Philip. But I wouldn't get in an airplane. I don't like airplanes. I've seen too many pilots drinking scotch in the bar. That, and I'm probably a control freak, and the pilots are in a different room. I'm also afraid of heights. And I don't like that flight attendants sound pretty when they give their inflight safety speeches. That bothers me.

I told my dad I was getting married, and that we were moving to Olympia, but I never told him the whole story. I never told him about Philip's conversation with the author of a book on my shelf, a book I didn't even know I had. I have so many books, there's no room for cereal anywhere on my shelves.

It all sounded too fishy, like a hoax. So I just told my dad that Philip got a job at a university out in the Pacific Northwest, and that we were going to go for it. That I'd try to teach out there too, even though I knew my certification wasn't valid in Washington. The story I told him sounded better than the truth. It didn't sound like we were desperately guessing at life.

I was cautious with what I told my dad. I never said a word to him when I got pregnant with Powerman. I always wanted my dad to think highly of me, different than I really was. I feared that anytime I wasn't sharp, or when I did something that didn't quite make sense, that he'd think I was turning into my mom. And my dad didn't stick around for my mom.

We had a small wedding. It was the first time I met Philip's mom. There were only a few people there. The Cohens showed up, and I told myself that if Mrs. Cohen pinched my arm we were going to fight. I didn't invite any of my friends. I didn't really have any friends. But I imagined the wedding was broadcast live from the room where everyone hates me, and they commented on my dress a lot, and the scabs on my arms that I pick, and my fingernails that I bite.

Unfortunately, my mom wasn't able to be there. I have grown very used to the way things turned out for my mom, the way her brain went against itself, the way she ended up. I don't hide from that. I'm used to it, but it's still sad for any girl not to have her mom at her wedding.

After selling off almost everything we owned, and convincing my dad to take Reggie, who would spent lots of time at my dad's bar, getting his belly rubbed by off duty police officers and health inspectors, we left New York on a beautiful, sunny day. The kind of day that makes you want to stay.

We drove across the country, and I fought the urge to turn the car around and undo everything. I wanted to start it all over. I wanted to go back to teaching at the middle school. I'd crawl back and beg what's-her-name for my job back. I wanted to go back to the day at the Cohen's cafe, and walk back out the door once I realized how busy it was, when an entire Midwest city decided to occupy it. Maybe I would have been fine staying in Glen Rock, teaching to the highly capable middle class. I could have taken better care of my mom, and lived with her still.

It was 1996, every mile marker reminded me I was further and further from home, and I missed my mom. The last time I saw her she looked like she was in a hamster cage.

Then my five, confusing years in Olympia began. And it doesn't end well. Jackie Fucking Robinson. I'm sure you were a great man, Jackie Robinson, but I've got to blame someone. So, I blame you. I'm sorry, but in a way, this is all your fault.

Gilb. The author of the book I didn't know I had. The man who talked Philip into interviewing at the college and moving out west. Gilbert Wiseman. Olympia will always be Gilb's city. There is no separating Gilb and Olympia in my mind. They are the same to me.

At first, I was confused by Gilb. I never understood why he was always around. He came over every weekend. He was clingy and he talked a lot. He was so loyal to us right away. He was so concerned about everything. He seemed to care about our well being more than he should.

But I slowly warmed up to him. He was interesting. He had an imagination to him. He was poetic when he spoke, and he was a good listener. Within a month of being there, he knew more about me than Philip ever did. He would come over and bring an interesting CD, like some music from Kenya, or a tool that the Eskimos used to hunt seals. I don't remember what it was called, but it basically scratched at the ice. It made seals think it was safe to come out of the breathing holes. He would explain how it was used. That was interesting. My kids back in the city would have thought that was interesting.

Gilb used to talk about the school bus he grew up in, and the way his mom and dad taught him everything he needed to know out in the woods. Any kid would have benefited from that kind of education, and you know which kids I'm thinking of.

I then told Gilb a lie, a lie that I have never admitted to him. I told him that I always wanted to open up a school out in the woods, but I really just thought of it right then, right then when he spoke about his childhood. He actually gave me the idea. I keep that to myself, still, and I smile like I just peed in the pool. He never knew the idea was his.

Without Gilb, this transition would have been impossible. I'd pretend to like

Olympia, but I couldn't have liked it less. Philip was so easy to please, he never complained about anything, and I sounded whiny when I complained about the weather, or the fact that there was nowhere to go eat in the middle of the night. If you could take New York, and change absolutely everything about it, you would have Olympia. Philip could be anywhere, and do anything, as long as he had a book to read and a corner to sit in. Sometimes it's a drag when someone is that easy going. You resent them when you need more than they do.

I did eventually find a job at a bar, and I tried to make friends at work, but I probably came off as uptight. I can't tell you how many people asked if I was from the east coast. I wasn't making any friends. I probably could have tried harder, or tried differently. Typical me. But as you can guess, I wasn't thrilled that I moved across the country to work at a bar.

That first month in Olympia was the rainiest June I had ever experienced, and I spent a lot of time looking at myself, looking deeper into myself, being honest with myself. I was judgmental. I was scratchy with other women. I was impatient. I was short, and self-conscious about it, so I compensated by being feisty, but feisty just means you give yourself permission to be a bitch.

I had life patterns that were in need of repair. I was a serial saboteur. I had sabotaged so many situations in my life. I could have taught in Glen Rock forever, and been fine, and met a nice man and had a family. But that seemed too easy. I went looking for a challenge, teaching in Harlem. That was challenging enough, just teaching there, but I went looking for a bigger challenge, I wanted to take on policy, and curriculum, and the cookie cutter education system.

Then I met Philip, and I tried to turn him into something that he wasn't, and I followed him out to the west coast. I was 27 when I left New York, and it was time I started to get to know myself better. I looked in the mirror, sometimes my own mirror, sometimes an Egyptian artifact mirror that Gilb brought over, and I didn't always like what I saw.

So, I did what I always do, I toughened up. I started taking care of myself. I started jogging again, and eating healthy foods. I found a yoga studio. And I started to pray.

Pray? Me? That's right, I started to pray. I wasn't down on my knees, palms together, not like that. I would just take long, slow breaths, and think positive thoughts. I would visualize beautiful things. I thought about the school in the woods, the one I wanted to open up someday, the one that Gilb never knew was his idea. I thought about Philip and me growing closer, getting past our differences. I thought about Gilb meeting a nice woman that I could be friends with. She'd like me because Gilb did. I thought about my mom, but I didn't have the imagination to make that situation better, I just tried to think about her finding comfort. I thought about my dad, keeping his cholesterol down, taking Reggie for walks. When things got bad, really bad, I was grateful to have my breath and my prayers.

Once, and only once, I asked Philip to sit and pray with me. He asked why, and who we were praying to, and what we thought was going to happen. He thought we'd just be talking to ourselves. I couldn't get him to understand that it wasn't a science experiment; it was about finding center and visualizing love. I was still new at it, I was still figuring out what it all meant for me, so I didn't know how to defend in words what I was trying to accomplish. I just wanted him to try it with me. I never brought it up again.

When Philip was off on the other side of the world, over in his reading chair, I started to read more too. I read about health, diet, foods I should avoid, foods I should eat more of. The environment. Plastics. Islands of trash the size of Texas floating around the Pacific.

Gilb had said that in the ten years he lived with his mom and Ray in their school bus, not once did they throw anything away. *What does that mean, away?* he would ask. So, I started bringing empty containers to the store and buying in bulk. It was easy.

Maybe this was what life was about. Change. It's not hard to make changes, it's just hard to recognize when you need to. I welcomed change.

Philip was never going to change. He was always going to be deep inside of himself, far from everyone else. That's where he wanted to be. And maybe it wasn't a bad thing. I needed to come to terms with the path my life was on. I had a job at a bar, and until I figured out what I was going to do next, I was going to be grateful for the job, and make the best of it. I had a very nice husband, who had his own, strange ways about him.

Five years of this went by. Gilb was like our son, although he was quite a bit older than us. He was always around. I grew to love him. He exposed us to parts of life that I didn't know existed. He even got us to protest in Seattle once, that is until we got shot at with rubber bullets.

As much as I wanted to accept Philip for who he was, it would sting sometimes when I realized how different we were. I saw him deliver a speech at a hotel downtown to the members of an astronomy club; a club that I didn't even know existed. He never told me about the event until we were supposed to leave, so I went downtown dressed in my yoga outfit, and I watched my husband deliver the keynote address before a packed room of people who all looked like they knew about the event for months.

He got up on that stage, stood behind a podium, and delivered a fantastic speech. I felt like I was watching someone else. I bounced back and forth between the gut-piercing reminder that my husband was a stranger to me, and the awe that I felt towards this stranger. He told jokes, and had access to a range of vocabulary that I didn't know he had. He was charming. He was confident. His voice was volcanic.

We drove home, and he slouched in his seat, and stared off. I tried to explain to him how impressed I was, but that I was also hurt. This was a special moment, and we didn't really get to share it. I wanted to lay it all out for him, and ask him, *who is that person? Do I know that person?* But I didn't need to; I already knew the answer.

I wasn't married to the man up there behind the podium, or the man who spoke to Gilb on the phone back in my Harlem apartment until the middle of the night. I wasn't married to the man who every college kid wanted to be like. Those kids would come in to the bar, and they'd be imitating Philip, sharing their favorite quotes from that evening's lecture. I wasn't married to that man. And I had to accept it, and I probably did some yoga when I got home from the astronomy meeting as a way to help me come to terms. I was already dressed for it anyways.

The next day at work a customer was pushing a conversation with me. She said she saw me leave the event with Philip the previous night. It sounded like she wanted to compliment me, but she was really just complimenting Philip. She said something like, *you must be so proud.* You'd think I would be *so proud*, but I wasn't.

I wasn't in touch with how intelligent he was. He was so deep in his own head, and you can't make conversation out of the things he thinks about. So, the fact that he is intelligent, it doesn't improve our marriage at all. It wasn't something that he shared with me. It wasn't something that he *could* share with me. I might have been the wrong woman for him. Maybe there was someone out there, like the woman standing in front of me, making small talk at the bar, who could have engaged in his intelligence more than I could. I didn't know how. I didn't know what the next question was to keep the conversation going, and keep him excited about sharing what he knew.

I would have gladly traded in some of his intelligence for some common sense. I thought to myself, *yeah, he's smart, but not smart enough to tell his wife about the astronomy event in advance.*

Gilb came by later that night and asked if we wanted to volunteer at a shelter with him, helping pass out food. I started to grab my coat, assuming he meant right then and there. He laughed, "Not tonight, Kennedy. A month from now. You think I'd just spring that on you like that?" I wanted Philip to hear him, but he was in the other room. I wanted so badly for Philip to hear that whole conversation from the beginning. Gilb then said, "Pretty big deal last night, Philip giving that speech, wish I could have made it. I heard he was fantastic." I wanted to scream.

My disconnect from the inside of Philip's head wasn't just inconvenient. If I was showing up at speaking engagements in yoga pants for the rest of our lives, I could learn to deal with it. But my disconnect from Philip proved to be dangerous. By the time I learned how dangerous it was, it was probably too late.

This is how it happened. I blame Jackie Robinson. Fucking Jackie Robinson. It's got to be someone's fault, so why not his?

One night in 2001, it was early spring, and Gilb was over. He was working on us to buy tickets to a Mariner's game a few weeks away. It was a special event, commemorating Jackie Robinson, and all the players would wear his jersey number. Gilb wanted to go as a way to show respect for Jackie Robinson. I would have gone regardless. I used to go to Yankee games all the time, and I enjoyed baseball. But Philip wanted nothing to do with it, and I knew why. I knew about the game his dad took him to, and the car accident, and the scar on his neck that he was self-conscious about, the scar he never wanted to talk about, but that I noticed the moment I met him.

Philip was off in the corner, being Philip, and we were both trying to talk him into it, and he shrugged us off. I knew enough to eventually drop it, but Gilb pressed on. I kept sending hand signals his way trying to get him to let it go, but he wasn't picking up on any of it. Philip finally said, "Look, I don't like baseball. I don't want to go. I had a bad experience as a kid and I'd rather not be reminded of it."

To Gilb, this was like an invitation to share our feelings, because Gilb wanted to share everything, always. We were Gilb's new family, and families always share. But I got nervous because this was new territory for us. Philip didn't like talking about his past, his childhood or his family. I've always respected that. I knew almost nothing about his mom before I met her. I knew her name was Stevie. That was about it.

Gilb pushed even harder, completely oblivious to boundaries, and Philip caved, and told us all the story about game 4 of 1977 World Series, every bit of it.

I had never connected all the dots before. I remember game 4, Reggie Jackson's home run. He crushed it. I remember being in my dad's bar, and the picture went out on the screen, but my dad poked the TV with a broomstick, just in time for us to see Reggie Jackson swing the bat. We all knew it was going to be a homer. I was eight years old. I remember it clearly. The bar erupted. I swear grown men were crying.

My dad met Reggie Jackson once. He came into the bar just to meet my dad. I even named my dog after Reggie Jackson, my dog who became the mascot at my dad's bar. And to think, when Reggie Jackson hit that homerun, Philip was in attendance, all the way across the country, and his experience was very different than mine.

It wasn't raining outside, which was rare for April, but it felt like it was raining inside, and when Philip finished telling his story, he told us he was tired, and he went off to bed. I waited maybe twenty minutes, and then got up and sat closer to Gilb, and I spoke quietly. I didn't want Philip to hear what I was going to tell him.

I had a vague memory that had been itching at me. I wondered if Gilb remembered it too. Recently, Stevie and her boyfriend had come up for a visit. I hadn't been paying attention to much of what Stevie said. She was quiet, kind of sheepish. You had to strain your ear to hear her. She and her boyfriend were so strange, they reminded me of no one in New York. It was uncomfortable watching Philip and his mother interact, and I thought to myself, *no wonder Philip turned out this way.*

But then Stevie said something, and I had been trying to make sense of it since. We were sitting down for dinner, Gilb was there of course, and she made a weird comment, something like, "...after the boys were born."

I can't be certain, but I thought Gilb and I made eye contact after she made that comment, both trying to sort it out. Philip didn't seem to notice. He went on eating. It was like he didn't hear it.

I wanted to know what Gilb remembered. So, I asked him, I said, "Do you ever get the feeling that Philip is hiding something from us, maybe even from himself?" Gilb wasn't following me. I needed to be clearer. I said, "Gilb, has Philip ever talked about his childhood to you?"

"No. Never. I just can't crack him open, he's a tough nut."

I couldn't dance around it anymore, I went straight back to memory of the dinner party, pulled as hard as I could at it, and as the words came out of my mouth, it became much clearer, and I remembered it better than I thought. Stevie specifically said, "We moved to North Hollywood after the boys were born." And Gilb remembered it too, slightly, but hadn't put much thought into it. That irritated me. *Jesus Fucking Christ, Gilb, aren't anthropologists, or archeologists, or whatever you are, aren't you supposed to investigate shit, figure out how entire civilizations lived after digging up one of their spoons?*

Philip had never once spoken of a brother. He was an only child. It was just him and his mom, in a little apartment outside of Los Angeles, hanging out in silence every night, shades drawn.

Gilb and I talked late into the night about the phenomenon we knew as Philip Duke. He knew Philip a little differently than I did. He had seen him lecture, he knew him in a professional way as well, they weren't just friends, they were colleagues. He celebrated how introverted Philip was. He thought it was a sign of intelligence. Everything Philip did was a sign of intelligence. Intelligence is overrated.

Gilb had spent the last 5 years trying to be Philip's best buddy. From my view, it was cute. They were like two little boys. Gilb would have some big, new idea, and he wanted to share it with Philip, and Philip was normally pretty easy going, as long as it wasn't a baseball game, anything involving alcohol, or a holiday. And then, I swear, it was like they wanted to ask me if they could go outside and play.

But what became clearer each day, was that Gilb accepted Philip. He just let him be himself. He loved him like a brother. I didn't have that luxury. I could have been a great pal to Philip, but this was my marriage. I needed more than a lifelong library visit.

Before Gilb went home that night, I asked him if he prayed, and he said something I'll always remember, and it warmed my heart. He said, "Of course I pray," as if I was asking him if he brushed his teeth.

When I went to bed that night, Philip was still awake, but he pretended not to be. In the morning, I got up to go to work, and he said he hadn't slept well. I'll always wonder if he heard Gilb and me speaking. That terrifies me.

The next night, it was the same deal. He couldn't sleep. And the next night. And the next night. And if I ever knew what the hell was going on, this wasn't one of those times. Philip seemed to stop sleeping completely. And he'd spend most of the next day on the couch. He stopped reading. I don't think I ever saw him pick up another book.

This went on for months. It got worse, and then a little better, and then much worse. It was horrifying watching Philip fall apart. It was an avalanche in slow motion.

There were good times and there were bad times. When it was good, I thought it would stay good forever. When it was bad, it was horrible. It was detrimental. I suffered. I'd want to airbrush him out of my field of vision. I'd see him rolling around on the couch, muttering something, and I'd want the floor to open up and make him disappear. I'd want to hear him fall, he would yell something like, "aaaaahhhhh I'm sooooorrrrry I was sooooo distaaaaant aaaaahhhhh." And then I'd walk into the bar, at work, and fold several copies of my resume into paper airplanes, and stand up on the bar and shoot them in every direction. And I'd be naked. I don't know why, I just figured, fuck Olympia. Fuck all this. I'm going back to New York. I'm going to throw paper airplanes in a bar naked. I'll go back to my side of the Mississippi River now.

But then the good times. Philip would spend any given part of his day uncontrollably hyper and scatter brained. I called this side of him Hyper Philip. I enjoyed Hyper Philip. I'd wait around all day, hoping Hyper Philip would show up. Hyper Philip would ask me thoughtful questions about my day, and he'd want to know about work, and anything else that was going on.

By this point, I was managing the bar, and I'd come home, and he'd want to hear everything about managing a bar. He would say, "Wow, a whole bar, you manage a whole bar, how do you do it?" Nothing could satisfy his curiosity. It was like he was making up for all the years where he never reached out. He'd want to know how we print the receipts, and what we do if someone gets too drunk, or if an employee wants to take the day off for their kid's birthday.

I wanted these conversations to go on forever and ever. In a way, during this horribly confusing and frustrating time, we may have had some of our better moments, too. I didn't know what was coming my way though.

I have deep scars. I look good on the outside, but turn me inside out and I'm carved up like a cutting board. My dad should have stayed by my mom's side. Not every day is a day at the bar. And you don't abandon people unless you absolutely have to. It hurts to admit that, because my dad is my hero, but what's true is true. My dad abandoned his wife. I know he didn't know what to do, but doing nothing wasn't an option either. I was forced, in a way, to confront this pain I had carried around about my mom and dad during these months with Philip.

I thought often about what Philip's mom had said. *Could I have misheard her?* I knew I needed to eventually ask him. So, at some random, unplanned moment, I accidentally found the guts to talk to him about it. I thought, *let's have this breakthrough moment. Let's do it.* He was sitting next to me, on the couch, looking out the window, and I interrupted whatever question he was going to ask me.

I felt my throat swallow my breath in a moment of anxiety. I just had to ask him, I said, "Philip, did you ever have a brother?" I heard my voice echo in my head. My voice wobbled like it was wounded. I'm not good at this. I'm not good at saying what I need to say. I'll yell at a stranger for cutting me off on the road, but I can't arrange meaningful combinations of words with the people that matter most, when I need to the most. I'm tougher than I am strong. I'm tough enough to deal with my problems. If I were stronger, I wouldn't keep creating them.

He only paused for a second, and looked at me, and I saw a flash of terror in his eyes. I know I did. I saw that. I'll always remember that frozen look. He blinked a few times, loosened his jaw, and went along as if I never asked the question. He started to change the subject. I was thinking, *no way, you can't just brush this off. I need to know these things about you.* I said, "Philip, please, did you once have a brother? You've never once told me about a brother."

I didn't know if he was going to laugh or cry, maybe both. He stared at me, took a few deep breaths, and said, "I don't remember. I'm not sure."

To me, that was a huge step. I let it go. I was sure we'd get around to digging deeper into it. I thought we made a huge first step. I was fine tabling that topic until next time. That tiny bit of a breakthrough, it made me feel closer to him than ever. A few minutes passed in comfortable silence, he laughed a little, and I let him change the subject. I wish I hadn't. I didn't know that was going to be the last time we spoke about it.

He went right back to Q & A time as if we never even brought this mystery brother up. I stopped being surprised by the questions he'd ask. Everything was on the table. So when he asked me about my two years teaching in Glen Rock, I was more than happy to talk about that time. Oddly, those are mostly good memories.

He said he remembered me talking about some ultra religious family that I had a run in with, and I was blown away that he remembered. I think I said something about it once, back when he didn't give a shit, back before he was the considerate, caring insomniac who rolled around on the couch for part of the day, and then spent the other part interviewing me.

I had a situation back when I was teaching in Glen Rock. I taught a science unit on the solar system. I didn't know anything about the solar system, I still don't. I'd give the assignments out of the book, and they were very basic. Kids left knowing how many planets there were, and that they orbit the sun. It was really dumbed down.

But I let the more advanced kids do some additional learning for extra credit. They weren't very challenged by the lessons from the book. One of the kids decided to do a project on the sun, and wanted to present it in front of the class. Sure, why not, go for it.

There was this fucking family, they were nuts. And they were always whining about Governor Florio taking away guns, and raising taxes, and they'd go to PTO meetings and call everyone a socialist. All of their kids were on IEPs, but they paid the same amount of taxes as everyone else. They never considered that contradiction. Whatever, they were nuts.

So, when my gifted student did a project on the sun, and stated that the sun was billions of years old, this nutty family called the principal, and wanted us to send home a formal notice any time their freedom of religion was going to get trampled on. I know nothing about the solar system, and I know even less about the Bible, and how the age of the sun trampled on their freedom of religion. I still don't know. But I hated these fucking people. They whined about everything, and I just wanted them to go fuck off.

I remember sitting in the office. My principal was as cool as the breeze, and he was nodding, letting these whack jobs have their moment. I was fuming. After they left, he turned to me and said, "That's their youngest kid right? And you're a fifth grade teacher, in a K-5 school, and we have two months left of the school year, right?"

Well, I wasn't a buck passer. I wanted blood. It was a Friday, and my principal said something soothing about going and having a pleasant weekend, and for a second, I thought, *he's right, just let it go.* And I almost did.

On my way out of the office, I took a look at the kid's file, which had the Wackjobs telephone number. I was stealth-like, no one saw me. It would have been perfectly okay for me to look at my own student's files, but I just knew I was going to do something that I shouldn't do, so I kicked it into ninja mode early.

When I got home, my mom was hiding cereal bowls on the shelves like an Easter egg hunt, and as soon as I was done cleaning that shit up, I went to a quiet room, and I made one hell of a phone call.

I'm a firm believer in the theory that somewhere out there is the best doctor, the best coffee, and the ugliest person. This phone call may have been the most kick ass phone call ever placed. Phones might as well have all stopped working after I hung up. No one was ever going to place a better phone call than this.

I dialed their number like I was loading a pistol clip, and Mrs. Fucking Wackjob answered the phone, I didn't even let her say hello. I said, "Listen, if you ever whine about something that your kid hears in my class again, I'm going to give you such a fucking headache you're going to think you have a fucking brain tumor. So some facts from an encyclopedia go against your fucking religion, that's your problem."

I went on and on about taking responsibility for their own kid, and how I was sick of their shit. I probably stopped making sense after a while. To my surprise, she didn't have a response. She just said something like, "Well, I'm sorry we caused you a problem, and we'll pray for you." I bet she's in the room where everyone hates me, but she's in there praying for me. Great.

I was halfway through telling this story when I noticed Philip was literally jumping up and down on the couch, cheering for me. He picked me up, or tried to, and carried me to the bedroom. And although he stubbed his toe on the way, he powered through like a champ and we had great sex, which had been a non-existent part of our marriage before that.

I would have never guessed it, but during this stretch of time, sex became a way for us to communicate. He wanted to have sex more and more. He'd ask me about my day, and I started to make up stories about things that I knew were going to piss him off, and then we'd go have sex.

But maybe I misjudged how bad things were. Maybe I never knew. I was being optimistic. I thought, *he'll get through this insomnia, and everything will be great, and we'll sit on this couch and talk about my day, and we'll have afternoon sex, and everything will be perfect forever.*

After Powerman, I had intimacy issues. I didn't enjoy sex for a long time. I didn't enjoy sex for most of my time with Philip either. It was like a chore. But during these crazy months in 2001, it was medicine.

But I didn't know. I didn't judge it right. I was blindsided. I was feeling happy and hopeful. And then it happened. And I'm not well when I think about it. I try not to think about it.

It happened right in the middle of having sex, right in the middle of me having a great thought, a thought that all this physical energy between us was going to save us. I was picturing myself, later in life, growing old with Philip, offering advice to younger couples who were struggling, urging them to hold on, that it gets better, that there's always going to be the rough patches. I saw it all.

Right in the middle of all that euphoria, all that prayer, and all that reaffirming validation, and all the beautiful emotions of having sex with the man you know you want to spend your life with, it happened. I never saw it coming. But it happened. He stopped and looked out the window, and he got that look of terror in his eyes, like when I asked him about his brother. He just froze.

And then he reached into a drawer, grabbed a handgun, aimed it in his mouth and pulled the trigger.

The Priest's Wimpy Assistant

I exist. Just not the way Philip thinks I do. I'm a nice guy in real life. But in Philip's head, I'm a monster. I'm a monster that he created.

At the conference each year, Father Suckerpunch Whiskeydick would ask me to help him with his briefcase and his notes. His hands would shake and he needed help with things. It was probably just symptoms of alcohol withdrawal. I never asked. I was glad to help him.

Philip created me from his own fears. He assumed that I was shook up by his rant at the conference, back in 2001. I didn't give a shit about that. I couldn't stop staring at him, because I'd never seen anyone so animated during all these conferences. I was probably giving him strange looks. I'm a strange looking guy. My pituitary glands don't produce enough growth hormone. People generally don't like the way I look. It confuses them.

Philip thinks I'm wimpy. He ought to know better. You have any idea how difficult it is being me? I'm tougher than nails and I stay nice to people. How nice would you be if people couldn't tell if you were an adult or a kid?

Philip assumed I went to Catholic school growing up and that I was a firm believer in everything Catholics believe. He assumed that I was consumed by this false view of the world, and that he was up there shattering it, and that I'd flip out and come find him and put a bullet in his head. Or maybe I'd take us both out. I'd tie him down, and drive us both off a cliff.

That's the kind of monster Philip thought I was. Only a monster can create a monster.

Philip was correct. I did go to Catholic school. I was raised by my grandparents, and the church was good to me. Father Suckerpunch Whiskeydick, he took good care of me. So, I helped him out in return. I even went to Alcoholics Anonymous with him. I remember the day he openly admitted to the congregation that he had a disease, and he asked us to pray for him. That was a brave moment.

But as far as the Catholic part, I never took it too seriously. Catholicism has influenced my faith, for sure, and I still go to Church, but it's more spiritual for me. I like to think of Jesus as this man that had such a beautiful view of the world, and He came here to spread His message, a message that was so powerful it reached me 2,000 years later.

So, I go to Church to feel closer to His message. I enjoy the community of Church. It's like a family to me. And Father Suckerpunch Whiskeydick, he's a genuine man who has given his life to serving others. He's caught malaria twice. Say what you want about priests, but Father Suckerpunch Whiskeydick is a genuine man.

I tend to think that Philip created me because of fear. He talks about dealing with the truth, with reality. He says scientists ask questions, and they aren't afraid of the truth. I call bullshit, Mr. Duke. This is reality. We're as faith-based as we are carbon-based. And that scares him.

He asked a question and he didn't like the answer.

Carbon steel wool reel? *Check.*

Ten inch balloon whisk? *Check.*

Rope? *Check.*

David Bowie? *Check.*

Dragonfly? *Check.*

Cupcakes? *Cupcake shop was closed.*

Philip

We went to the homeless shelter to help out. Maybe to help feel good about ourselves. But the obvious was maybe a bit too obvious for me. I couldn't ignore it. Did I think I was better than these people? Did they think so? Did they think that I thought so? These things are tough to ignore.

The gap between the quality of life of the people who were living in this shelter, and people like myself, it's too insulting to overlook. I couldn't maintain my ignorance much longer. I came there to help. Help what? No matter what I did, they would need more help. And why are these people living in shelters in the first place? I wanted to sit and ask each person how he or she got here. I needed to know.

I remember their flat tire faces. Jawlines defeated. Gravelly, angry voices. Grumpy man, repeating what the voice in the radio said, *democrats don't know the difference between a handgun and pistol.* Maybe.

Children yelled unprompted, not completely convinced of their own existence. Women flinched unprompted for opposite reasons. How they hated to be noticed.

I thought about the universe. Do these people know? Do they know about exploding stars? Do they know about our origins? I wondered if they cared. I wondered what role astronomy would have in their lives. Sure, the universe is beautiful, and it created a wondrous solar system, and an opportunistic planet arose. And these people are homeless on that planet. Sure, the axial tilt is fascinating, it creates seasons, but when you're homeless in the rain with a toddler, that axial tilt loses some wonder. I love comparing the moon to a bodyguard, protecting us from asteroids, but the moon doesn't protect you from landlords when you're several months late.

How would an astrophysicist explain homelessness? We like to say that we study everything. We study the cosmos. That's everything. What does an astrophysicist have to say about the economy? About drug addiction? About prejudice? About domestic violence?

A lot. Evolution. It's a cosmic occurrence. Evolution can add its two cents to any discussion here on earth, and the universe kicked evolution into gear. And what I was noticing right there in that shelter, that was evolution. We're creating several new species. We're splitting apart.

There was one uncomfortably obvious thing these people had in common, it's strange to say, but it's true. You'd never breed with them, they breed with each other, but you wouldn't dare. Yikes. Right there. That's a horrible thing to say. The people that you wouldn't breed with, give that 100,000 years, and you won't be able to breed with them. Classism is evolution in its primordial stages. We're slowly creating new species. I let my eyes swivel a panorama of the room, and I thought about the future of our species. Evolution is a lot like a lottery. Eventually you lose. Eventually we all lose.

I blinked and I was no longer at the shelter, but on a bus, heading up the hill. Strangers sat at safe distances, weary of each other. Humans, afraid of each other, afraid of themselves. People apologizing for unintentional body contact.

I blinked again. I was on the couch, my eyelids too heavy to lift. I rolled around hoping to find the opening in the couch where I could disappear forever. My mind shot off into the distance like an arrow. Everything was out of sequence. Days went missing.

Horrible, ugly things happened. Regrettable things happened. I landed on a beach, like an arrow would, the same beach near campus where I witnessed an archaeological dig take place years earlier, where I watched students dig up weaved cherry bark. I spectated, like I was at a sporting event. I should have cheered. The archeologist is the Santa Claus of science. But there was no dig on this day, just a quiet haze.

I blinked again and it was night, on the same beach. And I forgot everything I ever knew. And with that, I no longer blinked. I no longer needed to. I blinked to erase who I was.

High tide was an inch away, at most. I stared it down, and it receded. I looked up and took a tour. Orion's belt. That's where I go first. Up to Betelgeuse, then down to Rigel. I wander the constellations nearby. Taurus, Aries, Gemini. I have my favorites. I drew the sky with my fingers. I do this without thinking. The sky is my palm.

I wondered how I knew these things, but I didn't wonder too much, I might have accidentally found the answer.

It was perfect. I knew nothing. I couldn't make sense of anything. I didn't know where I was or who I was. Over the past several months there were times when I would drift into a haze, where thinking clear thoughts felt like squeezing and twisting a damp rag, trying to get the last bit of water out. But on this night, under a sky I knew better than my own reflection, thinking felt like squeezing a rock, a dry rock. So I chose not to. It was better that way.

I heard footsteps, and a girl dressed up as a dragonfly, giggling to herself, came up to me. She asked me if I had a fire. I didn't answer. *Did it look like I had a fire?* She said she had magic in her bag, but that she forgot fire, and cupcakes.

I saw a solution. I saw it all in several acts.

I had a gun. I didn't know why I had a gun, but I had one. And I drew it all up in my mind, and I realized, I could make fire with a gun. I couldn't tell you the date, or who the president was, or my name, but I knew I could make fire with a gun. Not cupcakes.

With the first words I'd heard out of my mouth in over a day, I said to her, without breathing, "I can help please don't be afraid I have a handgun I can make fire with it." She giggled again. Pebbles of who I was, where I was, it was coming back. I fought it. I didn't want to know, and I didn't want to know why I didn't want to know. I just wanted to focus on the task. I wanted to build a fire.

I was quick. I gave orders. We were a team. We crept around the beach, collected twigs and tossed them into a pile. We shaved some tinder using a shell we found on the beach. And not just any shell, we scanned the beach without a moon in the sky in search of the perfect tool. It needed to be round, with some depth, and sharp.

We made a cone of dry, fine, tinder. It triggered a memory, a dream I tried not to remember. A mountain, a volcano, but not on this planet. Enough. I was zeroed in on making this fire happen, nothing was going to stop me. I removed a bullet from the cartridge shell casing. I scattered some gunpowder from inside the casing over the cone. I then put the empty shell back in the gun, and fired at the gunpowder. I didn't warn the dragonfly girl, she jumped, she giggled, and we had flames. Small flames. We kneeled over it, together, taking turns whistle blowing air through our tube shaped mouths.

The fire jumped up, stood up. There were three of us now. And the dragonfly girl grabbed some steel wool from her bag. She wasted no time. I watched carefully. She was less careful, and lit the steel wool on fire, placed it in a whisk, and tied the whisk to a rope. She must have burned her dragonfly hands, but she didn't mind.

She looked at me with a pulling glare, cleared her throat as if she wanted my attention, and she bowed at the hip. This may have meant thank you. I kicked sand, because I was starting to piece more thoughts together, and I didn't like what I saw.

The dragonfly girl walked out into the tide and spun her fire rope, around and around and around, and my eyes followed the movement. In a very ancient and ancestral way, the movement of my eyes began to trigger memories. I couldn't look away. She danced, and spun, my eyes were fixed on the flame, chasing it. I surrendered. It could have been seconds; it could have been hours. it doesn't matter. Then the flame went out. She giggled. The show was over.

Heavy clouds marched. The night was dark and thick like a black crayon. I survived that round. Close call. I kept a torture of memories hidden in a safe location, safe from myself. Her dance had nearly picked the lock.

I couldn't see past my hand. I wondered if the dragonfly girl had flown away. She was nowhere. I exhaled. I was content on this beach. I could keep the fire going. I could fish, there were shellfish to harvest. I could smell them. If a rodent crossed my path, I could set a trap for it. There were sticks and rocks, all I'd need for a solid trap.

I could sit right here forever. There was a fresh spring. I could hear it splashing behind me. I could build a shelter. I would need supplies to stitch and repair my clothing. One trip into town, for needles, a sewing kit. But then, right back here. I'll keep the fire going.

My plan was simple and good. I would avoid ever remembering anything, and then I wouldn't have to deal with it. Why would I ever want to deal with it? Running away was a good thing. It was survival. An impala doesn't confront the lion; it doesn't try to resolve that issue. It runs, and it runs like hell, if it wants to survive.

But then I heard a giggle, eyes next to mine, face close enough to mine to feel her cold skin. She lit another swab of steel wool, wedged it snug in the loops of the whisk, and splashed out into the glowing water.

I thought this was over. You couldn't help but feel deceived at how dark it was. And when her dance kicked up again, I was entranced. A trance that brought me out of a trance. Thoughts and clarity, memories, pieces of me, pebbles of who I was. It was all coming back. I had wanted to hide this. I had earned a new start, to be someone else, to keep everything before this day blurry forever.

The fire was in orbit, a curvature of space-time, its geodesic trajectory pulling clear images of last week, last year. A slideshow, telling me about me, engined by inflamed steel filaments in orbital motion. Every image of my life threaded through my mind at the speed of light. I now knew. And I let my head fall back on the sand, and I looked up at the sky, and I wanted the tide to take me away, but I was at least a good inch clear.

This is my struggle. This is how I lost everything.

Damn. It was all going well. So well. All of my survival needs were met, which puts me in select class of people who have ever lived. I loved Olympia. Olympia was everything I ever needed in a town. I was right at home in this second hand city. And Kennedy. She was gorgeous, she had a bite to her, but she was nice to look at, and she was good to me. Gilb was a pal. He was loyal. He didn't make much sense, but I let him be him, and he let me be me. I was content, maybe for the first time in my life. I was living on the bridge connecting quantum theory with relativity. That was Olympia. Olympia was my string theory.

I thought it would stay this way forever. I thought we'd all be old, and Gilb would return from the South Pacific with an artifact that we'd think was fascinating, and then we'd eat hemp muffins and listen to some rare zydeco record. I'd still have my alarm clock that Mr. Leahy gave me. I'd teach until the day I died. I could just die right up at my podium. Call it retirement.

Olympia, Evergreen, the students, the occasional last minute speaking engagement, and that shitty book I tried to write about the mission to Mars, these were the pieces of my dream come true. I fit in here. This was home.

I'd run into students on the street, they would show me gratitude. They would say *thanks, thanks for everything you taught me.* How rewarding. How gratifying. Most people work hard their whole lives, and they never have that kind of moment. You don't run into your plumber a year later and share those kinds of words, even though you might use your plumbing as much as you use your education.

I had it all. Everything I needed. I landed right where I needed to. Coincidences, and chances, they had to occur just as they did. One in a million, one in a billion, I've experienced that *one,* that one result out of millions and billions of possibilities. I don't remember why I went to college in New York, but I did, and then working at the planetarium, and getting fired by Art, and that NASA job, I loved that job, or I thought I did, and the oil field cowboy who wanted to beat me into a putty. Maybe I missed Kennedy, or maybe I didn't want to get stuck in another far off corner of the world with oil field cowboys who want to take a cheap shot at a skinny scientist. Gilb's book, the *About the Author* section on the cover, Kennedy's idea that I ought to call the author. I would have finished reading that book, I would have put it back in the shelf, I would have never called Gilb had she not suggested it. Every aspect of my life would have been different. But what did happen was that I landed in Olympia, and I was happy, and I lost it. And it would have been ambitious at that moment to imagine that anything positive would ever come my way again.

Science had taught me to question. I loved the question. I loved it more than the answer. Finding a great question was my motivation. My focus during graduate studies was the electromagnetic spectrum everything to the left and right of visible light. I spent more time thinking about that question, *what do we not see?* And less time thinking about the answer, which was why I wasn't such a great student.

I trace these curiosities back to Mr. Leahy. I could only imagine that without his generosity, I would have picked up the scent and followed down the same path as so many other sensitive and shy kids, into substance abuse and isolation. Science saved me. And Mr. Leahy didn't just provide me with the means to explore and ask questions, but he gave me a reason to. I'd come home from riding my bike in the dirt, and he'd drop a hint that I could go faster with a cleaner drivetrain, and that he had all the tools I needed. He knew how to drop suggestions that activated my curiosity. After showing me how to clean and lube the chain, I'd think to myself, *what else can I do to make my bike faster?*

Mr. Leahy kept one of the storage units at the complex as a workshop, and kept all his tools in there. He never gave me a key, but he'd open up his workshop for me at all hours. Several times I'd wake him, and he made sure, made absolutely sure, that I knew it was perfectly okay to knock on his door at any hour. Although I never said thanks, I always cleaned up after myself, and maybe that meant more.

Mr. Leahy. He didn't have to be so kind. Most adults don't take the opportunity to reach out to kids the way he did. He didn't have to do that. How many kids can say that their favorite teacher growing up was the building manager at their apartment? He pushed me to keep asking questions, to gather evidence, all the things I still do. But he did all those things by being kind. I don't know how much he knew about science, we rarely talked about science. He was really just a generous handyman. In a world where I had to watch my step, I had a kind building manager. His kindness was the greatest teacher. His kindness taught me science. I bet he never knew how much of an influence he had on me.

By the time I was a teenager I didn't need him anymore. I grew up. My school had a lab, and I outgrew his tools. Then I went off to college one evening when my mom dropped me off at the bus station. My path was sent into motion by the generosity of Mr. Leahy, and I never told him goodbye, and I never showed my gratitude. I should have.

There is residual kindness left in me from those years of my life, and I feel the responsibility to treat every curious mind like Mr. Leahy would have. And it would have been just that simple. I could have grown old and kind like Mr. Leahy. I could have enjoyed my life more had I just stopped and appreciated what I had. But I found myself swinging at invisible enemies. I fought, and I lost.

I isolated myself. I thought the world around me was insane, suffering from delusions. Students of mine who would eat up every word during lecture, I'd lay it all out for them, and then they'd go check their horoscopes, buy dream catchers, and believe the dollar they gave a homeless person would bring them Karma. This tortured me. What good was an education, an education that was supposed to prepare you for the world, if you didn't understand the physical properties of the world?

I preferred teaching science to art majors and lit majors because I thought of science as a grand addition to whatever pursuits they had in their lives. I dreamed of a world where the poet knew her periodic table. *Hydrogen hyperboles and selenium similes.* Where the journalist reported on science. Not just a special guest column, but front page news, *Saturn is above the horizon at such and such time, here's the coordinates, here's the azimuth.* Maybe a gossip column that included a sighting of the rare yellow-rumped warbler, or what phosphorescent occurrences are happening in the Sound.

People say science isn't entertaining enough. I argue that its entertainment value is its greatest attribute. The problem is that the airwaves are crowded. Much like our food, we want our information to be processed prior to receiving it. Television and video games, religion, loud stadiums full of sports fans. This is the highly accessible diet of processed information, and we've forgotten about what is *actually* happening. Unfortunately, we're the descendants of animals that learned how to budget their energy, and we've blended that into our thinking patterns, gladly accepting all this processed information. *Why process it yourself if someone can do that for you?*

But worse than that, worse than the college kids that I only halfway reached, worse than teenagers wasting away in front of screens, and stressed out sports fans placing phantom importance on a game, on a fucking game, worse than all that was the injustice of brainwashing children. Childhood indoctrination. I see it as abusive. I don't know what else to call it.

That's a very heavy accusation, but it's the way I see it. I can't soften the terminology. Outside of science, we soften our messages, for the sake of making everything friendly, we don't want to hear the truth so we soften it, we sugar coat it, we dilute it, we sometimes blatantly change it. Not in science, in science we tell the truth. We're brave enough to tell the truth. All we have is the truth. What I see happening to children, I call that brainwashing and abusive, that's how I see it. It would be irresponsible to label it with anything other than the most accurate word I can find.

Beautiful, curious children, who would have loved to understand comets, and robin eggs, and light refraction, and tiny, water dwelling tardigrades, are filled with fear, judgment, and discouragement towards wonder. Some kids are exposed to nature *and* religion, but to truly understand the science behind nature, they eventually jaywalk through heavy Biblical traffic.

There was a religious recovery group at Evergreen. They met once a week, they probably still do. I was never religious. I attended out of curiosity. But I asked permission to attend, as a supportive and curious bystander. I felt for these college kids. These images of hell and of a god who is going to judge them, they were burned so deep into their senses that they needed to attend a support group to help them move on with their lives. They were taught that we didn't have enough good nature inside of us to morally navigate through life without religion, that we needed a savior. They felt exposed and vulnerable without the faith they placed in their savior.

These kids would talk to me after my lecture. They said they felt small when they considered the size of the universe, insignificant when they located our position in it. They felt irrationally guilty at even asking these questions, and the answers were often terrifying. They considered evolution, our stage in evolution, and that caused them to feel arbitrary in comparison to what they had been taught, that a god created us to be exactly how we are right now. It should never be underestimated how painful unlearning the lies of youth can be. I've seen these people suffer.

Millions of children grow up in religious homes, with supportive and loving church communities. I make the claim that these kids are being abused, but that doesn't make these parents bad people. Not at all. These families want to love their kids and they are giving them religion out of love. It goes back many generations. It is a continuous cycle of parents loving their kids. These are often very good, generous people. But they are brainwashing their children, just as they were brainwashed. Wonderful people do devastatingly careless things.

This was my struggle. When I really opened my eyes and saw how potentially damaging this was, I lost hope. I lost hope in the intelligence of our species. I replaced it with fear, the vacuum of exaggerated confusion. And you can't reason with a confused vacuum.

What I fear we miss out on though, more than anything else, is the solid grasp of understanding exactly how wonderful we really are. That is a human right; knowledge of oneself is a human right. Everyone deserves to know the truth. It is the only way to truly grasp how precious life is. We have evolved. That's beautiful. We share common ancestors. Every mammal on the planet, every animal on the planet, every form of life on the planet, we are all connected. People feel alone and small in the universe without their god. We're not alone; we have each other. We're not small; we're made of stars.

I don't hate the people that are responsible for this jam that we're in, this traffic jam of falsehoods. I don't hate anyone. What would I hate, their brains? Their skin? Their internal organs? When you understand what a human really is, what we're made of, there's nothing to hate. Humans are beautiful. It's the systems; the larger systems that we become a part of, these are the culprits. These churches, these companies, these bigger things that have domesticated us, they have forces stronger than we perceive ourselves to be.

We get pulled in, magnetically. There are metaphorical physical forces at work. The systems in our global society that make us dumb, they have star like properties. It's time for them to collapse. It's time for the corporate and religious stars to supernova. It'll be beautiful. More stable systems will emerge in the aftermaths. But those are just dreams. Just because it should happen, doesn't mean it will.

I felt the walls of this society close in on me, a society that linguistically obliges nothing to our scientific advancements. A sunset, a broken heart, good luck. We speak of last millennium's science. The sun doesn't set. Your heart is a hollow muscle; you can't love with it. Luck is just masturbating probability. We're so egocentric that we place ourselves in the center, as the vertex connecting event A and event B. *This* happened, and then *that* happened, and it's all connected through me. And that's what happens when our philosophies don't consider science.

I couldn't deal with it anymore. I didn't even speak the same language as the people I wanted to help. And then I caught myself saying things like *bless you* when someone sneezed, a phrase I've said my whole life because my mom taught me to, and I feel rude just letting someone sneeze and not begging some higher power to let that person live.

The religions and the superstitions and the pseudoscience of the world, they were chasing me. I never wanted enemies. I wanted to change people's minds. I couldn't live in everyone else's dream. But I was a threat to this system of ignorance. It was a force, not a singly conscious force, but a collective force, that webbed the most beautiful fairy tale these people could imagine, and I was a threat to it. If people only knew how much more beautiful science and truth are than any fairy tale we could concoct, if they only saw the universe, even just that tiny fraction that we actually know anything about, they would see for themselves, our imaginations are quite dull compared to beautiful genius of the cosmos.

Numbers are infinite, but maybe beauty isn't. Maybe science is beauty in its finite, maximum capacity. And it ached me to see people trade in beautiful knowledge for hopeful faith, and miss out on what I was experiencing.

In college, or at the museum, we were all scientists. It was so obvious to us that we never spoke of how important science was, just as we never spoke of how useful breathing was. We were indifferent to faith. Faith never proved anything. Faith was hoping in the absence of proof. Useless in a lab. But we got used to the beauty of science; we rarely defended it. We took it for granted.

This is where I wanted to be, in the fight between science and ignorance. But the fallacy was lost on me. Only an ignorant person would ever fight. I should have celebrated every curious kid on the street that came over to me and wanted to look at the moon through the telescope at night. Those were not victories in a battle. They were simple, positive experiences.

This was my struggle. We've been hijacked by the absence of science, the perceived irrelevance of it. None of us, anywhere, are unaffected. I wanted to fix this. I tried to fight it. I tried to take on the masses. You can't fight a majority and win. You can work with a majority, though. You can work with the energy of the majority, and lead it in a new direction. I didn't know that. I do now.

It wasn't always like this. I wasn't always at war. Before time stood still, and I started fighting, my mind was in a beautiful state of peace. Gilb and Kennedy and I were a family. The three of us shared space during the evening. I liked to read in my chair, while we burned a candle and listened to jazz records, and Gilb and Kennedy had nice conversations that I'd tune in and out of.

We had experiences. Gilb would come by when Kennedy was at work, and we'd go do something new and interesting every time. He would bring me over to his friends' homes to teach their kids about the sky. Sometimes when I'd bring my solar telescope downtown, looking to share the sun with people, he would come along and watch, even though he'd heard everything I had to say. He was proud to know me.

We had two experiences that stand out most. They both involved nebulae. I'll remember them both forever, and if I'm wise, I'll revisit them often to remind me of how beautiful life can be.

A few years back, Gilb called and told me to get a few of my telescopes together, that we were going to go see a friend of his and her kids. He didn't tell me much more. They lived up north by the military base, near Tacoma. This is a place where Gilb and I don't fit in. He drove his converted biodiesel truck, with the bumper stickers to prove it, into muscle truck country. "We're near the spot where Chief Leschi was hanged," he told me. *Who's Chief Leschi?*

Gilb's no patriot. I knew the way he felt. He didn't like conflict, so I got to hear all his opinions on the matter instead of some hillbilly that might not have reacted as nonchalantly as I did. I was surprised when we arrived near a military base, with American flags waving on every house, to look over and see that Gilb had actually driven us here, on his own free will.

We showed up at his friend's house, Donna was her name. She was dressed in sweats, but her hair was done, and her makeup was on. She was gorgeous. It was about seven at night. After she introduced herself, she ducked out, and Gilb and I were left with her three kids.

It was a clear night. When it got dark we took the kids outside and looked up. I just pointed some stars out, and told the kids a few minor facts about them. The smaller kids went back inside and watched a cartoon, but the older boy, who looked to be about ten, he wanted to know more.

We first found Betelgeuse, the red supergiant, my favorite star, and I told him all the reasons why. For starters, Betelgeuse is huge. It's a thousand times bigger than our sun, or about as big as the orbit of Jupiter. And in roughly a million years, it will supernova, and if anyone is left on this planet, they will see it outshine the moon.

We then drew a line to Beta Tauri, in the constellation Taurus. What I like about this star is that it is three degrees west of the galactic anticenter. I was actually able to explain this to a ten year old, and he understood. I don't know if I was more proud of him or me. I drew out the galaxy spiral, and explained that the anticenter is the opposite direction from the center of the galaxy. He got it.

About two-thirds of the way from Betelgeuse to Beta Tauri is the Crab Nebula. It's easy to locate. Here was a kid dressed from head to toe in sports paraphernalia, hat turned backwards so he could look in the lens, and he pumped his fist when he first saw the nebula, like he had caught a touchdown.

These were the kind of kids that made it clear that they were better than me back when I was a kid. Of course they were. They could play sports and speak quickly and proudly, they were dangerously confident. These kids exist in every city. Adults get them wrapped up in the competitive world of sports, and they often miss out on less competitive areas like art and science.

When I was the same age as this kid, I'd walk around the playground, measuring my shadow, thinking about the sun, the moon, and Mars. A ball might come bouncing over to me from some game that the more confident kids were playing. Sometimes I'd throw the ball back, wanting to help, and I'd get made fun of for how I threw. Or I'd accidentally kick the ball in the wrong direction and my shoe would fly off. They'd call me names. Sometimes they'd call me a girl. That one never made sense. Somebody spread a dumb rumor that calling someone a girl was a way to hurt a kid's feelings.

The first time I got called a girl, I told Mr. Leahy about it. I never wanted to upset my mom with these things; I wanted her to think I was getting along just fine. But every so often, I would ask Mr. Leahy a vague question, hoping to get a precise answer.

We were in one of the storage units that he used as a garage, and he was showing me how to use a band saw, and I asked him why boys call other boys girls, and he laughed. He challenged me a little, "Did someone call you a girl?" I said *no.* I was lying. I rephrased it with, "I've heard boys call other boys girls, and I don't understand why they do that."

As a scientist, already at that age, I looked at gender as a cooperating part of a system, but I never thought of one gender as better than the other. Of course I'd grow up and learn that not everyone cooperated in that system the same way, and even that was perfectly normal within science, despite all the insults we've created that suggest otherwise.

Mr. Leahy said something I'll never forget, and I've thought about it often. He said, "Some people are smarter when they're scared, and some people are dumber. And you'd be amazed at what scares people."

Out on the back porch with a ten year old kid who's athletic abilities were already greater than mine, who would have every opportunity in life to spike footballs and call other boys girls, here was a kid who was absolutely captivated by the glittery image of the Crab Nebula. He wanted to know everything about it. I showed him a picture of what it looked like in a book, and he put his eye back in the lens, and couldn't understand why he didn't see all the same colors. That turned into a conversation about the rods and cones in his eyes, and why we can't see the colors, but a camera lens could.

The other two kids, both much younger, were in the living room asleep on the couch next to Gilb, who was partially asleep himself. But the boy and I stayed up past midnight, looking at the sky. This was one of the most rewarding experiences with a telescope I would ever have. I made peace with every kid who ever called me a girl. I wondered how many less kids would have held such an entitled view of the world had they only been exposed to the universe.

Gilb explained to me on the way home how Donna's Army husband had got himself in trouble and she was left to take care of the kids by herself, so she did what she could, dancing at night for men to watch. And Gilb knew her somehow, as he knows a lot of people somehow, and he felt sorry for her, so he watched her kids at night sometimes. She was gorgeous and I asked him if he was interested in her, and he replied as if we were in grade school and girls still had cooties. When I thought about it, he hadn't dated anyone the whole time we lived in Olympia. In a lot of ways, he was dating us, Kennedy and me.

Then I made a comment, a dumb comment, about how that kid was curious and intelligent, and that it was too bad that his mom was a stripper, and I think Gilb took it the wrong way, or maybe he took it the right way, seeing as though it was a stupid thing to say. I couldn't tell. But Gilb was like a puppy dog. He shook it off and wanted to be best friends again.

Some time later, Gilb picked me up on another clear night, and we went over to his friend Jefferson's house. We brought the large 10-inch Dobsonian telescope over. Jefferson owned a few restaurants in town. Everyone seemed to know Jefferson. Kennedy knew who he was, too. She took a laughter yoga class from him. He was a popular character in Olympia, a town that loves characters.

Gilb had told me that everything Jefferson touched turned to gold, that he was blessed. So, of course I translated that in my head to him being a smart businessman, because blessings aren't real.

Their house was made of straw bale, fascinating, but very modest. All the art in the house was created by friends of theirs. And they had an entire room painted blood orange, with a xylophone. I liked these people.

Gilb liked to say I knew the sky well, and I do. This is true. But I like to think that I'm just very curious. If you took the most knowledgeable astronomers in the world, and compared what they knew to a five year old looking at planets in a cheap telescope, the gap of knowledge is quite thin when you consider how much there is to know. So, I never try to come off as an expert, just someone who knows a few things, simple facts, distances and sizes. Information that people can enjoy.

After dinner, we took turns looking up at the Orion Nebula. I liked explaining how far away it is, at 1,344 light years. It wasn't too close; it wasn't too far away. Everyone can name a dozen events that have happened over the last 1,344 years, and the concept of photons traveling through the galaxy at the speed of light for the past 1,344 years and reaching the earth, and through the lens, and into your eye, that's fun. That's fun astronomy. And you either get that, or you don't. There's no need to explain it any better. The simple definitions of the universe are the most enchanting.

Jefferson and his wife got it. They understood. They took turns looking at the Orion Nebula; they felt the emotion involved in connecting with the universe. They'd readjust the position of the telescope every few minutes, which was usually my duty with timid stargazers, fearful to touch another person's possessions. But since I wasn't needed, I left them alone, to enjoy the universe together, and I saw Jefferson rub his wife's belly in between gazes. Pregnant women and nebulae have a lot in common.

That summer I ran into Jefferson and his wife, and their little newborn boy, Orion, at the market. This is why I am at home in Olympia. This is why I know I had a good thing, and I lost it. You meet people in Olympia that name their children after something they saw in the sky.

You'd think with all the genuine experiences that I'd find a way to stay positive, and keep from getting sucked into a state of depression, insomnia, and paranoia, all sparked by each other. You'd think that turning a ten-year-old jock into an astronomy enthusiast, and introducing a happy couple to the Orion Nebula, you'd think I would be encouraged by this. But I was overwhelmingly discouraged by what I saw each day, in every magazine and newspaper, on the radio, and everywhere I looked.

I was slipping and I didn't know it. As magnificent as it was to bond with that ten-year-old on the porch, a sliver of a memory of something his mom said as she left the house kept poking at me, it kept irritating me the way a sliver would.

She was so beautiful, Donna. I'm normally put off by makeup, my mom never wore any, Kennedy rarely did, and it just seemed like another part of the bullshit fairy tale for me, but Donna was stunning. It was creative, artistic what she had done. I know nothing about makeup, so that's the best I can explain it. It was poetic what she had managed to do to herself in a mirror with kids hanging off her.

As she walked out, she told her son to get sleep, that if he was going to be a sports star some day he needed his sleep. I didn't understand the desperation of her situation at that moment, but it just sounded hopelessly delusional. What she was encouraging her son to dream about, the odds of that happening were microscopic, even if he was the most athletic kid in his school. Why set him up for failure?

When Gilb told me about their financial situation, about the husband who got caught up in some weapon trafficking scandal, it made me think about her comment in another light, which was also disturbing to me.

Money and sports. Donna was desperate. A college scholarship couldn't have been more than seven or eight years away. She was reaching for something she hoped would be there. It made me sad for her. And it made me think about the values we have in place in our society.

Here was a woman who needed help sending her kids to college. So, she prayed every night that her son would grow up to play a sport well enough that people would pay for his education.

Games are wonderful. Sports can be exhilarating. But what if, instead of packing stadiums full of tens of thousands of screaming fans, people actually got together and did something? Nearly every night, somewhere in this country, there's a stadium full of fans, spending money and energy, and all they do is make rich people richer. I've heard the argument that these sporting events are good for the economy, but that's very shortsighted. We can do a lot better than this.

What if all of those people, and all their money, and all their energy, all got together and planted gardens, and built homes, and developed sustainable living practices? That would be pretty damn good for the economy, and the ecology.

When a mom leaves the house at night to work, her kids in the care of two unlikely college professors, she should rest assured knowing that if her kid isn't the MVP of his basketball team he'll still go to college. If we're spending billions entertaining ourselves, there should never be another kid who can't afford to go to college, but wants to.

Stay with me on this one, I'll tie this up. I read a sci-fi novel when I was a kid about the last remaining humans becoming pets for a race of futuristic creatures. It was terrifying. But how different is our current reality? We're already pets. Trained pets. We're domesticated pets that anyone with two or more commas in their financial worth can own. We value their values. They tell us to pay attention, the big game is on, and we do just that. We sit. We roll over. We watch the screen. They tell us to jump. We jump. Our team just scored. We're pets.

That ten-year-old kid, Ty, his shot at getting an education depends on whether he can help your alma mater win a bowl game. And his mom had to worry about that when she went off to work at night. So she tells him to get his sleep, sports stars need their sleep. Instead, we stayed up late looking at stars. Maybe everyone was wrong and sports wouldn't be his only path. Maybe there was a scientist within him as well.

Science isn't just about looking at microbes, science is about thinking critically about life. Everything. Our religions. Our economic values. Our loyalties to corporations that do nothing for our communities. Everything. Our ignorance of the environmental impact we're causing. Our addictions to petty entertainment. These systems we have in place, when analyzed, are not sustainable over a long period of time. We're out of focus.

I think about our design, as mammals, with our forward facing eyes. We have to blend images. We call this stereopsis. I watched Mr. Leahy fix a pair of glasses once. He said one of his eyes was stronger than the other, so he needed special glasses to see distances. He explained to me that what we see is a blend of two views. We did some silly game where he had me cover one eye, than the other. I was pretty young. He called it stereovision. I remembered that term, because I've never heard it since. And in it, not too deep from the surface, was a metaphor that was lost on me. Two views, one understanding.

I'd had a long day of these kinds of rants in my head, dissecting society, and I came home one night and Gilb and Kennedy wanted me to go to a Mariner game with them.

Really?

Padding the pockets of millionaires? Why the hell would I want to go to a professional baseball game? We could do better things with our time and money. But these were arguments I'd be having with ghosts in my head, not with the people I loved in my own home.

We had protested in the streets a few years back, braving tear gas and rubber bullets, before sneaking back out of harm's way. We were standing up to this kind of bullshit, and now they wanted me to go to a ball game. I was literally working myself up that very day about how gullible people are, spending all that time and money at these professional sports games, and I came home and that's where they wanted me to go.

They said it was for Jackie Robinson. It was Jackie Robinson day, or something like that. It didn't change a thing for me. How about, instead of all us spending 20 dollars on tickets, we all did something that actually helped make a difference?

I pictured an African American kid. I had a very stereotypical thought in my head, I'll admit. I pictured her school as being less equipped, not having modern scientific equipment. I imagined all 30,000 people giving the price of their ticket to a few predominately African American schools in Seattle, and letting the Mariners play in front of an empty crowd, just once. That, to me, would be a great way to honor Jackie Robinson.

Right there, that thought. I knew it would never happen, but I entertained myself, and I let it play out in my head. Assuming the average ticket was at least 20 bucks, and that they would sell at least 30,000 tickets. That's a lot of money that the schools could do some good with. That would be something I could get on board with.

This wouldn't be a charitable cause, not at all. This would just be a bunch of sports fans realizing they could sit one game out to help fund an educational cause, and that we would all benefit in the long run from the differences these kids would make in the future.

My thoughts went further. Race. The illusion of race. Donna and her kids are African American. That ten-year-old that looked through my telescope was African American. When we drove up to the base, Gilb never mentioned anything about their race. He just said we were going to go hang out with a family. When I noticed they were African American, I had an unfortunate realization about myself, because I was surprised. I assumed they were white, because he hadn't said otherwise.

I've always known race to be an illusion. We have similarities to people who we are more closely related to, genetically. The color of our skin is one of those similarities. And yet, with all my background in science, I still generated a form of bigotry. It wasn't a harmful thought, it was just naïve of me. It was something I figured I should give some thought to, and try to improve on.

I was sailing away, letting my mind explore race and equality and Jackie

Robinson, who I'm sure was a very impressive man. I was pretending to listen as Gilb relentlessly tried to talk me into the game still. He kept saying *it'll be fun, c'mon.* Of course it would be fun. If I could get numb to it, I'm sure it would be. I bet I would even start to root for the Mariners, and all of sudden it would really, really matter. This is show business. These guys know what they're doing. They'd hook me in, no problem. I'd have a great time. That wasn't the issue. I'm a human, not a customer. I can have fun without buying something.

And the thing is, I know that Gilb feels the same way. He cringes every time he sees an American flag, and he's got all kinds of scars from when he was young, after Ray died, and he started going to real public schools and he didn't even know the Pledge of Allegiance. He's got as much venom towards the system as I do. He knows this country's history. He knows of events in our country's history that are so disgusting I wish he never shared them with me, so I know he gets it.

But the only way I could excuse myself from this proposed trip to the whorehouse was to tell the story about Game 4, 1977, and I milked it, I made it pretty dramatic. But that's not why I didn't want to go. I didn't want to go because it's all bullshit. Let's go watch a high school baseball game instead. I'll do that any day. Let's go cheer for some kids.

Gilb put two and two together. He saw the parallels. Kennedy's dad's bar benefitted from that World Series game. I didn't. I never saw my dad again, and ended up with scar that looked like a worm on my neck. He figured it out, and I went to bed. I'd had it. I was beat up from a long day of fighting demons. And on that night, the demons were in my home, too. This wasn't always the case, but it was on that night.

I can remember how exhausted I was. I was brushing my teeth, and I was so tired I couldn't wait to finish and go lie in bed. I thought I'd fall asleep right away. But that didn't happen. My mind kicked it up a gear, and horrible images flew through my imagination.

Plastic in the oceans, forests flattened, bombs, child soldiers, it got worse and worse. I had to remind myself to breathe. I tossed around in bed for hours, too tired to get up, too disturbed to sleep. I didn't think that Gilb and Kennedy would understand.

I could just barely hear them whispering to each other before Gilb left. Some paranoia kicked in. I imagined them talking about me, as if *I* was the weird one for bailing on the baseball game, and all the other things about me that people think are strange, but that I think are normal and human. I followed that thought into a bad place, for a long time, until I finally snapped out of it, and I remembered how much I love those two people, and how they love me. And I felt guilty for what I was thinking.

When Kennedy finally came to bed, I pretended to sleep, but I couldn't, and I stayed still while a train crossed through my head all night. I didn't sleep at all.

The next day felt like the first day on a new boat, in a hurricane. I couldn't take more than a few steps without recalibrating. I couldn't wait until the day was over so I could get to sleep. I was going to flush out all of these horrible thoughts with one good night sleep. Eventually I was in the bathroom again, brushing my teeth, staring into some heavy eyes in the mirror. I knew I was seconds away from sleep, but that didn't happen. I tossed all night and didn't sleep again.

This went on for three nights. I didn't get a wink of sleep for over 72 hours. I didn't recognize myself. My mind wasn't working. It was misfiring. I finally fell down on the couch, after dinner, right in the middle of something that Kennedy was trying to tell me, and I got a few hours of sleep. I had violent, stressful dreams. They were sharp and loud. I was grabbing at something, and I'd have it, but then I'd let go, and I couldn't figure out how to get it back, and I didn't know what it was. I was climbing up on things, doing everything I could to reach it.

I woke up later that night to find Kennedy already in bed. My mind was functioning better. It was clear outside, so I went out to look at the stars. No telescope, just my eyes.

Jupiter was as bright as ever, trying to pass as a star. I thought about a question that a student asked me once, whether Jupiter could have been a star. This is a pleasant thought. I'm happy when my mind goes here, when it stays away from thinking about things like that guy on the corner with the cardboard Ten Commandments, or the neighbor with the bumper sticker suggesting that if we burned an American flag we ought to wrap ourselves in it first. Crazy people. People I try to prove wrong in my head all day.

I remember the way she asked me the question. "This showcases my curiosity more than my knowledge, but is Jupiter big enough to become a star?" I love these questions. May we *always* be more curious than knowledgeable.

I have to admit, I'm a Mars junkie. That's always been my favorite planet. I remember doing projects in grade school about Mars. I was so excited I could hardly breathe. I would stand in front of the class and say something like, "You won't believe this, but the red color comes from Iron Oxide. Iron Oxide... guys, that's rust. Mars is rusty!" No one gave a shit, not even the teacher. Mars has a moon that sets twice a day, and because it has an axial tilt similar to ours, it has seasons, but the seasons are much longer because it takes 687 days to orbit the sun. And although there is no proof of it, there are credible hypotheses that life on Earth originated on Mars, and was brought here by a meteorite. True or not, that excites me.

I tremble with emotion when I think about Mars. Jupiter never did that to me.

But Jupiter is a fine planet. And because it's so accessible to our eyes at night, it's the planet I answer the most questions about. I remember telling this student how Jupiter formed very differently than a star would. Stars are formed from the collapse of dense clouds of interstellar gas. Planets are formed when these clouds take on the shape of a disk, surrounding the rotating star. Once the star is formed, the left over matter becomes planets. So, Jupiter could have never been a star. It has a similar composition, but it can't fuse hydrogen into helium.

It's interesting to me that people ask this question. Most adults I meet can't identify Jupiter in the sky. They assume it's a star. And because we don't sit around at night plotting and charting the sky like our ancestors did, we don't notice its orbit. So, in a way, Jupiter *is* a star, in the minds of many people. It blends right into the sky, and a person could sit back, observe the sky on a clear night, a person who admires the sky as an art, as a sort of canvas, and Jupiter is contributing as much, if not more, to that person's enjoyment.

For all practical purposes, yeah, Jupiter is a star, at least for that night. Why not? On that one night, I sacrificed some accuracy for the sake of a simple thought, a simple enjoyable thought. I was surprised that I was able to do that. My thoughts had been anything but simple lately.

This was a peaceful moment. My mind was in a good place. A beautiful place. Had it not been the middle of the night, I would have woken up Kennedy just to tell her how beautiful she was. I thought to myself, *whatever has been bugging me, it's passed. I should go back to sleep, and be more grateful for my time on this planet, and try not to get so caught up in all the little annoying details.*

I climbed into bed next to Kennedy, confident that I'd crash the second my head hit the pillow. But something else happened. I immediately felt lost in a rage. I went right back to my elementary school classroom, up in front of the class, with a solar system mobile that Mr. Leahy gave me all the parts for, and none of those little fuckers gave a shit because that Atari Video Game console had just come out, and it was the first day back after winter break, which meant every kid in my class spent the last week playing Pong. And Jupiter's not a fucking star. It's just a big ass planet. And it has probably only orbited the sun twice since I was in elementary school, yet on my mobile I spun it around and around, like I did all the planets, because I was excited about showing it off, because I got to use Mr. Leahy's bandsaw. What a job these corporate monsters with their video games have done in making the sky, the fucking sky, irrelevant, and less entertaining than a video game.

I didn't sleep at all that night. This went on, and on. Every night I fought demons in my head. I fought invisible demons. They whooped me. Fights are real even when your opponents aren't.

I'd have my moments, my *Jupiter is a star* moments. I'd pop up and I felt like a king, and I wanted to hug and kiss every inch of Kennedy, and tell her everything I have ever felt about her, how amazing she is, but mostly I'd just asked her questions I thought she'd want to answer. Isn't that what everyone wants?

We'd have sex. I spent my whole life ignoring my physical needs. In these clear moments, I felt like my brain was functioning better than ever. And sex was a need, a real need, and I was happier when we had sex.

But these moments would pass, and I'd be drowning again. My brain was going in two different directions, and the gap was widening. My days were split between positive, clear thoughts, and anger and paranoia. When I was clear and positive, I had energy, and I wanted to connect with people, especially Kennedy. When I was angry, I'd lie on the couch, hoping it would swallow me.

Gilb came by one particular Sunday when I was on the couch. I tried to pull it together, to be nice. I dreaded that I'd take all this rage out on Gilb, and he didn't deserve it. I must have looked like a zombie, but Gilb didn't seem to notice or care.

He said he wanted to go for a hike with me, to take some time and show that he was grateful for our friendship. It was always inspiring to see the way Gilb gave simple thanks for things. It was five years exactly since the phone call, the phone call that changed our lives, and he wanted to go hike this nature trail up north. It was a good idea. I was thinking, maybe I wasn't getting enough exercise. Maybe this would help. I was being hopeful. Hope is so passive.

But we got up there and I couldn't keep my focus. He was talking fast and he was excited. I was only catching half of his words. My mind was on other things. I knew I had a problem when he started talking about his mom, and how she died, and where he believed that she went after she died, and I made such a jackass move. I told him that nobody knows where we go when we die. He punched me. I don't blame him one bit.

What a jerk I was. I was a jerk that had hardly slept all month.

Miraculously, if I'm even allowed to use that word, I never had a problem keeping my work schedule. It was about the only thing I could do. It kept me sane. I'd look forward to lecture time, getting up there and speaking, I could hear myself, and it made me feel alive.

I've had so many students, so many wonderful, grateful students, but there's one that stood above the others, which is ironic since she was confined to a wheelchair.

I can't remember her name. I probably never learned it. I'd call on her every lecture. She had a scientific background, you could tell, but most of her questions were moral based. Like she was using science to frame her ethics. Perfect.

She was paralyzed from the waist down. Yet, you'd forget when you talked to her. You really would. It was not a part of her identity one bit. When I think of her, my memory tricks me, and she stands upright. I can clearly see her walking into my office, or the lecture hall. My memory gives her walking shoes, and a swagger to her step, because she was a bit cocky. This is how she exists to me. This was not a handicapped person. This person was not disabled. She had a different set of skills than most people, she couldn't dance on her feet, she couldn't run, but she more than made up for it. To call her disabled would be to point out all of our disabilities.

She'd stay after class and we'd talk. I felt the obligation to treat everyone the way that Mr. Leahy treated me. Yet this wasn't really an obligation. I enjoyed it. I would look forward to it. I learned from her as much as she learned from me. She was much more intellectually capable than I was. I just had a head start.

These were positive experiences that I had with this student, and it reminded me of why I teach. I was failing in every other part of my life, but I was always able to get up and teach, and she was why. Her purpose in that classroom was so evident, and her presence impossible to ignore, that when I planned my lectures, I pictured her in the audience, and it inspired me to make every lecture as interesting as I could.

I wrote about her in my first book, Between Yellow and Red, in hopes that if she ever picked it up and read it, she'd know I appreciated her being my student. I had dedicated the book to Mr. Leahy, as my finest teacher, but I wrote an introduction where I expressed gratitude to all of my students, and in one in particular. If that book ever landed on her lap, she would immediately have recognized my gratitude to her.

Every year, Gilb helped put on this event that never really made sense to me. He helped host a debate, although it wasn't a debate. Nobody agreed, but everyone was too afraid to admit it. It centered on the topic of life after death. He had asked me if I wanted to be involved, and after he told me the line up, I felt obligated, because not one person on that stage other than me had a scientific background. I never really wanted to be a part of it, but I had to.

We always met at a very expensive looking private Catholic high school. Every year I kept my cool, and just went along with the format. I would get up there, and talk about science, and if I was accurate, then all these clowns were full of shit. There's no gray area. I almost felt worse not addressing just how contradicting my facts were to their beliefs. But I went along with it because Gilb was a buddy, and I really couldn't imagine just how sorry that forum would be without a scientist up there.

So I'd go, I'd try to be a good sport, and we'd stay in a fun hostel in an interesting part of Portland with intriguing people that Gilb knew. You could count on Gilb for that.

He'll never bore you.

The forum was scheduled, whether I liked it or not, during this chaotic time I was having. And it was a disaster. I should have skipped it, I was sleeping an hour or two a night at most, and most nights I got no sleep at all. I have no idea what I said, but it was bad. I know it was rough. I'm sure everything I said was true, something that I meant, but I probably went overboard, and made up for the past few years where I was more tame and sterile on that stage.

The only thing I remember was the Irish priest's assistant. He was there every year, but I noticed him more that particular year. He was an adult but he looked like a kid still. I think he had some kind of growth hormone deficiency.

All of it made me uneasy. I didn't like the Irish priest. Gilb swore he was a wonderful man, but I had a poor opinion of priests, and I didn't have it in me to try to fix that. Priests looked like walking suckerpunches to me. I felt like they were going to suckerpunch me when I wasn't looking.

On this night, the priest's assistant was staring at me the whole time I was speaking, like he was putting a curse on me. I was watching him, making eye contact. I felt like I was shattering his world. And in some sick kind of way, I kept pushing it. I wanted to shatter his false reality. It was sadistic of me.

Most of the time, it's empathy that drives me to want to debunk a person's entire faith system, and introduce them to reality. But on this night, I was being spiteful. I finally had to look away from the assistant. The hate I was feeling was consuming me. I'm sure my tone changed once I looked away. It had to have.

After the forum, I wandered into some weight lifting room, collapsed on a bench and fell asleep. It was the deepest sleep I'd had in a few months.

But on this night, I dreamed. It was a bad dream. I dreamed about the assistant. I dreamed that I was his age, and that I was making fun of him. I was calling him wimpy. And then he pulled out a gun, a Derringer, like the gun that killed Lincoln.

When I was a kid, there was a replica of the gun that killed Lincoln in an exhibit at a museum, and it made me nervous. Lincoln had to have known what was coming. He had to have been paranoid. I'm no historian, but I'm guessing maybe half the country wanted him dead. I can't think of Lincoln without thinking of that gun, and for some reason the assistant had one just like it. He looked at me, and we both said at the same time, *like the gun that killed Lincoln*. He was reading my thoughts. He pointed the gun at me, and I woke up.

For the next few weeks I was paranoid. I was convinced that I had unlocked the assistant's inner psychopath with all of my heathen words up at the podium. I would imagine him finding me. I was terrified. I opened every door slowly, or sometimes very quickly, expecting to see him. I don't know how I got through the last month of that semester. I'm not sure I did.

Before I knew it, all of my evaluations were over, and we were on summer break, and I went to the couch and put my head down. Without the routine of required work, I was in deep trouble.

I was experiencing uncontrollable rushes of energy at weird times during the day, and then I'd crash and hide on the couch. I would hallucinate. I'd come out of my hallucinations, and I'd be in the middle of a conversation with Kennedy, and she was smiling. Or sometimes, I'd come out of my trance and we would be in bed. Sometimes

I'd roll over and Gilb would be reading to me, trying to get me to eat something or go to the doctor. I was never sure if I was coming in or out of a trance. There were wormholes to my existence. I'd get sucked in, and I'd pop out somewhere else.

On my clear moments, I'd be downtown, at a coffee shop, trying to be around people. Kennedy worked during the day, and I was still having anxiety about the priest's assistant, so being around people was comforting. I felt sharper when I was near people. I was afraid to be alone.

I got to know a lot of street kids. I started to make friends with them. Some of them had drug problems, but for the most part, they were living in resistance to the destructive systems in our society. I very clearly remember feeling close to these people, I felt like I understood them.

The girl with the tire marks tattooed down her back, I talked to her. I didn't say *hey, nice tattoo*, because that's not what she wants to hear, like when people point out my scar. Instead, I sat down next to her, and brought her some coffee, and wanted to hear her story, and if the tattoo was something she wanted to share, then the tattoo was worth hearing about. She had a lot to say, and she did explain the metaphorical meaning behind the tire marks, how she feels like those are society's tire marks, and I listened. I wasn't even trying to understand. I just listened.

She showed me the dates tattooed down her arm, attempts at sobriety. The last date wasn't crossed out. I figured it out. She'd been sober for a few months. She hoped she never had to cross that date out. We hugged. And she remembered my name the next time I saw her.

The thug with the tattoos on his face. His name was Accid. We became friends. I took my 10-inch telescope downtown, into the alley, where he was spray painting. I snuck up on him. His name is all over town. No one else's name appears on more buildings and signs in Olympia than his, and he puts it there himself. He climbs up over barbed wire, hangs from overpasses. He's like a spider. I see his name up high and I can't put together how he managed to land his name there.

I said, "Hey man, you're Accid? I want to show you the universe."

He thought I was joking. I said, "No, really, come look." He dropped his can of paint and walked over. Looking back, I don't know what made him trust me, but something did, and I showed him Saturn's rings. After about a minute, he looked up, and said, "Are you fucking kidding me? What else is out there?"

He was smart, good at math, real sharp, and we started talking about constellations, orbits, how fast the earth is traveling. 67,000 miles per hour.

I spent an hour in an alley with that guy, interrupted him in the middle of his spray painting. Why not? We're two humans, looking at the universe. Beautiful. And he walked away with a different understanding of the universe than he had before.

But I still wasn't sleeping much at night. I was still hallucinating, popping up in weird spots. I was still paranoid about the priest's strange looking assistant. I thought about him more and more. I had moments everyday when I was convinced that he was going to find me and gun me down. My hallucinations were centered on him. And the worst part of all of this, sometimes I'd look in the mirror and see him.

I'd drift in and out of reality. I'd wake up on a city bus. I'd wake up and I'd be walking around downtown. And one day, I woke up at a pawnshop purchasing a handgun, looking over my shoulder for the priest's assistant the whole time. I knew enough to even ask for one that was vacuum sealed. I heard myself speak gun talk. I got a good price, and I knew it was a good price.

I had a clear moment later that week, where I questioned the safety of a gun in the house. I decided I would need to hide the bullets from myself. If I kept the gun in my drawer, and the bullets in a locked cupboard in the garage, I'd probably be safe. I even threw the keys to the cupboard in the sewer. I could have just gotten rid of it, but even in my clearest moments, I wasn't convinced that the priest's assistant wasn't after me. So, this was a safe plan. Keep the gun, hide the ammo.

But the next day I opened my eyes and I had a receipt from the rental store for lock cutters, and the lock was on the ground, and with one hand, I was searching for the bullets, and with the other I was jamming a handgun in my mouth. I gagged and I dropped the gun on the floor, and I brushed my teeth. This was the life I was living. This was the mess I was in.

I was seeing the assistant daily in the mirror. In between beautiful, clear moments with Kennedy, I would be coming up with ways to hide the gun from myself. It finally came to me when I was on a city bus. A good plan, as good as my sleep deprived, paranoid mind could derive.

When I interviewed for the job at the school, five years earlier, we walked down to the beach, on a trail. I used to walk that trail, and sit, just to be alone to think. I did it often. There were several large, hollow logs in the woods on the trail, and I once hid my camera in there when it was raining and I didn't have pockets.

So, I hiked down there, without the gun, just with the ammo. I could never travel with both of them at the same time. I found a nice hollow tree, and I stuffed the magazine in there as far as I could, with as much grass and leaves as I could find as well.

This was toward the end. My paranoia was eating me. I was still wormholing though each day. I was still seeing the assistant in the mirror. I was still perking up for good parts of the day, and sharing meaningful moments with Kennedy. I'd still go downtown and meet homeless kids. I'd still wake up to find an empty gun down my throat. No bullets, no problem.

This was my routine.

And then, it all came loose.

I blinked. I saw my reflection in the bedroom window. It was the assistant again. I wanted him dead. I wanted him to go away. Far away. I thought if I killed him, I could sleep again. I didn't want to end up like Abraham Lincoln.

This was it; this was the end. I knew it. I reached for the gun in the drawer, the drawer near the bed, and I grabbed it. Dammit I wanted him long gone, dead, forever dead. He was haunting me. I grabbed the gun, put it in his mouth, and killed him. I killed him dead. I blinked.

I heard a sound. The sound of the pulled trigger woke me. Kennedy was screaming. I had never heard her scream before. I knew what I did. It was all so clear and real. I saw the gun in my mouth. I looked down the barrel. I knew it wasn't loaded. The magazine was missing. But Kennedy didn't know that. We were in bed, and I saw the assistant in the reflection of the window, and I put the gun in my mouth. And she screamed. It gets circular at this point. I saw the gun, and I saw what I had done, and I saw the assistant in the reflection, and Kennedy was screaming. And I saw that the magazine was missing. I saw the assistant. I pulled the trigger. Kennedy screamed. Every detail of this moment swarmed me, but I never saw the assistant again. It must have killed him. By killing a piece of me, I killed him.

I evacuated. That's how it felt. Me, my bag, my alarm clock, my handgun. It happened like the house was on fire. I grabbed what I could. I ran. But not before I heard Kennedy say the very last thing she would ever tell me.

I was trying not to remember it. I was trying so hard not to remember any of it.

Every pebble of who I was had come back, the giggling dragonfly girl had wound up the cassette tape of my memory. I was me again. I knew me.

Then I heard another voice. Two of them, actually. Friendly voices. Happy to see me. Relieved. It was all over.

Stevie

I finally got the courage to ask him, *were you drinking?* Nah, it wasn't the courage, it was ... it was something else. I was sick of what I knew. I always thought it was an accident. I wanted it to be something else.

Back when I first met Jerry, he was so handsome and charming, too charming. He was so smart. I knew he could do so much more. He was constantly getting behind on some gambling debt. He should have been running his own shipping business. He knew everything about the business.

He was at the bar a lot during the week. He used to say nice things, and bring me gifts. I didn't want anything to do with him at first, but he made sure I changed my mind.

When I told him we were going to have a kid he froze up and I didn't see him for a short time. We didn't know we'd be blessed with twins. But then he came back around. He wanted to do right. He tried to sober up, quit gambling, and keep his affairs in order. We got a place out in North Hollywood after the boys were born. He had a good thing going for a while, and that gave him the mindset that he could start up again, gambling off some of his wages, wages we couldn't afford to lose. He started up again with the alcohol too. He got too comfortable. He had a disease. Addiction is his disease. But he'd never admit it.

One day, a busy day, I had to go to work. I got called in. I was cleaning at the hospital. Jerry was off work for a few days, and he took the boys to the beach, and maybe you read about it in the newspaper, or saw on the television that night, that a little boy drowned in the water. Well that was my baby boy. Joshua. Joshua died on the beach that day.

Philip and Joshua, even at age four, were inseparable. They'd play all day together. They would fall asleep on the couch and take a nap together. Those were my little boys. And Jerry, that dumb son of a bitch, he got careless at the beach, he took them in the water, and he slipped, and he only came out with one. The lifeguard got to Joshua, but it was too late. It doesn't take long for a kid that age to drown. That's what they told me.

Jerry couldn't handle it, and he split. I'm sure the drinking and the gambling got worse. We didn't see him for a couple of years.

Philip and I moved across town. I was working several jobs. Canoga Park was a better location to where we needed to be. My mom knew of a nice man who owned a hardware store, and he managed an apartment building. He told my mom that he'd keep the rent low if we'd be willing to stay long term. He liked to have people stay long term, as opposed to having people in and out all the time. And if they were a nice family, he didn't mind making the place more affordable.

Well, we were nice, and he made it affordable. That Mr. Leahy was a saint. I was working at a few different hotels up near Studio City, and then I worked in Chatsworth at a restaurant a few days a week. My mom and her boyfriend lived in North Hollywood, so when I worked in Studio City, I would drop Philip off with them. But he didn't like it there.

Philip changed after the beach accident. He had been the more talkative one. He was so active and aggressive. But after Joshua drowned, he turned inward, and he never came out.

Philip used to ask what happened to Joshua, and I didn't know what to tell him.

I'd go in the bathroom and cry, I'd ask strangers to watch my kid so I could go in the bathroom and cry. And when I came back out, Philip would ask me again. I never knew what to say. I didn't know how to explain it. I tried to explain heaven, and Philip just looked at me.

And then I said something that didn't make much sense. I said it was like another world, where Joshua went. And then he never asked again. I cried every night for years. I still do. I took down the pictures. I couldn't stand to see them. It was like he was never born. And we never talked about it. And I know that was a mistake now, but at the time I was just too heartbroken.

Our building manager, Mr. Leahy, he was so good to Philip. We were coming home from the grocery store, and the sun was setting, and Mr. Leahy was looking at Mars in his telescope on the grassy field near the parking lot to our apartment. Philip was curious, and he walked over to him. I remember Mr. Leahy explaining what Mars was, that it was like another world. You couldn't take Philip off that telescope, and I often wondered if he thought he could find Joshua there.

Jerry tried to get back in the picture when Philip was eight. He wasn't able to keep it going though. He'd say he was going to be around, and then he wasn't. He was here for a few months, gone for a few months. He moved around a lot. It was hard for him to find work. He had burned all his bridges.

He wanted to come move in with us, and I had to threaten to call the cops one time. And Mr. Leahy came over and talked everyone down, and walked Jerry back to his car. He had those calming words, Mr. Leahy did.

Jerry was far behind on any sort of child support. He was trying to be a part of

Philip's life, but he wasn't helping us out, and I got tough with him. He needed to lock down some work, and quit messing up.

Philip's tenth birthday. What a mess. Jerry was supposed to have given us some money, and I never heard from him for months, and then he called, and I don't even think he remembered that it was Philip's birthday. He called and told me he would have the money by the next day, and that he had some tickets to the World Series game, and he wanted to take Philip. I bet he had money on the game. So, I prayed that the Dodgers would win. I watched that home run late in the game on the television. I knew we'd never see Jerry again.

I had already screwed up Philip's birthday enough by promising to take him to the museum, and then my boss called and told me I was going to get fired if I didn't come in, and I couldn't say no, and I didn't want Philip to think I had a mean boss. I didn't want him thinking about how hard everything was, so it was easier just to act like I forgot. Philip was awfully mad at me. He loved the museum so much. There was never anyone to take him. Had I known he'd go off one day and become a scientist, and work at a museum, I wouldn't have felt so bad.

On the way home from the baseball game, Jerry wrecked his car with Philip in it, and I had to rush down to the hospital to pick him up late at night. That was the last time we ever heard from Jerry. He was gone. This time I know he was drinking. They filed a report.

I never went looking for him. I just figured he needed to be out of our lives. He was bad for us from the beginning. He couldn't ever get a grip of his drinking and his gambling.

Not once before Philip went off to college did I ever have a man around. I thought he'd hate me for it. But it couldn't have been more than a few weeks after I dropped Philip off at the bus station that I met Dave.

Dave was a schoolteacher at Philip's high school. He called me up one day, and told me that Philip had done a presentation about nautical star maps that sailors had put together hundreds of years earlier. Dave owned a boat, a 41-foot sailboat that he kept out in Venice Beach. He was inspired by Philip's presentation. He spent the summer fixing up the boat, and he wanted to tell me that my son was something special.

He said that my son had built a telescope that the school was planning on using, would probably use for a long time. I started to cry, because I knew it, my son was something special.

Jerry Duke

I was bad luck. I'm bad luck to everyone around me. Always was. Still am.

It stopped raining. Then the winds came. Then we left. That's how my family talked about the 'dirty thirties.' They traveled from Oklahoma to California. They roamed from farm to farm, picking fruit. I was the twelfth born kid of two migrant workers. Nothing came easy. Mostly never came at all.

I learned how to get by. As long as I can remember, I've had to put my own food on my plate. I started fixing things, and people would give me food.

It was 1950. I was eight. I knew how to patch the tires of the trucks, and I had quick little hands. I knew how to work fast, so I'd ride with the drivers into the cities. I'd be gone for days, but I was fed, so my parents didn't worry. I never went to school past the age of 10, but I learned everything I needed to know to get by.

I met Stevie at a familiar truck stop. We were young. I had a pleasant thought that we would all move out to a nice home and we'd have a normal life. My mom and dad crossing from Oklahoma, they would have thought at least a few of their kids would find something worth living for.

And I probably could have made it work. I could have saved up, and bought my own trucks, and had a business of my own. I tried. I tried to be the family man, good dad. But everything I did, I busted it up somehow. Bad luck.

I took the boys out to the beach on a nice day, was thinking to myself, being a dad sure is great. We were playing in the sand, and one of the boys kept asking about the water. I think it was Philip; he kept so curious about everything. Well, I'd never been in the ocean water before, I didn't know about it. I saw all kinds of kids swimming around.

Couldn't have been too tricky. So, I held the boys tight, and we walked out a bit, and that's when I lost my footing. I wasn't much of a swimmer, and of course the boys couldn't swim. I slipped and I didn't have either one of them. I grabbed a hand, and I searched for the other. I yelled for help. Swallowed a mouthful of saltwater.

Folks on the beach were screaming. A lifeguard had Joshua on the sand. He was this kid, just a teenager, trying to save my son's life, breathing in his mouth, and he kept on trying. I just stood there, holding Philip, and Joshua never woke up. Paramedics came, and then Stevie showed up. Could have been hours. She took Philip with her, and I just stood there, and I didn't know what to do. It's all a blur, I don't think about it. I can't think about it. Worst thing that ever happened to me.

Stevie asked me if I was drinking, sometime later. I always had a flask on me, that's not really drinking.

I drifted in and out of their lives after that. I couldn't live with myself. Then I had a plan, I placed some bets on the Dodgers. It was 1977. They had a great team. And I stood to make a lot of money.

I called Stevie to tell her I'd have her money for her, I just needed a few more days. I needed the World Series to be over, and then we'd have a lot of money, and we'd finally get back what we always wanted. We could have had the life we wanted. I had close to 20 grand on that Series.

I had tickets to Game 4, and talked Stevie into letting me bring Philip. Luckily, it was his birthday. Honest, I had forgotten. I had a lot riding on that game. My nerves were hopping. And then that son of a bitch Reggie Jackson, he really crushed that ball, and that was it, I knew the game was over. I knew the series was over. I was out a lot of money. I knew it.

And then I about got us killed, again. Bad luck.

It was best for everyone I just went away. I went away for good.

On the road. Foot on the pedal. Hand on the wheel. All he had to do was drive south. That's all. Anyone can keep their foot on the ground. Hand on the wheel. Simple thoughts. Just drive.

Jimmy Eagle rolled a cigarette, smoked it out the window.

Early stars were out. Jimmy Eagle had his own names for them. The brightest one, low in the eastern sky at this hour, he strained to see it. It was his favorite star. He knew nothing about it, but he felt like it was good luck.

Just keep driving south. This road takes us south. Ignore the dancing lines in the road, floating up to eye level, lassoing the mile markers. Don't think.

Smell of cattle, sound of crickets.

Gilb

Puddles skipped past me overhead. That's what it looked like. Air joggers, thirty feet above, wearing shoes, similar to miniature inflatable pools.

A delicate day in the nation's capital, Los Angeles, came to a cautious end. A fully grown adult with a child's voice held tight to the side of an even more fully grown adult. *Holy shit, what am I witnessing?* Trained dolphins appeared, signaling the 90 degree swivel of two dimensional buildings anchored out past the surf. More citizens gathered, speaking mostly in touches and children's voices, and watched the ocean swallow the sun. The dolphins returned soon after, and the buildings swiveled back to their widths.

Blades of grass as thick as Komodo dragons began to rattle as a whisper thundered from the hilltops. The gathered citizens poked each other in excitement. They hummed a chaos of static, which slowly blended into order, and cycled into childlike harmony.

Tall female figures marched in perfect formation over a marble path, down the hill, approaching the marina. Not one man stood as tall as these soldiers. Dimorphism.

A woman, taller than the rest, carried a glass box, and a captive animal was flapping its clawed wings inside. The excitement was unbearable. My shoulders, my arms, behind my ears, all poked by youthful adult citizens. Rapid pokes, pokes like a lockstitch sewing machine. I was afraid to speak. I spoke like an adult, but surely looked like a kid to them.

A painfully low voice, octaves lower than any voice I'd ever heard, calmed the gathering crowd, and halted the soldiers. The columns of soldiers merged, allowing the woman with the glass box to reach the front of the line. The voice announced to the citizens that the creature in the box was a bird, the first of this class of animals to have been recovered in their lifetimes, dug from it's nest deep underground.

The voice assured the crowd that the animal would be returned, unharmed, by the morning. A virtual screen appeared in the sky, with images of birds flying. The crowd had never seen birds. They poked. They poked. They couldn't stop poking me.

Jimmy Eagle was poking at me, trying to wake me. *I found Stevie, I found her.* I could hear him, but I didn't answer him. I hadn't entirely left my dream yet. He poked me again. I finally swatted at him.

I had fallen asleep under the sun in Venice Beach. Jimmy had gone off to grab some coffee for us. He grabbed the key to use the bathroom in the coffee shop, and accidentally left the key in the bathroom, locking it in there. When he returned to tell the barista about his mishap, he asked her if she knew of anyone named Stevie, or her partner Dave, who lived on a 41 foot boat. She did.

We didn't have a plan. Nothing that resembled a plan. How did we end up 1000 miles south of home on some beach in California? I followed my gut, not a plan.

I went into a corner of my mind after Kennedy explained the incident with Philip. I couldn't deal with it. I only partially accepted it. I became tunnel focused on finding Philip. That was all. I didn't eat. Nothing. I had one thought. Find Philip.

Jimmy Eagle and I searched downtown Olympia, we'd bust into coffee shops and bookstores, startling customers. "HAVE YOU FUCKING SEEN HIM?!" Jimmy Eagle would clean up after me, and explain that we were looking for a man named Philip Duke, and he'd describe a man he'd never seen before, based on a description I gave him. Five years of friendship and I didn't have a single photo, and I wasn't going to go bug Kennedy for one.

We spoke with homeless kids. I'd describe Philip. "Beetlejuice? Nah, we haven't seen him lately." *Beetlejuice? Oh Betelgeuse.* The street kids named him Beetlejuice, after his favorite star.

We scoured every street and alley before Jimmy Eagle finally stopped me, told me to breathe, and handed me a cup of coffee. I was panicking. I was muttering to myself, interrupting myself. I was in a shaky place. I was breaking apart. Jimmy Eagle was rubbing my shoulder, coaching me on basic human functions. *Breathe. Think. Drink this coffee.*

I had been looking for a sign. There would be no hornet's nest. That story was enhanced anyways. No hailstorms. I needed a real sign. Philip was somewhere. He was somewhere we were not. There had to be a sign somewhere. We were missing something.

Jimmy Eagle shot me a neutralizing stare. I knew what he was trying to tell me.

Philip wasn't downtown. His energy wasn't down here. Nobody had seen him. He was a traceable guy, and there was no trace of him.

We sat down outside a cafe. Jimmy Eagle rolled a cigarette. He was so calm. He had something to say, I knew that about him, so I let him roll a cigarette and waited for him to speak.

"We make a good team," he finally said. "You love this man, like a brother, you love him. But you're not capable of doing this on your own. I don't know Philip, but I know you, and I will always help you. So, you need someone who cares about you the way you care about Philip. This may take several degrees of help, just like every emergency."

He was right. All of it. This reminded me.

Help. A memory. An important memory. So many years ago, divorce papers from Aishwarya sitting on the counter. Jimmy Eagle appeared in my blurry view, inches from my face, trying to wake me, trying to reach me. "Trust me," he said. "I'm going to take you somewhere, somewhere I believe you need to be."

I remember. Years ago. We drove all night. I'd ask where we going, he'd say "Just a little longer," which didn't answer my question. A river hopped up next to us. The road began to wiggle. *Just a little longer.*

Hours. Heavy hung over hours. So many of them. We drove all night. All across the night. And then, I could feel the truck decelerate, and a jolt of energy straightened me out, I tried to stand in my seat. Wherever we were going, we were there. We arrived.

But I couldn't tell where we were. I saw Jimmy Eagle scan the highway, looking to turn left, but I couldn't see a thing. I couldn't see anything that resembled a possible turn off the highway. So many years later, and I still remember that moment of doubt I had. I never doubted Jimmy Eagle again after that.

The top of a ponderosa pine, years ago, wrapped in a Tibetan prayer flag, hardly noticeable in the deep, digested hours of the night, marked the entrance to a road. It looked more like a deer trail. I would have never driven a car onto it. *Wherever we're going, these people don't want to be found.* But Jimmy Eagle found it, and hit the gas hard. It was good that he did, because we met a sharp incline, and it almost stopped us. The road was as wide as the car, at best, and tree limbs scraped the doors.

We bumped along this path for twenty long minutes. This was the worst part of the drive. I held my hand over my mouth, begging the night's worth of whiskey to stay down. I yelled, over the sound of rocks and road and horsepower in the mighty dozens, "Is this a road?"

Jimmy Eagle smiled forward. "We're driving on it, ain't we?"

"I can jerk off in my hand, doesn't make it a woman," I replied.

"Wouldn't that be nice. You might want to snip that kind of humor where we're going."

"Hey, seriously," I got straight faced with him, "where the shit are we, Eagle?"

"Gilb," Jimmy Eagle slowed the car down to a complete a stop, to emphasize his point. "Just... relax... bro..."

Something about the combination of words and tone, and maybe the fact that we weren't moving anymore, it calmed me. I did relax. And I felt better too. I didn't feel hung over anymore. I noticed that he parked right next to a broken down tractor, as if it was just another car. On this important night, so many years ago, it made me laugh.

We got out, and Jimmy Eagle asked me, "You brought a tooth brush right?" *No, I was sleeping in my own vomit when you arrived, I didn't know where the shit we were going.*

"Just kidding, man, you'll be okay. Follow me." *Follow you? Was that ever in doubt?*

We walked through a field of short, tame grass. Thicker, but calmer than I'd ever seen grass. I felt the faint tap of a drumbeat far, far off. We walked some more.

Jimmy Eagle knew where to walk. He knew what to do. I followed him without thinking. Instinctively, I followed. No thoughts, just my pace matching his. He knew where to go.

The drumbeat kicked up. It was louder with every step. By the time we crossed the field and reached the trailhead, the drumbeat was deafening.

The trail was more of a gravel walkway that eventually became a stone and brick mixture, embedded solar LED lights, and lined with perfectly placed logs, all cleaned and carved out. Golden sage and feverfew, some other herbs I couldn't recognize, rose from the dugout garden beds these logs became. *Who did all this?*

And then, finally, for the first time in so long, we stopped. We really stopped. The trail came to an end. The drums were so loud I couldn't think. It ricocheted and thudded throughout my whole body. It felt like it was in me, in my heart. I got caught up in its design like a spider web.

I took it all in. Everything. It was beautiful. I'd been all over Mexico, and India, and I had never seen anything as magical as this farm in the middle of Oregon on this night so many years ago. I noticed the wooly yarrow ground cover, shy at my feet. The trees were decorated in weather withstanding bird feeders, more Tibetan flags, and shiny metallic objects. People danced around a fire; I distinguished shadows of all ages.

And a child, a seated little girl, who's tiny hands looked like they were folding laundry over a djembe, slowed the beat down to a halt, and the hypnotic, deafening rhythm I had heard since we parked near the rusty tractor, fell silent.

The dancers stopped. The moon was low in the sky behind me, inches above my head. One by one, every man, woman, and child that had been dancing around the fire, walked up to me and welcomed me. Men's grips reached past my wrist to my forearm, and they lowered their heads below mine, maintaining eye contact. Most of the women reached both hands out before me, and I held them, but they didn't lower their heads, and I realized that I was supposed to. Their hands released themselves once I lowered my head, all the while maintaining eye contact. Some of the women shook like the men did. Children shook like we had closed a business deal. Quick, tight squeezes. They didn't value eye contact the same way, and they'd cluck and gawk as they ran back to the fire. The little girl found her drum again, flattening my thoughts with the sounds that filled the whole sky, and I tried to make sense of my first moments at The Farm.

Jimmy Eagle put his hand on my shoulder. He's a bit taller than I am. Everyone is. The drumbeat was loud. He didn't try to speak. But he gave me a look that must have meant, "I know you've been through some dog shit lately. Stay here and be human for a while. I'll take you back to Olympia when you're ready."

Senses dulled, I was caught a bit off guard. The largest man I had ever seen, a grizzly man, stood before me. A man they call Logjam. It was like a dump truck snuck up on me. His hands were far too large to shake. Fields of red hair spread across his knuckles.

Logjam was a myth of a man. The kids told stories of him, that he wandered off at night to teach bears how to wrestle Greco-Roman style, or that he was a Viking that wandered upon the Fountain of Youth. I don't know the true story behind Logjam. All I ever learned was that he was an army medic in Vietnam, was held prisoner in a POW camp for a year, and has lived on this farm ever since, rarely leaving. As an anthropologist, I needed to know more. This was unacceptable.

Ten years earlier, Jimmy Eagle was just a teenager at the time, and his truck started acting funny heading north on that road, that same long road that brought us here, so he pulled off to take a look under the hood. Miraculously, he pulled off at the exact spot of that deer trail they call a driveway. And, miraculously, Logjam, who almost never leaves The Farm, happened to be driving down the deer trail, and had to slam on his breaks not to hit Jimmy Eagle's truck.

Jimmy Eagle says they got acquainted real quick, realizing that their families knew each other, both having grown up in the area, and by the end of the day Jimmy Eagle was helping install solar panels on their roofs. Most of the projects around The Farm came about because of Jimmy Eagle. He built the straw bale homes, and the gardens, and he raised the wind turbine. Jimmy Eagle was like family to Logjam after that summer. So, when he learned he was meeting Jimmy Eagle's cousin, the usually stoic Zen Master that we know as Logjam launched into a hug that almost killed me.

I've asked. I say, *what's his real name?* People look at me strange, as if Logjam isn't a perfectly normal real name. I asked Jimmy Eagle, and he says, "What do you mean, *real name*?" I wanted to know, needed to know, *who is this man*? How is it that this enormous person, this man that you could only describe with hyperboles, how is it that he shares this spread of land so generously with anyone who stumbles upon his poorly marked deer trail? That's not how it works in the real world. The rest of the civilization lives by a different set of rules. How is it that children climb over him and giggle, yet he remains so still and calm? You would take his picture if you saw him in the street, just to prove how big he was.

I stayed a week. I should have stayed longer. If I was supposed to sober up at The Farm, I didn't. I found the liquor store in Olympia right where I left it.

Philip tried to explain string theory to me once, the missing link between quantum mechanics and general relativity. He explained that the small things, the elementary particles, they play by a different set of rules than the big things. He used this theory as a metaphor for civilization, comparing people to the small things, and organizations of people to the bigger things. I never fully wrapped my mind around it, but I think I knew where he was going. He liked remaining small, living by his own set of rules. He didn't want to belong to anything.

At The Farm, this was a collection of people acting very differently than any organization of people I had ever witnessed. Often, in the span of time that I knew Philip, I wondered what he'd think of The Farm. And when we were searching for him that warm day all through town, I imagined Philip's long and skinny body tangled up in a Logjam hug. Philip needed The Farm, and he needed to stay longer than a week.

This was years ago. Years before I met Philip and Kennedy. This was help. I needed help. And Jimmy Eagle helped me. He brought me to a place where others could help me. And we both knew, Jimmy Eagle and I, as we sat outside in the heat, and Jimmy Eagle rolled a cigarette, and I drank my black coffee, that Philip was not downtown, but that we *would* find him, and that he needed help. We knew where we would take him. And in the acuteness of my desperation, the thought of seeing Logjam again in his overalls dragged a smile across my face.

Spirit provides. Ray used to say that. It provides everything. It's much simpler than it sounds. The answers to every question. Clues and hints that we ignore, because we're not tuned in enough. It's a hornet's nest. A hailstorm. It's an old dirt road; a faded foot trail. It's a kid bringing his resume into a coffee shop, hair combed like he's never done it before.

I missed it. At first I missed it. Spirit provided, but I missed it. Jimmy Eagle rolled his cigarette thin like a Q-tip, and he said, "Think of all the places you've seen him, start all the way from the beginning." I missed it. I was distracted by the kid with the resume walking past us into the coffee shop. Sometimes we're too distracted by the answer to notice the answer. A skinny, awkward kid with a resume.

We spent the rest of that day and night just dragging along. My vision, my thoughts, all narrow. I was scared, and I'm not very smart when I'm scared. I didn't have much of a plan. *Find my friend, take him to The Farm.* That's not a plan. That's a hope. That's a wish. I didn't want to get the cops involved either. Neither of us did. My gut told me they wouldn't help, not the way we could.

We drove through Olympia all night. We'd stop for gas, ask strangers if they had seen a man we could only describe. Jimmy Eagle must have learned I wasn't listening to him. He got up out of the truck and grabbed the fuel pump from me, and said it again. "Think of all the places you've gone with him, start from the beginning, the very beginning."

It echoed inside my head. *The very beginning. The very beginning.* Memories of the day Frisbeed across my mind. *That pathetic looking college kid hoping to land a job at the coffee shop where Jimmy Eagle and I were sitting.* The sun reflected off my black coffee. The image rippled. I couldn't hold my coffee still. Not in my memory either.

I replayed that moment over and over. Jimmy Eagle waving his cigarette around. Nervous college kid walks by, holding his resume. Sun shining off my black coffee, weak hand trembling, rippled image.

If we're connected enough, if we're paying attention, there's always a sign. I was stuck on that image. College kid. Cigarette. Sun coffee. Looped, over and over. Each time the kid walked by, he became more and more Philip-like. Clothes started to hang off him like Philip's did. His hair got messier each time he passed; like a tumbleweed, the way Philip's hair looked until Kennedy told him to get a haircut. His scar slowly appeared, his ugly scar that looks like a small snake down his neck. Faint at first, but eventually, impossible to ignore.

The coffee slowly changed color, from crime black to a more industrial blue. The ripples slowed, came washing in as waves. The day Philip interviewed for the job, and we walked down to the beach. It had been gray and damp the whole time he was here, but for just a brief moment the clouds parted and the sun was shining off the water, as it was off my coffee cup earlier that day.

Jimmy Eagle's lit cigarette twirled around his fingers, looking more like a rope than a cigarette, and Jimmy Eagle looked more and more like some horned insect. That wouldn't make any sense until later. But, the spirit provides. It always does. There's always a sign, if you're willing to look for it.

When Jimmy Eagle tried to grab the fuel pump from me I didn't let go, and we both stood there pumping gas while I was working it all out in my head. I turned to him and said, "I know where he is, I know exactly where he is."

The spirit provides. The spirit that connects all of us. It had to have been 2 or 3 in the morning when we set foot on the trail without lights or a moon and anything more than a hunch. Jimmy Eagle must have had his doubts. I know I did. I'd wobble back in forth between the present and the memory of the interview, five years earlier, when we all walked down to this very beach. Philip had trimmed his tumbleweed, had slacks, a polo shirt, and a tie. He looked ridiculous. You don't wear a polo shirt and a tie. But that added to his intrigue. It astounded us that this astrophysicist from New York that couldn't dress himself wanted to work at Evergreen.

They asked him what he loved most about astrophysics, and he said he could explain why we are here. But when he explained why we are here, he really just explained how we got here, not *why* we are here. To him, that was the same thing, and he had so much energy to his voice, that the other members were convinced he had it all figured out.

But even then, back when we hired the oddity that is Philip Duke, I knew he'd always see the universe differently than I did. He explained how a star exploded, and there was disk, which had heavier elements, or something, and those became the planets, and all the stuff that you and I are made of, it's all traceable to that explosion. He had us all mesmerized. And that's all a beautiful explanation for how we ended up here. It doesn't begin to explain why.

I'm no scientist, not the way Philip is. I believe wholeheartedly in the Big Bang, and evolution, but I think there's more to it than we understand. Life is a spirit that exists on this planet, and it exists inside of all of us. We all share it. We are one. We are one spirit. Love of others is love of oneself, one greater self.

Love. Love is why we are here. We're here to love each other. And as I was sprinting down that path, bouncing back and forth between hallucinations and reality, burning fumes to stay awake, drinking gas station coffee in the middle of the night, I knew that I loved Philip like a brother. I never had a brother. But if I did, he'd be a lot like Philip. Brothers are two lines past their intersection. We come from the same place; we're not always heading in the same place. Philip believes in the science of all things, and I believe in the spirit of all things, and we both use them to reaffirm how precious life is. And that's why I was running so fast, not concerned with the roots sticking out of the ground, or the tree branches at eye level that I couldn't see, but I knew were there. Life is precious. Like the woman on the beach in Mexico told Ray, *we've got a lot to live for.*

And then we found him, right where we stood five years earlier and watched the clouds break, right where he told us all the reasons why Mars was his favorite planet. Reasons I've forgotten several times. Mars is boring.

We didn't see him at first, but instead we saw a girl twirling a rope on fire, standing knee deep in the water, dressed up like a horned insect. She had been spinning Jimmy Eagle's cigarette in my mind's eye. But not far from where she stood, above the tide, was a smoldering fire, and Philip sitting right next to it. He wasn't surprised to see us. He just looked at me and smiled.

It didn't take much convincing. It felt like we found our missing dog. We got back to the truck, squeezed in, and drove south. Before falling into a deep sleep, Philip said he forgot his bag down at the beach. I told him he probably didn't need it. He didn't put up much of a fight, didn't even ask where we were going. He looked at me, and he said, "I trust you." And then his head fell back, and he slept with his Adam's apple up in the air.

We drove south, and then east over the Oregon Cascades, along the river, up through the deer trail, parking next to the rusty tractor. It was morning, and the sun was already over the horizon. We were exhausted. I had never been that tired. Jimmy Eagle knew where to take him.

Everyone went to sleep except for me.

I had a stupid thought. A memory. When Stevie was visiting, she let slip that after the boys were born they lived in North Hollywood. I heard her, I heard her clearly. Kennedy heard her too, and she asked me about it once. I played dumb. I had to.

After Stevie said what she said, it spun around and around in my head. I caught a moment where she and I were alone, and I confronted her about it. I said, "What was all that back there about *the boys?* Did Philip have a brother? None of us had ever heard Philip talk about a brother."

She was embarrassed; she didn't realize what she said. She mentioned that she and Philip don't talk about it, haven't since he was a kid, but she told me the story about how Philip's twin brother died at the beach with their drunk dad, the same dad that took Philip to that Dodger game back in 1977. Then she asked me not to mention it, that Philip probably buried that memory so far that it was best forgotten. I can't say I agree with it, but I had to honor what she said. She was Philip's mom.

With Philip and Jimmy Eagle catching up on sleep in a hut somewhere on The Farm, I sat outside and let my mind race, and I decided we needed to go to Los Angeles, Venice Beach, and find Stevie, and see if we could get a few old pictures of Philip and his brother. If Philip was going to heal, he was going to need to confront the truth. Being back at The Farm gave me a strange feeling of invincibility, like I could do anything. So, I drew it out, I figured, we'll just go down to Los Angeles, find Stevie, get a few pictures, and come back to The Farm. Easy. Los Angeles. Stevie. Pictures. What a stupid thought.

From the start, this whole rescue mission was a satire of what a good plan would look like. Had I been thinking logically, all the way back to when I first came home from my cousin's wedding and went to visit Philip, expecting him to be rolling around on the couch, or a hyperactive polar opposite, I would have at least grabbed a picture of him, and planned and executed a better strategy for finding him. I wouldn't have driven around all day and night, wearing myself out. And when we did eventually arrive at The Farm, and Jimmy Eagle found a comfortable spot for us to sleep, I would have slept too.

Had I been thinking logically, we would have stayed a few days, enjoying the atmosphere at The Farm, making sure Philip was going to be all right. Instead, I woke Jimmy Eagle up, told him we had to go; we had to go quickly before I changed my mind. We had to get some road behind us before logic kicked in. I was racing against my better judgment. Jimmy Eagle never put up a fight. We left Philip a note, explaining where he was, telling him, "Hey, I've been here too. Stay as long as you need to. These people will take care of you."

Had I been thinking logically, when we got back off the deer trail, I would have turned right, north, back up to Olympia. Back up to Olympia to check on Kennedy, and help her get her life together. Surely she was headed back to New York or New Jersey, wherever she considered home. She would go back and try to find a teaching job. She'd be gone, and I'd never see her again.

But I wasn't thinking clearly, lack of sleep, I suppose. Just a few days of this, and my mind had lost its grip on reality. Philip had been suffering through months of insomnia, no wonder he fell apart.

We turned left off the deer trail, guessing the highway would eventually find Los Angeles. It probably did.

We arrived in Venice Beach the next morning. And that's when the nightmares began. I don't remember the drive. Not one bit of it. I know I drove, Jimmy Eagle confirmed that, but I don't remember a mile of it. I just know we ended up in Venice Beach.

I found a park near the beach, and I sat in the grass, and tried to collect and organize the details of the last few days. I put my head back, and looked up, and I closed my eyes. I lost track of it all. I forgot about Jimmy Eagle, and our illegally parked truck, and Stevie and her partner who I knew was Philip's old high school teacher. Philip didn't tell me that though. Stevie did. Philip doesn't tell us much.

The last thing I remember was feeling colder than I thought I would in Los Angeles in the summer, and a breeze rushed over me that smelled like seaweed. I was gone. My mind dematerialized. I floated away.

Deep inside my head I saw a crazy man. Grey and yellow hair all over his face.

Wide brimmed hat like a gold miner. Horrified teenage girl shackled inside a shack. Tattered clothes. Mouth cut, eyes swollen. He tells her to stay put or he'll find her family, he'll cut them. A crazy man. One too many Indian massacres along the Russian River, and not enough gold in his pan.

A sheriff stumbles upon them. A sheriff and his men, and a horn, and a few dogs, and some horses, all majestic and polished silver. And the cuts heal and the swelling recedes, and the girl, along with hundreds of other town folk watch the crazy man's lifeless body sway in the wind below a swing set made of wood, and they cheer. A public execution. It's in their minds. They cheer the man's death. His body sways in the breeze, a cool breeze, like the one that pushed against me while I slept in the grass near the beach in Los Angeles.

I saw their faces, young and old. A circus of faces, out of century, faces that have never seen a television screen. Limestone faces. Children, as young as they get, celebrating the death of the crazy man. The good guys killed a monster. They danced. And they all knew something, whether they said it or not, they couldn't wait until the next one. They wanted it to happen again. They prayed for a monster, so they could kill him. It was inside of them now. The violence was inside of them.

I woke up panting like a dog. A homeless man, and his panting dog, wobbled past me, pushing a grocery cart. The man wore a wide brimmed hat. Yellow stains in his beard. They stopped to look at me, I was boring to them, and they continued down the beach.

Where was I? I put the puzzle pieces back together, sort of. There were a few extra pieces left over. There always were. Jimmy Eagle was nowhere. I thought to look for him, but instead I peed under a tree, leaned against it, and felt my head start to break apart again. I had to sit down, and I sunk again, deep into more dreams. I wasn't awake; I wasn't asleep.

My mind was off again. I saw in different colors, and I moved quickly without thinking. Something small fluttered in the near distance, and then it was in my mouth. I crawled around. My skin was scaly. Hands and feet, short and quick below me. This wasn't thinking, this was reacting. This was instinct.

I felt a laser scan behind my neck. A uniformed man informed me of my violation, I was using my reptile brain. He took a vial out and injected the contents into my neck. It took no time. I was back on my feet. The landscape gained a dimension. The colors spread and thinned out. I could breathe, and I was thankful to the uniformed man. I compensated him. I knew to do this.

Strapped to my arm was a thin polyurethane bag that looked like a bladder, and it was filled with liquid metal. I uncoiled a hose and the uniformed man began to drink from it. And it didn't confuse me at all. I even asked him if he got enough. But then he started yanking on it, annoyingly. He was pulling on it, apologizing, but pulling on it roughly nonetheless. I couldn't get him to stop. I snapped out of my dream, and Jimmy Eagle was trying to drink from my Camelback, hoping not to wake me, apologizing.

"You didn't sleep at all did you, at The Farm? You didn't sleep. You're losing your mind a little. Stay here, I'm going to find Stevie and her 41 foot boat. Just rest, I got it. I'll come back and get you."

Jimmy Eagle has always been a pal. So loyal. Anything I've ever needed, he's been there. In my blur of consciousness, I asked him, "Eagle, why are you so loyal to me?" I'll never forget what he said.

Ray told everyone he knew before he died, to take care of his son, me. That's what family does. In a way, Jimmy Eagle was surprised I even asked. "Family, man. You're family. You're Ray's kid." That's all I needed to hear. I rolled back over on the ground into a fetal position, and left my mind again. Dreams. Visions from the past, present and future.

My visions continued all morning, exploring half theories about the past and future, about human nature, until finally, Jimmy Eagle returned with the news. He had found Stevie, and Dave, her husband. Or, he knew where to find them. So, I shook it all off, the last few days, the visions, and the exhaustion. In a way, it wasn't until we found Stevie, that I felt like it was all finally over.

Jimmy Eagle handed me a tall coffee, and he rolled a cigarette. I took a few puffs of it as well. The nicotine buzz helped bring me back down. And we followed the map he wrote on his arm down to the marina where Stevie and Dave lived.

Just a photograph, or two, to bring back to Philip. He needed it. I felt like he needed it. A photograph of him and his brother. If he was going to heal, he needed it. I keep some sacred photos in an envelope. He needed a photograph and an envelope too.

It wasn't too difficult to find the marina. The ocean acts as a great landmark. And Stevie and Dave's 41-foot sailboat was also easy to find. Dave was there, working on it, had a miter saw out and was cutting some fiber board. I could see Jimmy Eagle's wheels turning. The boat looked like it was under construction.

Jimmy Eagle didn't even introduce himself. He just walked up and started asking about the project. Dave was friendly and spoke as if they knew each other. I thought, *this must have been how it was with Logjam, the first time they met.* Within no time, Jimmy Eagle had a bucket and was staining some wood trim. *Is this for real, do people just walk up to each other and start helping them out with their home projects?* Neither man was fazed.

Finally, I interrupted and introduced ourselves, and explained that we were friends of Philip's and that we were searching for Stevie. He explained that she was helping Susie out today. *Susie?* Susie was a young woman that had been in a bad car accident, and once a week Stevie helped her get some errands done. She was confined to a wheelchair.

Then, before I knew it, I was also helping with the boat. I had a power drill in my hand and Dave was holding some boards in place while I drilled into them. I didn't know what we were doing, but I was helping, and because it was the home of Philip's mom, it felt right. It felt so right that I started to tear up. All I ever wanted to do was show Philip how grateful I was that he called me back five years ago when I had that bottle of whiskey on my desk, even if it was Kennedy's idea. The debt I owe Philip is infinite. Every time I try to pay it off, I'm no closer.

A few hours later, sun all over our faces, Stevie came home. She was pushing Susie, a beautiful young woman who could only use half her face. Susie liked to come sit on the boat.

I couldn't stop looking at Susie, how gorgeous she was, how gorgeous half of her face was. The other half fell motionless. We sat and spoke, and she told me she was a schoolteacher, was engaged to be married, and was hit by a drunk driver a few years back. It all went away. She couldn't teach, and her fiancé left her. Now, Stevie took her around town once a week, and it was all she had to look forward to.

Eventually Stevie and I had a moment alone. I told her everything. I told her about Philip, where he was, what happened. Everything. She cried. And she agreed, it was time Philip was at peace with his brother. She had an envelope already, filled with pictures of two little boys running around in the grass, sleeping next to each other, blowing out candles. "It's best he has this. Please, tell him I'm sorry. Tell him I'm sorry I let this happen."

With the envelope in my hand, there was nothing left to do but leave. A Farm in Oregon waited. But Jimmy Eagle, wearing a tool belt and running the operation on the boat as if it was his own, he shot me a look, and I knew exactly what it meant. He wasn't coming back with me. Stevie and Dave were planning a trip out across the Pacific, and they needed some help getting the boat in shape. And you don't let someone like Jimmy Eagle just disappear when you need help. The guy was born to help.

I'll be fine. I'll get back home somehow. I believed him.

I bid everyone farewell, Stevie, Dave, Jimmy Eagle, and Susie, who I had a feeling I'd see again. And I drove north. I had one place to go. North. To The Farm. It was time to give Philip a few photographs, and let him heal. Then, off to Olympia, and help Kennedy get her life together.

She needed to return home. Olympia wasn't her home. I had to go where I was needed. I could feel the pull at my waist. I knew where I was headed.

Now I had a plan. It was a good plan. But it didn't happen. The exit that would have taken me east over the mountains to The Farm, I saw it ahead, 3 miles, 2 miles, 1 mile ahead. And then, it was in my rearview mirror. I missed it, intentionally.

It wasn't time. Philip wasn't ready. He would be, eventually, but he wasn't yet. It had only been a few days since we dropped him off. He needed some time. He wasn't ready for these photographs. I could return in a month or two.

I got to Portland; I was tired. I had driven without stopping. The only sleep I had gotten was on the beach in Los Angeles, and it was more of a series of psychotic episodes than it was sleep.

I had an itch. It was a familiar itch. I ignored it. It would go away.

It didn't. It spread. I ignored it. I ignored it as best I could. Putting energy toward not thinking about something, that's like trying to disappear.

An hour later, I was sitting on the windowsill of a cheap hotel downtown with a bottle of whiskey. This hotel was perfect for what I knew I was going to do. The button on the elevator sparked when I touched it. This was where I was going to do it, where I was going to fall apart.

Philip was gone, and the bottle was back. I knew it. This was where I was going to give it all away. I couldn't go back to Olympia. That bridge, over the Columbia, out of Portland, I couldn't drive over it.

They say it can come back at anytime. It's in my blood, a fight I can't win. I hadn't been to a meeting in years. I thought I was cured. No, you're never cured. It's not something you cure. You treat it your whole life.

I looked out over downtown Portland, bottle of whiskey in my hands, opened, but not on my lips yet, and I wanted to throw it. I wanted it to hit a car, a fancy car. I wanted it out of my hands. I'd put the bottle down, pace around the room. The bottle would fuss.

I'd pick it back up.

I did this for an hour, two hours. I was only prolonging the inevitable. I knew where every ounce of that poison was going to end up, and I knew the monster that was going to drink it. Philip and his magical phone call wasn't going to save me.

Another memory. New York City. A long time ago. The first sip reminded me of New York. It reminded me of the libraries and museums that I used to speak at, back when I was doing a book tour for *Iridescence*. Tweed wearing professors with apologetic accents introducing me to only half familiar audiences.

The second sip reminded me of Port Authority. The subway. Trains flying by, yanking the ties out of business suits. Musicians so talented, you'd pay to see them, so you ought to.

The third sip a gulp, God I love whisky. It reminded me of a bar in Manhattan. Stairs fell from the street level down to a basement where I heard I could get a good, quiet drink. I asked a police officer who was directing traffic. He told me to step back, and then he smiled and gave me directions to *this bar*. It wasn't good or quiet, I get why he was smiling.

But I came back, day after day. I must have liked the atmosphere. And the day before I flew out, I left my book on the bar stool, slightly on purpose. Maybe I hoped I'd leave a little culture in that sports bar. I don't remember. I was in one of my functional alcoholic stages. I remember what I did; don't remember why I did it.

On my fourth sip, I put it all together. Everything that Kennedy had ever said about her dad's bar, even down to the young woman that came and wiped up my spilled beer.

On the fifth sip I pictured Kennedy taking the book home, jamming it into her crowded bookshelf. Philip had spoken about how it poked out, like it didn't really fit. She had so many books, so many books she didn't read.

By the sixth sip Manhattan was gone. It didn't exist. I had solved a mystery, but I didn't care. In fact, it was a bad sign. My sobriety came from a phone call, which came from a time when I wasn't sober. I left a book in a bar, Kennedy's boyfriend found it, called me up, and I got sober. Her boyfriend becomes her husband, he goes crazy, we leave him at a farm, and I ended up in a shitty hotel room in the middle of downtown Portland.

My seventh sip was a sip to forget, and I sat halfway cocked out of my hotel window, yelling anti-American obscenities at people. I was that guy. *Slaves built the Wall in Wall Street...* I was that guy.

This went on a few days. Bottle after bottle. Each bottle cost about as much as the room did. On the third day, the door knocked open. I don't know how else to word that. Someone knocked on the door, and it opened. It must not have been closed all the way. I was starting to sober up, was getting ready to walk across the street for another bottle. At this point the bottles were hiding from me like new pets, they wanted nothing to do with me. They knew they'd be half empty before we even reached my hotel room.

I was out of whiskey, my head felt like two street gangs having a knife fight. The door knocked open. There she was.

Not tall enough to wipe the dust from the corners of the picture frame, but old enough to notice it, and every other detail of the photograph. Curious enough to ask an endless amount of questions.

Who are they? *Those were your grandparents.*

Where was this picture? *At the beach.*

Which beach? *Westport. It's in Washington.*

Was I alive yet? *You were in my belly still, silly.*

Why did you take their picture? *I wanted one last picture of them together. I thought this might be my last chance.*

How did you know? *I just knew.*

Who's the woman in the corner with the mean face? *I don't know, she didn't seem to understand that I wanted her to move out of the way.*

Did you ask her? *I think so. I don't remember.*

The child often wondered who the woman was, if she was a nice person or a mean person, and what she would think if she knew she was immortalized in the corner of a photograph which hung in the living room of a typical family a thousand miles away.

Kennedy

"They're trying to tell us something we're not ready to hear."

Every crow I see reminds me of my mom. Maybe I'm not always conscious of it, but it happens. I see a crow, I see my mom. I may never know if my mom was a genius or a crazy person. I don't understand crows, and I really don't understand my mom. The older I get, the less sure I am of anything.

There was life after the incident, the incident I can't explain because I can't talk about the gun I can still see in Philip's mouth. For years, every night when I closed my eyes and I would have been, should have been sleeping, I'd see that gun in his mouth.

After the incident I'd lose many hours revisiting the nonsense my mom would say, crow talk, or the haunted buildings she knew about growing up in New Jersey. *Oh don't go in there, that building's haunted.* Or after I'd remind her not to leave her dirty dishes on the shelves, and she'd explain that there was *no sense making sense.*

There were times when I thought she was aware of the state her mind was in. She would joke like she was a witness to it. She would show glimpses of a more sane side, a side to her that we could reason with, but it would go away, reminding us that she was delusional, unreachable. I'd wonder if she even knew she was crazy.

Maybe it was ancient mother-daughter instinct, but in these hopeless months after the incident, I sought the words of my mom, tried to decode them, like hieroglyphics. I didn't know I could be that desperate.

Most mornings I stayed in bed, not sleeping, but not entirely awake either, just letting minutes pass until it was absolutely necessary that I got myself out of bed and off to work. I didn't have any other reason to get up, and even my job seemed less and less important.

I remember a morning lying in bed, annoyed at first by the sound of what I assumed had to be ninjas crawling around on my roof. Back then, I wasn't surprised by anything, I was too disengaged to ever feel any sort of panic or alarm, but I was annoyed. If there were ninjas on my roof, why'd they have to make so much noise?

One of the last things I'd do each morning before my drive to work was to go out to the deck and grab the dinner plates from the night before. I'd eat dinner outside, because a dinner table may be the loneliest place to find yourself, and then I'd lie in a hammock that Gilb had left a long time ago, a hammock I told him he'd never get back, something from one of his trips to Latin America.

I'd stare in the sky and if it was clear out, I'd notice the stars, they were all Philip's. He left them here, along with a lot of other stuff, papers, journals, and telescope things. I wondered if he looked up at the sky, and felt a little less joy, and maybe some remorse, some guilt. I can't picture the hippie farm down in the middle of Oregon that Jimmy and Gilb brought him to, and I couldn't say I agreed with it either, but I knew he was staring at the same stars. I think of the horrible thing he did when I see those stars.

After lying in Gilb's hammock, looking at Philip's stars, I'd leave the plates outside overnight because I learned that critters would come and clean them for me. When you're depressed, it feels normal to let the animal kingdom help you with your dishes.

On the morning I was invaded by roof ninjas, I went out to the deck, and didn't see any plates. I then remembered that I hadn't eaten outside that night, that I was probably too lethargic to even make dinner, and that the ninjas weren't ninjas, but were crows. They were deliberately making noise on my roof. They seemed to be communicating to me, that I had broken the pattern. They were not very happy about it.

These crows were benefiting from my laziness, my funk that I was in. At least *they* were. It made me smile, the sloppy kind of smile that felt like my face was going to spill. And I started leaving more and more of my food out for them each night, and I got better at smiling. I used to have a lovely smile. Smiling isn't like riding a bike, you *can* forget how.

But the crows were definitely telling me something. It's difficult to interrupt consistency without insult. Those scraps, the ends of sandwiches, pizza crust, apple cores, unwanted mac and cheese, those did not belong to me, they belonged to the crow ninjas. They were entitled to them. Once theirs, always theirs.

Life got weird before that day, the roof ninja day. If you would have asked me what day it was, I wouldn't have known. I had no way of knowing that I'd remember the date forever. It was just a morning, a Tuesday, I believe. A roof ninja Tuesday morning and I knew I had to be at work soon.

I knew that September 11 had something to do with Chile. Gilb used to talk about it. But now we had our own September 11. What an ugly word, September 11. Life got weird before that day.

September 11, 2001, where the skyline in my mind was rearranged. I showed up at work and all my co-workers were crying, and I didn't know why because I was unplugged from society, but I saw them crying on the sidewalk, smoking. We didn't have a television in the bar, so I walked over to the Mexican restaurant next door, where they had the news on a big screen in Spanish, but that didn't make a difference. I saw the planes hit the towers, those towers that I kept in my backyard. Manhattan was my backyard. I watched it over and over. The buildings would reassemble, only to be destroyed again. I kept hoping that the planes would eventually miss. I still don't know why the networks felt like burning that into my memory. You must have seen the same looped footage. You must have heard the same dramatic news breaking music that I did.

Life got so weird before the attacks on 9/11 that I may have even tried to get a hold of Powerman. His confidence and steadiness was overwhelming when I was a young adult, but I wondered if he cooled off a bit, if he mellowed out. I imagined he was successful. I wanted to call him, have him send me a jet, and fly me out of this place called Olympia, and out of this year called 2001, and I'd erase it all, one big eraser, I'd erase everything. I'd be shallow and narrow and fool myself into thinking that was good enough. Damn, I really just wanted to fool myself. I wanted to receive gifts at dinner tables on patios near rivieras.

But I couldn't find him. I probably didn't even look him up. I just hoped he'd find me. I'm glad he didn't. I would have jumped on the back of any horse out of that place.

Life got strange before the horrible attacks that forced my dad to sell his bar. Maybe it didn't force him to, but he lost a lot of friends that day. He didn't want to reopen. It wasn't a very long conversation. He just told me about Tim, his firefighter buddy who had his own stool at the bar for years. He told me there would be a funeral. I'd have to fly on a plane to go back to New York. The thought would have crippled me earlier in my life. But I had lost my fear.

You have to love things in order to fear them. I wasn't afraid anymore. Flying had been the most terrifying thought in my head for years, but when my dad told me he was closing the bar, and that Tim, whose daughters I used to babysit, had died in the attacks, I booked the next flight. I wasn't afraid of anything. I wasn't happy enough. I didn't even pick scabs or pluck chin hairs anymore.

No fear at all. Life got weird. I'd drive with my eyes closed. Sometimes for just a second. Sometimes longer. I'd push the limits. Sometimes I wouldn't look when I crossed the street, more curious than nervous about my own safety, unconscious of anyone else's. Life got weird.

I didn't have any answers, I still don't. But the attacks will always symbolize something very important to us, as we live on, here in the Catskills, where Gilb talks about his dad every time it hails, at the school we built, with the money we earned from the bar after my dad refused to reopen. He sold it quickly. He got a lot of money.

On the downside, the investors knew what they were doing; they basically bought my dad. They bought the idea of him, and opened several Yossi's all over New York and New Jersey. He hasn't set foot in that bar since the attacks on 9/11. I can't stand it. They made a cartoon out of my dad.

Life got weird before I flew back to New York, and I found myself sitting in a field with a pretty dress on. It was stormy. My dad sat next to me. It was a funeral, or a wake. I don't know the difference. I couldn't help it, I enjoyed the bagpipes.

It was a home video that someone took. Some New Yorker, who happened to have a camcorder, and turned and caught what was happening. A man we knew, I knew him as Tim, Firefighter Tim, I knew him and he knew me and now he's dead, and some anonymous voice said to him, "Hey, you can't go in there, you might die."

I've seen the footage several times, his wife and two middle school aged daughters, they felt it was important to show his last moments alive at his wake.

And I don't know how to put myself in his mindset at that moment. He went back in. He went into a place where others were trying to escape from. And he never came out. He had to have been thinking about his family, and that everyone in that building was someone's family. I don't think those first responders died because it was their job, I think they were just brave people who cared an awful lot about strangers. Only someone brave would go back in the way he did. Most people wouldn't do that. I was proud to be at that funeral.

Not everyone becomes a firefighter, which is why my dad held such respect for these people, and why he couldn't reopen the bar, and why he sold it and we now all live here in the Catskills at the outdoor school, with our welding equipment, and our goats, and our kinesthetic learning environment. Even my mom is here, in a cabin that Gilb's cousin built for her, and my dad is taking full advantage of his second chance to be a good husband. Even though she's crazy, even though she would embarrass me as a kid, and I worried that I'd become her, and that my dad would reject me too, even though she's a lot of work and we went against the doctor's orders, here she is. Here she is living comfortably, at the place I thought would only exist in my dreams, a place where inner city kids could come and get a useful education, in an environment that would have otherwise been unavailable to them. It was Gilb's idea, and I never admitted it. But it got weird before all this happened.

I went out to the beach one day, August-ish, it was a gray day. I didn't mean to do it. I missed the exit and kept driving, I didn't have the energy to turn around, I just kept going. I got to the coast and sat on the beach and stared at all the families, and I was sure I was going to grow old and do nothing with my life. I was sure this was it. I didn't see how I'd pull it back together. My life was a kite that flew way behind the gray clouds, once so colorful.

I wasn't even sad. I was just numb. A cute baby splashed around with her dad in water and I felt nothing. A woman finally snapped at me as she was trying to take a picture of her parents holding hands on the beach, and I wasn't moving out of the view, because my mind kept drifting away. I ignored her. I just wanted to sit where I was, undisturbed, left to wonder how I ended up on this beach, and why my husband lost his mind, and shoved a gun into his mouth, and how I was going to settle this whole marriage thing. Five years wasted.

The sand in my toes reminded me of something Philip told me once, that there are more stars in the universe than grains of sand on every beach, and I don't know how you could know that. I don't understand how anyone could know that. But he said it. And it never mattered to me. It wasn't even interesting. If that's true, those stars are so far away. Why would that matter to me? Things that are far away don't matter to me.

The clouds over the ocean got heavier, and the sky greyer, and it reminded me of a trip we took to the beach when I was a kid. I think about this experience from time to time, and, as most memories go, I don't know if I remember it completely as it happened, but this is what I see when I think back on that day. It was cloudy. It wasn't summer. It was cold. It felt spontaneous, like we just jumped in the car and no one said a word, and we were at the beach. If there were any other families there, I don't remember them. They didn't preserve well in my mind.

I remember a bathroom that looked like a bunker, and crows hovering over it, and a receptacle with trash spilling out over the rim. I had to go pee, but I held it in most of the day because the bathroom scared me. Inevitably, I had no choice, I was probably drinking Coke all morning, and I went to use the bathroom, but I was nervous. I don't know if it was the crows hovering, or the unattended trash receptacle, or the war bunker appearance of the building, but I was nervous.

I think the worst part of being a kid is that sometimes your fears come true, and when I walked into the cold, brick bathroom, I saw a monster. But, what surprised me is that I didn't go running, I actually went pee, and tip toed around him, and went quickly back to my parents on the beach towel, and the way I remember it, the beach towel really wanted to fly away.

I don't remember if I was scared, but for some reason, I didn't share what happened with my family, and I considered that when I was teaching, that kids don't always share everything with adults, so we don't always know everything that happens to them. We don't know about all their monsters.

I've lived a lot of my life with anxiety, just everyday anxiety. I'd get anxious on subways and having to call complete strangers to deal with a bill, things like that. They terrify me. Flying used to horrify me. Some of the safest, normal things scare me, yet I seem to keep my cool when I'm actually in danger.

The sky at the beach was so gray and so familiar. That's what five years in Olympia can do. It makes you familiar with the color gray, and reminds you of so many gray days.

Like the day we joined the protests up in Seattle. I sat on the beach alone, still ignoring the woman's plea to move out of the way, and the clouds reminded me of that day of the riots. They wouldn't admit it, but Gilb and Philip were scared. Rubber bullets screamed past us. It didn't bother me at all. I liked being there, in the chaos, and the danger. I think more clearly in those moments. I remember a man, so big, so enormous, huge muscles, tattoos everywhere, like out of a comic book. And he was just growling at the riot cops. He had a shirt on that said *Challenge Authority*, which he was doing a wonderful job of. I know Gilb and Philip saw him too, but I was pulled to him, I wanted to stand next to him, and growl and challenge authority with him. I can still remember how large his shoulders were, propped way up behind his neck, very intimidating. And the cops, covered in armor, they were puny. I wanted to team up with this guy. He looked nice too, like he knew Shakespeare. He was a different kind of Powerman, the silent, sensitive, rip your face off Powerman. You see millions of people throughout your life, weird how a stranger can inhabit your memory.

I wasn't sure why I was at the protests to begin with. I don't have too many strong political statements, and I love cops. But I got wrapped up in the scene, and the little white lengths of rope that the riot cops had dangling at their belts, I suppose for the purpose of tying us up, those enraged me. I would have stayed and taken a mouth full of pepper spray, and gotten tied up, and thrown in the back of a van. And they won't admit this, but really, Gilb and Philip got scared. They did. And I didn't. I wasn't scared. I'm never scared when I should be.

I challenged authority. Or, I was just being a grumpy bitch, and this nice lady was trying to take a picture of her old parents on a piece of driftwood and I wouldn't move. She was right, I was wrong.

I just sat there all day, nowhere to go, staring at the waves crashing in, thinking about different times in my life. Bad times, good times, strange times.

During all my memories, waves were crashing on this same beach. When the Yankees won the World Series back in the 70s, or when Philip and I first met, those were happy times, and I bet there were waves crashing on that beach. And I can remember this exact thought, I was thinking, *maybe if I ever get it together, there will still be waves crashing on this beach.* That's nothing, but it was a something similar to a positive thought, and I still wonder if I ruined the picture the pregnant woman was taking.

So we bought the property in the Catskills. I don't know how it happened. Someone knew someone, who knew someone. All of a sudden it was ours. And it was a mess. A lot of work. Gilb and his cousin Jimmy did most of it. Actually, Jimmy did all of it. I grew to love that strange man, born on a farm in Oregon and never had a social security number. He and his wife, they loved each other. Of course, I doubt they were legally married, but I remember when they showed up at the outdoor school, and Gilb was waiting with anticipation, and Jimmy showed up in a little truck with a woman in the passenger seat. Gilb was in shock. She was stuck in a wheelchair, and Jimmy just loved her. He loved her. I've never seen anyone love a woman like that, here at the outdoor school that we purchased after Tim the firefighter perished in the attacks of 9/11. They said, "Hey, you can't go in there, you could die." And even though he had two daughters at home, he actually looked straight at the camera, before going back in to try save people, where there were a lot of sons and daughters who needed help, right before he went back in there, before he died, he turned to the bystander with the camcorder, maybe knowing that he was saying goodbye, knowing that the footage would reach his family, he turned and said, "I know, but I'm needed."

It's too bad I needed so much help. It's too bad. I had big dreams. Day to day, I don't do as well. I can remember my teenage years, and teaching at the school in the city, and my five years in Olympia, but I don't remember yesterday too well. I had a lot of dreams. So much that I wanted to do.

But it got weird before that day, before 9/11. After Gilb dropped Philip off at the farm, he ended up in a hotel in Oregon. It was more like a pit. He fell into a pit.

I got a phone call in the middle of the night, had to have been about 3 or 4 in the morning, and it was Gilb, talking about some American monster destroying the environment, then he started singing Bob Dylan's *The Times They Are a-Changin'*. It took me forty minutes to get his location out of him, two hours to drive to Portland, and another hour to actually find the hotel. It looked like an abandoned apartment complex. I checked the address several times, the strange people who were breezing around early in the morning looked at me oddly when I gave them the name of the hotel I was looking for. There were newspapers floating, and people floating, and rags everywhere. That's how I remember it.

I showed up, opened the door to his hotel, and he was surprised to see me. Mortified. He had no idea he called me.

I had never known Gilb to drink alcohol. He had said once that he used to have a problem, so he stayed away from it, but he'd come in the bar and order a cider. It never seemed to be an issue. It was sleeping, deep down inside of him, that's what he says. He thought he had cured himself, that his problem was in the past. He tells me now, *that's not how it works.* You don't cure an addiction, you treat it, and then you die.

That makes me sad for him. Gilb lives for others. He didn't ask to be an alcoholic. It chose him. He reminds me often that he'll be an alcoholic the rest of his life, and then he hops on a bus and heads to town and attends a meeting. And students ask where he's going, and he tells them, he says, "I'm an alcoholic, I'm heading to my meeting." He says it with such pride, and now I understand why. He's proud that he seeks help, and he wants the kids to know it's okay to get help. He's been sober several years, but that demon inside of him could come back anytime, so he hits a meeting once a week. He takes a bus into town and he's not shy about telling everyone where he's off to. I think he sets a good example. A lot of people are afraid to get help.

There's a sign not many people can see, when it's almost too late, that my mom told me about, when she used to live in the Bay Area when she was young, when she was married to her first husband. If you climb up on the railing on the Golden Gate Bridge, there's a sign placed in a dangerous spot that pleads with you not to end your life. But some people don't get help. So, I'm proud of Gilb. He's proud of himself.

Before he moved to the United States, my dad was in the Israeli Army, and he was stationed at a prison, where the prisoners used to rig up tattoo machines. They'd melt the heels of their shoes, mix it with their urine. They'd use wires and guitar strings. This isn't something you do unless you're mechanical. Imagine the job potential of a guy who can rig up a tattoo machine in prison. He told me, bad people are just as smart, sometimes smarter. When the hijackers flew those planes into the towers, I thought about what he told me, about those prisoners in Israel. There's a lot of bad people doing very intelligent things.

When he told me he was selling the bar, I knew exactly what we'd do with the money. It was a lot of money. The bar was worth a lot. I wanted to reach those smart kids, before the world turned its back on them.

Back when I was staring at dust particles, suspended in sunlight, creeping in through a dirty window, remembering how Philip had told me that a speck of dust is halfway between the size of an atom and the size of the Earth, remembering that Philip was a genius who had lost his mind and stuck a gun in his mouth, I would have never thought we'd end up here, at the outdoor school. But life got weird, and I needed help.

Even my lawyer brother, out in California, my half brother who I never talked to, even he helped us out with some of the legalities. He was born out in California, when my mom lived out there. I sometimes wonder how my mom knew about the signs on the bridge.

I never saw Philip again. Gilb helped me get the paperwork signed. We all know what became of Philip. I wish I could be happier for him. But I'm happy enough for myself, and the hundreds of students we've had come through here over the years, with the grants that my brother helped secure for us. I don't really understand any of that. Legal talk. Legal stuff.

I take the kids out to the river and read Shakespeare with them, and I giggle because Philip once told me that most of the moons of Uranus are named after characters in Shakespeare's plays. There's actually a joke that I don't totally remember, something about Uranus, and the King of England. Uranus used to be named after an English king.

And every time that Gilb sees a hornet, or anything that looks like a hornet, he tells me an exaggerated story about when he was searching for a place to spread his mom's ashes, rest her soul. He doesn't think I listen but I do. I listen to his stories, and he enhances them every time he tells them. Gilb's a storyteller. Which is a nice way of saying that he's full of shit.

I may never forget when I opened the door to that horrible, disgusting hotel in Portland. It was basically a brothel. I'll never forget the look on Gilb's face. Everything had come undone. Philip meant a lot to him. He meant a lot to me too. I don't know that I ever saw him for who he was, but instead how he fit into my life. The men in my life are all very different. Powerman had hair with horsepower. It was slick and strong and got the job done. Philip had hair like a tumbleweed, and I had to convince him to cut or it would balloon out. I loved Philip. But Gilb got to know him. I loved what Philip was to me.

Gilb just loved Philip.

Sadly, we both fell apart after Philip went to go live on a farm.

On the last day that I worked at the tavern, two of my favorite customers came in to say goodbye. None of my coworkers cared, but the customers did. A few of them at least.

Don Mackenzie, from Canada. He always said he was Canada. Some tiny town called Coombs, where people keep their goats on the roof. He'd tell me if I ever got myself in trouble up there, to call a Mackenzie, and I'd laugh trying to picture what that would look like, to put Don's offer to the test. But I never made it up to Canada. I don't even know where Coombs is. I just know that Don would come in, order a beer, barely sip at it, and make small, tiny talk all night. It would bother me at first, and other servers didn't want to deal with him. But I grew to appreciate Don. Never complained about anything, always in a good mood. Yeah, he'd find ways to keep the conversation going, and I guess that's what you do when you're lonely and most of your life is behind you.

But I noticed something he did once. He was a gentleman. He was talking about his time up in the Canadian tundra, when he was a pilot, and he was carrying explosives, something called tetranitrate. I don't know how I remember that detail. But he was talking about how stressful it was to fly with this stuff, and the little villages needed it. Apparently the hunters needed it. When Don had something to talk about, he was an animated storyteller. But he noticed that I was uncomfortable with the story, the explosives, the hunting, the small bush planes, all of it, and he made a smooth transition out of the story, despite the audience that he craved, and all the attention. And I appreciated that he did that, and I thought he was a gentleman for noticing. It wasn't like

I could get up and leave the bar. I was working at it. He was my friend after that.

Don used to like to sit next to another character, Jefferson. Everyone knows Jefferson. Mr. Olympia, Washington. Gilb knew him. Philip knew him. I knew him. He would teach laughter yoga up at the community center, or sometimes at the park for free. He liked making people laugh. He was like a medicine man. My favorite two customers. Don and Jefferson would sip at their beers, hardly ever order anything else, tip poorly, and basically take up good space at the bar. But guys like Don and Jefferson, they were the history of this tavern, before the well-dressed lawyers and politicians started coming in. So I appreciated them, and I missed them when I left.

They came in on my last day, and I told them about the plan we had, opening up the school, and that Gilb was heading out there with me. And Olympia has been in my rearview mirror since. I quietly left. Gilb and I drove off early in the morning, before the city was awake, and it was creepy how quietly we left. And when we crossed the Mississippi, I decided, the west coast isn't for me. I won't return.

But here we are in the Catskills, with Jimmy's wonderful woman and her face that only half works. I can never remember her name. She's been here for years.

My life means something. When I was on the beach, and I was reminiscing about protests and bathroom monsters, and I wouldn't get out of the way when the pregnant woman was trying to take a picture, and I was watching the families play and I didn't think the baby was cute, I would have never guessed my life would turn around and be so meaningful. We're doing something important here. I needed a lot of help though.

This is important. For every student who lost faith in the system and ended up in jail, for all the misguided intelligence, for all the drug dealers that could have easily been

CEOs, we're doing something here at the outdoor school. We have welding equipment. Every kid can harness up and take a bow saw and trim the trees on the property. They can all milk a goat. They can all score glass, solder copper pipes, and recite Shakespeare. Van Gogh matters here. We have solar power, wind power; the students can fix and install all the equipment. Jimmy taught them how. Jimmy can hardly read.

Me, Gilb, Jimmy, Jimmy's woman, my mom and dad, we're all here. Even Reggie, my old dog. He lived for a few years here. Every kid spoiled that dog. He had a heart attack. We should have told them not to feed the dog.

Gilb keeps a stack of Philip's books, and always takes one with him when he rides the bus into town to go to his AA meeting.

My dad observes Jewish holidays. Gilb notices, fond and curious.

It's unfortunate that I need so much help. Gilb takes good care of me. But I don't think about the room anymore where everyone hates me. I don't feel short. I'm not feisty anymore. I joined a book club full of teenagers and I read a lot of young adult literature. A lot of Gary Paulsen.

We have a good school. I don't think anyone hates being here.

Mr. Leahy

I am as old as the summer of 1902. I was born on a farm in Oregon that had been in my family since before the Civil War. Less than five generations of men separate myself and a man who helped administer rattlesnake remedy to a Shoshone woman named Sacagawea during her painful labor. His name, from start to finish, is the same as mine. I am the first born male in a line of first born males who share the same name.

But none of that matters. What matters to me are the relationships I've experienced in my life. What I've learned and what I've shared. Most of what I have at this age is a memory of an experience shared with others. People are important to me, even if I don't know what ever happened to them.

When Philip moved on to college, I poured myself a glass of whisky, not a lot of ice, and I had a good cry. I hadn't seen much of the boy in years, and every time I saw him he was an inch taller. And then Stevie came by one morning, I asked about Philip, how he was doing. She told me he hopped on a bus and was on his way back east to study at a major university. That he was going to be a scientist.

Thirteen years this family had lived in the apartment complex. I saw this little boy grow up. You couldn't slow him down. Watching this boy grow up, having a hand in it, having an influence on his life, there's nothing I'm more proud of. Nothing I've enjoyed more. And then he was gone.

He hadn't been a boy in a long time. When I'd see him, as a teenager, helping his mom with groceries, I'd still see the boy who thought I was Santa Claus, who would park himself in the storage unit where I kept my tools and ask every imaginable question about every tool, whose face would light up every time I let him make a cut, or turn a wrench.

I never had any kids. So, this was special to me, and after he grew up and he was gone, I replayed all the memories, and I thanked God for the opportunity to be in that boy's life.

It was all dumb luck. I had an unlikely ally. This was so many years ago. The church had turned against me. They told me I was invited to a meeting, not just any meeting, but a meeting about me, about whether someone like me could be a member of their church. So I came. I figured I ought to have a say in it too.

The congregation got together, talked about me as if I wasn't there, and decided that because of my lifestyle, I ought to stay away. I left quietly after the meeting, I went home, and I prayed. I prayed for them. My faith has always been strong.

But I had an unlikely ally. A man I knew as Hal, a stoic man that looked as mean as they come, he walked into the my shop down in North Hollywood and said if I ever wanted to come back to church, that he'd walk through the door with me, and that if anyone had a problem with it, they could come talk to him.

I was shocked. I never took him up on it, but I was so touched by it, that months later when his stepdaughter needed a place to stay, I told him she ought to come talk to me, we'd keep the rent where she could reach it. And that was how Stevie and her boy came into my life.

Hal and I remained friends. He would come into the shop, make small talk. I don't know that he ever bought a thing. He could be a bit of a grump. That never meant he was a bad guy.

But once he stayed longer than usual, and he pulled up a chair, and told me a story. It explained a lot to me. It helped make sense of how this bull faced, drill sergeant kept a soft spot in his heart for an old man like me.

Hal

I always knew my daughter was different. She had no interest in makeup or dolls. I chalked it up to her never having a mom. My wife died when Anne was just a baby. And I didn't know a thing about raising girls.

The most difficult day in my life wasn't July 30, 1945, when my ship was torpedoed and I spent the next two nights floating in the Pacific, dodging sharks. I couldn't bend my legs when I finally got on deck. My throat was swollen and I couldn't swallow, and my skin is still scarred from the sun we couldn't hide from.

The most difficult day wasn't the day my wife died in a cold hospital bed after mysteriously coming down with a fever, sending me home to begin my life without her, never finding peace in knowing what actually happened. I left that night wondering how I was going to raise this girl up to be a woman on my own, how I was going to feed her and buy her new clothes and help her get her schoolwork done. But we made it through.

The hardest day of my life was the day Anne, my only daughter, packed a couple of sandwiches and picked me up and took me on a drive through the hills in her pickup truck. When she was just a kid, I'd pick her up from school with a couple of sandwiches in that same pickup, and we'd drive all through the Santa Monica mountains, admiring the views. That was something we did. For no reason at all, we did it just to be with each other.

Only this time, she came to tell me something big, something important to her. For most parents, this would have been a beautiful day, a day to remember.

She handed me a sandwich and said that she met someone, someone important that she loved very much, someone that she wanted to spend the rest of her life with.

She came to ask me for my blessing.

And I didn't give it to her. And I sure as hell didn't eat my sandwich. I felt sorry for myself. I asked God, why this? He already took my wife away. Why this?

I can't take back what I said that day. I live with regret. Every day. Not a day goes by when I don't try to redo it, when I don't put myself back in that truck, and tell her I love her, no matter who she is. I give her my blessing, and I tell her how proud I am of her. I take a big bite of my sandwich, and I thank God for the beautiful daughter He blessed me with. That's how I should have acted.

I'll live the rest of my life having to remember how I failed my daughter at that moment.

My memories of floating in the Pacific are peaceful and playful in comparison to this day. Like a rafting trip. Like a fun rafting trip with friends.

We made our peace, but I'll never get back those years. And if she's forgiven me, that makes one of us.

Usually well mannered, usually very even-tempered, that's what people would say about the kid. He'd laugh and smile unprompted. People liked being around him.

His dad got him a job driving the delivery van right after high school because he was familiar with the routes, having grown up on a farm in the area, and because he was such a likeable kid the manager handed him the job.

He knew that stretch of highway. He had never lived too far off it. So, he couldn't figure out why the beat up Volvo ahead of him kept slowing down every few miles, almost to a halt, with the turning signal on. There was nowhere to turn for miles. He knew that, everyone knew that. After so many miles of this unexplainable driving, he figured the driver of the Volvo was trying to mess with him. He lost his cool and started honking. His delivery van, carrying close to 5,000 pounds of cargo at the time, was unfriendly to sudden stops, and the stress started to mount.

But as he honked, he realized that the Volvo actually was turning, and to his amazement, there was in fact a tiny dirt path, just barely wide enough for the width of the axle. The Volvo hit the gas hard and flew up and over the dirt road and was gone.

His whole life he had ridden this highway and had never seen that path. He felt guilty for honking, and wished his delivery van was thin enough so he could follow the driver of the Volvo and apologize.

Gilb

Spirit provides. Spirit takes away, too. I don't claim to know how the universe works. Maybe so many billions of things happen on a daily basis, that, if we're paying attention, a few of them look like miracles, and a few of them might lead us to be believe we're cursed, or that God has a bad sense of humor.

Kennedy had a dream to build a school in the woods, a place where kids could meet their potentials, kids who couldn't learn in a traditional classroom environment, or kids whose home environments were too disruptive. She used to talk about her time teaching in New York City, watching all these intelligent kids lose faith in the process of education, and get caught up in the street life. So this was her dream. And it came true. It somehow came true.

Everything aligned. The tragic events of September 11 caused Kennedy's dad to sell his bar, which made him a very wealthy man the second he signed his name. That money allowed Kennedy to buy the land.

Ironically, there were tragic events of September 11, 1973, the Chilean coup d'état, which was why my Chilean friends were travelling through town, and I met them during a hailstorm at a gas station. That inspired me to finally get up off my ass and finish the book. Then I went on a lecture tour on the east coast, New York in particular. While in New York, I purposely left a copy of my book at Yossi's bar, the bar that the cop sent me to when I interrupted him while he was directing traffic. Just that guy, that cop, directing traffic, if I hadn't interrupted him, and asked him where I could find a quiet bar to get a drink, and if he hadn't, in a moment of well aimed humor, directed me to a very loud bar, Yossi's sports bar, then my book would have never ended up in Kennedy's book shelf, and in Philip's hands. Philip would have never called me, and I would have drunk the bottle of whisky. And I would have drunk myself away.

I don't claim to understand how the universe works, I just try to make as many connections as I can, and keep my mind open. It's hard for me to feel like this all just happened by chance. Everything Kennedy wanted, it all happened, but the thing about Kennedy, is that tragedy seems to follow her everywhere. At the table where her dreams come true, there's always a seat reserved for tragedy.

This was all Kennedy's vision. What a beautiful thing. And I find it horribly ironic that by the time we rebuilt the classrooms and cabins and redesigned the entire campus, and by the time Jimmy Eagle arrived and lent his magical hand to making this all come together, and by the time I got my certification to teach, which was Kennedy's suggestion, and by the time her brother, who I didn't even know existed, appeared out of nowhere and started securing funding for us to provide scholarships for all the students, and by the time we thinned out the thousands of applicants and filled our staff, by that time, Kennedy was no longer mentally fit to participate.

Sure, she reads to the kids down at the river, and she helps them with their art projects, and she takes care of the farm animals, but it appears that with a strange twist of fate, she would follow the same footsteps of her late mother, and succumb to the same mental illness. And I don't think that's very fair.

On most nights, Jimmy Eagle walks Susie down to the river and they sit and enjoy each other. I don't know what they say to each other, but they laugh. They are at great peace. Jimmy Eagle agreed to stay here in the Catskills with us and look after maintenance, and he and Susie made a nice home in one of the cabins near the garden that Susie helps looks after.

Jimmy Eagle needed to settle down, and he doesn't exactly have a social security number. I don't think that the government even knows he exists. He was born at home and schooled at home. All my cousins are like that. They don't open bank accounts; they don't have any official documents or pieces of identification. They just exist. And now he exists here, and I like that. I like having him here. I'm not sure what else he was going to do with his life. He needed this place as much as this place needed him. He needed to stop and stay put and love someone.

Susie has a toughness to her, like the student I remember back in Olympia so many years ago. She'd be sitting in a wheelchair, right next to you, having a conversation, and you'd forget she was unable to walk, that she was confined to a wheelchair at all. Jimmy Eagle loves to help others, but I don't think that's why he loves this woman.

From time to time I get a postcard from Stevie, Philip's mom. She and Dave set sail eventually, not as soon as they hoped, but they did it. A postcard arrived from New Zealand, and Stevie, doing the best she could in her own reserved way, thanked me for being a good friend to Philip, and thanked Jimmy Eagle for helping with the boat. We all need a Jimmy Eagle once in awhile.

I'll always remember the look she gave me when I asked her for the photographs to give to Philip. It was the look of a mom that loved her son, but never really knew how to help him. She had done everything she could her whole life for Philip, worked jobs that no one else wanted, but she couldn't replace what had been lost. When she handed me the envelope, filled with pictures of Philip and Joshua, she had a look of trust on her face. It validated me. That whole experience was like a rollercoaster, and I was losing my grip on reality. Driving all the way down to California was impulsive and ill advised, but we did it, and that look she gave me, I can still see it. It meant something more than I can describe.

Stevie is very featureless, almost peasant looking. She's very plain and reserved, and doesn't express herself with facial movements. But she has a deep heart. I saw pain and joy and hope and regret. And she trusted me. She could see that I was simply trying to help my friend. At that moment, I needed a sign that I was doing something right.

But, inevitably, it all came undone, as much of what was holding it together was now missing. I didn't go to The Farm, not then. I landed in that sleazy hotel. If I had found a sleazier one, I would have stayed in it.

In my drunken frenzy, I apparently called Kennedy and ran my mouth for a while. Hours later she opened the door, and I can only guess at just how disgusted she must have been. I'll never know why I chose that moment to relapse, I don't have a good enough grip on it, which is why I take the bus once a week into town and catch a meeting, still to this day I do this. I always bring one of Philip's books with me. His energy has always helped keep me stronger than my addiction. Philip and I have that thing in common. We have lost a lot because of alcohol abuse.

I have been playing catch up since I was ten years old. Ray died slightly before my tenth birthday, and I've never gotten back what I once had. That was a family we had. When Ray died, a part of my mom died too. Moving in with my grandparents in Seattle, with their traditional Jewish customs, that was helpful, and I'm grateful, but it was never quite the same. And I've been searching ever since then for my family.

I don't feel like I'm missing anything anymore. I teach history on a spread of land out in the woods to some wonderful children. I've got Jimmy Eagle five feet away and I haven't fixed a single light bulb since he showed up.

This is what I know. You can't bury a tire. Impossible. Ray tried once. You can't waste your life away on a beach in Mexico either. An old woman will get you every time. Show you how dumb you look. The color orange. Crowded buses in India, hair in my food. One single strand, a foot long. Hailstorms. Chilean refugees. And now the Catskills. We find hornet's nests everywhere we look. I don't even think about

Aishwarya. I try not to think about whisky. I visit with my parents, my mom and Ray, daily, with a candle, some saffron incense. I've got a banjo I can't play either, although I've never let a Komodo dragon sneak up on me while doing Yoga. I've got all ten fingers. Ray, my dad, was missing a few.

I have a fondness for Kennedy's dad, Yossi. He's just a goofy man who, after selling off the bar, found his inner Jewish, and keeps pictures of his late wife, who he abandoned, all over his cabin. He wishes he had been a better husband to Kennedy's mom. He got too caught up in his business. It was healthy, she wasn't. But he's quick and he's funny. I've always liked him. Even way back during the book tour, I liked him. Otherwise I wouldn't have stuck around his loud sports bar. He's magnetic.

But every magnet pushes away as much as it attracts. He didn't stick around for Kennedy's mom, and now that Kennedy is heading down that road, I wonder how much he'd take care of her if I weren't here to do it. But I am here. I'm going nowhere.

Kennedy and I take long walks through the woods at night. Sometimes I think she's still got it, she'll be sharp and observant, she'll analyze something poetically, but then she talks about her mom like she's still alive, and she unwraps hours of rambling stories about crows and a guy she calls Powerman, who she thinks lives in Europe now. She seems to remember things that happened ten years ago perfectly clear, but can't remember what she was doing ten minutes ago. She could fool you, you could sit down with her and you'd think she was pretty sharp, but she's getting worse. I would know.

She leans on me a lot. I don't mind. I like looking after her. We'd have none of this without her. This was her vision. None of us would have any of this without her.

We never talk about Philip, but he's with me, always. I hold out hope that our paths will cross again. Philip tried to describe entangled particles to me once. Some strange phenomenon of quantum mechanics. All I remember was that he said these two particles will react to each other even if they are light years away, and that even Einstein was baffled by this. I like to think that Philip and I are like that, like those entangled particles. I can feel his happiness.

I finally did drive back down to The Farm, and I had him sign some papers for Kennedy, to get her out of the marriage, and I brought him the rest of his telescopes, too. It's strange what I remember from that day. A delivery truck almost killed us as we turned onto the thin little deer trail on our way to The Farm. And I remember all the children playing, new faces that I had never seen before. But I forget most of what Philip and I talked about. And I can't remember if he even asked about Kennedy, how she was doing. My gut feeling is that we avoided that topic altogether.

Before I left, I handed him the envelope. I had rehearsed, over and over, how I was going to do this, what I was going to say. But when it came time to do it, I just handed it to him. And I said nothing.

He opened the envelope, possibly assuming it was more legal paperwork, and I was frozen, knowing that I was about to witness the alteration of a man's reality. I could tell he was surprised to find photographs in his hands, having no clue what the envelope contained before opening it. But he didn't outwardly express what he was thinking or feeling. He stared at each photograph, and maybe a few minutes went by, and then we hugged and I left. Kennedy was in the car, parked all the way back near the rusty tractor, and we were on our way across the country, so I felt the pull, and I left. And I still have no sense of what that experience was like for him, to see those photos. We've never spoken about it. Whatever happened, I was not a witness to it.

Still, I have faith that it was the right move. That look that Stevie gave me, I rely on that often. That look of trust she gave me, I picture that often.

Ray still makes it hail. Not like he did back in the Rockies, but we still get hailstorms. And every time I hear that sound on the roof I'm reminded of the magic we all have. If a ten year old remembers a hornet attack as a good memory, then you're magic. Ray and my mom are with me here at the outdoor school. Maybe that's what Kennedy means when she talks about her mom like she's alive.

Philip

I felt like a buried tire. I didn't realize yet how impossible it would be to bury me.

My bed was like a treadmill; I'd roll over and over, going nowhere. When I wasn't resting, I was restless. When I wasn't thinking, I was thinking too much.

Next to the bed was a nightstand, completely flush. I'd wake up, roll over, and notice little flakes of dust at eye level. Or a spider, less than six inches away from my face, which I fought the initial reaction to swat at. I've killed an infinite number of spiders in my life, without thought, just doing my part as a member of the animal kingdom, keeping the size and population of arachnids from overtaking us, only delaying their inevitable conquer of this planet. It wasn't until the dinosaurs went extinct that our ancestors had the freedom to bolt in every evolutionary direction. So, what is inevitable is inevitable, but each species needs to wait its turn. This fortunate spider, since I knew it was harmless, I let it live, and I lost track of it. It left its station.

Eventually, it was the surface of the nightstand that caught my attention, not the spider crawling around on it. This is where my alarm clock would go. Mr. Leahy's alarm clock, it's been everywhere with me, in every one of my homes since I was a kid. The nightstand looked odd without it. That spot, where the spider was mapping out its trap line, it was missing an alarm clock. It reminded me I wasn't home. At least not yet.

Sure, it was an ugly alarm clock. It was an old, out of date ugly alarm clock from the 70s. But I missed it. Mr. Leahy had given it to me. It didn't survive the rescue mission. I must have left it on the beach when Gilb and Jimmy grabbed me and brought me down to The Farm. I'll never know what happened to it. Whoever found it would have no idea how much sentimental value it had for me, and might discard it as trash.

I had negative associations with the little duct tape experiment on my floor back in our apartment when I was a kid. I'm sure it would have been a successful operation, but it reminded me too much of my birthday, and waking up earlier than I had planned on, and going to community pools and Dodger games and hospitals. So, when Mr. Leahy gave me that alarm clock, I placed a kind of symbolic importance on it. It was a way to advance myself past the events of that day.

But besides the clock's value as an artifact from a person I admired, it kept my interest as a statement about society. Functional and modern are two unrelated things, and make very different statements. The alarm clock was fairly modern when Mr. Leahy gave it to me, and it still worked up until the day I unplugged it and evacuated my own home after staging what had to have looked like a suicide attempt in bed with Kennedy. But it looked so out of place in this century, and everyone that came into contact with it would ask why I still had it.

Two reasons: It still worked. There was no need to improve on it; it woke me up. The paneled numbers still glowed at night. And then, of course, Mr. Leahy gave it to me. I just simply had to keep it. It went to New York, Alaska, and Olympia with me. And then I lost it. And I wonder how many people have ever *lost* an alarm clock.

That alarm clock may have been the only thing I ever lost that Mr. Leahy gave me. I never lost my ingenuity. I never lost my thirst for knowledge. These are comforting thoughts, but I'd still like to have that alarm clock back.

After Gilb and Jimmy dropped me off at The Farm, it took several days to gather myself and actually come to terms with where I was. At first it was just a round, orange, fabric place, where a woman would arrive throughout the day with fruit and tea, and kind sounds. I slept entire days away, waking up at weird hours and staring at spiders and invisible alarm clocks. I wasn't yet interested in dealing with reality. I was indifferent to it.

Eventually, the sleep and the nutrition fused the working parts of my brain back together, and I had to deal with the issues that reality had presented. I couldn't keep turning it away. And this wasn't enjoyable. An unfortunate part of my healing was the clarity through which I could view just how ugly I was. I had work to do, heavy lifting.

Like flies, or hornets, if Gilb was telling the story, several people in my life were buzzing around me, little memories and images of people I cared about, important people, some I knew well, some I just admired, some I feared.

I needed to sort it all out. I needed to locate where I stood with them. Unfinished business. Double knots and bottle caps that needed tightening. Just some unfinished, necessary dirty work.

I could hear new life outside, between the drums, the people dancing, laughing. New people with names I didn't know yet, kids that I'd want to teach all about Mars. I could smell food. I knew that important events were ahead of me, here at the place that I'd come to know as The Farm. I knew that something new was about to begin, but I was stuck in the primordial stage.

So, one by one, I'd visit with these buzzing images, have dialog, and when I felt like I had double knotted it, and tightened the cap, I'd move on. I was the only person in that orange, round room, but I had company, and it was helpful. Hurtful, but helpful. It had been a rough 5 or 6 months, and this was a way to check inventory before I moved on.

My mom. Stevie. I pictured her. She materialized from the circulating buzz, and she sat in the corner of the round room, something only she could do, and we quietly shared space. This is how we spoke, this how we've always spoken.

I see my mom so infrequently that I never get used to her face. Some might say she's featureless, but I think her face looks like survival. She used to clean hotel rooms, the kind of rooms most people wouldn't want to stay in; she cleaned those up. That couldn't have been rewarding. She didn't see a clean hotel room. She saw a paycheck, a winter coat, a bag of groceries, a rent check delivered on time, most of the time.

There's a sort of cosmic justice, when you consider what she's been through, and where she is now. With Dave, my old teacher from high school, the two of them with their organic foods and their Eastern medicine, she has a new life now. She's earned it. If you can accumulate enough credit to earn a new life, she did. And maybe I did too.

I used to think that she wasn't very guiding in my path as a scientist. I likely didn't give her enough credit. She stayed out of my way. She didn't slow me down. She'd let me break things and build things. She let my room be a lab. She must have had some faith in me.

She expresses so little, people can't get a read on her, but I learned the intelligence of her silence. You don't have to say a lot to communicate. I look back and I feel like I can still hear her message, giving me the space necessary to become myself. She had to have known I was capable of making something out of myself. I must have picked up on it. It encouraged me to go out and be me.

There was a dead silence between us too. The kind of silence that would never wake up. Most nights, after a long day of work, she preferred to sit and be still.

Sometimes she'd read, and sometimes the book sat, like a hat, on the armrest of the couch, while she stared off. There was a death to these moments that I felt, deep within, like something was missing.

The silence hollowed us, and I never felt emptier. I'd have the same daydream, I'd reach for something, begging for it to appear in my hand, and it never would, and I'd give up on it, shake myself out, and notice my mom on the couch snoring and coughing, asleep in an uncomfortable pose.

Reality is more subjective than I like to admit. I'll tell you I don't believe in demons, and flinch every time I see them. I didn't know, not until months later, holding a photograph, finally reaching and grabbing what I had been missing in my hands all those years, I didn't know how real her demons may have been. Now I do.

Maybe we were never meant to be close, but we did have a positive effect on one another. I'm happy for the life that she has. I know that I don't have a place in her life, and that I'd have even less of a place as the years pass. But she had been good to me and I was indebted. I looked at her, sitting in the corner of the round room, I told her I was grateful for her, and I meant it, and I believed it. I trusted that I'd see her again, and she would read it on my face, how I felt, the same way I read so many subtle truths on her expressionless face.

You can skip this part but it's important to me. Density is mass divided by volume. Things like sail boats, they float because they have less density than water. Whatever the density of that sailboat is, when you subtract the density of the boat from the misplaced water, that's the precise thickness of freedom. I ought to submit that formula.

This planet has water. We all know how unique that is in this solar system.

Humans don't float, and we can't swim for long distances, so we have to assemble a vessel with less density than water in order to travel safely through the oceans. I know it took Dave and my mom quite a few years before the sailboat was seaworthy. But after several thousand dollars and hours, they did eventually set sail, and when I was catching up on sleep in the round room, I swear I could see them out on the ocean. It was a prophecy. I must have gathered enough evidence to know that nothing was going to hold them back. I saw the wind hit my mom's expressionless face, chapping her lips and eyes. Freedom. She was gone. She floated away. Double knotted, cap tightened, we were at peace.

I rested, but eventually my senses captured what guilt must sound like, when buzzing through the click mechanism of a fly. I never saw the priest's assistant after I jammed that gun in my mouth, the day I killed him, and I still can't picture him now, but I visited with him.

It was so dark. Neither of us could see each other. I couldn't conjure up his image, and I didn't want him conjuring up mine. I wasn't comfy, and I never would be, but we had the room and the means to find peace. So, we went for it.

In a condescending manner, I patted the spot next to me where I was sitting, motioning for him to have a seat. He may have. I couldn't see.

I asked him who he was, where he came from, but he didn't answer. These weren't questions to be answered. They were questions that needed to be put to rest. There's a difference. You can answer some questions, and they are solved, and they don't exist anymore. *What did I have for lunch?* Cornbread, and some melons. There. That question is dead. It no longer needs answering. But questions stem fear and confusion, they feed on us. They only get hungrier when we try to answer them.

The assistant. I was at war with the questions that arose from this man. *Who was he? Where did he come from?* Everything and everywhere that I don't believe in. I couldn't identify this man. I rely on reading people, and when I can't, I don't trust them. And when I give them a reason to hate me, I fear them. When I don't sleep for several months, I become obsessed with that fear, and when I continue not to get sleep, that fear starts to drive the hallucinations and the paranoia.

My intentions were more and more orphaned with every night of sleep I didn't get. I didn't mean to kill him. More precisely, I didn't mean to fear him enough to hate him enough to kill him. I didn't mean to misunderstand him so much. I didn't mean to let the flesh eating questions bite at me like horseflies.

It confuses me when I see people cling to their religions, when all I've ever known is science. It's a confusion that doesn't come from an angry place. I care a great deal about each and every person on this planet, that they live life to the fullest, because I know how amazing it is that they are even here, that they survived billions of years of evolutionary trimming, and it confuses me that people don't see it that way. I often think the world must seem so strange without science, without constantly referencing science, the periodic table, or the laws of physics. Time, space, energy. Non-scientific people must see the world very differently than I do, and that confuses me. I never wanted to be so angry, but confusion is blind, and when it drives an emotion, it has no problem finding anger. I got angry.

The track record shows we almost always mislabel our enemies. The opposite of science isn't religion. The opposite of science is indifference and satisfaction. It's no secret; religion can lead to indifference and satisfaction. Religion can cause people to stop searching, and it can confuse people, it can mislead people. But without enough curiosity, science can lead us in the same direction. And we all know an answer junkie that masquerades as a scientist.

Dialog is a step. Like Gilb said, like he tried to say, but I wasn't listening, there needs to be dialog. If I've found myself arguing over the differences between science and religion, I've miss-stepped, and bruised the potential of dialog. It's important to remember, not everyone is open enough to even have dialog, so arguing with a religious person is an argument with someone who at one point was willing to have dialog. Newton's third law, every action has an equal and opposite reaction. You treat people with respect; they'll give it back.

Deep down, I had to have known all that when I was up there on that stage in Portland, mouthing off about how ignorant I thought these religious people were, I had to have known I was going about it wrong. I had to have known that.

Guilt. I felt guilty. I was foolish. I had to have known that I was wrong. What I said was correct, but what I did was wrong. The burden of being correct is running the risk of acting incorrectly, and allowing the truth to be irrelevant.

The priest's assistant was the mascot of my errors. I killed the bastard, but I had to resurrect him, and make peace with him, because I'd likely have a long life of potentially frustrating experiences with religious people, and dialog would have to be a tool, not a weapon. Arguments repel, but careful, peaceful dialog embraces. So, I sat up in my bed, in the dark, and I said, "Wimpy Priest's Assistant, I'm sorry. I'm sorry I directed my anger towards you back at the Catholic high school in Portland. And I'm sorry that I created a fictional character based on you, convinced myself that you were after me, and then shot and killed you in a paranoid hallucination." He may have forgiven me. That's not what's important. What I did feel from him, I can still remember it very clearly, it was a plea for acceptance.

Never mind forgiveness, never mind sorrow. Acceptance. He was a man of faith, like so many other humans. If he was the only person on the planet who was religious, I could pull him aside and say, "hey, assistant, you're making an ass of yourself, do you realize you're the only one here who has faith?" But he's not the only one. This is what humans do; we rely on faith. We always have. I disagree with it, just like I disagree with birds that build nests in the ground. But generation after generation, they keep doing it.

The need to believe, to have faith, exists inside of all of us. I accept it; at least I'm trying to. It's the scientist's job not to hate the religions, but to offer new hypotheses. *I see your Bible, and I raise you a peer reviewed, published paper written on the origins of our solar system.*

And with that thought, he was gone, he buzzed off. We would never cross paths again. And I don't remember what guilt sounds like.

I never taught again, not in the capacity that I had before, where I had students and lessons. And in that final year of teaching, I had a student that left a mark on me. I can't remember her name, and I don't know much about her, like where she was from or what she wanted to pursue as a career, but in that awful stretch of time, spring of 2001, her presence in my audience was a battery, a source of energy for me. Hands would pop up through the crowd, waving like sea grass, but I knew I'd prefer her question so I disproportionately called on her. She was brilliant. More brilliant than I realized at the time.

I read about Einstein. He's amazing, come on, we all know that. And then, of course, the story about his professor that told him he ought to pack it up and go home, that's fascinating. That makes for a great story. No one wants to be that guy. No one wants to be the professor that thought Einstein was a failure. But what keeps me up at night, what terrifies me, is that I'd be the professor that was indifferent to Einstein, the one he never remembered. That's worse.

It was encouraging to meet someone her age who was using science appropriately, like a compass, like a system for making an array of decisions. She was a bright spot in a dark time. And I wish I could have been more than just a rambling insomniac for her, but that I could have been more influential, more Mr. Leahy-like.

What amuses me is that I know she was in a wheelchair, yet I can vividly recall her walking around, tall and proud. I remember her that way. People live on in our memories. A day will come when I'll have no recollection that she was ever anywhere near a wheelchair.

She didn't buzz into the round room at The Farm. She walked in through the door. I was confined to a bed. I recognized her by the way she walked. She came right up to me, and I caught her eye, and I told her that she never got the best of me, that I wish I was in a better headspace so that I could have connected with her more.

It was at that moment that I decided to write a book. She would be my motivation. This book would be successful, she'd pick it up one day, and she'd have very little doubt that I remember her. This book would be the way I'd reach her, the way I'd fix it. I'd have to invest myself in it. I'd build the typewriter if I had to. I'd write the whole thing there in that round orange room.

Her eyes glowed because we both knew this would come true. And it did. It's exactly how it happened.

She left like she entered, out the door, eyes glowing, locked with mine, knowing we'd cross paths again. A double take was sure to happen, years later, as I'd forget she used a wheelchair.

I remind myself that I had several students, many of which never stepped foot in the lecture hall. Back in my insomnia, I soothed myself by walking around downtown with my telescope, talking to homeless kids. I've always enjoyed taking telescopes into crowded settings, but it wasn't until I completely lost my mind that I started taking the conversation out into the creepier rings of the population. Anyone can spark up an interesting conversation with people that use soap and dress well, that you know have no intention of snatching your purse off your shoulder, but I got bored with that, and I found a common thread between me and these kids. We were both dangerously close to the edge, and maybe I was closer.

The girl with the tire marks tattoo, with the sobriety dates on her arm, it's her universe too. The universe doesn't value you and me more than it values her. The universe is indifferent to our differences, our perceived differences. It created us all. And then it created something else.

I like to think that she never added anymore sobriety dates to her arm, that the one I saw remains, without a line through it. But there were several. So the probability isn't high. The odds of her living a long, happy life are not high. That brings me a great deal of pain. Not just for her, but for every drug addicted kid on the streets, in every city.

I couldn't picture her; she never came buzzing around. I would have wanted to talk to her. But I'm not a drug addict, and I'm not an expert on drug addiction, so there I was hoping, that strange and useless thing we do, that she found a professional, someone that could help her. Unfortunately, too many people don't feel entitled to help. So, I did something at that moment, something that I had never done before, something I never did again. I prayed for her. There was nothing else I could do. It was a moment of desperation. I tried it on, and I don't imagine I did any harm.

There were many street kids, and I can picture all of them, but I had a special warmth for a psychopathic ex gang member that could have been your boss.

I had no problem picturing Accid. Let me tell you about him. This man could have been a CEO, You would have bought stock in his company. He would have invented something that you'd use a lot, a household item, and you'd wonder if your teenagers were old enough to use it. You're lucky he went the route of gangs and drugs, because he would have put your company out of business.

Accid climbed down through the top of the round room somehow, the way he'd climb up above the freeway signs, spray painting his name. His face was smeared with tattoos, more than I remember. I used to show him the stars, and he couldn't hide it, he was an astronomer. The sky mattered to him.

He had that thing that people have when you know they're smart, street smart. You weren't going to get one past him. He thought quickly, spoke faster. He knew what he was saying. You give this guy a suit, a high school education, a clean face, and he would have you buying something from him.

Accid had been a drug dealer, a filthy drug pushing thug, but he stopped doing that. He seemed content living out his days with his hood up and a bag of spray paint on his back. He was glad to be alive. He told me the story. He may not have known I was listening. I didn't know I was either.

He told me, "Hey Beetle Juice," he called me Betelgeuse, a lot of the street kids did. "I got a story for you, Beetle Juice. I want to tell you about the person I once was."

Start to finish, it's an ice cube down my spine. He was abandoned as a toddler, left at daycare, thinks his mom had an overdose. He was adopted by an American family, brought here in an airplane, but ran away, over and over. He said they wanted a punching bag, not a kid. Foster families, same problem. By then, the abuse went both ways.

But he remembers a time in high school, he was learning about physics in class, about how the ground pushes back when we jump, and he wanted to stay for the lesson, but a car came around that he could see from the window of his class, a car that wasn't supposed to be there, and he knew what that meant, and what he had to do. His gang was the only family he ever had.

That was the last time he was ever in class. But, the story gets worse. Years of gang violence, drugs, rival gangs, blood spilled over a city block, over who controlled that city block. And it makes me wonder why the corporate world doesn't come in and swoop these guys up by the armload. If they think it's hard to open a coffee shop across the street from another coffee shop, and start siphoning profits, these corporate heads ought to see what a day in a street gang is like.

The boiling point for Accid, short for accident, as he figured he was born on accident, his boiling point was when he was in the backseat of car, rolling down the window with one hand, and throwing the severed arm of another man, with aim, towards the front door of his mom's house. That's a competitive business. He said he never killed anyone, but he tightened the belt over the exercise bench while his buddy took a machete and amputated a man's arm.

Start to finish, this is how it went down. They drove by, dragged a rival gang member off the street, took him to an abandoned storage unit, drugged him, tied him down just in case he woke up mid amputation, and had a doctor, yes, a real doctor, come and treat the wounds, really. The man had a tattoo on his forearm, a black and white portrait of his mom, and Accid took that arm and spiraled it out of a moving car right onto the doorstep of the gang member's mom.

That was the boiling point for him. He stood on the bridge near West Seattle, the one that so many people jump off, the last thing they ever do. And he thought about jumping, he thought about the physical act of it. The lesson he only half learned in high school. And it was at that moment that he caught himself wondering how it could be, that if he pushed off that bridge, the bridge would push back. And he didn't want that to be the last thing he ever did.

I know very little about how he ended up in an alley with an insomniac like me, but I had no problem finishing that physics lesson, with a little help from Isaac Newton. You should have seen us jumping in the alley. To this day, when I find myself in Olympia I'm charmed when I see his name around town, or impossibly placed on the overpass.

Before Accid climbed out of the round, orange, fabric room, I told him he was all right. I liked him. I don't hold it against him that he threw a man's arm out of moving car, because, like Newton says, every action has an equal and opposite reaction. He didn't ask for all that violence, it came looking for him. He was just reacting. I'd be proud to call him a student, and I told him, maybe our days looking through telescopes and testing the laws of physics weren't over.

The buzz in the room was much lighter. Most of the noise had already left. And there were many people and experiences that I didn't even bother with. Their numbers were never called. Art and his bolo tie, who fired me under the Andromeda Galaxy, but got me a gig taking ice and soil samples from above the Arctic, while avoiding the temper tantrum of an oil field cowboy, tense over my remarks about the Vietnam War. I didn't revisit these things. They don't matter to me. I didn't revisit Dodger games, and dads who wrap cars around trees, or telephone poles, I don't even remember. I don't care. I'm indifferent to it. I've swallowed that pill. I was the least qualified doctoral candidate in recent history, according to one of my professors. I don't remember his name. It's water off my back.

The smells and the sounds of this place, somewhere in Oregon, they were trying to pull me out of bed. I wanted to get out and join the crowd. I knew what awaited me out there, that Gilb wouldn't have brought me here if this place wasn't going to be good for me. Bathroom breaks and the occasional peek at the moon was the most excitement I'd had in days. I was ready to get out of bed. I'd never slept this much in my life. I was ready to wake up. I was at peace.

Which is exactly why I still had work to do.

Kennedy. I see a silhouette of her. I have very little to say to her. I didn't want to slow her down with my apologies. What is an apology? Can you apologize to the glass plate you broke? She didn't come inside the round, fabric room, but she stayed outside, and I told her that for as long as I live, I'll revisit her memory, I'll think of the day we met at the cafe, the crowded cafe. I'll remember that it was her who suggested I call up Gilb. I'll revisit the positive experiences we had with each other, I'll think of them forever. Those memories need to be kept alive. I told her that she'll never be forgotten. Then I told her to go.

Even then, before I learned about the money from the bar, and the school in the woods, I knew she had somewhere to go. Olympia slowed her down enough. And her idea about the school, I had every chance to get on board with it, to be excited and show support, and I never did. And to be honest, it's the best idea I've ever heard. A school in the woods. What I would have given to be a student at that school. We put kids in a classroom for 12 years, to prepare them for the real world, and the classroom looks nothing like the real world.

But I didn't know anything about the school when I was saying goodbye to Kennedy from the inside of the round, orange, fabric room. I didn't know that Gilb's cousin Jimmy, who argued that I couldn't have started a fire the way I said I did, and he was probably right, I didn't know he would help build the school, and bring a woman across the country that he met on my mom's boat, after helping rebuild that boat. I didn't know any of that because it hadn't happened yet. But I knew that Kennedy had important things to do with her life. And she had to go. And after she left, after I knew she had walked far away, it fell quiet.

Quiet.

I wanted to say something. *Next. Next?* But there was no one there. And for reasons I couldn't explain at the time, I knew, at every level, that I was done. That it was time to wake up, that the bottle caps were tight, the knots were doubled. I was done. I had made my peace with the important people of my life. Of course, I knew then, like I know now, that there were two very powerful people, very powerful forces in my life that never showed up to my peace gathering in the round, fabric room. But, I knew I was done. It would all come together later, in a way that would test my grip on the universe. But for that moment, I was done. I knew it.

It was time to start my life. I had a new life ahead. And it smelled like everything I've ever wanted to eat was cooking outside over a fire. A band of drummers was piecing a beat together, complex but slow and pulling. A story telling beat. A beat like a story I'd tell. The moon was overhead, just slightly waning. And I took a step out.

Everything stopped. Every sound, every movement, it all came to a halt. And every person I would come to know at The Farm welcomed me.

Logjam

I don't think it was a very difficult lesson to learn. We treat people how we want to be treated. We don't impose our will on them. The word *should*, it's a useless word. It's an empty word. It means nothing.

Philip is my friend. Philip Duke. I imagine him walking up the hill from his orange yurt every morning to welcome the sun's rays with me. Because he was once here, he is always here. Because I remember him, I am still with him. In so many ways, he is still here.

His stay here lasted two years. It feels longer. Many people have stayed longer. Many beautiful people have made a home of this farm, and have stayed for years. Philip needed to be here for two years. That was all. He almost left after one year, and I searched all morning for the best way to ask him to stay. I knew it would be important to him. I was loading up the truck. I was heading out of town, to California. I'd be back after a week. I asked him to stay, just until I returned.

Philip trusted me. He knew I wouldn't have asked him to stay unless it was important. He stayed another year after I returned. There was a reason to. It was the right decision to ask him to stay. He would agree.

The first time I saw Philip he was broken. Life is hard. It's hard to be a human being. Something out there in the world broke him. Eagle and Gilb were right to bring him here.

It was several days before he left his yurt. A woman brought him food and checked on him. She said she'd never seen someone so tired. I didn't know that man. The man I know came out of the yurt one night during a roast. The families greeted him.

I approached him. We became friends quickly.

It was easy to be Philip's friend. I can read people well. Anyone who is content standing in the cold welcoming the sun every morning with you, that's a friend.

I'm grateful that Eagle and his cousin Gilb brought Philip here. Eagle has always had a positive impact wherever he goes. Eagle is a man of good intention, and he leaves places better than when he arrived. I almost ran him over, so many years ago. He was stalled down on highway right at the end of our road.

I learned not to expect things to be the way they often are. Never has there been a car at the end of our road. I didn't expect it. Had I run over him, I may never have gotten to know him, and he has contributed much to The Farm. He also brought Philip here. Eagle is a blessed man.

Philip needed to be here. The world is rough, I don't go out there much. Noise, and anger. I stay here at The Farm, so I understand when someone needs to stay put. I've never asked anyone to leave. If they've got to stay, then they've got to stay.

This land has been in the family for longer than it matters. Not much left of the family now, just me, and a hawk that comes to say hello every morning. I've spent most of my life here, although no one really knows where I came from before that.

I'm an old man, and it's an old story, but the way I heard it, a family was traveling through Oregon and there was a violent storm. That highway down near the river, at the end of our road, that was just a dirt path back then. This was 1944.

The traveling family asked if there was any shelter to spare, and since this was a Christian home, the answer was yes. But when the storm passed, and the morning came, the family was gone, all except a baby. And if I heard that part right, that baby was me.

I grew up here, and no one was ever sure if anyone was coming back for me, but that didn't matter, I was raised like I belonged here. They raised me like family, and now I'm all the family that remains.

Some people said those travellers had an accent, European or maybe Russian. I've never been too curious. I don't chase answers I'll never find. I came from somewhere, I ended up somewhere else. This is home.

I spent a year in a POW camp in Vietnam, but no one is better off by reliving those memories. I didn't survive it so I could retell it. I did learn one thing though. We can never be too sure who is capable of kindness. I can say with confidence that I wouldn't be here without the kindness of a man I met in a POW camp in Vietnam. Sure, he helped capture me, and I suffered a great deal from his actions. But I am correct when I say that he saved my life. The kindness we receive from people we dislike has great value.

One by one, all the family here either left or died off, and I've just gone ahead and done what they would have done, and I share the land.

I got to know Philip real quickly. If he looked horrible the first night out of the yurt, then he didn't look half bad by the third night, and after a week, he was beam of sunshine.

I'm known for not saying a lot. I'd rather listen. I'd rather enjoy the silence too. There is much to enjoy in silence. Life is silent. If noise is made to remind ourselves that we're alive, than silence is the sound we make when we don't need to be reminded.

I've always been large. I've never met anyone as large as I am. Most people who meet me have never met anyone as large as I am. I've found that a large, gentle, quiet man can blend very peacefully into any setting. I wish for people to feel safe around me. Because of my size, that requires action on my part. It's important to me that people feel safe around me. I know what it's like to not feel safe.

Philip was a quiet man. He was introverted and he disengaged from most social interactions. It was a sign of honesty. It was a way to preserve honesty. He would engage when he wanted to. I can trust someone who does that. There is much meaning behind the words of an introvert. I knew that when Philip chose to communicate, he was going to share something honest and important.

Two weeks after he arrived, he started exploring The Farm, and he wandered into a dwelling where I've kept old machines from the family, some of them are old and broken and I don't know what I'll ever do with them. They'll be here when I die, I can imagine.

I watched him leave the dwelling with a cash register. He walked over to me. I was digging a ditch. I suppose he was approaching me to ask if he could use the cash register. He must have read me well. I didn't stop digging. He took that as a sign that I had no objection to him using the cash register. It was old, decades old, and we had no use for it. I very much appreciated that he interpreted that exchange the way he did. If I had wanted to discuss the cash register, I would have stopped digging. In no way did I wish to slow down any plans he had for that cash register.

Maybe a week later, I visited him, and what he had in front of him was no longer a cash register. He had rigged it up to be a typewriter. The cash register didn't have enough keys for the entire alphabet, but he took the metal off of the remaining typebars, melted them with magnets, and reshaped them enough to look like the characters he needed. I got to watch him melt the metal with the magnets, otherwise I wouldn't have thought it was possible. He coiled some thick wire, and ran a current through it, and then placed the metal in the housing of the wire. It floated. I'd never seen anything like it. But then it started to melt, so he quickly grabbed it. He burned his hands. Then, with a pocket knife, he reshaped the numbers into letters.

That was his will. It was important to him that he did it this way.

I still have the typewriter here, years after Philip has moved on, it's here. It's not a cash register, it's a typewriter, and he used it to write a book. We have the original manuscript here, which we read often. We laugh when the Z and S are the same, the L and I, a 6 is a G and an E. But he did it, he wrote a book. I say this with excitement. You can find it in any bookstore, and he wrote it here, on a typewriter from many decades ago, that wasn't even a typewriter. It was a cash register.

I told him that we could have found all the supplies in town if he needed to write something so badly. But this was his will, to do it the way he did. He felt like the process was compromised enough with us buying him ink and paper. He struggled with that. It took days before he finally asked for help. He had no means to make paper, and he tried to concoct ink, but did not have the means for that either. Eventually, having exhausted all options, he asked for help.

He told me stories about some of the amateur astronomers that he admired, how they built their telescopes with farm equipment. He had something he needed to do, he needed to write a book, and he was compelled to be as utilitarian as he could. I suggested that asking for help is a form of self-reliance. He nodded.

He told me he had a lot to say, that he wanted to write a book, and was hoping someone he used to know would find it. That's all he ever said about it. That was all I needed to know. And I guessed that when he finished his book that his time here would come to an end. I grew to enjoy his company. If it was his will to leave when the book was finished, then it was my will to enjoy my time with him while I could.

Something unpredictable happened. Philip had a visitor. It was Gilb, Eagle's cousin. He had some of Philip's possessions. Some beautiful telescopes, most of which are still here, that we all use regularly. But there was something else that Gilb left with Philip, and I don't think it made Philip too happy, not at first.

Philip came and sat near me at dinner that evening. He was looking at several old pictures of two little boys, two happy little boys. But he looked troubled.

I knew that if he wanted to discuss it with me, he would have. He chose not to. Philip was upset, the pictures of the giggling little boys didn't cheer him up, and he wanted to sit close. That was all. Nothing too complicated. He reached out, on his terms. That's all you can ask of anyone. By the end of dinner, his head was halfway up my shoulder, resting, and he looked exhausted.

At one point, he slid the photos over to me, and so I looked at them, and I could tell that one of the boys was him. I don't know why he did that.

And then I noticed something. I had to search deep, very deep into my memory to make sense of what I saw. I wasn't able to make the connection right away, but when I did, days later, I sprung up out of my bed. And at the moment, I knew something beautiful was going to happen.

Philip

A boring, cone shaped ant hill. A fully functional society. Don't get me wrong, ants are brilliant, but we've all seen an ant hill. We're used to it.

This was the day Gilb came back to The Farm. The day I heard the familiar sound of a Volvo engine. It was rare that we heard the sound of an engine. The far off, familiar car engine stole my attention away from the ant hill. I knew that sound. I knew that engine.

The sound made me nervous. I wasn't sure what it meant. But as soon as I saw Gilb walking down the path towards the orange yurt carrying my telescopes over his shoulder, I was overwhelmed with emotion. It was wonderful to see Gilb. I was grateful that he and Jimmy had brought me to The Farm.

I hadn't visited with Gilb during those first few days at The Farm when I was making peace with the important people of my past. He never buzzed by. I concluded that it wasn't necessary. Gilb was a constant figure in my life. Even in his absence, I felt his presence.

There were two people I skipped on, Gilb and Mr. Leahy. I carry them with me. I'm never without them. They remain in a place where I only know peace.

Gilb was happy. He explained his relapse, but he sounded positive about it. He was seeking help. It was important to me that he saw that I was healthy and happy, too. I knew he was worried. Of course he was. I was relieved that he got to move on in life with that peace of mind. Having a mental picture of me, healthy, that was important to him.

Even when I signed the divorce papers, we were able to get past that potentially strange moment. I understood. Kennedy would be happier. It was good for her to go back home. And when Gilb told me about the school in the woods, and how they secured the money, I was thrilled. Beyond thrilled. These were positive things. And if it was his will to be a part of Kennedy's life, to be out in the woods on the other side of the country, I had no intention of standing in the way of that. I had learned quite a bit from Logjam, about the will of others.

When the attacks of September 11 happened, we at The Farm didn't hear anything about it. A neighbor who was aware that we were slightly off the grid felt that we should know, and we gathered around at dinner, and he explained to us that the jets had been hijacked. He gave us the death toll. There was an outpour of emotion that evening, and most of us didn't have the appetite for dinner. We never wasted at The Farm, but on this night, food wasn't necessary.

But because we never saw the images, we were free to interpret it as it was, a horrific tragedy. We never saw the buildings collapse. Anger didn't build inside of us. We mourned for the victims. That was all.

The children started a fire, down in the pit, and we were sad. That is really all I can say about it. We were silent, we were fairly still, and we were sad. Life went on after that night, and I never heard anyone speak of the attacks again until Gilb showed up. It's my opinion that we properly mourned.

When Gilb explained that the money from Kennedy's dad's bar was going towards the purchase of an old Civilian Conservation Corps camp from the 1930s, out in the Catskills, and that he sold the bar because many of his patrons had died in the attacks of September 11, that ignited a confusing feeling, a realization of the reach that this tragedy had. I was aware that people had died, but never considered that people I knew would be affected. Then, to learn that an outdoor school would come about, directly because of the attacks, I interpreted that as a great metaphor for how the world has always worked things out, the cycle necessary for evolution. Things have to go away. Without death, there is no birth.

Evolution is indifferent to our emotions. It goes without saying that the attacks were tragic, and now, years later, having seen the images on screen, there is no part of me that is insensitive to the pain that these attacks caused. I carefully slip this statement into the conversation though, for so many kids who have attended that school out in the woods, a very positive thing happened, and it happened as a result, a direct result of the attacks on September 11. We have to be open to the idea that tragedy can bring about positivity. The tragedy occurred whether we come to terms with it or not. It happened. And this school is a positive thing.

I took inspiration from this. I had been working on the novel for a few months at this point, and this was something to be written about. From the laws of nature, of physics, of the universe, there are metaphors that we can use in our daily lives. That is what the book was intended to be, a case for thinking scientifically. The book was a way to use science to help address our social needs, our emotional needs, all the while considering science, both literally and figuratively.

I experienced both positive and negative emotions when Gilb spoke of the school, and I feel that was appropriate. I still feel that way. I take great pride knowing that two very important people to me opened a school out in the woods for inner city kids to receive their education in a natural learning environment. Wonderful things will happen as a result of that school.

But Gilb had one more issue that was important to him. Something he thought was important to me. I would eventually be thankful for his act of kindness, but that wasn't my first response. I suffered during this moment. I experienced great pain after Gilb presented me with the envelope that he had driven all the way down to Los Angeles for, months earlier, before his relapse. When I opened it, and I saw what was inside, an emotion exploded inside of me, an emotion greater than my understanding, so I said nothing. I was incapable of expressing anything. This was a moment that changed my life. This was a moment that would test all of my theories.

So often in my life, I felt urgency. It was irrational. I'd squeeze my hands. I'd feel the need to grab at things. When I was younger I'd daydream about reaching for something. I could never satisfy this urge. It was so deep within me.

The brain is a powerful machine. We may never completely understand it. Its capabilities never fail to amaze me. It's a habit of mine, when identifying the behavior of an animal, plant, insect, or any organism, to ask what role in survival this behavior has.

I imagine our ancestors, back in the Serengeti. Something tragic happened, half the clan is wiped out. Dead children everywhere. Those who could quickly bury it and continue on, those were the survivors. We have a part of our brain that tricks us. The power of denial should never be underestimated.

I'm a descendent of survival. I am a descendent of whatever it took to survive. We all are. That's a truth worth remembering.

But I didn't see it that way when I saw the photographs of my brother, when we were children. Every single moment of my life, after he drowned down at Zuma Beach when we were five, I kept that secret locked up from myself. Every negative sensation that I had protected myself from, they all came back right at that moment.

Gilb left. He knew enough to leave. Even Gilb knew there was nothing left for him to do. He handed me the pictures, and he said nothing, in a very non Gilb-like manner. Gilb, who was rarely quiet, just slipped away after handing me the photographs, and I spent the rest of the evening looking at each one of them, remembering my brother.

Five years old. I remember Joshua. I remember him well. I remember his voice. I remember when he shit his pants at the park and it smelled the whole drive home. I remember that he didn't like vegetables, even when my mom put butter on them.

I remember when he drowned. I mean to say, I remember the exact moment he was no longer alive. I remember reaching for him. My dad had me in his arms, and I remember having a perfect understanding that we were not safe, and I tried to reach for Joshua. We shared a womb together, there's nothing more intimate than that. I knew he wasn't alive any longer.

I became a lot quieter after his death. No one would ever understand me as well as my twin brother would have.

At dinner that night, in the hearth room, I sat next to Logjam, unusually close. I was frozen. My eyes had not left the photos. I was slow. I was experiencing shock. The best I could do was to eventually nudge the photos over to Logjam, in an attempt to say, *I'm not all right, and this is why.*

That was the best I could do.

But something positive happened, a positive thing arose from the negative thing. It was hard for me to look at it that way at the time; it tested my theories. Looking back now, I now know something beautiful happened at that moment.

But I still had an important book to write. In a world where people make wishes and cross fingers, I offered this, a practical guide to using science to improve our lives. That book, it became such an obsession. Everything I ever felt. Every struggle I ever had. I'd spent so many years fighting against religion, and the damage I perceived that I attributed to religion. This book was my peace offering. It was my testimony. I was at *their* doorstep this time.

I knew she would understand, the former student of mine. The one in the wheelchair, who I'd forget was in a wheelchair. She had come from religion. I remember that. Or I derived it from the questions she asked. I knew she would appreciate the book. I imagined her reading about the laws of physics as metaphors for healthy living, or the chapter I wrote about life as an elementary science fair, how we can teach kids to test a hypothesis, and arrive at a conclusion, and that using that model throughout our daily lives could be beneficial in our decision making.

As much as I imagined the satisfaction she would experience in catching the references to her that I placed throughout the book, I equally felt the responsibility to consider an audience of readers who had very little scientific background, if any. This book was equally written for them. There were people who would benefit from science, and so I had a book to write. And I named it after Gilb's favorite color, which is why I believe he found the only orange yurt on The Farm to put me in when I arrived at The Farm on that wild night.

Orange is a color that holds spiritual importance in nearly every religion. Gilb wrote about it in his book, *Iridescence*. Many Eastern religions reserve the color orange specifically for clergy and religious authorities. But I offered a scientific explanation, a way of looking at it scientifically. Our minds process colors, color wavelengths, and a variety of psychological and neurological reactions ensue. This isn't news. People know this. Advertisers know this.

Orange lies between the primary colors yellow and red on the spectrum. And orange, just like every other color, invokes very unique reactions. There is much scientific research to back this up. But we can test these theories on our own.

Red and yellow arouse a sense of wanting, a sense of feeling empty. Restaurants often use this combination in their advertising schemes. But not so much orange. Orange provides a balance. It offers a more soothing and satisfied sensation. Exposure to the color orange increases oxygen to the brain. You don't go rushing to spend your money when you feel at peace, when you feel satisfied. It's not a color you use when you're trying to trick someone.

The book practically wrote itself. And, the rigged up typewriter that I had to assemble, that was a part of the process for me. I came across a perfectly functional typewriter in that old shed, but I wasn't looking for a typewriter. I figured if I had to build it, then I knew I would put everything I had into this book, starting with the instrument used to write the book. It was that important to me that the book be successful, that it end up in my former student's hands, the one in the wheelchair.

I think Logjam understood.

I so desperately had a book to write. I woke up the day after Gilb left, and I melted into that book. I had ant hills to admire, and compare, in their nature, to our human structures. I had sunrises to enjoy with Logjam each morning, failing to see the hawk that he claimed visited each morning; the hawk he named the field after. I never once saw that hawk. He'd point, and I wouldn't see it.

I was distracted. I'd welcome the sun, and I'd be exploring the origins of the term *sunrise*, an artifact from when we knew less. An entire chapter was dedicated to terms we use in our language that have survived more advanced scientific knowledge. It was an observation, not a critique. We know that the sun doesn't rise. We still use the term. I thought I'd point it out, for entertainment.

There was a night when I realized two things - that I had lived at The Farm with all the beautiful people for close to a year, and that I was finished with my book. It was late, and I normally didn't like staying up late, as I grew to value the importance of keeping a sleeping routine, but I was so close to finishing the book that I stayed up later than usual. And then, as if the whole year was a dream, I blinked and the book was done. It was done. I had a finished book on my hands, and I had no idea what to do next.

I'd probably need to leave The Farm and seek a publisher. I didn't know. Perhaps Gilb knew what to do next. That aspect of the process never quite occurred to me. But I fell asleep before I came up with a plan, and I woke up the next morning, having slept through our morning ritual. I hadn't missed a morning of welcoming the sun in almost a year. It was a vital part of my day. But I had my reasons.

Logjam caught on. Our communication had become very instinctual. We had a year to work on it. We were transparent to each other. When I walked up to his truck later that morning, yawning the whole way up the hill, I saw that he was packing for a trip. In a playful way, I did what I could to slow him down.

What he said next wouldn't have been too memorable, had it not been Logjam saying it. He said he'd be back in a week, and he asked that I'd stay until at least then before taking off. It was the first time Logjam had ever asked me to do anything. He had a pretty strict policy about never imposing his will on anyone else. And since I had no intention of taking off that soon anyway, it was easy for me to agree to that request.

That was a long week. Everyone at The Farm felt an absence. He hadn't left the property for that long since I'd been there. Take the sun out of the solar system.

With the book completed, and Logjam away, I took another stab at coming to terms with the photographs in the envelope. Everyday I thought about Joshua, and I hadn't yet sorted out my fugitive emotions. The book was an excellent distraction.

I knew all along. It's not as if I didn't know I had a brother. I knew. But the brain is a mysterious machine. I took that knowledge, and I put it in a place where I would never come across it. And for 30 years I did exactly that, I never came across it. And I lived in a home where my mom and I didn't speak about these things. She wasn't dealing with it either. We're descendants of survivors. That's how we survived. And I imagine she had no idea just how suppressed my memories of Joshua were.

I took a photograph out of the envelope, it was the only one with my mom in it. All three of us are wearing Santa Claus hats. I left the photograph on the nightstand where my alarm clock should have been. And I just let it sit there. It was a beautiful photograph of my family. When I was still in shock, and I nuzzled up next to Logjam at the dinner in the hearth room, it was that particular picture that he put all his attention on. I remember that. He couldn't take his eyes off of it.

A week later, I'd know exactly why.

Stereovision

Philip searched for a soft spot in the woman's appearance. Pressed clothes and pearl jewelry, magically tight hair pulled back and out of sight. She fidgeted during his reading from the front row, but otherwise sat uncomfortably straight in her prize-winning posture.

"My question is concerning the chapter about Mr. Leahy," she said.

Philip nodded.

"You claim not to believe in miracles, yet I don't see what else you can call this. If I recall correctly, you were living on a farm in Oregon, am I right?"

"Correct." Philip played along. He knew he was being interrogated. He didn't mind. He knew this would end well. This was his favorite road to go down during book readings.

"And, the owner of the farm recognized your mom from a picture you had, is that right?"

"He recognized both my mom and me, yes."

"Can you explain that?"

"Well, the owner of the farm, he's an interesting man. He has a great memory. He's a very observant person, he's --"

She interrupted, "And he just remembered your faces, somehow, from a photograph that his uncle sent him, randomly, twenty or thirty years earlier?"

"Yeah, like I said, he's a pretty unique --"

"And you don't believe in miracles?"

Philip looked at his watch. Time was running out. He had a cab to catch from downtown Seattle to the University District, so he decided to wrap this up, for everyone's sake. "Alright, let me lay it out for you. I was living on a farm, working on my book, and the man who owned the farm had seen one of my photographs, a photograph of my mom and me from when I was a child. And yes, he's got a photographic memory, which is convenient when you're looking at photographs."

The crowd chuckled, sensing just a thin layer of conflict between the author and the audience member. She chimed in, "Not a miracle though?"

"No. So, he recognizes the photograph, but it takes him several days before he can make sense of it. And then it hits him, he had an uncle who managed the apartment building that my mom and I lived in."

"Mr. Leahy?"

"Yes, Mr. Leahy was the uncle of the man who owned the farm I was staying at. And Mr. Leahy was a very important person in my life. Very influential in me becoming a scientist."

"Still, not a miracle?"

"Not to me. So, anyway, I grew up always feeling a bit guilty about not showing more appreciation to Mr. Leahy. And Mr. Leahy was an old man when I finally left for college, and I never said goodbye, thanks, none of that. I just left. I was a teenager, I wasn't concerned with other people." The crowd chuckles again. The woman in the front row sat still, just daring Philip to try to explain how this, if true, could have happened without some sort of divine intervention. Philip felt the squeeze of having very little time to travel across town to the gymnasium at the University of Washington.

"So, one day, I finish my book. I'm done, and I'm feeling like it's time to leave the farm. By the way, I wrote the whole book on a typewriter I built from scratch, which is something Mr. Leahy would have been very proud of. But I don't have time to tell that story... So, the book is done, and I feel the need to get going, to leave, but my friend who owns the farm asks that I just stay until he returns from California. And he doesn't tell me why, he just asks that I stay. He says he'll be back in a week.

"So, I stay. The curiosity is killing me. That week took a lifetime. Then..." Philip's face shifts expression. His tone goes from speaking like a beach reporter to a much more solemn and serious manner, with a hint of emotion, "So, this man, this old man named Mr. Leahy, who I owe the world to, I knew it was him right away. The dirt clouds settled, and my friend walked around and opened the passenger door, and there he was. All 100 years of him."

Philip paused, succumbed to the emotion, cleared his throat and tried to muscle through it, remembering that he's almost out of time.

"My friend who owned the farm, he had always kept in touch with Mr. Leahy, while the rest of his family didn't. But they were the only two Leahys left. And when Mr. Leahy turned 100, my friend convinced him to come up and live his last days out at the farm, the farm that Mr. Leahy grew up on. There was a chapel on the farm, it was old, and abandoned, but while I was busy working on the book, my friend had restored it, knowing that Mr. Leahy would have liked to see it in good shape.

"The day that my friend was packing his truck to go down to California and pick up Mr. Leahy, and I noticed that the chapel was completely restored, like it was built yesterday. And then he drove off and returned a week later."

"Not a miracle?"

"Sure felt like one, but no. Not a miracle. And so, as you can imagine, it was the most rewarding experience I ever had. I spent the next year at the farm, and I just put my manuscript in a safe spot, and gave Mr. Leahy a year of my life. We looked through telescopes, we talked about science, and I made sure, I made absolutely sure that he knew how appreciated he was. I'm not a scientist without Mr. Leahy. He died a year later in a hospital in Eugene, and I was there, holding his hand. It was the most important day of my life."

The woman dismissed the sentiment and continued searching for holes. "Mr. Duke, you mean to say that of all the millions and billions of people, that the one person your friend's uncle turned out to be was your mentor, Mr. Leahy, and you completely ignore the work of God in that miracle? You were blessed with the opportunity to make peace with someone that you assumed was dead, and you can't see God at work?"

Philip didn't answer. He didn't need to. He could tell that she was about to speak and wouldn't have heard him anyway.

"He was a Christian man, if I read correctly. Is that right, Mr. Duke?"

"Yes, he was. He had a cross around his neck when he died."

"And, Mr. Duke, you are quoted as saying that the cross is a disturbing symbol to you." The audience became uncomfortable; the mood was awkward. The woman was challenging Philip.

"Yes, I said that, and I still believe it. To me, *to me*, it is a bit disturbing. It's a torturing device. That's all I see. But maybe you see it differently. We can have different views. And Mr. Leahy was a very religious man, up until the day he died. He died believing that he was going to meet his creator, in heaven. And I don't have to remind you that I'm less convinced of that.

"And we had amazing conversations, enlightening conversations about the origins of the universe, about stars exploding, dust clouds collapsing. How our solar system was formed. About the origin of our planet, the remaining particles orbiting around the center of the dust cloud. Centrifugal force forming an accretion disk around the star. We spoke about that while looking at planets along the ecliptic. He was proud that the little boy from the apartment complex grew up to be an astrophysicist.

"Where did Mr. Leahy think our planet came from?" A little girl, not older than the age of eight, asked.

Philip paused before answering, and a powerful look came over his face. "I don't know. I didn't ask. He was just very proud of me. He still saw me as a young kid, I'm sure, and he was proud of me."

Philip held eye contact with the little girl while answering her question, as if she was the only person in the room. He shifted his focus back on the rest of the crowd and said, "I have the feeling this was very rewarding for him to live old enough to see me grow up to become the person I am. You see, there's something else you don't know about Mr. Leahy. I never wrote about it. Mr. Leahy was a gay man. He didn't have any family left, he didn't have any kids of his own, so, I was the closest thing he ever had to a grandkid. And he never had any trouble believing in God, reading the Bible, building a relationship with his God, all the while living life as a gay man. This was a man who was kicked out of his church for being gay, and he went home and he prayed for those people, the people who told him he couldn't return. So, he could handle some scientific talk that may have contradicted his Biblical views. We observed the universe together, we were looking at the same stars and planets at night, and maybe we differed on how it came to be, but we were looking at the same objects.

"But I know I haven't completely answered your question," nodding to the woman in the front row. "You believe this was a miracle, that a divine force brought Mr. Leahy to that farm, and that I'd be a fool not to believe that. Let me offer this, and it may or may not satisfy you. It's not my responsibility to.

"In science, we deal first hand with extreme odds. One in a million, one in a billion, one in a trillion. We deal with that *one*, the one in a billion. Imagine a lottery, one winning ticket, billions of losing tickets. We deal with that one winning ticket.

"Consider evolution. We are four and half billion years into it. We are the winning lottery ticket holders of billions of years worth of lotteries. The fact that we are here, that the dinosaurs were wiped out exactly when they were, and that our mammalian ancestors were more free to reproduce, and 60 million years later, our line of primates finally come out of the trees. You see, you give molecules billions of years, and you and I are up here in Seattle at a bookstore talking, in oral language, about miracles.

"So, I submit this, that no greater miracle can occur during our existence than the miracle *of* our existence. Very little surprises me. We are the winning lottery ticket holder of billions of years worth of lotteries. If you want to call that a miracle, and it helps you stay grateful for your time here on this planet, then I say great. Do that. But we're looking at the same thing. We may have different views, but we're looking at the same thing. A metaphorical stereovision.

"I won't convince you that it wasn't a miracle. I'll simply suggest that everything in life, everything we experience, everyday, is the result of near impossible odds, that if anything in life is a miracle, then everything in life is a miracle, and I have a different word for it than you do. I call it science."

The audience, disproportionately supportive of Philip's views, fans of his literary work, his views on science, immediately responded with the applause that he has come to appreciate at every book reading. He apologized to the crowd, explained that he must catch a cab, and that he was dangerously close to arriving late to a very important event, the final college basketball game of a senior at the University of Washington. His stepson, Ty, was the only member of the team on an academic scholarship.

As he sat in the back of a sharp turning taxicab, placing his blind faith in a stranger, he opened an envelope, and looked at the photo of himself, his mom and his brother, all wearing Santa Claus hats. He'll never understand. All those years, he never mourned, he hid the truth from himself. He'll never recover from that. It will hurt him forever. And he smiled, grateful for the ability to feel the loss. He rubbed his finger over Joshua's face, and wondered what kind of man he would have been. He will suffer the rest of his life at the loss of his brother.

He skimmed a letter from a student in the past, a woman named Sam, which he brings with him everywhere he goes. Her work in the field of neuroscience is worthy of notice. He feels a sense of pride when he thinks of her. They've discussed at length his ability to block the death of his own brother all those years. She even published a paper on it.

He handled the next item in his envelope, a recently received postcard from an island in the Pacific. He's memorized the private message written very openly on the back of the postcard, with the words *I'm sorry* scattered several times, an acknowledgement that the photographs of Philip and his brother were decades late.

As the cab pulled up to the university, searching for the gymnasium where Philip's stepson's name would be called in the starting lineup for the first and only time in his four year college basketball career, he took a glance at the last item in his envelope.

Gilb must have hired a helicopter for the shot. A student body of close to 300, gathered in the field of an outdoor school, forming the humorously abbreviated THNX!, with a ten inch Dobsonian telescope clearly visible, centered in front of the grateful crowd. There are many schools just like it now, all very similar. He visits them. But he stays away from the one in the Catskills. He knows it's better that way.

Philip arrived at his seat. Donna, his wife, shot him a look. *You barely made it.* They smiled, both knowing their son will be back on the bench soon. Ty, a physics major on a full academic scholarship, missed his only shot from the field, and sat back down on the bench. His basketball career quietly came to an end.

Donna glanced at Philip's scar on his neck, knowing that if he had wanted to explain it, he would have, but she smirked knowing that her two daughters think it looks like a worm, and that they are bound to ask him at some point, having grown to know him as more than just their mom's husband.

Meanwhile, at an art gallery on the other side of town, an Icelandic visual artist known for her dragonfly costumes, her David Bowie themes, and her love of cupcakes, displayed her latest work, a gun aimed at an alarm clock, with a bullet in mid trajectory, between the two. The piece of art, which she calls *Wake Up!*, is constructed entirely of items she found on a beach in Olympia while she was in college. The high-end art collectors were forced to ask themselves, *who finds a gun, a bullet, and an alarm clock on the beach?*

Each day, the Field of the Morning Hawk is flooded with sunlight. Children tumble and giggle. Nearby, a modest grave is marked with a pile of rocks. The initials JL are carved into a flat stone at the foot of the grave. A man they call Logjam, relying heavily on a cane as thick as a tree trunk, quietly admires the sky.

This story is dedicated to my mom, Nancy.